ONE WOMAN'S WAR

ONE WOMAN'S WAR

A novel by

Natalija Nogulich

ADVANCE PRAISE

"This stunning novel reminds one of a symphony comprised not of notes, but of words. The first movement evokes Tolstoy-like depiction of Slavic peasant life, idyllic that turns ugly; forcing the heroine to flee to New York City for an interlude of promise and love. The last and third movement is a return to the 'old country' where revenge and redemption make for a gripping climax. A truly remarkable read!"

James Trivers, Author

"With ONE WOMAN'S WAR, Natalija Nogulich has written a timeless and profoundly moving first novel – a story and characters which will reverberate long after the last page is turned. In a style and prose that is uniquely her own, ONE WOMAN'S WAR reads as if the words had grown from the very soil itself, so authentic is the voice speaking from the pages of this book. Rich and powerful ONE WOMAN'S WAR touches one to the core – this book is a MUST read!"

Susan England, Producer

"This book demands attention to the personal side of conflict, to the innate damage and profound healing that accompanies war. But, for Nogulich, war goes much farther than political strife – she handles the carnage of divorce and betrayals of friendship in the same detail, with vivid acumen, that she frames clashes between cultures. Her work is moving in its honesty and delicate in its style. Her characters are at once strangers and loved ones, reminiscent of all of our ancestors and of ourselves."

Yael Prizant, Ph.D.

I dedicate this book to my family.

You are always in my heart.

"Out beyond the ideas of

wrongdoing and

rightdoing,

There is a field,

I'll meet you there."

RUMI

PART ONE

The Village

CHAPTER ONE

MOUNTAINS BREED POETS, bishops and soulful women, queens of the land that walk and work, hiding their magic behind babushkas and radiating love. Mountains hold secrets for centuries, hatred or a sacred passion planted like a naturally entitled prince stays safe in silent granite. A mountain can heap human error upon itself, daring a man to drown his most unpardonable acts, under the weight of a divine force, leveling sin to a gentle field in the valley where tenderness grows. In that field, afternoon clouds hooded four Balkan beauties from the moist heat, while they worked their rich harvest of hay, determined to get it down and up before the rain came. Four blousy bodies bent over their latest victim: a fistful of hay, sliced clean from its mother earth with swift scythes in confident female hands. Their bare feet were clinging to the earth as if to quell its rebellion against their aggressive act of pillage. A perfect rhythm of bend, grab, slice, fling, then feet inch forward a fraction and bend, grab, slice, fling, rolling on for hours with nary a grunt from the lady laborers, only an occasional song, ripples of laughter, and the glint of a naked gold tooth. They hung together like four grapes left on the vine, juicy and capable of becoming something oh-so-intoxicating, yet each occasionally contemplated breaking free to uncover an unmarked destiny. But who knows what; perhaps solidarity or the simple task at hand, kept them together like notes on a page dedicated to completing the phrase.

Zorka, the oldest and most voluptuous of the lot, clearly felt that at fifty, she'd put in her share of decades of devotion to the field work, and wasn't it time for retirement, or at the very least, a coffee break? She had married quite young, to a night watchman at the local brickyard. Somehow the uniform confused her, for she thought her Vlado to be a man of means, but alas thirty years later, he was still looking at the same bricks from ten o'clock in the evening till four o'clock in the morning. What he lacked in ambition, he made up for by having a heart as big as the entire Shar Mountain range.

When their daughter, Dushka, was born with brain damage, Vlado was a tower of strength. While Zorka drank and fell apart, he took care of the child, and helped her break the medical prediction that she'd be dead at fifteen. The story goes that the timid, unassuming Vlado turned Dr. Vukich's office upside down the day that the good doctor gave him the bad news. Vlado had the wisdom to have Zorka and two-year-old Dushka wait in the reception area, while he went in to speak to Dr. Vukich alone. Zorka claimed she heard a loud crash, then shouting, then a thud. She figured Vlado had fainted, for he'd always been a little frail, nearly passed out on their wedding night, from the sheer excitement of mounting his mountain woman. To the rescue, as usual, Zorka rushed into the office, and found the X-ray light board had been shattered, apparently by an airborne metal chart.

The doctor's desk had been turned upside down, sending X-ray films and patient files to the floor. The doctor, nearly a foot taller than Vlado, was pinned against the wall. Much to Zorka's surprise and admiration, Vlado had the good doctor by his tie, and was hissing at him, "Don't you dare tell me lies about my daughter! What kind of man are you? You are supposed to heal people, not break their hearts..." and so on until Zorka thought it wise to pry him off the doctor's neck, before her hero husband ended up in jail. Dr. Vukich is said to have left the practice. Dushka was never taken to another doctor. She survived whatever they thought was wrong, and left all their medical premonitions in the dust.

Though quiet and slow, Dushka was utterly content at thirty. She'd worked side by side with her mother since the age of ten. Her education stopped at the sixth grade, the teachers were unsuccessful in getting her to read, and they didn't know what to do with her. So she became her mother's partner in all things, and was actually quite handy.

Dushka, her name derived from the word "dusha" meaning soul, took profound care with each task given her. She was devoted to making beauty out of ashes. One Christmas, she had just learned to embroider, and so naturally got busy embroidering everything in sight. Christmas tree ornaments, potholders, towels, scarves, anything that could bear her emblematic threads. That same Christmas, the elder of the village, everyone's Aunt Sofia, had crocheted house slippers for all the women, some two dozen pairs. Dushka decided to surprise them all, by embroidering a floral pattern on each one, which she accomplished with delirious dexterity. But somehow, in the fervor of creativity, she carefully yet unknowingly, had stitched the top and bottom of the toe of the slipper together, making it impossible for any woman to get her foot all the way into the slipper. No one said a word about it. In the spirit of sisterhood, all the women wore their new Christmas slippers with their heels hanging out the back, like it was some new Parisian fashion. They sported them proudly and had nothing but praise for their darling Dushka. Such was the sisterhood of Shar village.

CHAPTER TWO

THE WIND WAS PICKING UP, threatening rain and cooling their brows. As the cutters swept across the field, Dushka trailed behind, gathering the hay into large piles to be loaded on the wagon later. This was their last cutting for the year. Autumn had arrived early. And they were late. Yet there was always time for chatter.

"How did we get this job?" Zorka moaned. "This is man's work."

Miriana, the chubby, cheerful, eternal optimist, with a laugh like a bubbling brook, replied, "The men are busy."

"Or dead." Zorka retorted.

"Even some live ones are dead!" Miriana spilled more inexplicable ebullience. At forty, with four children and a young husband to care for each day, Miriana was blessed with a buoyant outlook that could only be explained by what must have been constant sexual attention from her randy husband, Miroslav, ten years her junior. That being the case, her remark was a bit mysterious since clearly Miroslav was one of the live ones. In any case, everything was *always* all right with Miriana, and frankly, every pack of field workers should have one of her - complete with the contagious laugh and the glass half full attitude.

"Because of the war," declared Dushka, miraculously folding into the conversation, with a mention of the unmentionable. It was a indeed a time of Civil War in their troubled country, and their beautiful mountain village, sandwiched between Bosnia-Herzegovina, Montenegro and Kosovo, near the Morovica river, was in the cradle of Old Serbia. It lay amidst the ancient, cherished Orthodox monasteries, enveloped by the exquisite Shar Mountains, at the cross-section of the terrifically hot-headed, hot-bedded, historical, hysterical Balkan civil strife. Some called it the Jerusalem of Eastern Orthodoxy.

"What war?" Zorka professed, finally using this change of topic from henhouse to epic, as an excuse to stop work, straighten up, and deliver the denial that kept the entire history of the world from coming clean. "It's far away." And so it was in her thought. The stakes were too high to think of the war being nearby. That the atrocities could be more than exaggerated hearsay, that they could even remotely approach her precious Vlado, or cherished Dushka, or beloved village, that in a moment the whiplash of a spiteful history could tear apart her life as she knew it – it was more than she could bear to let into her thought, even for a second. So she pressed on and enlisted the support of Yelena. "Right, Yelena, six hundred years ago, maybe, yes, in this village there was...well, you know...a war....but not now, no.....no, right?"

To be a Slav at that time, 1990's, was to learn to live in longing, obstinacy and love. It was a time when they'd seen enough, but not all that they would come to see, though they knew it not. Unwilling to give up their passionate love for their land, for their home, for each other, for their customs and for their simple but meaningful life, they hung on. It was like stretching a filament so thinly that it could only be a supernatural faith in the Supreme that kept it from snapping. Like a relationship shattered yet one party still grabs on to the slim hope that it can be restored. Perhaps that staunch stubbornness to defy defeat, that absolute fierceness to face down error and stand up for love, could indeed restore what was broken, and one and one could begin again to equal oneness or unity. This was the confirmation Zorka sought but did not get from Yelena.

Yelena, the shining star of the village, the diamond in the rough, the beautiful, energetic, intelligent, multilingual, woman of the field, clung to the piece of earth she identified as home like a lion to her cub. Yelena, who for all her virtues, possessed straight arrow thinking and an armor of honor that often made her daunting to accompany, so loud were her unspoken principles. Yelena, who was meant to be a boy, sprang from her mother's womb feet first, as if to say, "Okay, so I'm not a boy, but I refuse to let the disappointment in your eyes, keep my light under a bushel." Yelena, who subconsciously sought to overcome the let down she figured she'd caused her expectant father, with her unbridled ability to break a horse better than any son of his could have, carried a pocket of sorrow deep inside her soul. And she had no intention of letting anyone ever visit it.

Yelena's sister Ljuba regularly begged her to join her family in America and begin a new life, and each time Yelena declined because the plum trees needed pruning that day, or the cow was about to calve or the morel mushrooms needed gathering. Yelena, the high tower of strength, the promise of reason and understanding, secreted her daily wrangling with deep seeded fears of being separated from the village she adored. Still, she was the only one who could affirm for Zorka and for them all, that there was no danger here right now, only a faint memory of terror, buried beneath their denial from long, long ago. She was the one whose word carried impact, for she lived the truth.

Not wishing to accommodate Zorka's desire for delusion, Yelena proclaimed, "Six hundred years ago is yesterday in this village, Zorka, and you know that." Sensing that her soothsaying might have discouraged Zorka and the others, she quickly added, "But anyway, how about coffee," then called out, "Aunt Sofia, please, some coffee!"

Zorka, wavered, wanting to penalize Yelena for not taking her side, but then relented as if to say, *tomorrow is another day in court,* with "Coffee, hell, I need a Slivovitz." And the four women plowed up the hill, swinging their scythes at their sides. Zorka chose not to dwell on Yelena's pellet of truth. She only briefly mused, *why did I even ask her...who cares, that's her view.* Then Zorka broke into song to dilute what she knew to be the case: that Yelena would no sooner cloak the truth than she would strike her son. So Zorka let her belting voice ring out loudly, as she sauntered through the freshly piled hay, recklessly scattering their last hour's work, causing Yelena to marvel yet again at how her beloved people could so nonchalantly create chaos out of newly created order. What is that impulse to undo the good done? She would never comprehend it. *Accept them or leave them because you aren't ever going to change them,* she thought, then followed them up the hill, pausing to restore the toppled hay piles, satisfying her very own personal and sometimes annoying obsession for order. Zorka had eyes in back of her head, for without turning around, she finished the refrain of her song and shouted back, "Yelena, you missed a blade of hay, hurry up and get it back where it belongs!" Laughing, at her cleverness while justifying her own slovenliness, Zorka quickly commenced the next verse of her bawdy folk song, before her witty friend could top her.

CHAPTER THREE

YELENA ALEXIS ZELENICH MANDICH, an anachronism in the village, held there by her love and devotion to the small patch of terrain she possessed, was beautiful beyond reason. Rarely was such radiance found amid the peasant population of the remote village where Yelena's Aunt Sofia, her mother's sister, had raised her and her older sister Ljuba. Aunt Sofia was now their only living blood relation. Truth be told, where would Yelena go, anyway? Her own husband was killed in a truck accident three years ago when her son, Marko, was only seven years old. Aunt Sofia and Uncle Anton made a healthy household for little Marko, otherwise Yelena would have been without family at the table. She didn't want that for her son. So she stayed in the Shar Mountains.

Yelena was thirty-three years young, emanating the full bloom of womanhood. Born on a cold, snowy December night in the very house she lived in now, the house her great grandfather built, she was the second daughter to a macho father and an affectionate mother. Her father Marko was a farmer, a great horseman, a blacksmith, and a voracious lover of life. Her mother Nadya, ever the dutiful wife, was gifted in her handiwork - crocheting, embroidering, and knitting. She could make anything with her hands, and so became known in the village as having "fingers of gold." But Nadya's main delight was her two daughters, Yelena and Ljuba. She lived for them, breathed for them, could not imagine sunlight without them. It was the standard Mediterranean sense of motherhood.

Yelena's sister, Ljuba, six years her senior, inherited Nadya's talents, while Yelena followed in her father's footsteps--strong, lively, with the gait of a young colt from the day she learned to walk. Her mother was by no means a softy herself. She played the good farm wife with steadiness, reason and quiet obedience, but could fight like a mountain lion if need be. Her family was her life. She adored her husband massively, served him happily, and mourned him devotedly.

So much so, that when he died of a heart attack, hard at work at his anvil, Nadya contracted pneumonia and passed on within a year. She left the earth with only one regret, not to have lived to see her daughters marry and have children. Ljuba and Yelena both thought their mother had wanted to be with her man. Nadya always thought of what others needed. This was the pleasure she gleaned from life, answering the call of her loved ones. So it was no surprise, her willingness to follow that call to heaven.

That left the Zelenich sisters to be mothered by their Aunt Sofia, who stepped up to the plate with pleasure, especially since she was now childless. She had lost her only daughter, Snezhana eight years earlier. The girl ran an unexplainably high fever one morning at the age of two, and death branded her by sundown. The doctor had been sent for but couldn't be located in time. Aunt Sofia and her husband, Anton, had no idea how to bring the fever down. They had no refrigeration back then, and it was a warm spring. In a furious effort to save his only child Anton ran a direct vertical to the top of a mountain to fill his pack with snow to cool the baby's flaming little frame. Pitifully, it was nearly melted by the time he reached his child, since his own body produced such heat. It was like carrying the snow in an oven. His heroic failure broke him in two. A man is not a man if he cannot save his seed. Baby Snezhana would have been exactly Yelena's age had she lived. They were born a week apart. Life. Just when we've been cut to the bone and every layer of skin has been peeled so far back that the flutter of a butterfly wing could scald us, it comes to our aid. In this case, it was Aunt Sofia who was saved from her unutterable grief, by being granted her life employment – raising her two nieces, Yelena and Ljuba.

So Aunt Sofia had come by her caretaking qualities naturally. She anticipated the needs of others, just like her sister Nadya had. She was already at her kitchen counter, filling the four demitasse with good, strong Turkish coffee and placing them on a tray with a clear liter-bottle of homemade plum brandy - the famed Slav Slivovitz, and a bowl of cherries, before she even heard the call from the women in the field. A small woman with a large person's courage of conviction, Aunt Sofia peered past Machka, her fat cat planted on her window sill, to see her niece and the other women coming up from the field. She nodded and muttered to Machka, congratulating herself on her prescient and perfect timing. She popped a sweetened cherry into Machka's purring pucker, and stuffed her own jaw with a chunk of chewing tobacco, stored in a Dushka-embroidered pouch, dangling daintily from her apron strings. The cat played with tissue paper from a cardboard carton, with a return address label from America, reminding Aunt Sofia to put the package on the tray for show and tell.

"Bad cat," she feigned reprimand the same time she rewarded Machka with another cherry, thus typifying the quick change artistry of the feminine Slavic soul. One moment - I am furious, you have broken my heart, forget you know me, and in a millisecond, come to dinner, darling, all is forgiven. It was not insincerity, but rather a kind of existential hopscotch that was quite genuine, despite the velocity with which it often occurred. If only that enlightened attitude of casual acquittal were rampant in the ongoing civil war, there wouldn't be one.

CHAPTER FOUR

THE FIELD WOMEN PADDED UP the dusty path primed to soak up the coming rain. Taking off their babushkas, they mopped their faces and glanced over to their neighbors, who were donning their scarves for their afternoon prayers in the village mosque. Would that the differences between the Muslim world and the Christian world were as simple as the usage of a babushka, sacred or mundane. The same piece of cloth could rent a gash between friends, split the globe into pieces, or blanket them in peace. The field women sauntered past their neighbors, revealing indifference or disdain, and glanced fleetingly at the Muslim households, a mere twenty meters from their own cluster of homes. All but Yelena, who had kept her long, black, shining tresses wrapped for a while longer, and lingered to greet her Muslim friend, Zima, who was on her way to prayers. Yelena liked the sound of the "call to prayer" that emerged from the mosque five times daily. The yearning cry felt somehow familiar to Yelena. Unlike her fellow-Slavs, she refused to let bitterness or intolerance toward her neighbors creep into her heart.

"Zima!" she called out. Zima turned, letting her Muslim friends proceed to the mosque ahead of her, and greeted Yelena, her childhood friend, with the Slav tradition of three kisses on the cheek.

"How are you doing? How are the boys?" Yelena continued.

"They're boys, you know," Zima replied warmly, brightening at the mere mention of her sons, melting away her usual reticent manner. "And Marko?" she added.

"Good." Yelena smiled. She and Zima had grown up together, as neighbors, schoolmates, best friends. Zima was a boney, somber version of Yelena. Both with black hair, dark exotic eyes, high cheek bones, a proud gait, though Zima's beauty lacked the fire of passion that Yelena possessed. Instead, Zima reflected a sober resignation to her fairly young life, as something already written, that no expansiveness on her part could change. Yet there was a soulful grace in her ascetic stature, almost that of someone who's been out in the desert wilderness searching for something they don't find, so they return carrying the wisdom of the wilderness inside them, but still harboring the longing. Though less than two years older than Yelena, Zima's face betrayed more hardship. Both had endured losses, and both had helped each other grieve with an unspoken contract to share any burden like sisters.

Zima's father emigrated from Albania, where he was a farmer on a plot of dusty land that did not fulfill the needs of his livestock, let alone his family of eight. He sought richer, fatter land, and he didn't have to go far to find it. Southern Serbia opened their borders, made room for his family, and hundreds and hundreds like his. The strangers were ignored, tolerated or befriended, and a peaceful co-existence between Albanian and Serb, Muslim and Christian sustained for decades. That is, as long as it was clear to the newcomers that they were living on Serbian land, by the grace of Serbian hospitality, then all would be well. But try to take from a Serb what is his - like his land, or infringe upon his freedom for his family to grow and prosper in the Serbian Orthodox way, and that hospitable hand could suddenly become armed and dangerous. So when Mahmud, Zima's father, fell in love with a Serbian villager, Zeljka, he risked the fury of his family by marrying her. He was quickly disowned, as a matter of course, until Zima and her brothers were born and raised up in a strict Muslim way, a huge and not particularly willing concession on the part of his Serbian wife. Only then was Mahmud restored to his tribe. The village Slavs were certain that was not an easy sacrifice that Zeljka made and many waited for the other slipper to fall. Nevertheless, she kept her word, raised her children as devout Muslims, and as far as Zima was concerned, her mother was as loyal a Muslim as she vowed to be on her wedding day.

It mattered not one drop to Yelena what religion Zima was. She had a good girlfriend, close to her age, whom she loved. Yelena was brought up by her selectively liberal-minded Aunt Sofia, who completely ignored the then muffled Muslim-Serb feud, and was forthright in her acts of kindness toward Zima and her family. She had learned well from her aunt.

Zima scurried over to a wooden bin in front of her house, and scooped out several ripe pears, as many as her apron would hold, and handed them over to Yelena, who caught them in her own apron. "That's too much," Yelena protested, while receiving the near ripe fruit, and recollecting how Zima had always shared more than half of what she had, including her Muslim prayer rug, which, at the age of nine, Zima cut in half to divvy up with Yelena, and caught the wrath of her father for it.

Zima nodded, "Maybe you'll make your brandy with them." Yelena thanked her and thought about the word *your* brandy, knowing that with a Serbian mother, Zima must have known a time when it was *her* brandy too. "I have to go. Prayers. Omir doesn't care, but I do." Zima flashed a quick smile, then rushed down the hill to catch up with the other Muslim women heading obediently toward the mosque. Yelena watched her go, and wondered how it was that Zima's husband, Omir, Muslim by birth, cared less about prayers than his half Serbian wife. Yelena supposed Zima possessed the zeal of the convert.

The field women were huddled around the table under the grape arbor outside of Aunt Sofia's farmhouse with the glee that men have at a poker table. Zorka straddled the bench with the bottle of Slivovitz nestled between her legs, pouring shots for one and all, ignoring the fact that she was the only one drinking. If that bench could talk, one can only imagine the gnarly tales it would tell. Yelena unloaded the pears from her apron and let them roll freely across the weather warped wooden table. The women looked but did not touch, a silent statement of their separatism from their neighbors, a stand Yelena refused to support. So Yelena downed her coffee in one swallow, turned over the cup, grabbed one of Zima's pears and headed up the hill to the church. The turning over of the cup allowed the residue of the coffee grinds to drain so the fortune of the drinker could be told by a prophetic eye. Zorka's third Slivovitz deluded her into thinking she had one such eye and called after Yelena, "Don't you want to sit for a cup reading?"

Like a mountain goat, Yelena had already scaled the hill. She turned back, "Yes, later. Church first, then my favorite Turkish custom," Yelena laughed, overlapping Zorka's bristling snort at the mention of the Turks. Yelena carried her head high and her principles higher. She would not go along with the ignorant prejudices ingrained in the villagers. She loved her village family dearly, but detested their racism. Albanian Muslims had been their neighbors for as long as she could remember. Marriages mixed Muslims and Serbs together on many occasions. Some Serbs were Muslim, more often than either group would ever admit. But the line of demarcation between the Christian world and the Islamic world remained solid as a prison wall. Yelena chose to leap over that wall, and maintain her cherished childhood friendship with Zima, overtly recognizing that many of their customs they had come from the Muslim Turks. She put down the belief that the belligerent goings on in Bosnia had made one side any more right than the other. She condemned all violence.

Nevertheless, her father's words sometimes haunted her, "Beware of strong convictions, my daughter" he used to say to his headstrong offspring, "for you will either have to surrender your life for them, or be shamed by them should you ever attempt to save your own life at their expense. They'll make you a hero or a hermit, or both," he would say, "but they'll never make you happy." Yelena furtively disagreed. She did that a lot. It was almost a trademark. Never perfunctory and often annoying to those of a more supple spine, Yelena would ponder things, tear them apart, and chew on them interminably until she understood them. She did it with the ferocity of a jungle feline, and then having done so, she would dive into her convictions with a somewhat perturbing passion. It exhausted everyone but her. At that moment, she fueled up the hill toward church, her favorite hunting ground for chasing down a greater comprehension of life as Spirit. This she craved.

CHAPTER FIVE

YELENA'S SON MARKO WAS A SPITTING IMAGE OF HIS FATHER, in brawn, brains, and manly beauty, but he had his mother's fast feet. Yelena's gazelle genes were passed on to her son, and he loved to run, for the fun of it. He was a gifted child. Things came easily to him. He read at an early age, probably because Yelena recited poetry to him while he was still in the womb, and read to him every night since his birth. Though an excellent reader himself, Marko loved the sound of his mother's voice, and insisted on her reading to him, even at his ripe old age of ten, going on eleven. He was nursed to the poetry of Njegos, renowned Montenegrin poet. Yelena clung to the poet's writings like she did the Bible. When her husband Radmilo died, she inscribed a passage from Njegos's famous opus, *The Mountain Wreath* on his grave stone:

"And all this vast array

Of things confus'd

Hath yet some rhythmic Harmony and Law."

This was more a testimony to her insistence that she had not been abandoned by the Divine, than a true acceptance of the tragedy at such an early moment in their love.

Little Marko was a love child, born of the romantic ardor his parents had for each other. Perhaps that was why for all his gifts and ease with the hurdles of growing up, no narcissism or laziness ever got hold of him. He made his way through his ten young years, with the grace of a finely carved paddle parting the water, doing whatever was necessary to move the boat forward, but never expecting the water to do it for him, nor leaving behind anything but a subtle after-smile on the wave. Yelena knew he was special, but what mother doesn't see that in her son? The night she and Radmilo made Marko, he whispered to her. May he have all of you and none of me, except that part of me, which is from you, for you are the best of me. Amen. She was sure she would never love another man, after Radmilo. She reasoned that we were rationed one great love per lifetime. Radmilo had filled that portion a thousandfold.

They met in the Greenwich village of Belgrade - a section called Skardarlija - an old, wide, cobblestone street, colorfully bejeweled with galleries, studios, cafes, restaurants, and gypsy violinists luring patrons to dwell in their dream for a night. Closed to automobiles, it was plentifully populated with tourists and natives alike, sauntering, chatting, imbibing the balmy evening air. Yelena was spending the summer of her twentieth year studying English in Belgrade and working in a cafe in Skardarlija at night. She had planned to go on to study nursing, but that never developed into more than weekend volunteer work in a children's hospital. She roomed with her sister, who'd been living in the capital city for five years. It was a lonely summer for Aunt Sofia without the girls; but for the sister duo it was a divine adventure. In her typically directed manner, Yelena focused on conquering the English language in one summer and toward that end, she spoke English to every customer she had, whether they were from Berlin or Brazil. Half of the time it worked, the other half, it threw the customer into the position of trying to help their waitress to communicate, as if she were the stranger in a strange land, and they, the natives.

When a certain handsome, virile man, soon to become her Radmilo, came in and ordered a beer in English with a heavy Slavic accent, she figured she'd met her match. Like her, he loved poetry, but quoted Bob Dylan not Njegos. Turned out he was a truck driver for an express shipping company, and he had lots of time to memorize lyrics, whether he understood them or not, that played on the radio or tape en route from Skopje to Belgrade, his usual run. Completely mesmerized by Yelena's spirited beauty, he made a point of coming to the cafe every weekend, staying till closing, then helping Yelena clean up. They'd sit for hours, after closing, talking the language of love, and dancing to the juke box, while the janitor whipped the mop around their ankles, dodging their fancy footwork.

At the end of that summer of love, Radmilo came to Yelena's village and asked Uncle Anton for her hand. They were married in October, and they lived in the village, in a little cottage near Aunt Sofia's farmhouse. He planned to build them a palace one day, and fill it with as many children as she desired. They were drunk with joy.

She sometimes accompanied him on his trucking hauls, but when she had to stay in the village to do the farm work, their reunions parted the heavens. It was three years before she became pregnant with little Marko, not for lack of joyful efforts. It was simply that God blessed them with plenty of time to themselves before the little prince arrived. So at twenty-three, nearly twenty-four, Yelena became a mother. She wore the mantle like a proud and protective lioness.

On the eve of Marko's seventh birthday, Yelena was planning a big party for her son in the village. Radmilo was making a run from Skopje to Belgrade, but decided to turn right around and drive back down to be there by the morning of his son's birthday. He was due at midnight. Yelena had perfumed herself, and waited for him in undiminished anticipation of a night of love with her husband. By three o'clock in the morning, she knew something had happened. Her heart feared she would never hold him again. At dawn, two policemen came to the door. She was still up and sitting on the front step, smoking a cigarette, as if she were expecting them. She spoke to them as if they had come to look at her cows for purchase, and escorted them out toward the barn, so as not to alarm Marko, in case he was already awake. Radmilo had been speeding to get home, and jackknifed the truck in the rain. He was killed instantly.

Yelena stood stone still at the news of what she'd already known in her gut since midnight. She stayed down in the barn milking a long time that morning, answering the demands of her bovine dependents, and stowing away to weep into their hides as she milked them. She sent Marko to school that day, gave him his birthday party that afternoon, and left that evening to do the arrangements for Radmilo's funeral, leaving young Marko with Aunt Sofia. When she returned, she sat her son down on the front step and told him what happened. It was such a big tragedy for a little boy to take in. He sat silently for a long moment.

"I knew my Dad would never forget me on my birthday."

She held him as he convulsed with tears, then took him inside where she insisted they work on some homework together. And, of course, she read to him that night, but she could never remember what story it was. All life had been excavated from Yelena the night Radmilo died. It returned to her slowly, day by day, through loving her son.

It was unclear whether it was early widowhood, or her fascination with the mysticism of the Slavic version of Christianity,

Eastern Orthodoxy, that made Yelena a regular at the village church. As Christian faiths went, this one offered an unusual combination of the passion of Christ and the mysterious monasticism of the monks. It was curious that such ascetic devotion could be so heavily laced with rituals that bordered on paganism. Yelena was intrigued by the paradox, wherein one often finds the Divine. She loved God, worshipped Him sincerely, and believed in the power of prayer to move mountains. She practiced her faith to her best understanding so she could honestly teach her boy about his true Creator at an early age. Yet there was almost something heathen about her devotion to this tiny Byzantine Church.

There was a scent of gypsy magic in it. Yelena often knew things before they happened, and she'd take these intuitions to prayer, often transmuting a dark premonition into a healing. God's alchemy, she called it. This was the way she circumvented the principles of true Christianity which would not permit embarking on the superstitious practices that tempted her. She lightly touched the ceaseless invitations to read fortunes at the bottom of coffee cups, where somehow she was able to gaze impeccably into another's future and past. It wasn't easy to resist these rituals. She'd grown up with them. They were part of her. Yelena found sanctuary in the church on the hill; the Church of the Holy Mother of God, Sveti Bogorodica, literally, *"the Holy One who gave birth to God."* It made her feel serene and safe. The still, dark eyes of the Byzantine icons comforted her; the smell of the incense and burnt candles calmed her; and the prayerful mutterings of the old priest, Father Voyn, reassured her. Those centuries-old repetitions from behind the door of the altar, the sacred area forbidden to women, enchanted her. Father Voyn confessed that keeping women out of the altar area was a silly rule, and one that he had ignored years ago when Yelena's mother was permitted back there to clean. It was surmised that he may have had a school boy's crush on Nadya, Yelena's mother. In any case, dogma had not petrified Father Voyn's heart. He had a deep, leavening, vital love for God, his church, and all who entered it.

Yelena knew very little about the details of Father Voyn's life, only that he'd been married once, as is the privilege of Orthodox priests, and that he had an unshakable faith in God, and a capacity for love that made him sing. He was like a mysterious wedding guest at his own wedding, both the blesser and the blessed, the bridegroom, and the Lamb of God. Within the walls of this little church, in quiet contemplation, Yelena witnessed fears turn into hope, like water to wine, inspiring and motivating her daily trips up the hill. She needed it like a fix. It was her oxygen, her sunlight, her elixir for life. She required it daily. She had a holy "jones."

So it was a natural occurrence for Yelena to be hiking up the hill to the church, that particular day. Driven by a sincere desire to know more about the ineffable matters of Life, she'd grown certain those revelations were caked in the musty smell of the cavernous sepulchre that withstood the moisture of five centuries. Like tears, the chips of the fifteenth century frescoes fell on the cement floor and became part of the baptism of love that rarefied her afternoon visits.

Yelena grabbed a small bunch of flowering basil that grew wild around the church. As she approached the door of the cool sanctuary, she paused to wrap her head in her babushka, then stepped into the one place she felt undeniably inseparable from God's love. She prayed with certainty that there was some divine plan in place that would one day include a perfect peace to replace the current chaos of her beloved Balkan landscape. With the aristocracy of soul and the humility of a saint, she knew deep inside that it was Soul that governed her way. She cherished all life, all living things, all that Spirit offered each day.

On entering the holy canopy, she crossed herself, walked forward to the icon at the front of the church, kissed it, and placed the flowering basil around its gold frame. The custom of honoring the holy image with spices was an ancient ritual, possibly an effort to win favor with God, or perhaps a faint echo of the Wise Men at Jesus' birth. Then she lit three candles, each burning with a specific prayerful request; first, her husband's soul to be at rest, then peace and harmony in her homeland, and third, for her son's good health and well-being. She lingered on the third prayer a little longer than usual, as if there were some gossamer web of concern that had to be burned off. After her speechless reverence, she climbed up to the choir loft, to her special place where she came to think and dream. She opened the window and looked out over the grandeur of the Shar Mountain range, smiling at the splendor she'd inherited by simply being born in this little hamlet, surrounded by simple joys and glorious beauty each day.

The greatest of these was now running up the path to greet her. It was her son, her only child, Marko. What mother wouldn't gloat at the sight of her boy, running free like the wind, happy and strong, with her own self as his destination? She descended the loft to meet him.

CHAPTER SIX

MARKO AND YELENA WERE CLOSE. Maybe because she was both parents to him since Radmilo's passing, or maybe because they were so much alike. They spent precious time together; riding horses bareback, hiking, fishing and best of all, reading. Both of them possessed a healthy hunger for books. They read together, they read to each other, they read aloud, softly or boldly, they were hooked on the written word. Smitten by the sound of his mother's voice, Marko was indulged to the extent he desired. "No," was not a word he heard very often from his mother. She prayed daily that she would raise him right, not spoil him too, too much, and fulfill her mission of motherhood honorably. She asked daily for God's help to keep her on His path.

At that moment, all her joy galvanized in the image of her young boy, a bundle of radiant energy, racing up the mountain. Her communion with Spirit was about to be raided by the love of her life, her son. Her cherished peace she happily sacrificed as Marko burst through the church door like a wild mustang heading for the barn, like he couldn't quite identify the edifice as a church, like he was creating the space as he moved through it. She could chastise him till judgment day, but in truth she loved his unbridled spirit. She knew she was responsible for his undisciplined ways, which she loved because they reminded her of his father.

Barefoot, disheveled, with his proper school clothes unbound, released and untied, Marko rushed in and brought the wonder of the world with him. "Mamma," he panted, "can I go play soccer with the high school boys in the far meadow." He wasn't really asking, as much as announcing to his mother what her next concession would be. Not that he was arrogant, for that was not his way, but he knew his mother accepted his need to reach higher, do better, excel, advance every chance he got. He learned it from her, so he knew she wouldn't deny him.

"Where are your shoes?" she asked, delaying her inevitable compliance, so she could prolong her enjoyment of her son, already

With bowed head, but undimmed glee, Marko replied, "Yes, Mamma, I will. I promise. Next time for sure. Thank you, Mamma!" And he was gone.

She looked up at the beautiful Byzantine icon of the Holy Virgin Mary, and shook her head, "Mother of God, when will they learn we are all one?" She listened, expectantly for a reply from the centuries old varnished surface radiating the image of Mother and Child in serene acceptance of All Good. None came. Then Marko bolted back into the church.

"Mamma, where are your shoes?" He liked having the last word. She smiled and guessed that was part of being a feisty almost-eleven year old. She resumed her prayer, picturing her son flying down the hill like the wind to join his soccer mentors for a game. After a few moments she got up from her knees, took the broom from behind the front door, and began sweeping the church, where some dried basil seeds and old candle wax had littered the floor.

Then she heard, "Yelenaaaaaaaaaaaaaaaaaaaa!" *The call of the wild,* she thought, the call of the helpless and lazy gaggle of Zorka, Miriana, Dushka and even Aunt Sofia. "Yelenaaaaaaaaaaa, we need you!!!!"

Indeed.

CHAPTER SEVEN

WHAT WAS IT THAT MADE SOME WOMEN CAPABLE, conscientious and complete, and others fragmented like the edges of an unfinished tapestry, waiting for the weaver to organize their path across the warp and woof of their own existence? One can guess genetics, bad habits, or worse still a conscious choice to let the world serve them, presuming they're here for the duration to occupy an unearned throne. *"Don't step on my robe while you bow to me, thank you very much."*

Yelena didn't necessarily see her friends that way. Well, not always. She did her best to cultivate a glass half-full mentality, and looked for and found the good in every soul she encountered. But the mountains educated her to have the keen awareness of a coyote, and she couldn't help but note that these bovine beauties, she called her life-long friends, couldn't pick up a fork without her help. The village life taught her to serve the common welfare, so critical judgment took a back seat to her mantra of *"what do we need to do, to do what we have to do, to get things done, ladies?"* At that point the task at hand appeared to be unloading the wagon delivering their grain supply.

There may have been times when Yelena could have strangled Zorka and Miriana for their consummate laziness, but today she abided in a channel of love. It was a good day. She felt expansive, and generous spirited. It was only mid-afternoon and so much good had unfolded; they heard from her sister, Ljuba, in America, always a special treat; the work in the field was nearly finished; she had visited briefly with her close friend, Zima; she'd had her time to herself in the church; and of course best of all, young Marko had lit the lamp on her face with his bubbling boyish being. So what's a little extra work to a woman with a strong back and cheerful spirit?

Surely she could manage the bags of grain on her own. Poised with a true appreciation of being, Yelena practiced acceptance of her slow-moving friends. She was happy to be of service. In fact, she practically danced down the hill to rescue the bags. She flung them over her shoulder with the ease of Ginger Rogers in the arms of Fred Astaire, her favorite American movie stars.

When she lived in Belgrade, she had devoured whatever videotapes of that dancing duo that she could find. If circumstances had permitted, she'd have chosen to be a dancer, if for no other reason than to defy gravity on a daily basis. Yelena's insurgent nature was not confined to the spiritual matters, she often thought it appealing to overturn a few laws of physics as well.

The wagon driver was a neighbor from another part of the village. He came to them twice a month with grain for the animals. Access to Aunt Sofia's place was limited to horses, mules, wagons, and those fancy four-wheel drive vehicles. So Mr. Shriqui and his horse drawn wagon were both necessary and welcomed. He answered a need, and he did it with the grace of a fine gentleman, which is to say, he did not comment nor critique Zorka and Miriana's character flaws, whereas Yelena felt like kicking those two broads in the back of the head sometimes. But not today.

Mr. Shriqui knew they refused to help with the grain because he was Muslim and they were Serbian. That age-old conflict crept into the most mundane moments of the day. They knew it. He knew it. But his view of Yelena was different. She always looked him in the eye, asked after his family, offered him water, and helped him unload the grain. Normally, he would not have minded waiting for Yelena to show up before he unloaded, but that day the clouds were gathering, and he was impatient to finish his deliveries before the rain came.

He was a small, wiry man, with a terribly attractive face, high cheekbones, deeply set dark eyes, thick black brows, and a shock of hair hidden under a well-worn felt cap. His smoky smile suggested he had a sensuous side that he kept covered with a flannel shirt, lambskin vest, and silky mustache. He pulled his wagon up to the edge of the gate near the arbor where the women sat drinking and cackling. "A little help with the grain, please, ladies, the rain's coming soon." They didn't budge. He didn't ask twice, but joined their afternoon siesta by letting the leather reins rest on his knee, while he rolled himself a cigarette and observed the predictable response from the laggers.

"Yelenaaaaaaaaaaaaaaaaaaaaaaaaaaaaaaa." In perfect unison as if rehearsed, their cry shattered Yelena's serene sweeping of the church, and sent her skipping down the hillside.

She greeted the chore with alacrity, as was her wont. "Mr. Shriqui, how good to see you." He tipped his hat and helped her unload the grain. The field women suffered conflicting emotions going off inside them. They felt relief that Yelena showed up to do the job, but they recoiled watching her continue to be so friendly to the Muslim community. *What could she be thinking, making nice to him. Doesn't she know what's happening all around us with these people,* Zorka silently wondered. Ah the game of blame, the momentary reprieve to allow one's elbow to bend one more time and throw down the slivovitz, without shame. That was Zorka's specialty. She then flipped on the tape deck Ljuba had sent in the package from America, providing musical accompaniment for Yelena's hard labor. Undaunted, Yelena managed a quick dance step between loads. "Where do you get that energy," Zorka inquired and admired.

"God," Yelena replied, knowing that answer would shut Zorka up for a little while, so she could listen to the engaging folk music wafting into the moistening air.

The momentary levity of Yelena's dance step, the pause in the middle of farm chores, the stillness before the storm reflected the palpable paradox which was the essence of their tribal life. The women of the village were true existentialists. They had no choice but to be fully alive each moment, as if that moment were all that existed, because maybe it was. They were like angels on the point of a needle, poised for flight, if duty called.

Duty did call. Yelena caught a look at the clouds gathering overhead and swiftly shifted gears and went back to the bags of grain still to be loaded into the barn. As Yelena resumed her work the tape deck suddenly clicked off, and Zorka snapped at the ever-innocent Dushka, "Now you broke it." The delusionary reality brought about by the plum brandy, *it's everybody else's fault.* Yelena smiled knowingly, shaking her head as she trotted off to the barn.

CHAPTER EIGHT

THE BARN. After the safe haven of the church, the barn was Yelena's favorite spot. She loved them both. Two caverns of security, where specific tasks were performed. From their vantage point, all looked right with the world. She pushed open the barn door with her hip, dropped the last bag of grain into the bin and closed the lid, stopping briefly to catch her breath before her next maneuver. The doves greeted her, the chickens scattered, the cows readied their haunches for imminent, tangible relief, and the rabbits remained silent in calm certainty that dinner was coming along with the soft touch of the hand that fed them.

They were a two-cow family and Yelena chose to manage the milking by hand twice a day. "Krava" and "Katya" as they were named, much preferred her warm hands to the cold metal milking instruments they would have to succumb to if the modern age were ever to reach Shar village. As there seemed to be little or no danger of that happening in the foreseeable future, the manual ritual began. The animals were at ease with Yelena and vice versa. There was a sense of purpose and perfect completion with animal chores. You milk the cows you carry away buckets of milk. You feed the pigs eventually you get bacon. You give grain to the chickens they produce eggs. Concrete cause and effect, nothing abstract nor confounding, just pure, sure-fire results you could count on.

Same held true for household chores. You iron a shirt, you've made a difference in the integrity of that piece of cotton for that day. Oh the bliss of do-able actions. It's not that Yelena didn't have a keen intellect, she did. In fact, she spoke three languages and was a voracious reader in two of them. It's more that she had an understanding of life as cyclical, not linear. Her happiness lay in the repetition of daily tasks that created the fabric of her life, and the life of her child, and his to come. She was content to place a single piece of mosaic in the picture to contribute to the ultimate masterpiece.

Like a true Byzantine woman, she walked with the same dignity in the barnyard, as she did in church, a mountain path, or might in the presence of a king. All of Life was a divine design and she was devoted to it, took nothing for granted, lacked nothing, yet longed for something more. That was one of the blessed incongruities of her Serbian soul.

A cold wind blew over her shoulder as she burrowed into Krava's haunches to drain the last few drops from her udder. Yelena raised up her head and gazed through the barn door. Rain clouds were gathering, the animals stirred. Autumn was already upon them. She finished the milking and looked out again, studied the sky, the patterns of the clouds, as if she were trying to read their message. In the distance, she heard the cackle of Zorka and Miriana, who'd probably drained the bottle of slivovitz by now. What would their culture have achieved without that fire-water? One can't help but wonder. Much, she surmised. It was hard for a Slav to learn moderation. It did not come naturally to any mountain inhabitant. After all, a mountain itself was an extreme act of nature, a piece of ground that said, *"I shall rise up so far above you, earth, and I shall live where the air is so thin and delicate, that every minute change shall be profoundly felt."* Vulnerable is what the mountains made you, and tough is what you had to become to survive there. So the field women were spared any harsh judgment for imbibing. What they were doing, they had deemed necessary given their clime. The sound of their distant voices comforted Yelena. They were something predictable and sure.

The rabbits showed their appreciation of her care by the ceaseless movement of their noses. She figured that was the same as a wagging tail, though maybe it was more. *"Gimme another carrot if you please?"* Who knew? They drank in her petting and scratching like a blind man takes in the sun.

"Are you hungry for love or food, Mala?" she asked the baby rabbit, then deduced it was both. It's impossible not to cuddle their silky coats. She held the little one close to her chest and snuggled him. *"Who was comforting whom?"* one might have asked.

Again the wind blew through the barn and cut through the calm she felt there. Again Yelena was drawn to the barn door to look out, scrutinize the horizon and listen. What was she hearing? A whistle of wind, an indiscernible something. Then suddenly, quiet again, she must be imagining things. She turned back about to replace the rabbit among his own, when this time, the sound sliced through her heart.

"Mamma!" she heard clearly from afar. "Mamma!" an urgent, terrifying cry, one that a mother never wants to hear, but lives in fear that one day she might.

Dropped from the safety of Yelena's palm, the baby rabbit scurried to its own mother, making way for Marko's mother to race out the door to her son. Her heart pounding so hard it was as if it preceded her body, desperately reaching to meet the cry that came again and again, "Mamma! Mamma!" She felt her heart crack, but no blood fell. She kept pumping toward him, her son, her soul, her life.

"Coming son, coming," she cried out, in a voice hoarse with horror. The long awaited rain chose to fall right then, showering her in tears that she was soon to claim forever and always for herself. She slipped on the newly cut hay, the fruits of her unfinished field labor today cost her critical moments in getting to Marko. She cursed the hay, the sun that made it, the rain that pulled her down.

In the distance she saw her son, seemingly headless, buried into the chest of a masked man. Marko was flailing with his fists, fighting for his young life. Her vision blurred; the rain, her tears, the impossibility that this was real. Her heart panted as she cut across the field like the scythe she used earlier that morning. She flew. "Coming son, coming," she wailed, wanting him to hear her voice and for him to know she heard his. Her heart bid, "Hang on, hang on, I'm there with you, my boy, my dear boy. Almost. Almost." Love, fear, hate, terror propelled her legs. Capital nouns. Immense emotions. To get to her son in time, she moved her legs faster than they knew to go in order to get there in time, in time to throw herself between the predator and the lamb, in time to fling her body to buffer the blow, in time to kill if necessary, the evil that would strike her son. Perhaps her mistake was looking up. Why did she do that? He was in front of her, straight ahead of her, the sole destination of her very being. She slipped again on the wet hay, the damnable remains of their sloth. *If only they'd skipped the coffee and picked up that hay, she'd have had more traction on the ground, and could have increased her speed by seconds, precious unretrievable moments.* If only, if only, if only, if only, a treacherous mantra pounded inside her like thumbs on the skin of a taut drum. Her bare feet were cut and bleeding from her rapid-blaze across the vast field. She regained her rhythm in the run for her life. She couldn't forgive her fall, the slip, the moment lost that kept her from her son a cosmic second longer than desirable. She rose in time to see what looked like a lead pipe in the hand of the masked man. He raised it up over her boy's head, raised it up to blend with the grey sky, raised it up to threaten the innocent one.

Where was Abraham's angel now to still the strike of death, to whisper in the killer's dumb ear, *Thus far and no farther!* Didn't he realize murder was unnecessary in God's world? Cease. Be still. Walk away. Leave the lambkins to their fold. No more blood dare be shed. Let them be. Where was that damned angel now when it was most needed? Yelena's entire being rang out for that angel to do what she could not, but it heard her not. The iron fell, the child took the blow, the boy called again for his mother, sure that his salvation would arrive. She did. She did arrive. She did indeed. She never broke speed, as she watched the masked evil disappear into a covered truck, pushing some older boys in the back. She thought she saw that, she was sure of nothing but reaching her son.

Marko was a thoughtful boy, he waited for his mother's arms to encompass him, beneath, above and around, before he uttered his last for her. "I knew you'd come," he said. His eyes were peaceful, unafraid. The storm had passed and he was in his mother's bosom.

"I'm here, my son, I'm here," she whispered, stroking his brow, his oh-so-young blood flowing freely from it.

"Ma," he started, as if he were about to tell her of some adventure, or make some modest request for an extra cookie.

"Yes, my darling, yes, my son, yes, yes, my soul," she managed through her tears, wanting to disguise her alarm. "I'm here, honey. I'm here with you, my boy, my good, good boy." Tenderly wiping the blood from his eyelids, "Don't you worry, Marko. You're all right now, you're safe, my darling boy. There's nothing to be afraid of, my son." And then he closed his eyes forever.

A wail that came from the bowels of the earth ripped through her body and cracked the sky. Raging thunder was drowned out by the mother's grief. She demanded the God of her understanding reach down and reverse this with His All-Powerful hand. She screamed for the Almighty to awaken her from this nightmare of unbearable horror. She pleaded to be spared this loss of her blood, that is, the blood of her son, which gave her life. Her request remained unrequited.

CHAPTER NINE

THE ENTIRE PLANET FELT YELENA'S PLEA. Two men from the town tavern jumped into a jeep and journeyed across the wet field toward the agonizing scene. From a distance, the way Yelena was holding Marko in her arm it looked like he might still be alive. Yet eternal grief had already set in as she was rocked her son to and fro, keening. The sound of a jeep penetrated her sobs, then heaving nostrils of a horse carrying an old neighbor friend to the scene reached her ears and made her quiver. All her senses were peaked to the height of the Himalayas. It was as if four layers of skin had been stripped away, and pain like flames from Hades were licking at the core of her being. She felt, heard, smelled, tasted, witnessed every minute to the maximum. This was the slow motion she'd witnessed only once before in her thirty-three years, the night she was told of her husband's accident. By now the rain was gushing down. It made things at once indiscernible and crystalline. Where did her tears stop, and the rain begin? When did her son's heart cease, and hers wrench? What was this rush of saviors in jeeps or on horseback racing to her side? Where did they come from and wherefore? The lamb had already been slaughtered. Abraham's angel was late.

By the time these men of great heart skidded toward the heap of tragedy, under the canopy of the olive tree, Yelena had a firm hold of her Marko, her beloved bundle, her life, her very life. She began the walk back across the field to bring him home. No dirge could be deep enough to accompany this death march. Each step was branded in her heart as a measurement of the field too great in length for her to traverse it in time to take the blow for her son. The weapon might have struck her instead. She might have landed in time to do what mothers do, give their lives for their children. Each stride was a slice of her flesh left on the vast field under her feet, like a punishment to herself, for not being there in time to save her son. Each stagger was a reverberation in her gut of the desire to hear the rest of the sentence her Marko started when she knelt over him, stroking his bleeding head. She imagined a thousand different endings to that phrase that would have made this whole thing a mistake, a charade, a rotten prank, a foolish aberration of war games, of boys being boys, anything but actual. She heard herself saying over and over, *This didn't happen, it never happened, it isn't real. It can't be. It couldn't be true. It's too horrible to be true.* The men mistook her murmurings for a petition for help with her bundle. She walked in a mesmeric state. They attempted to alleviate her of her load.

She snapped at them like a crocodile, "Leave me! Don't you touch him!" Fire flew from her mouth. She could not recognize their gesture as one of assistance. She only saw what was left for her to do to now, to keep a shield around her precious boy; that he should not be touched by anything but love, ever, ever, ever, ever again, for all eternity. Oh dear God, how can this be? God.

CHAPTER TEN

DINNER PLATES RESOUNDED WITH THE STRIKE OF FORKS AND KNIVES, slicing and scooping up the funeral meats into mouths at a loss for words. Glasses were set down hard on the tablecloth, as if in defiance. The gulp of wine they provided did not make gentle the hand of the drinker. Every mourner who sat partaking of the lamentable luncheon hated what had happened, detested the day, despised the doom, and denied the terrifying powerlessness deep inside each one of them that rendered them impotent before the finality of death. Each wanted to scream, lash out, but against whom and where? Weren't they there to be a comfort to the bereft mother? Where was she, the mother of the dead boy?

Zorka aided Aunt Sofia in preparing the coffee. Over the sink they both paused as if suddenly put on hold by an invisible hand. They looked out. Still it rained. Darkness came early. "Where is Yelena?" Zorka inquired. All that Sofia could muster up was a nod in the direction of the hilltop cemetery, tucked behind the church. The simple nod of Sofia's babushka-clad head told of the centuries-old knowledge that came from walking the earth, and listening to it. The smallest of movements, without a syllable attached, told Zorka what she already registered in her heart, that Yelena was where she would be the rest of her life, in that grave with her son. That was just the way it was.

She would come down to the house when she was ready, or maybe she would stand there all night. The women had too much respect for the chasm of grief Yelena carried to attempt to coax her down to the funeral table. Her table was set in the wilderness now. She had entered a vestibule of loneliness that was a prelude to rooms upon rooms filled with tears, a veritable Versailles of sorrow that awaited her. Sorrow, the one thing in life besides love that never leaves you where it finds you. The morphing had already begun for Yelena, she was ankle deep in wet earth. Fine. It brought her inches closer to her son. She wanted to stay there forever.

All this floated through Aunt Sofia's thought, for she knew Yelena like she knew her own self. She felt for her, and suffered her own pain soundlessly. She would have taken on Yelena's pain too, if there'd been a way to do that. The deafening silence was simply and suddenly snapped by Uncle Anton's direct command, a blessing under the circumstances.

"Sofia, coffee!"

Across the way, their neighbor Zima heard the hum of the funeral dinner muffled by the downpour, as she double-latched her front door against the wind, then popped open her umbrella and headed up the hill, with the effortlessness that comes with urgency. If anyone could get through to Yelena in her grief, it would be Zima. Zima and Yelena were like sisters, more than that even, soul mates, more, they were like the same person. That's how well they silently and surely read each other's thoughts. When they were growing up together, Zima would arrive at Yelena's doorstep at some odd hour of the evening, and gather small stones to wake her friend with a tap on her bedroom window, when the doorknob would already be turning and Yelena would step out. How did she know? It was never questioned. They were what could be called, *in synch*. They built things as a team, planted seeds together and broke the rules in perfect unison. Swimming naked in the Danube in their youth, it was as if Yelena was the arms, and Zima, the legs kicking. Blended like one bird on a branch, the right wing and the left. When Yelena's husband was killed, it was Zima and her husband Omir that took care of Marko while Yelena took the much-needed time alone to mourn.

Now Zima felt a double portion of Yelena's loss. She had two sons of her own, and the twinge that went through her womb when she heard the news was unbearable. It could have been one of her sons. Naturally she had been at the funeral, and was invited to the dinner at Sofia's afterward, but the overzealous vigilance that emerges when tragedy strikes next door kept her home feeding her husband and sons and giving thanks for their safety for today. Allah Akbar. God is Great.

That Zima was Muslim and Yelena Eastern Orthodox Christian never split them. Why should it? They were friends indeed and in deed. Never succumbing to the belief systems that separate, never denying that they broke the present day mold when they ignored religious differences, never blindly trusting that blood was necessarily thicker than water, they swam together in the same pool of life. Their mantra as girls had been simple, *"Jump!"* Do it whatever it was. Risk, dare, do, and do it all the way, most of all, do it from the heart. That was their safety net, leading with their hearts. It bound their friendship, dissolved centuries of grinding axes, and allowed them to dream from the mountaintop of hope. They were clear that they would always be there to catch each other if necessary, should the Great Spirit that held us all happen to blink.

Zima kept her footing with the same mountain goat grace that all the village women possessed. She scaled the slippery hillside to reach her friend. Unrelenting rain veiled the sky as if in shyness or shame for what the universe had wrought on this village, as if the firmament could not let itself be seen for fear of revealing its own vast vulnerability. The soft sky surrendered merciful rain to cloak the tears that flooded the grief stricken mother. Zima moved swiftly, as if Yelena might at any time join Marko in the freshly dug plot and call an end to the pain of separation.

The Eastern Orthodox burial rituals drum out mesmeric repetitions of prayer meant to temper the torture of the bereaved, and replace it with a concrete feel for God's presence. It hadn't worked for Yelena. She raged like a tiger inside, railed against God and His so-called Divine plan. On the outside, she could barely stand. Or was it vice versa. She couldn't tell. Reality had radically receded since she dropped the rabbit in the barn the moment she first heard Marko's call.

Zima intuited everything going on in her friend's heart. One could not rejoice without the other, and suffering surfaced in both their hearts as immediately as it touched the one. Yelena stood shivering in the cold autumn wind when Zima wrapped her own shawl around her and held her in her arms. She wanted to make it all go away for her friend, to comfort her into a complete healing of the hurt. Yet as she held her and patted her shoulder, there was a chilling feeling she wished she could have suppressed, but she had no power over it. It was that insidious human response to tragedy, "Thank God this didn't happen to me." In Zima's case, she was sure it was Allah that had spared her two sons of similar age to Marko. Allah is Great indeed. Allah Akbar.

That thought quickly evaporated when Zima actually caught a glimpse of Yelena's ghostly face. She stood shimmering over the mound of dirt which was all that remained of her Marko. Holding Yelena's shoulders firmly, hoping to quell her erupting grief, she attempted to still her terror for a moment. Yet, like a volcano waiting a millennium for just the right moment to be explode, Yelena suddenly yielded up eons of despair, past hope, past fear, past anything she could have imagined. The crater hollowing inside her suddenly widened, and she collapsed on the wet ground.

The two women eventually reached the doorstep of Sofia's home. Sounds of subtle slurping of food and drink spilled out of the windows. The troops were still eating. The funeral dinner meant to be a comfort for Yelena, was an irritating distraction. How many of these funeral dinners had Yelena herself attended. For the first time she could see the loss of a child was beyond that ritualistic reprieve. There was simply nothing to say. The family, neighbors and friends showed up to be present for Yelena. That's all they could do, just be there, in the infinite now. Breathing in and out, alongside the breath of death, eating without appetite, the guests quietly embraced Aunt Sofia and Uncle Anton, then shuffled to the hallway, slipped on their shoes, ready to navigate the rainy night.

Zima and Yelena stood outside the house, oblivious to the rain. "You should rest," Zima advised.

"How?" muttered Yelena.

"Try to eat something," Zima persisted.

"You want to come inside?" asked Yelena, unwilling to relinquish her best friend's company. Zima freed her hand from Yelena's.

"No, honey, I have to get the boys to bed."

Yelena lifted her head for the first time that day, and looked her friend directly in the eyes. "Keep them close, Zima, keep them very close." No one understood what had happened to Marko or why, and so the danger felt ubiquitous. She patted her friend's hand, turned and trudged up the rain soaked steps into Aunt Sofia's warm home. As guests were leaving, they paused on the stoop, offering words of comfort to Yelena, who nodded robotically.

Yelena shed her shoes, heavy with mud, in the hallway, replacing the footwear of the funeral guests. She'd hoped to invisibly journey up to her room, but she was stopped by a few more embraces, gentle words of kindness from the stragglers. She felt like a specter, without substance, without response, without human civility. Nevertheless she stood and received the expressions of sympathy that vanished as quickly as they were uttered. As she traveled through the kitchen she passed her Aunt Sofia, the only one who knew better than to put a band-aid of words over the hellish hemorrhaging that would not be staunched.

The enormous love and deep humility of Aunt Sofia allowed her to dare to offer, "Soup, child?" Yelena patted the top of her aunt's babushka as she floated past her, thinking she hadn't remembered her being so little. The great oak tree of maternity walked up the wooden stairs, a hollowed out spirit carrying the weight of a thousand worlds in her heart.

"Not now, Auntie," she managed to mutter, as she stumbled up the loft stairs.

She'd barely reached the threshold of her bedroom when phone shrilled, scattering the dense molecules of sadness like an ax to the down feathers at the neck of a Christmas goose. It startled the household. Uncle Anton knocked over a glass of red wine. Even his deaf ears heard it. It rang again, and then Zorka finally rescued the phone from its cradle.

"*Dobro Vecer*," Zorka offered a solemn "good evening" in her most somber Serbian, then a split second later, shouted into the receiver as if she were at a soccer game, "Ljuba!" She turned and announced to the stoic household in her best circus voice, "It's Ljuba from New York!" Zorka wailed so loudly into the receiver, it was as if she thought that sheer volume, not the implement she held in her hand, was what transmitted her voice across the continents. She continued excitedly, "Oh Ljuba, we need you here, darling, you must come!" urging her as if it were an invitation to a ball. She listened to some response, then shouted out, "Yelena! It's your sister...." Finally, with uncharacteristic tenderness, Zorka gently called from the bottom of the stairs, "Honey, can you come down?"

Yelena was already heading down the stairs when she heard the first syllable of her big sister's name. She took the heavy black receiver from Zorka's hand. It steadied her.

"Oh, sis…" she faltered, then flooded the phone with tears. The dam broke.

CHAPTER ELEVEN

THE NEXT MORNING YELENA ROSE EARLY to do the chores. It had been a sleepless night that culminated in her nodding off near dawn for about twenty minutes before the barnyard animals proclaimed the day. It was hopeless, she thought sleep would be forever a memory. Her soul was destined to stalk the night eternally. As she stooped over to don her mud-caked boots, she felt hung over, not from slivovitz, in which she rarely if ever imbibed, but from the wrenching grief that flooded her gut. She breathed in and out, involuntarily. It didn't matter, nothing did. The steel grey clouds overhead were mirrors of her lungs hardened from weeping. There was a lumbering acceptance in her movements. She lacked the lithe step of the thirty-three year old woman that she was only one day ago at this time of the morning.

Today she carried an anvil of darkness on her shoulders, as she pressed the hay beneath her feet and fixed the milking stool next to the hind of the restless cow, waiting to be milked. Her breath heaved in consonance with her bovine friend before her. She needed to connect with something. There was nowhere inside her soul where she could flee for refuge. So she furrowed her head into the side of the cow and mixed her tears with the morning milk.

Brushing the flies away from her bare ankle, she looked down to see the rabbit she'd held safely in her arms before she ceased to believe in safety as a reality on this earth. It was nibbling at her ankle, as if to say, *Remember how you were cradling me the other day? Let's pick up where we left off.* At first she flicked it away. It was her first reaction to the anger inside her that could not come up with any compassion in a world that had just hollowed her heart. Then her true nature overruled that judgment as she gently picked it up, stroking it, placing it back where it belonged, by its mother's side.

The chores took longer than usual. Each task seemed to serve as a way of not dealing with the hugely changed picture of her life, a looking more mountain goat than student, even though it'd had been only minutes since school had been dismissed. Caught like a cub in a trap, he surrendered, "They're, uh, at the field, already."

In an effort to retain some dominion in their two-person family unit, she insisted prayer precede her permission. Marko, like his father before him, was given a double dose of charm and it was never lost on Yelena. He graciously and somewhat gratuitously removed his cap, bowed to her like he would to a queen, and knelt before the altar and recited the fastest version of the Lord's Prayer in Old Slavonic ever known to man. His mother thought she detected a millisecond of sincerity in the "Our Father," and she took that as sufficient reassurance of his spiritual devotion, and promptly gave him leave to play soccer. He sprang from his posture of contrition, flung his arms around his mother in thanks, and bolted out the door.

"Marko!" she called.

"Yes, Mamma," he stood in the doorway, beaming with joy, backlit by the glow of a late afternoon sun behind him. He looked like an angel, she thought.

"Why don't you take Nassir with you?"

He knew what she was getting at, and didn't want to reply. He'd grown up with Nassir and Namik, Zima's sons. He loved them like brothers. They had bonded like family. They were good boys. Yelena loved Zima's boys; after all they belonged to her best friend.

Now the genuine contrition came, as Marko confessed what he knew to be wrong, but felt powerless over. "Mamma, the older boys don't want to play with Nassir and Namik, because they're…." His own sense of principle made the reality of wrong gag in his throat. *Because they were Muslim*, Yelena finished the sentence in her thought. The ugly dragon of unwarranted prejudice reared its wretched fangs even in the purity of this mountain village.

"What did I teach you about that, Marko?"

"I know, Mamma, I know, I promise to make them take Nassir and Namik with us next time, but just this once can I go by myself with the older boys, they hardly ever let me play with them, and how am I going to play soccer like my Dad did, if I don't learn…and…and…." He was out of gas, because he wasn't brought up to justify a wrong. "I'm sorry, Mamma."

"All right," she relented, "but next time you invite Zima's boys, for sure, okay?"

life without Marko. How could she define that, let alone imagine what it would feel like? He was her son, her soul, her reason to live, her life lesson on Love. It was impossible to think of it. There was no reference point for this loss, no compass for the wild desert surrounding her.

So Yelena brought down the hay from the loft, cleaned out the chicken coop, hosed down the hogs, brushed the horses, milked the goat after draining the two demanding cows, collected the eggs from the happily productive hens, gave the ever-under-foot rooster a swift but easy boot, and made sure the rabbits were all accounted for and fed. The sweat of the labor eased her pain one millisecond at a time, and before she knew it days passed, under the protective umbrella of her daily routine. Up early morning after morning, despite sleepless night followed by sleepless night, she performed the chores for as long as possible, then steadied up the hill to sit by Marko's grave; to sit and sit, in complete and utter silence.

Shunning Father Voyn's gestures of comfort, refusing Aunt Sofia's healthy cuisine, tolerating Zima's presence, she simply chose to spend the days as close to Marko as she could get. This would be her life. She was resigned to it. She heard Marko's voice in her mind while she sat and mentally spoke to him of how she loved him, occasionally whispering softly as if the grass that covered his grave could not be trusted with her secret.

Many days passed in this way, maybe a weeks, maybe more, maybe less. Yelena could no longer gauge the mortal measurement of time. Only when she felt the chilly autumn winds sweep through her did she realize winter was approaching and her boy would spend it covered by the cold earth.

One day, in the midst of her extensive round of chores, Yelena was startled out of her meditative tasks by the sound of a jeep coming up the path toward Aunt Sofia's home. Two young policemen where winding their way up the road with the arrogance of kings, surmising that the weather and elements affected the plebeians of the planet, but certainly not them.

The mudslide caused by typical autumnal rainfall would not and could not possibly prevent their precious jeep from gaining appropriate traction to take them to their mission. They were young, handsome, feigned a bit of authority, possessed with a drop of decency and a modicum of conscience, but were shy on climatic wisdom on that particular day. In short, they were stuck in the mud.

One of them was not the brightest bulb in the bunch but cute, while the other was vain as Valentino, but displayed a dollop of discerning intelligence. Unfortunately, the less than brilliant driver was revving the engine, digging them deeper into a rut, while Handsome, who was standing outside the jeep to direct his partner, got splattered with mud. As he was the superior rank of the two, he did not bother to edit his rage, while the other egghead, oblivious to his crime, kept the pedal to the metal. Up close it was comical. From the vantage point of the barnyard, it looked like trouble. It was clear a third musketeer was called for, and one with brains appeared.

Zima's husband Omir, loaded down with schoolbooks, was en route to his position at the high school where he taught history. A solid, muscular man, who normally strode with the gait of royalty, was trudging through the mud, head down, with the weight of world history between his shoulders, and clumps of wet dirt clinging to his shoes. The recent tragedy had affected all the neighbors, perhaps Zima and Omir the most, as they had boys the same age as Marko. Nevertheless, seeing the difficulty of the officers, he stopped to offer assistance, as any neighborly man would.

"Thanks, Professor," said the good-looking Vladimir. "I appreciate it." They performed the job of releasing the jeep from the soon to be quicksand. Vladimir continued, "Say, could you do me a favor? Let up on the homework, my son can hardly keep up." Omir chuckled as together they produced the final shove that freed the jeep.

"Hard work is the road to greatness, Officer," Omir replied. With that, he recovered his books from the back seat of the jeep, and marched down the path toward the village school, head a tad higher. The genius cop behind the wheel, nicknamed Popeye for his surname Popovic, watched Omir walk out of earshot, then turned to his partner.

"Greatness! What does he know about it, the smart-ass."

"Never mind," Vladimir clipped, directing their focus to the task at hand. "Here comes the boy's mother."

Popeye was rather wowed at the Slavic beauty coming up the path, and briefly forgot that they were there as bearers of more bad news, as he slipped into his barroom mind set.

"Nice!" he whistled and nudged his superior, who frowned at him disapprovingly.

Yelena witnessed the encounter from a distance, and waited to collect herself for what she dreaded, dealing with more legalities of her son's murder. There had been a steady flow of calls, paper work, police, questioning and bureaucratic baloney leading nowhere. Their inability to solve this crime added salt to the wound. Now she had to face more of their incompetence which she loathed. Somehow in the barnyard amidst the smells and sounds of the animal realm, she could block her grief for a few minutes at a time and gain brief reprieve, before she took it on again like a holy mantle.

Now the two new cops pulled up to the front of Aunt Sofia's house in their muddied vehicle. She braced herself and strode toward them, stopping directly in front of them, as if daring them to speak. Vladimir jumped out of the jeep, Popeye followed.

"Mrs. Mandich?" Vladimir said as he approached her. She looked him straight in the eye, steeling herself for whatever he had to report. He reached into his shirt pocket and produced a gold chain. She began to tremble and everything went to slow motion again. Tragedy has a way of making time stand still. She gently placed the bucket of milk on the ground by her feet, and then cupped her hands to receive the final vestige of her son. How could such an infinitely joyful soul fit in the palm of her small hand. It burned as it touched her, like his final scream for his mother, like the last line of an epic poem. "Did this belong to your son?" Vladimir continued. He hated this job.

Yelena nodded, murmuring, "There was a cross on it...where did you find it?" Unprepared for the size of the sadness he was brushing against, he stammered, as if before a great work of art.

"Uh, there was a...well...it was on a...uh, the bush near the location of the...." His wavering was like a slap into wakefulness for Yelena.

"Where, exactly?" she demanded. "I thought you searched there already!" He grabbed his notebook from his back pocket, and began rifling through it to feed her information he was sure he must have written down somewhere. At least he could appear to have some semblance of professionalism before this towering demand for facts diminished him. His notebook gave him nothing, but a few seconds of vamp time.

"Uh, it was near the...uh...place where your son was...." Too little, too late; time was up. Yelena grabbed the notebook and began tearing at it like an animal, looking for someone to blame for the death of her young.

Finally, she threw the notebook down in the mud. Her fury unleashed. "Did you find the other boys yet? What about the truck?

What have you been doing? It's been weeks already and you bring me my son's gold chain and not the killer...." The handsome, young cop was mortified, and genuinely wished he had something to say to ease the pain of this tortured beauty, but he had nothing.

"Mrs. Mandich, there's been other cases like this lately like the woman in Srebenica, others. On both sides, you know...it's become impossible...."

Again she lashed out. "Don't tell me about Srebenica, tell me about my son's murderer!" With this, she flailed at him, pounding against his chest, as if the force of her blows would yield up some hidden morsel of truth explaining what happened to her Marko, and how and why. The bucket of milk spilled; the other cop, mistaking that as the real problem, jumped to salvage half of it, while the other one continued his attempts to comfort the mad mother.

"I know this doesn't make it easier, ma'am, and I wish I had something to tell you, but I don't, and with no leads, well, there's not much more we can do on this case. We came to tell you that."

This stilled Yelena, but didn't quiet her insides. She stared at him in disbelief. He averted her look. The other cop handed her the pail, "Sorry about the milk, ma'am." She took the pail from him, and turned and walked up the path toward the front steps of the house, and hurled the pail against the wall, splattering the already white stucco wall with the whiteness of the cow's milk.

Yelena then bolted up the hill toward the church. The two policemen had already managed to turn their jeep around and head down the hill, more afraid of a further encounter with Yelena than of getting stuck in the mud again. Fear propelled them, fierceness of heart moved her. All the while Aunt Sofia stood at the kitchen window witnessing the exchange, stroking her cat, chewing her tobacco, sensing a curve ball coming.

CHAPTER TWELVE

FATHER VOYN WAS PULLING WEEDS FROM HIS HERB GARDEN behind the church. The rain, like most things of Nature, had a yin and a yang, and it had both nourished and trampled some of his plants. So he was in garden repair garb, which is to say, black trousers, pulled up to his calves, black shirt, without the white yoke of his profession, and an oversized straw hat with a small hole in the top, allowing his bald spot to be forever suntanned. He cared for his herb garden, the same way he tended to his parishioners, tenderly. It was this kind touch of love he brought to all living things that made him mysterious to many in the small congregation. They thought even a priest ought to lose it sometimes, but his gentleness never failed him. It was ever-present. Orthodox priests were permitted to marry and have families, but Father Voyn had been widowed long ago. That was common knowledge, though no one really knew the details of his personal story. He lived his life in service to others and set a high standard of principle and love for his community. More than that, one cannot ask. Yelena had run to that lap of kindness and understanding on many occasions in the past. He was not surprised to hear her panting up the path, then throwing herself on the bench alongside the church.

"Good morning, child," he called from his garden, glancing up to gauge the gravity of her need. No reply, only deep sobs from Yelena as she banged the back of her head against the church wall and wept.

"They'll never find them, Father, they never will…."

He gently put down his gardening spade, took off his gloves, removed his straw hat, and went to her side to comfort her. "All right, child, it's all right…you have a right to your tears…." He stroked her head. "The sunlight will always follow the rain, always." Yelena lifted her head and looked out across the village to the far range of mountains, and thought how much she loved her village, her home. Not just her home, but her ancestral birth place. The Zelenich's had been there for generations, her great grandfather built Aunt Sofia's home with his own hands, planted the trees, plowed the land, tended the sheep. This earth was hers, she came out of it and she knew it with every cell in her being. Whichever way one turned, there were mountains, encircling, enveloping, promising a sure protection. And now, with the loss of her son, it felt like a prison. There was no sense of safety anymore, only lurking danger and confusion.

As if Father Voyn could read her thoughts, he said, "I understand the name of your sister's village in New York is Queens. It must be very beautiful with a name like that." Yelena kept looking across the meadow veiled in sunlight. He continued, "Go to see your sister, Yelena, it's not good for you here right now." Silence. "You must, dear." Yelena intuited a warning in the last remark, and wondered how Father Voyn knew that she was feeling more than the all too familiar grief, but a palpable sense of mortal fear.

"Why must I, Father?" she asked with her signature importunity.

"Because, my dear, you are right, they probably will not find these men who did this, and so you must go away from here in order to heal." Yelena opened her cupped hand and revealed the gold chain the police had given her. Again, Father Voyn tracked her with characteristic sensitivity. He took the chain from her hand and placed it over her head, around her neck, "Marko will be with you always, Yelena. And anyway, you don't have to stay there forever, but go for a little while."

He embraced her with the reassurance of a spiritual father. She could smell the incense from the church that had settled into the cloth of his shirt, mixed with the scent of the black tobacco he smoked, and the fragrance of the basil plants he'd been tending in his garden. The earthly smells were a potent comfort to her, calming her and causing her to wonder for the first time in her young life, what was beyond her treasured mountain village. It's true she'd lived in the capital city of Belgrade one summer, and had traveled to the beautiful Adriatic coast on her honeymoon, but this was her country, her home, these were her people. She never had the desire to leave, even now with all the civil strife, she felt loyal to her land.

How did her sister Ljuba do it? And why? She'd often asked herself. Then she'd remember why. It was for the love of a man who became Ljuba's husband. Yelena might have done the same thing for Radmilo. But at that moment, sitting on the bench with Father Voyn, it was hard to imagine. She loved the bench, and the cool, moist wall of the church supporting them, and the unspeakable dignity of the horizon. Her fingers touched the gold chain around her neck. All that remained of Marko, all that bid her stay, all that bid her go.

CHAPTER THIRTEEN

THAT NIGHT YELENA LAY AWAKE replaying Father Voyn's words, and wrestling with her willful soul that wanted to change the facts of the reality she was living. Yelena would have liked to transform the whole world into a place of peace. Her heart sang a haunting lullaby that night, with lyrics of "I want and I want and I want and…."

She didn't recollect the actual moment when she made the decision to go see Ljuba. But she suddenly found herself up and dressed in the middle of the night, packing. Reaching into her dresser drawer, Yelena pulled out her passport and an envelope of money which Ljuba had sent her over the years. There were hundreds and hundreds of American dollars she had been saving for Marko's college education. She grabbed her knapsack, sufficient baggage for a short trip, and filled it with basic necessities: socks, sweaters, her crocheting, and other simple amenities. She made the bed, straightened the room, and got down on her knees and prayed. She needed guidance, she needed strength, and she needed grace. Amen.

The steps creaked beneath her feet, destroying her efforts to not awaken the household. Her efforts were for naught. She found Aunt Sofia at the stove in the kitchen, preparing coffee for her. Her dear, dear Aunt Sofia, as caring as her real mother ever could have been, had dedicated her life to Yelena and Ljuba, raising them, rejoicing in them, rewarding them with unconditional affection. How do you say good-bye to a woman like that even for a little while. Aunt Sofia was pure kindness, ever enveloping her nieces in everlasting arms of love.

Now in her later years, when she needed the girls around her, they would both be in New York, at least for now. At Aunt Sofia's age, *now* was all there was. The future loomed like an early winter, unwelcomed and inevitable. As Yelena reached the bottom stair, she looked over at Aunt Sofia and thought how old she looked. She had gotten smaller. When did that happen, yesterday, a week ago? Or had she always been so diminuitive? As she hovered over the stove, stirring Turkish coffee, grasping the long handle with her curled fingers, Aunt Sofia glanced up at Yelena and nodded, as if to say, *I know, I understand, I saw this coming,* but then quickly returned her gaze to the pot that was about to boil over with that magical, thick, black substance that was the blood in their veins in this household. It was that which bound them together when they met; comforted them when they were blue; picked them up when they were tired; and permitted a glimpse into the future in the grinds when they needed some hope. They would drink from the demitasse in honor of all of the above that morning, and for the momentous event about to occur. Yelena was leaving the village. Only for a while, she reassured Aunt Sofia who figured that she and Uncle Anton didn't have too many *"a whiles"* left. Yet Sofia wouldn't make known these sentiments to Yelena. She would never deny her niece a chance for some relief from her grief, any more than the sun could deny the earth its warmth. Still her stomach rumbled in sadness.

"What are you doing up so early, Auntie?" Yelena gently queried. Aunt Sofia knew when spunk was called for, as a benign pain reliever.

"Look who's talking!" Yelena smiled and her heart ached for her aunt's imminent solitude. They each knew exactly what the other was going through and both worked hard to spare the other any added discomfort, though it was impossible, considering how intertwined they were. Distance may not have the power to separate their hearts, but it would hurt nonetheless. "I'm going to see Ljuba for a little while." Yelena offered it up, like an unwanted clue to a mystery better left unsolved.

"I know. That's good, little bird. Now drink your coffee," her aunt replied, and with that she served the coffee at the table she'd already set for breakfast; fresh baked bread and cherry jam, and a shot of slivovitz for the road, not to mention a packed lunch. She must have gotten the message before Yelena did. They ate in silence, and in the spirit of selfless love.

When it came time to go it was not yet dawn. Yelena downed her brandy, slipped into her boots and gathered her bag. "It's dark out, child," Aunt Sofia pleaded.

"I know, but I'm going up to the church before I go." Of course, she would bid farewell over Marko's grave. Though Aunt Sofia wanted her to wait, she knew better than to stop her. Yelena embraced her aunt for a long time, until her aunt's chest heaved with sadness. Yelena held her shoulders, looked her in the eye and made a promise. "I'm coming back, Aunt Sofia, I'm only going for a short time." They both fought back their tears, each out-braving the other. Sofia nodded. Yelena added, "Kiss Uncle Anton for me."

"Kiss him yourself, when you come back," Aunt Sofia replied. That quickly, their tears turned to laughter, and there you have the Slavic soul. With that, Aunt Sofia removed her babushka and placed it around Yelena's head, as if she wanted her to remember where she came from, then handed her a sack of food, bread, cheese, fruit, chicken, and kissed her forehead...her final blessing. Yelena reached the end of the walkway in front of the house and turned, knowing Aunt Sofia would still be standing in the doorway. She waved at her aunt, a shorn lamb without her babushka, who nodded and raised her chin, as if to say, "I'm all right. Go."

Yelena charged into the chilly morning air, considered running back to sit with Aunt Sofia and talk about this crazy notion of going to America, but no, she had begun. She would not waver. She trudged up the hill to the church, pushed open the door as quietly as possible, so as not to rouse Father Voyn from his cabin, a stone's throw away. The sliver of predawn glow that slipped through the crack in the church door allowed her to see enough to grab two candles and a matchbook. The first candle she lit and put in the candle stand by the door, the other she took outside with the matches. Yelena walked around to the small cemetery in the open field behind the church, lit the candle and placed it at the head of Marko's grave, then kneeled and prayed. She took her off knapsack and placed it next to the grave. It became her pillow. She curled up next to Marko, stretched her arm across the mound of dirt, feeling as close as possible to her son. The candle flickered, as she drifted into sleep, her first real sleep in weeks.

The sun was slow to creep over the mountain ridge, where it'd stayed hidden till mid- morning. Once it broke through, it shot right onto Yelena's face and she awoke with a start, forgetting where she had laid her head a few hours ago. The candle had burned down. She slowly arose, smoothed the dirt where her body had made an indentation, brushed herself off, kissed the cross that marked her son's grave, and then patted the mound of earth with the palm of her hand, letting it rest there a moment as if she were touching her son's cheek as he left for school. With that, she straightened and started her journey to America, destination - the village of Queens.

She walked barefoot, but with the dignity of a queen, following the path behind the church that led to the next town. It was the long way around to catch the bus that went to the port city of Bar where she would board a ship, but she wanted to avoid meeting any neighbors who would surely have a myriad of questions, for which she had no answers. She was sorry to leave it to Aunt Sofia to explain her sudden departure, but Sofia had a clipped tongue when she needed it, and would have no problem stifling the flapping ones. There was a purposeful spring to her gait. What it was she knew not, only that it was there.

By mid-day, Yelena was boarding a bus for Bar, Montenegro along the Adriatic Sea. She'd been there before for a holiday with her husband when Marko was a baby, but never imagined it a launching pad to an unknown world. America. Though she'd studied English in school, and received countless letters from her sister, begging her to come visit Queens, she had no idea what to expect. They'd often spoken on the phone in English, to keep their secrets from Zorka and the rest of the hens that hovered whenever the phone rang, yet she still felt ill-equipped for the task of a new language.

Yelena had never craved America like Ljuba had. She'd been perfectly satisfied in her mountain village. She felt attached to the land, and thought she'd be content to be sitting on the bench under the grape arbor in twenty-five years, holding the grandchild she'd hoped Marko would give her. One rainy afternoon it had all changed: the grand metamorphosis, a transformation beyond imagination. But into what was she morphing? *Certainly not an American, never that.* For now, she was a traveler, a stranger about to enter a strange land. She would join the ranks of the many pilgrims wandering the earth, wondering why they had left their homeland, and spending their days longing for it. At least for her it was temporary, which did not explain the ache in her heart.

Before she boarded the bus, she brushed the dust from her feet, and put on her sandals. She'd walked the distance barefoot to feel the land she was leaving, as if to kiss it farewell. Stepping up on the bus, handing over her ticket, finding a place to sit near a window, she was caught off guard by a strange sense of excitement, for which she felt momentarily ashamed. Nestled into her home on wheels for the next ten hours, she leaned her head against the cool glass and closed her eyes. Sheer exhaustion promised some welcomed rest.

CHAPTER FOURTEEN

MYSTERIOUS, MAGICAL MONTENEGRO unfolded all around her while she slept. The black mountains that bore sturdy men, wizards, berserk heroes and strong hearted females were not just pages in a school book now, but real entities enveloping her. There was an enchantment to the place, if nothing else, due to the sheer miracle that anyone could live there at all. Rock upon rock defied the possibility of a seed to take hold, not to mention a home to be built. And yet they did it. How? Perhaps the pure passion and undaunted drive of the southern Slav got it done. The blessing and curse of the people that never gave up. She was one of them. Her father's side were Montenegrins and she felt their fire coursing through her veins on many occasions, when the demure, feminine aspect was completely absent. The Montenegrin image of womanhood was the sister who would die for the brother or the passionate love of the bride that would carry water across a battlefield to her wounded husband. Sacrifice was all. Was she dreaming this or did it come to her when she awoke from the switchback turns the bus was taking to weave through the mountains toward the shore? The beauty that surrounded her was like taking a bath in a bewildering hope that the power of Nature would somehow set everything right again. Harmony would prevail. *But how would it. How?*

She awoke hungry, also a first in weeks, and reached for her knapsack on the floor of the bus, and only then did she notice that seated next to her were a Muslim woman with her baby at her breast, well-hidden by her traditional garb. They must have boarded after she fell asleep. Not an easy journey for a newborn. Yelena smiled warmly at the sight of them. The Muslim woman nodded. They exchanged only a few words at first, but then the delicious lunch Aunt Sofia had packed formed a bond between them, as they broke bread together.

The young matriarch let Yelena hold her baby girl, while she partook of the offering, needing strength for feeding. It was odd to see a

Muslim woman traveling alone, and Yelena was sad to learn that because the child was a girl, the woman had been disowned by her husband, and was headed back to her family in Albania. The woman confessed that she had wanted a girl, willed it, and that she was sure Allah blessed baby girls the same as boys. That statement cost her a blow to her head, which was scantily covered by her head dress. She had escaped his ire the next morning, with no danger of his pursuit of them. She admitted she felt free, and that she could tell this to Yelena, who was not Muslim, because she could understand this freedom. The Albanian woman had never known it until this moment on the bus, eating the bread of a Serbian woman who rocked her little daughter to sleep. In a way, they were both experiencing a new liberty born of loss and suffering, and they nourished themselves and each other like sisters, during the remaining journey to the port of Bar. Yelena never spoke of Marko. The words could not be formed on her tongue. She needed the shroud of anonymity about her a while longer. Holding the little baby comforted her, and let her feel what she sensed she never would again...motherhood.

As she rocked the little baby girl gently in her arms, Yelena witnessed the stark contrast out the bus window. The raging black mountains of Montenegro, their elegance etched against the grey vault of heaven, threw Yelena into the shadows of her predecessors, who bequeathed her an ancestry of the warrior spirit particular to this land. The lore was that the Montenegrin ancestors were always watching you, protecting you, and their spirits were carried inside you as a constant reminder of your true identity. Yelena felt that was true. It had to be. The secret of who she was on a deep level was embedded in the rock of these mountains that scraped the sky. If only they could be cracked open and the message of all the angels that may have heard her prayers and desires could be presented on a scroll of instruction, of what to do, of how to live, of where to find refuge from her pain.

A stirring of self-righteous pity began to erupt inside her. She gazed down at the little child she held in her arms, while the Muslim mother slept against her shoulder. Yelena caught a glimpse of the continuity of life, then despite the current blockages of grief that burned inside her, she slept. They all three slept in an unusual triangle of mutual peace, a peace that surpassed understanding and unified a mixture of minds and hearts that were in certain parts of this land meant to be enemies.

When the bus ended its winding trail, it bumped into the town of Bar, which bustled with merchants, workers, travelers. Greeks, Italians, Albanians, Serbs and Montenegrins clamored to meet the bus, to board it or to rescue an arriving relative. It was complete chaos.

Yelena shepherded her new found friend with child to the bus that would take her down to her home town in Albania, where one could only pray she'd be welcomed and fed. The woman bowed to Yelena when they part. Yelena kissed her on the cheek three times, as is her custom; and the woman bowed again, following her own custom, and then they embraced. They had shared a passage together, a huge chasm was crossed, and now they were changing horses and heading in different directions. A Muslim woman was returning to her home as a single mother of a baby girl, and a Slavic peasant, widowed and now childless, was traveling alone to America. Finally, Yelena bowed to the young mother, the borders of customs were rapidly fading. All is one. That's what sorrow does...it levels the playing field.

It was late afternoon when she left her friend at the bus station and made the short walk to the port to secure a ticket. All these American dollars she had saved over the last fifteen years so Marko could go to some great university, were now to be used to teach her a way of living without him. It was unimaginable. Nevertheless, she bought the ticket from an Italian ticket agent who spoke to her in Italian, then Albanian, and finally settled on English. Might as well, she needed the practice. The ship left in three hours. She was lucky. She was afraid she'd have to wait days for a ship, which she was more than willing to do in order to avoid boarding a plane. Strange that Yelena grew up in high altitudes, but harbored an unhealed fear of flying.

Now with only a few hours to spare, she would easily fill the time with a strong cup of Turkish coffee or three. A nearby café provided a vestibule for the next leg of her trip. She sipped the black gold and gazed out at the Adriatic Sea, the powerful element of nature that would transport her into her sister Ljuba's arms.

CHAPTER FIFTEEN

LJUBA. HER SISTER'S NAME MEANT "LOVE." She deserved the appellation. When was the last time they saw each other? Six years ago Ljuba came when Aunt Sofia had been unwell. Ljuba's daughters were quite young then, but she brought them anyway and left her husband Henry at home, working in New York. The girls and Marko chased chickens, ran from the rooster, and raced across the meadow in a daily game of tag. They were just children, but still they bonded enough to cry when they parted, and made promises to speak on the phone in their invented Serbo-American language at birthdays and Christmas. Yelena was anxious and afraid of walking into their home and greeting her nieces without Marko. *Would they even remember?* She asked herself.

The final boarding bells rang as she was about to glance at her turned over coffee cup to get a look at her future in the grinds. It was a foolish custom that everyone criticized at the same time they reverently believed in it. She picked it up, and put it down just as fast. She was afraid to know. Instead Yelena boarded the ship, settled into her tiny, second-class cabin, and began to crochet. It would be a two-week trip. She was glad for the time to think, or not think, to feel, or not feel, simply to be alone and to learn to be unafraid. Besides it was a good alternative to an airplane. A virtual mountain aerialist, she would tip the ridges of the highest crest, but put her in a metal tube and take her up to 35,000 feet at the speed of 700 mph...no way, no thank you. She'd rather eat the dust off a Turkish carpet. She'd told herself she would take a plane only when absolutely necessary, some kind of emergency, like for Marko's graduation from Harvard or...she swallowed hard, took out her crocheting, shed her shoes, curled up on her cot, and began her meditation of counting stitches. It would carry her across an ocean or two.

Eventually, her roommate, an American woman of about twenty-five entered, loaded down with beads, bracelets and earrings, and a bandana around her forehead, a throwback from the 70's. "What's happening, mamma," she said to Yelena, tossing her bag on the upper bunk.

"It's okay, thank you." Yelena replied and continued counting. Janice Joplin's look-alike just shook her head and chuckled.

"Whatever you say, mamma."

"Okay, thank you!" Yelena felt the gratitude phrase would be a safe way to end almost any sentence, so she used it liberally. "Thank you!"

"You're welcome, mamma. Thank you!"

Yelena had unintentionally brought some manners into her hippie roommate's vocabulary, and the two women got along fine with just those two words.

Several hundred thousand stitches later Yelena and her roommate, whose name was China, looked out at the port of New York. With Aunt Sofia's babushka now tied around her head like a bandana, echoing China's style, Yelena leaned over the edge of the railing and stared at the Statue of Liberty. She had a letter from her sister clasped in her hand and glancing at the return address, she read aloud, "Queens, New York." Then, putting two and two together and coming up with five, she proclaimed, "Oh boy, there's the queen!" Her own sense of irony made her smile for the first time in forty days.

When she parted from China, she learned yet another departure ritual, some kind of fancy hand-shake with fists and thumbs and minor grunting. She accomplished it with aplomb, and bid her friend farewell, and placed her bare feet on American soil. Now what?

PART TWO

The City

CHAPTER SIXTEEN

STEPS TAKEN ON A FOREIGN GROUND, different turf, throw the balance off. Feet behave strangely. The center reorganizes itself to relocate gravity. Yelena was dizzy. *"Where in the world am I?"* she wondered. The rhythm of the streets made her feel like a bassoon in a jazz band. *"I'll never get used to this, that's for sure,"* she thought. No books, news programs, maps, pictures, nor postcards or photos from her sister Ljuba could have prepared her for the awesome experience of the sheer size of New York City. The medieval presence of the buildings, the endless throngs of people rushing to get somewhere and the shrill screeches of traffic were all wildly alien to her. She felt a sudden longing in her bones. *"My village, my bench, my church, my son, I want to go back home. Why did I come here? I need to be with my son,"* she murmured to herself in a tongue she could safely assume would not be understood by a fellow pedestrian breathing down her back, hogging his share of the sidewalk.

Like waking up with buyer's remorse, Yelena choked on the regret that she'd ever left Shar Village. She reached into the pocket of her sweater and felt the thin paper envelope of her sister's letter, a membrane of familiarity. She took it out and again read the return address aloud, reciting it as if it were a mantra or magic spell which, when repeated numerous times, would transport her back to Kansas. And in a way, that's what happened. She later learned that New York was a place where you have to be willing to be lucky.

A young man and his two buddies, burdened with book bags, nearly bumped into Yelena, begged her pardon, and perceived that she was lost. "You need some help, lady."

"Yes, please…help…please," she stammered, handing him the envelope. He glanced at it quickly.

"Oh, I see, you're going up to Queens." When she heard that word, she nodded eagerly. Finally something she understood, Queens! "Okay then lady. Look, you go down those stairs," the young man instructed, pointing to the subway entrance across the street, "and take the L train. You understand L?"

"L," Yelena repeated, easily enough.

He pulled a pen out of his book bag and wrote the directions on her envelope, talking the whole time, "Change trains, then cross over..." all of it faster than she could follow, but she caught enough to thank him, give him a smile, and continue on her way. "Good luck, lady!" he called.

She turned and waved, "Good luck, boy!" Her first New York encounter. Funny how that can change a person's posture, just to have accomplished the comprehension of the "L" train.

The New York City subway platform at five o'clock on Friday afternoon, and for all Yelena knew, at any time of day, made the peak hour of market day in her village look like an empty schoolyard. There was a crush of human forms occupying every inch of space. Then one more would somehow find a way to squeeze into the fold. *"So this is New York,"* she mused. Yes, this was New York indeed. The subway. The main artery of this burg, the mysterious loud metal snake that slithered through the underground, delivered the travelers back to the earth's surface after they dwelt in the dark cave of the city's subconscious long enough to yearn for light. That was New York.

Yelena managed to find a spot to stand, her very own four square inches of territory, where she could pause to study the directions the boy had written on the envelope. She looked up and saw the sign "L" confirming what she'd heard from her young guide. Good, good, so far very good.

Over the din of the crowd and the scream of the approaching train, she noticed a man standing in front of her yelling into the palm of his hand. Cellular phones had not yet reached her village. This made her pause. She heard, "That's impossible...I've been home all day..." as the man paced back and forth in front of her, with the restlessness of a thoroughbred. "That's right," he continued, "I am going to work at this hour because I like to work at night." The train was pulling into the station, causing him to raise his voice, so that even jaded New Yorkers were beginning to stare at him. "Look, Sig, back off. Did you forget we're not married anymore?" Suddenly the man looked at his phone and snapped it shut. She'd hung up on him. A fellow traveler, pushed his way toward the open door of the train and commented, "That's telling her, brother."

Yelena witnessed the exchange, as a wave of people enfolded her. The man on the phone, Jake Thompson, had squeezed in just before the doors closed quickly behind him.

Jake stood over six feet tall, nostrils flaring from the fight with the ex-wife. He was always under attack from her, divorced or not. She had a rope around his neck because of their son, who was struggling with a drug problem. Jake loved the boy more than himself, but felt helpless in the face of his addiction. Fatherhood, he'd come to realize, was when the happiness and well-being of a child determined his own.

Jake had been the promising young star journalist at the City Journal when he met and married a New York socialite at the vainglorious age of twenty-four. When it all blew up a couple of years ago, he crashed mentally, couldn't produce at work and started doing some day drinking, while his nineteen-year-old son sought solace in cocaine. His wife had taken up with her personal trainer...how tawdry. Jake fancied himself a Hemingway type of guy, who deserved to be dumped in a more exotic way. Rivalled by a sugar cane potentate from Cuba, that he could have lived with, but to be trumped by a mere muscle man, please. Sigrid had found the most mundane infidelity to slap him with, including the proverbial, "It didn't mean anything, Jake." Hell, what did he expect, he was away on assignment so often she was lonely, a woman has needs, yeah, yeah, yeah, he'd heard it all. Understatement of the century.

Then one morning the baloney hit the fan, as it were, and he woke up with the clarity of Christ. "Honey," he said, as he made himself coffee and poured it into one of the Styrofoam cups she kept on hand for the help, "I'm going. I'm not living this lie anymore. I don't want your money or your messy life. I'm out. Sayonara, baby." That was more the kind of Bogey break up he had in mind for himself. And much to Sigrid's surprise, Jake left.

Sig, rather addicted to appearances, didn't like the way this would look on the society page. She had a more than mildly misplaced sense of entitlement and expected Jake to swallow her infidelity. Shaken, she attempted the age old manipulation, "What about our son?" Jake was already packed and ready to respond. When an idea finds its perfect moment in time, nothing can stop it.

"I'm driving up to UMass this morning to tell him." That's when he first learned of his son Tony's drug problem. Jake got Tony right into rehab, where the young lad refused to stay. His beautiful boy, Tony, a perfect reflection of his father, left and went back and left and went back to rehab six times under the close watch and surveillance of his devoted dad, unrelentingly determined to have his son heal. Sigrid had her own selfish set of addictions, and if Jake had cared anymore, he'd have found a chair for her next to Tony. But oh well, she offered him too little, way too late, and when a man is done, he's done.

Jake was forty-five years young, handsome and gifted, although convinced he was washed up as a writer and maybe as a man. Nevertheless, he got himself to the office every evening and stayed through the night, working on the second-rate assignments given him; doing a little writing of his own; and watching the Yankees on the small television he had in his cubicle at work. Despite the relief of night baseball, it ate him up inside that things had ended up this way.

A romantic behind the armor of a tough guy from Brooklyn, Jake expected *happily ever after* from life. For all the ugly reality he faced on the newspaper job, he still believed things would all work out and people were basically good at heart. Not exactly an Anne Frank philosophy per se, he held her in a class all her own, he simply thought better of the world than what met the journalist's eye. He refused to admit that mankind could dwell willingly in ignorance and prejudice, and he expressed that conviction first with his fist, as a rebel youth, and then with his pen, as a conflicted and conscious adult. The divorce shattered him, but it didn't shut him down. Jake's heart cracked open, not closed, and a kindness flowed from him that he didn't understand. *Pain never leaves you where it found you,* he had heard that somewhere.

Jake kept moving, never broke his stride. So his wife hung up on him on the subway platform. Big deal, he barely blinked. He stood behind Yelena on the subway and looked down at her gold cross, admiring the carving in it; he had an eye for detail, could have been a detective or a cop. He looked up and noticed two young punks eyeing Yelena's gold cross and chain. They gave each other a nod, and moved in for the heist. One put his hand behind his ear pretending to scratch in order to position his hand to grab the gold. The train was already braking into the next station.

Yelena was oblivious to the imminent assault, as she stared at the advertisements above the windows of the train car. Busy practicing her English, she mouthed the words on the ads, "Preparation H...stops...itching..." wondering what she just uttered.

The train jolted to a stop. The punk's hand went for the back of her neck, but Jake grabbed his wrist before it touched her.

"Don't even think about it, pal," Jake hissed, happy for the chance to get Sigrid's venom out of his system.

The perpetrator quickly covered with "Whatcha talkin' 'bout, man, ain't doin' nothin' but movin' for the door, dis my stop, get out dis stop."

"Good idea." Jake replied, taking a handful of the guy's shirt and giving him a helpful shove, "Here, let me help you out." Jake stepped out on the platform and watched the guy run up the stairs. He got back on the train as it started to move. Yelena had disappeared. As the train picked up speed, he caught a glimpse of her walking away in the opposite direction on the platform toward the connecting trains. He shook his head, hoping she wouldn't run into the punks again, but he decided he'd succeeded at scaring them off for the time being. New York City. Why in the world does he do it, day after day after day?

This subtle act of heroism heartened him for a beat or two. The primal rules of the jungle had kicked in and man enjoyed rescuing a maiden in distress. To redeem them from the jaws of the lion, hell, it was Biblical. Save the pure and innocent. Then Jake's mind wandered back to his ex-wife, his marriage, his list of failures, all the reaching and missing, the valiant slipping that wore him down and diminished him in his own eyes, his wife's, the world's. Did he change or did she? They fell in love and married. She became a fishwife, and he, indifferent. What kind of crucible is marriage to cause so complete a chemical transformation of one's individual identity? His soul evaporated at the sight of her now. He neither feared her nor loved her. He simply no longer knew her or himself for that matter. Now their only son was struggling again. And they had to battle that out one day at a time. Jake took a deep breath, and exhaled with some modicum of comfort that today he performed a noble act. He saved somebody from something. Of course, the benefactress of his daring didn't notice, but Jake didn't care. Well, he cared, but it didn't matter. He had done one thing well that day, and he might feed on that for a decade or maybe a day or at least till the train pulled into the next station. His stop. Awareness is all.

CHAPTER SEVENTEEN

MIRACLES DO HAPPEN. Or maybe they don't. Maybe it's all quite natural in a divine sort of way, when the impossible becomes possible on a particular day. Yelena looked at the address on the envelope for the hundredth time. It was now crumpled and wilted from the New York humidity, causing it to resemble more of a secret cuneiform etched on Etruscan papyrus, than the blueprint of a Balkan widow's new life. She matched the numbers on the envelope with those on the brownstone before her. A sigh of relief that could have moved a mountain escaped her. She had found her sister's home with only a few dozen words of English at her command. She had made it all the way from Shar Village to Queens, and she was more than a little proud of herself. The building loomed large and imposing. Not realizing that Ljuba and her husband, Henry, and their two daughters, Nadya and Anna, lived in about 500 square feet of this edifice, she stood impressed by the enormity of her sister's American dwelling place.

The third doorbell had the name Henry/Ljuba Meyer next to it, as clear as day. She wondered *who were all the other names,* and pressed the one for Meyer. Then she pressed it again, and again, and again, hoping to hear it ring. The door buzzed to let her in, but she missed her cue more than once and so she kept ringing the bell with the 3B next to it. Finally, Henry came running down the stairs, fork in hand, mouthful of food, mumbling, "Whatdya want for Christ's sake, quit ringing the damned bell. We're not buying whatever you're selling, damnit...you can't even eat in peace anymore...." By which time, he'd opened the door to behold Yelena standing there with Aunt Sofia's babushka wrapped around her head, her backpack at her side, and a stunned look on her face that broke into a smile through tears, once she saw her brother-in-law.

"Henry?" she uttered.

"Oh my God, Yelena, honey, I'm sorry, come in, come in..." He embraced her, still holding the fork between his fingers. "We expected you tomorrow, sweetheart. Oh my God, how are you....come on, let me take that sack from you. So glad you made it. My God, we've been worried about you! We wanted to pick you up...how the heck did you find us...huh?" He rambled on as he grabbed her knapsack and began escorting her up the three flights of stairs. Then Ljuba came running down and threw herself into her sister's arms. They stood totally still and inseparable for what seemed like eternity, until one of them finally came up for air. It was hard to tell which one. Tears flowed like a summer rain.

"Oh Yelena, honey, I can't believe you're here. Oh, sweetheart, I'm so sorry for what you've been through. Oh my God, but you made it here, thank God!" Ljuba went on. Yelena couldn't speak. She was overwhelmed to have landed in these comforting arms. It was as if she had been holding her breath for four weeks, and finally let it go.

From the top of the stairs, two pairs of dark Mediterranean eyes belonging to Yelena's nieces Anna and Nadya peered down, fascinated and unafraid. Theirs matched the eyes of her Marko. Those Zelenich eyes, deep, dark, like endless wells of water, yet warm as the sun in May. When she got to the landing, she embraced them, and they murmured a welcome, prompted by their mother. In their view, this strange lady with a babushka and dark hair and dark eyes, looked nothing like their now blonde mother, who spoke near perfect English. Sisters were supposed to look alike, they certainly did, so why not their Aunt Yelena and their mother, the two cherubs wondered.

Yelena, sensing their hesitancy, offered, "I brought something from Shar Village, especially for the two of you."

"Where's that?" Nadya, the younger one, asked.

Ljuba jumped in, "It's a long way from here, I showed you on the map remember, and it's where I was born, and where I grew up and went to school. Remember, we were there when you were very, very little. I told you all about it, remember?" The two girls nodded in unison. "And your Aunt Yelena traveled a long, long way to see you, so what do we say?"

"Thank you, Aunt Yelena," they chimed. Two angels, right before her eyes. Yelena could hardly keep her heart from bursting.

Then Nadya added, "You're supposed to say, 'you're welcome.'" Anna, the elder of the two, elbowed her for correcting their new guest, but Nadya insisted, though with a whisper, "Well, in school, Miss Ley always says if someone says, 'thank you' you're supposed to...." Anna had had enough, and grabbed her Aunt Yelena's hand, ignoring her little sister, as big sisters do when exercising their first born privileges.

Yelena was finally shepherded through the threshold of the tiny apartment brimming with smells of an inviting dinner and sounds of a TV in the other room. There was an undeniable atmosphere of affection and safety. The wandering sparrow had found a nest for a while. Ljuba took Yelena's hand, "Welcome to our little home, sis." Yelena looked around at the warm, cozy home that her sister had created out of four small rooms. The entry way had the same customary rug with boots, shoes and slippers piled on it as did Aunt Sofia's hallway. Shoes off, slippers on. It was like a lullaby they'd never forget. Even Henry was in the rhythm of that practice, by now. With two young girls in school, they had pounded extra hooks on the hallway walls that held the jackets, hats, and sweaters, school bags, all loaded on top of one another. A hook was freed up for Yelena's sweater, which Henry took from her and hung up. Only then did he realize his fork was still in his hand and catching the back of her sweater.

"I was wondering where that went," he muttered as he freed his fork and licked it clean, with the panache of a plumber.

Stepping into the living room, Yelena's focus went to the large screen television blaring in full color and stereo sound. America. On the opposite wall was a copy of the traditional painting of *Kosovska Devojka,* the famous picture of the Serbian girl giving water to a fallen soldier in the famous battle of 1389, between the Turks and the Serbs.

The story goes that the Serbs lost the battle, but had fought so valiantly and inflicted so much damage on the Turkish imperialism that it spared the rest of Europe the not so genial Ottoman rule; or the more callous version of their grandfather was, "If it weren't for us, the whole world would be speaking Turkish today!" And so the historical battle was revered, remembered and celebrated even though it was technically a Serbian defeat. That detail was rarely mentioned. It was their stand for freedom, and their unreserved persistence and passion that was portrayed in this painting. The famous image was embroidered on pillows and wall hangings in almost every Serbian household. So naturally this emblem of love for liberty hung in Ljuba's living room opposite the flickering images of a quiz show that captivated viewers with the promise of winning, perhaps not liberty, but large sums of money that might buy the illusion of it.

This was Yelena's first startling juxtaposition of her immigrant experience; one side of the living room, the *Battle of Kosovo,* the other, *Jeopardy*. In that space between the two worlds was the pull-out sofa, where this nervous mother bird could rest her wings, on the air of the winds of comfort that filled her sister's dwelling in the strange village of Queens. Perfect. In that unresolved space between the old and the new, Yelena would lay her head, securely sheltered for that night, and many nights to come.

CHAPTER EIGHTEEN

LOVE WAS THE VERB OF LJUBA'S LIFE. She was indeed the keeper of her namesake. She loved ceaselessly and unreservedly. Most especially, she loved her little sister, Yelena. When Yelena was eight years old, she had a puppy she named Sertsa, which means "heart." She told Ljuba that she named the puppy in honor of her, because Yelena felt her big sister had a huge heart. Ljuba thought it was sweet, though at that time she was sixteen years old and rather more caught up in the world of boys, make up and rock 'n' roll. To the extent that she was able to arouse that particular triad in their "old-fashioned" village, she stayed focused on her precious teenage interests and couldn't be bothered with things like puppies.

One day Ljuba got permission from Aunt Sofia to go into town to shop with her hard-earned babysitting money, on the condition that she take Yelena and the ubiquitous black and white, scruffy, spunky Sertsa with her. Aunt Sofia thought it criminal for a young woman to go anywhere alone, especially wearing lipstick and blue jeans, so she calculated that the presence of Yelena and the puppy would keep Ljuba tethered to resist the temptations of the town testosterone bearers. God forbid the attractive, long- legged Ljuba should be caught smoking a cigarette, or drinking in public, or, heaven forfend, performing any other carnal sin.

As Aunt Sofia watched her two nieces walk down the path to the main road with that little scamp of a pup behind them, a maternal tremor of concern shot through her body. What if her sister were alive to see them now, so independent, so grown-up. Maybe it was too soon for such an outing. Maybe she hadn't been strict enough with them. They say one often isn't, when the children aren't actually one's own. What could she do? She raised them the best she could, they knew right from wrong. She shook it off, affirming she had nothing to worry about. Nevertheless, she reached for Uncle Anton's bag of tobacco, and for the first time in her life Aunt Sofia began to chew tobacco. It calmed her and she stuck with that little habit, like it stuck to her, well into her golden years.

The girls walked out of eye shot of Aunt Sofia and immediately put out their thumbs to catch a ride. They weren't about to wait for that lazy old bus and waste good money that could be more wisely spent on a chocolate soda or a sequined t-shirt.

Once in town, Ljuba lead the way, never letting go of Yelena's hand, which never let go of Sertsa's leash. The three of them were like a chain gang clearing a path through the crowd at the open market in the main plaza of the center of town. Market day found endless vendors jammed up next to each other; sandwich stands, magazines, book stalls, clothing dealers, hand-made leather goods, silver jewelry, hats, curry tools, chestnuts, knitted scarves, crocheted blankets. You name it, they made it, they sold it, and often bought it back the following week. The posted sign stating, "No Dogs Allowed" inside the market area eluded the girls. So into the fray they charged, pausing at every stand to sample, taste, and even purchase what their modest purse would permit. As they approached the meat stand, a rather plump woman caught Sertsa's tail under her foot. Sertsa yelped. Yelena picked her up and comforted the pup as she also assured the perspiring woman that no harm had been done.

Yelena's arms created a new vantage point for the furry little mutt. Sertsa was suddenly up high looking down on the stands instead of watching everything from below "see" level. If a wagging tail is testimony to canine ecstasy, she was one happy dog. She sniffed longingly at the meat stand, eyeing everything a pup could ever hope for in life. Then just as the butcher was placing the heart and gizzards of a freshly cut lamb on a slab of ice, Sertsa sprang out of Yelena's arms with the force of a dozen Russian sled dogs, landed on the lamb's heart and took a juicy bite out of it. The meat vendor went wild and grabbed his chopping knife, raising it above his head as he took aim, giving Yelena the millisecond needed to pull Sertsa from an undesirable destiny. The chopping knife landed on the lamb's heart, splattering the vendor with blood, while the organ slid off the ice onto the ground. Sertsa dove under the stand, releasing herself from Yelena's grip, but not from the end of the leash. Yelena yanked until she had Sertsa back in her arms. Ljuba parted the sea of customers so the trio could get out of Dodge fast. The butcher had lost a fresh lamb's heart, not to mention soiling his shirt and apron. He was sure to seek revenge, so the two sisters and their four-legged trouble hound ran like the wind. Finally, they took refuge in a park around the corner, caught their breath, had a few giggles and gave an unconvincing reprimand to Sertsa, who received it with a wagging tail and panting tongue, as if to say, "Aren't you glad you brought me? I'm making this trip a real adventure."

The sisters tied the pup to a park bench and walked over to the water fountain a few yards away to clean their hands and get a drink. They turned away from Sertsa long enough for the city dog catcher to pull up in his van, grab Sertsa and throw her into the back of the van, slamming the door. Sertsa was fooled by the attention that a dog biscuit offered her, so it wasn't until she was trapped behind the grated windows of the van that her yelps could be heard. Yelena turned and saw her. "Oh my God, Ljuba, look!" Ljuba glanced up from the fountain and saw the van halfway down the block already, running a red light. She bolted like lightning into a full sprint and followed that van for five blocks at top speed. Yelena stood frozen at first, in disbelief at the ferocious velocity of her sister, then she ran to catch up, but they were far ahead of her by then. The dog catcher saw Ljuba and took the opportunity to speed up in his little vehicle. Surely he would lose her. Ljuba didn't stop. Sooner or later, he was going to have to stop at a red light and she would gain then. He did, and she did.

When he was at a full stop, she grabbed onto the bumper, jumped up and road it, while attempting to catch her breath enough to figure out how to open the back door to free Sertsa. The dog catcher knew she was riding the vehicle, and stopped suddenly. Ljuba fell off and the driver got out, and came over to her, scolding her as she got up off the pavement. She was smart. She feigned a limp, and went into a tirade about how he'd harmed her and how his boss would fire him for hitting a pedestrian. Mr. "Trapper of Man's Best Friend" flipped out. He was being black mailed by a sixteen-year-old with platform shoes, who had outrun his internal combustion engine. Oh, the shame of it all. Meantime, Sertsa was yelping and scratching at the door of the mobile jail. He banged on it and shouted, "Shut up, you mutt!" seeking dominion over something.

"Let her go, mister! Please!" Ljuba cried, abandoning her cunning scheme and opting for flat out begging. The man just scowled at her and took out his ticket pad.

"You'll have to pay the fine," he said.

"How much?" she asked, pulling the remaining bills out of her pocket. He looked down at her.

"That much," he sneered.

"Let her out first," Ljuba demanded. He unlocked the door and Sertsa ran out. Yelena had caught up to them, just in time to see Ljuba give over every last cent of her shopping money to free Sertsa. The man shoved the loot in his shirt pocket. Ljuba was still out of breath, but managed to say to the guy, "I'd like a receipt, please."

"Oh, would you, now?" he said, and climbed back into the van, pretending to reach for a receipt book, but instead he took off with the back door of the van still unlocked. It flew open, freeing a few other dogs. Yelena put her arm around Ljuba and they walked over to an old oak tree on the side of the road, which Sertsa immediately baptized.

"Oh, Ljuba," Yelena said, and put her head on Ljuba's shoulder. "You're the best sister in the world! Thank you, thank you, thank you!"

Yelena knew her sister would never in a million years make her feel bad for the costly rescue.

"Forget it," Ljuba said.

"Is your foot all right?" Yelena asked.

"Sure," Ljuba smiled, "that was only a scare tactic."

Yelena beheld in her sister an angel for life. Ljuba was awesome.

"Well, it worked, Ljuba!" Yelena beamed.

Ljuba chuckled at the unwanted victory, and put her arm around her little sister, "Yeah honey, it worked. Now let's go home."

The threesome trudged up the hill, two thumbs out, one wagging tail.

CHAPTER NINETEEN

LANDING IN LJUBA'S QUEEN'S APARTMENT was great medicine for a broken heart. The protective instincts Ljuba possessed at sixteen hadn't changed in twenty-five years. Yelena hadn't slept in days, nor had she been able to weep or properly grieve. Her village felt far away. She was in America now. She buried her pain under the concentration required to put a sentence together in English, and figure out the way of life in New York. It served as a giant curtain covering the real show going on inside her, the one her soul was governing, the one that featured the never ending hemorrhage that, drop by drop, memory by memory made her accept that Marko was gone. She would never see him again. It was impossible to comprehend, far too much for her to bear. It needed to be cloaked behind a heavy velvet drape that would muffle the images that could drive her senseless at the drop of a pin. Sheer madness awaits the mother who loses a child. She was a glass mountain being scaled by a savage beast called grief.

Yelena pulled the quilted cover over her and rolled to the other side of the lumpy sofa bed, searching for a different picture to put in her brain that might give her the courage to close her eyes. Fifteen minutes felt like forever. Traffic, a distant siren, the flush of a toilet from the upstairs flat, another comrade fighting insomnia, perhaps. Or maybe they were one of the fortunate ones who fumbled their way to the bathroom, then floated back to bed, half-asleep, robbing the sheets of their chance to cool off before warm, steady, secure snores inhabited them again. Yelena surrendered, sat up, switched on the bedside lamp while sending the alarm clock flying, slicing the night silence like a machete through butter.

Henry rushed into the living room, carrying his bedtime reading glasses, rescuing the alarm clock on his way in, snuffing its aria with a quick tap on the off button. "Yelena! You all right?"

From the bedroom, Ljuba called, "Henry, is she all right?"

"It's okay, honey, go back to sleep, she's fine." Then conspiratorially, he leaned in to replace the clock and assess the situation, "Can't sleep, eh, kid?" She nodded, unable to resist a once-over of Henry's sleeping garb; pink sweat pants and a dago-tee. Henry reached for the universal panacea for all human ills, the remote. He caught Yelena staring at the sweats. "Never mind, Ljuba bought 'em. Believe me, pink's not normally my color. What was she thinking? You gotta ask, you know what I mean?"

She let that one go, it was too sotto voce, too fast, too much Bronx accent. Would she ever learn this foreign tongue?

"Here ya go." Henry handed her the remote like it was the Holy Grail, or a baton for the last lap of the relays at the Olympics. "You'll find something to watch that'll put you to sleep."

She watched him as the sweat on his nose created a slope for his reading glasses to ski down. She wondered which would hit the ground first, the pebble of perspiration on the tip of his nose or the glasses.

He rescued both with his plumber's thumb and headed back to the bedroom, throwing a "'Night, Yelena," as he disappeared.

She thought that it was probably those pink pants made him sweat like that, then turned her attention on the remote. She found the "on" button, but then accidentally pushed the volume which nearly sent her to the ceiling and brought Henry back in a flash. Nadya also appeared at the door of her bedroom grasping her teddy bear, Pooh. Henry showed his sister-in-law the proper "buttonage." Yelena was a quick learner.

"Thanks, Henry, I know now."

Henry nodded, somewhat unconvinced, then noticed his daughter was awake.

"Nadya, honey, back to bed, school tomorrow." The rebellious second reluctantly born obeyed.

"Yes, Daddy." Then, the limits tester kicked in, "But Daddy, can't I sit with Auntie Yelena for a few minutes? Because, Daddy, you know what? She might want Pooh to keep her company, so she doesn't get lonely without her baby?" Out of the mouths of babes, thought Henry.

"Five minutes," he yawned and stumbled back to bed, tossing his National Geographic aside. His reading was over for the night. Nadya snuggled in next to her aunt. They watched the images wrought by Yelena's fast fingering flash before them. Henry had muted the sound. So all they could hear was the sound of Nadya sucking her thumb with one hand, while she held onto Yelena with the other. In sixty seconds she was asleep against her aunt's shoulder. Yelena, mesmerized by the television, paused to look down at her niece breathing that steady child breath that says, *all, all is well.*

Yelena reached to cover Nadya with the quilt and accidentally hit the volume button again, but mercifully it was on low. Good thing too, because the sound of laughter spilled from the television like endless confetti. Yelena was captivated. On the screen she saw a woman with light brown hair and a tiny waist waiting on a man in a large clothing store. It appeared he wanted to buy a tie. Yelena listened carefully to what they were saying, but couldn't quite understand them. She dared to raise the volume half a level, but came no closer to comprehending why there was so much laughter after almost everything the woman said. And where were the people who were doing the laughing, anyhow? Almost involuntarily, Yelena began repeating the words she heard coming out of the mouth of the woman with the tiny waist. It was fun to say the words that floated out of the television screen and into her mouth. She listened carefully.

"Yes sir. Well yes, you certainly do need a new tie."

"I do?"

"Don't you think you do?"

"Well, Miss when you put it that way…are you always so candid with your customers?"

"Oooh no, I can't accept candy from my customers, it wouldn't be right." Loud laughter followed that line from somewhere. What was so funny?

"Okay, Miss, I'm sold. Now do you have anything on sale?"

"Oh yes, Sir. Everything here is on sale. We'll sell you anything you want. After all this is a store. But if you don't mind my asking who were you sold to?"

"What? Sold? Oh. Never mind. Let's see, I think I'll take this blue tie."

"All right, I'll just wrap it up. That'll be twenty dollars."

"Twenty dollars! That's a little high, isn't it?"

"Well, sir, I shouldn't tell you this, but if you buy the red one over there, you can save twenty dollars. So if I were you, I'd buy that one, and with the twenty that you save, buy the blue one you like, and forget about the red one."

Yelena heard more laughter go on and on. She was fascinated and delighted to be figuring out, little by little, what was going on in that magical world inside the television screen. Finally a funny design came onto the screen and a high pitched noise. No more laughter. She clicked the TV off and fell asleep.

Yelena awoke before dawn. Nadya was still asleep beside her, and somehow, sometime between the funny lady on television, and the sound of the first traffic horn, another little angel appeared in the form of Anna who had snuggled in on the other side of Nadya. A happy threesome, indeed. Yelena peeled out of bed without a sound and walked to the kitchen sink to get a glass of water. Gazing out at the iron bars on the windows, the iron fire escape, the iron water tower on the roof across the way, she saw nothing but hard metal and cement rooftops for miles. Metal gates, barbed fences, brick walls, not a patch of green save the branches of some potted plants Ljuba had put on the landing of the fire escape.

Mid-October found the plants without their bloom, though the leaves held on tight. She poured herself some water, drank, winced. It tasted different from the mountain stream water at home, but she had to admit it wasn't bad, not as fresh, but not bad. A spasm of homesickness wrenched her gut. So far from the rolling meadows of her home, she was frightened by the iron permanency of this place. When a woman crosses half the globe into the arms of her beloved sister, she's altered inside. She's not the same. Maybe it was the radically different topography or the trauma of her recent trials that caused the restlessness in Yelena. She felt a repeated longing, reaching, grabbing and not getting, an overwhelming desire to be somewhere other than where she was, gnawing at her like a haunting melody she couldn't get out of her head.

So now what? she thought, then eyed her salvation, the Turkish coffee pot, the demitasse and the can of coffee, right there on the counter, staring at her and proving her wrong. Ah-ha, good, something familiar after all. Something she was capable of doing, not like that darned remote.

Yelena filled the pot with water and turned on the burner. Before placing the pot over fire, she stopped, gazed at the water in the pot, poured it out, refilled it three times, and then returned it to the flame, just to be on the safe side. Good water makes good coffee. Coffee, the sacred bean, was distilled inspiration by her book. Unlike most Americans, for Yelena, coffee was not taken to "wake up" or "give one energy." It was simply what one did, daily, like a holy ritual. To drink of the dark black liquid made thick with residue causing one to nearly chew the last swallow was a link to a tribal tradition, a generational convention, a damn good habit. Yelena drank it down silently, wondering what Aunt Sofia was doing at that very moment. *What time was it there? Had anything been learned about the men who killed Marko?*

She downed the elixir and gazed out at the village of Queens, a very different kind of village from her own, where, in her thirty-three years, she had known moments of peace. Not anymore. Now there was stillness in her, but no real serenity, and there probably never would be again.

She finished her coffee and climbed back into the sofa bed, in between her two nieces. Holding them in her arms, with no hope of returning to sleep, she quietly watched the first rays of the day sweep across the sweet faces of Ljuba's children. She had made it through her first night in America, and survived.

CHAPTER TWENTY

CAREFUL NOT TO WAKEN HER NIECES, Yelena patiently waited until they felt the sun on their cheeks and arose to greet their aunt with a bounty of kisses. Surrounded on all sides by affection, Yelena found herself giggling and playing with the girls, who jumped on her, uttering words of joy in perfect English. What a world cupped her now. She had no plan, no idea what came next, and no net. Standing on this precipice of new possibilities, an inner voice urged her to put one foot in front of the other and walk through the pain. When you're walking through hell, you don't pitch a tent. Laughing with her nieces brought tears to her eyes, and the turmoil of the topsy-turvy night fell away.

The angst that blackened her conscience, being so far from Marko's mound of earth, had lifted briefly. She looked around the room, noticing its character had changed in the morning light. Its flaws veiled by the gauze of evening were now as blatant as clown's make-up under hot lights of a big top. Naked walls, chipped paint and torn, ragged wall-paper were covered up with family photos, symbols of genuine affection drowning out the deterioration of a *very* "lived in" pad. Landing on a photo of herself holding up her newborn son, her eyes snapped shut again and a wayward war erupted inside her like acid through silk. I should be home with Marko, lying on that mound of dirt that has become his eternal blanket. I want to drink the rain that makes heavy the earth upon him. I want and I want and I want and I want. How do you heal want? How? Just then Nadya shook her, "Watch this Aunt Yelena!" she demanded as she performed a head-stand right there on the sofa bed, with Anna spotting her, as big sisters do.

Henry emerged, eyes half shut, and within minutes Ljuba had American coffee ready for him. The girls scrambled to get ready for their Saturday morning art classes at a nearby community park. Henry worked on Saturdays too, which he obviously resented as he slurped coffee from a saucer while his wife packed a box lunch for him. Ljuba stood upright and sure, even in the early morning, loving every small task that she performed. That was her nature, nothing but love.

Yelena closed her eyes again, as jetlag seemed to be setting in. She drifted off and saw Aunt Sofia standing at the stove in her mind's eye, stirring the Turkish coffee on that morning of departure only a short time ago. In her dream state, Yelena realized what it must have taken for Aunt Sofia to let her go. She'd obviously understood the need for Yelena to visit Ljuba to restore herself, and she wouldn't have hampered her for the world, even if she may have secretly dreaded being left alone to mourn. Uncle Anton had been given the divine reprieve of senility to carry him through the dark passage of his grand nephew's exit before his time. Either one of them would have gladly taken his place. But neither grief nor Aunt Sofia's seventy-eight years would keep her from her daily chores, or her prayerful visits to the church. Her personal code of honor was: *keep going, don't dwell on the hurt, find a way to keep loving.* Too much, Yelena thought, way too tall an order. Way. Nevertheless, she herself ventured forth, foot to floor once more, until she heard Henry break the morning silence, and she froze, retreating under the covers. What she heard would change her life forever. She had no idea.

"So what's with sleeping beauty? I thought they get up early on the farm?" Henry murmured between mouthfuls of toast with jam landing more on his chin than into his mouth. He was in a hurry.

"Don't start, Henry. I doubt she slept a wink."

"You're telling me. She was up at 12:30, 1:30, 2:30, around 3:30 the girls must have joined her, and by 4:30 she was pacing off the joint. I'm telling you, we could get her a paper route, if she keeps these hours."

"Henry!" Ljuba protested.

Henry was on a roll. "Then I think she actually slept for thirty minutes, got up at five, made herself a cup of strong Turkish coffee, chewed that down, and while most of the planet would be up for a week after that she was out like a light. Go figure."

"Ever heard of jetlag, baby?" *Two could play the irony game,* Ljuba thought.

"I know, I know," Henry conceded. "I'm just saying...hell, never mind, forget it... my people write backward, yours live backward."

"Making us a perfect fit," Ljuba ended the parry, by filling Henry's lunch box with potato skins, a kind of benign punishment, or rather a reminder of who had the last word. The actual potatoes landed in the skillet, filling the kitchen with a wonderful smell of hot olive oil.

"Hmm, smells good," Henry sniffed the air, "how come the breakfast entrée is being served after the king of the castle leaves for work, I'd like to know."

"Bye, Ralph, have a good day," Ljuba pecked him on the cheek, and placed his lunch in his hand.

"Bye, angel, see you later," Henry returned the kiss, then: "You know what, honey, I'm gonna keep my eyes open for a job for Blanche DuBois here, it'll be good for her."

"Henry!!! She's been here twenty minutes, would you please back it up a bit?!" Ljuba chastised him.

"Sure, honey, whatever you say." And as he went for the door, Yelena sat up in bed, like a ghost, startling even Henry, though he managed, "Good morning, Yelena!"

And she, from the depths of a disheveled, sleepless, restless night, quipped, "I don't know about you, Henry, but I can't get used to America."

"Uh-huh," he responded, shot a look to Ljuba as if to say, 'welcome to the asylum', closed the door, headed down the stairs, and released "Ay gevalt!" just a tad too loudly, so that Ljuba started humming to cover it. Meanwhile Yelena finally took the leap of faith, one small step for womankind, and got up, made a conscious stride of choice, off the sofa, on to the rug, trusting that the great Spirit of Life would carry her through this day. That, and another cup coffee.

Ljuba poured a mug of "American" coffee for Yelena, and served it up with milk and sugar. Yelena was stunned by the size of the cup.

"It's like a lake," she commented. Stifling a laugh, Ljuba recollected her own immigrant experience fifteen years ago, the walking misunderstood. "What?" asked Yelena, noticing Ljuba's shoulders shaking with laughter, "You think I'm funny?"

Ljuba shook her head and put on her poker face, and announced in perfect English, "Sister of mine, after I get the girls off to their art class, we are going to participate in America's greatest pastime...shopping!"

Yelena understood perhaps every other word of what her sister had just said, but nodded anyway, because this day, this particular early morning, she was choosing to live.

CHAPTER TWENTY-ONE

LJUBA TOOK THE DAY OFF from her at-home tutoring job and she and her sister hit the streets of Queens. *What a village, what a village,* Yelena kept repeating to herself. The size alone was outside her concept of a village. This was more like Belgrade, her capital city where crowds of people waiting at each corner for the light to change to green and the unrelenting noise of traffic were the norm. This was radically different from Shar village where one's eyes could rest on the horizon, rather than on the back of someone's coat collar. But with her sister by her side, she would be fine.

Ljuba helped her negotiate her first purchase, cabbage, the staple ingredient along with garlic in most Eastern European cooking. The vegetable vendor found Yelena both amusing and annoying when she touched and squeezed nearly every head of cabbage he had in his stall.

"You gonna make love to it, lady, you gonna have to buy it!" he snorted.

Yelena smiled and made her first attempt at American chit-chat. "In my country, gold!" she said, holding up the winning head of cabbage that she would purchase.

The chubby, unshaven, black-haired vendor shook his head, glanced at his wife next to him to make sure she caught him being clever, "Gold, eh? Yeah, well in this country you can have it for thirty pieces of silver!" He cracked himself up, gave his wife an eye roll, while Ljuba rescued Yelena by exchanging three quarters, for the head of cabbage.

"Another nutcase comes to New York," he muttered to his wife.

"Never mind, Joe, just give the lady her cabbage, already," his wife demanded.

"Wha-at, I'm giving, I'm giving, don't worry about it." The vendor obeyed, unhappy to be reminded his ancestry was matriarchal, and the cabbage couple commenced their long day of "gold" sales.

"Thank you," waved Yelena, marking this transaction a major victory on foreign soil.

Ljuba decided to treat her sister to New York's special cuisine, a footlong hotdog. Standing at a corner stand, Yelena experienced another first, an encounter with a homeless man, who barely had to look at her before she emptied her pockets into his hat. He was thrilled and gushed with "God bless you's" till he noticed they were dinars, worthless, even in their country of origin. He was deflated, and she inspired, figuring she was beginning to get the hang of things.

Finally Ljuba escorted her to their ultimate destination, a women's clothing store, where she planned to give her sister a new look. She thought it would be good to get her some more up-to-date clothing, something to gently lift her out of mourning.

Yelena was in the fitting room trying on a black turtleneck and a pair of black slacks, when Ljuba came to the door and handed her a red sweater. "What's that?" Yelena queried, never associating herself with the color red, especially not now.

"Just try it," Ljuba replied. "It's a nice color on you." That was true. Yelena's long, silky black hair was well framed by red, but that didn't matter. She couldn't imagine putting on such a bright color while she was still in mourning. And when would she not be in mourning? It would last a mere lifetime. But to please her sister, Yelena donned the red sweater. No sooner had she pulled it over her head that a levee of tears gave way. The threads of the sweater got caught in Marko's gold chain; she was stuck inside the tent of red wool. She became hysterical. Ljuba tried to open the door of the fitting room, but it locked automatically from the inside, so Yelena was left blinded by her grief and trapped in the sweater. Ljuba crawled under the door and put her arm around her sister, and freed the sweater from the chain so that it slipped easily over Yelena's head. Yelena collapsed on the floor in a puddle of hangars, tags, safety pins and plastic. "I want my son back, Ljuba. I want him back, I want him back."

Ljuba joined her on the floor and wrapped her in her arms, and rocked her, as she had many times before in their childhood, stroking her ebony head, whispering, "Shhh, shhh, honey, everything is going to be all-right, shhh...."

The saleslady pounded on the door, "Has something happened? Is her son lost? Shall I call security?"

"No," Ljuba assured her, "we're fine, we just need a minute."

"Well, okay then," the woman said, reluctantly leaving them to their business.

There they stayed, two sisters on the cold floor of the fitting room, safe in each other's arms. Ljuba quieted her baby sister's fears, as she always had. But this was different. This was not about the baby rabbit that died when accidentally crushed under the hoof of a heifer when Yelena was only six, or over their cat caught in a tree one Easter Sunday, or even the puppy taken hostage by the nasty dogcatcher. This was a veritable crater of pain. There was no way to comprehend the size of it. It was like the earth, you couldn't get around it.

The ice had cracked on the frozen pond of underground grief. Yelena's sorrow slowly began to thaw. The sisters walked back home, arm in arm, each saddled with packages, yet in perfect synchronization of step. They possessed the unity that comes from understanding each other, due to endless shared experiences as well as that undeniable double helix that mapped their mutual ancestry in every cell of their being. The cool autumn clime energized their strides. With genetic determination and learned dignity, they walked chin up and out, while inside their two child-like hearts, driven by an adult need to survive, they were desperately seeking to trust in the mysterious and great God of their understanding.

That night, Yelena turned the cabbage into gold by preparing a delicious dinner that had Henry asking for thirds, despite his complaints that the stuffed cabbage stunk up the whole building. That comment earned him a love slap from Ljuba.

Life in the Meyers apartment didn't move linearly, they clashed and whacked up against each other. Pieces fell together in a new configuration every ten minutes, like a kaleidoscope. The place was small, things were piled on top of each other, colors fell from the top shelves, strange stuffed animals created by the children and chewed on by a runaway pup since deported to Henry's Mother's house, tumbled from unseen lodgings. A constant hum of ordinary life mixed with street noise, appliances whirring from dwellings above and below, and the energy of Ljuba ever in fifth gear, all converged to transform this tiny collection of rooms into a panoply of love, a perfect design for living.

Days passed, nights lingered. At bedtime, Yelena regularly shared the lumpy pull out sofa with her beloved nieces, they with their teddy bears, she with her remote. Her nightly channel surfing became a mandatory ritual preceding sleep, should sleep choose to come at all. This particular month featured comedy specials on cable, and among them was the funny lady with the tiny waist that she'd seen her first night in America, and who soon became her hero and prototype for American life, the one and only Gracie Allen. Yelena was hypnotized by her and began an in-depth devotional study of Gracie's every antic, gesture and phrase.

When Gracie was singing to a potential paramour, an amusing ditty called, "'I'm a Whole Lot Wilder Than I Look,'" Yelena decided to learn it. She had a fair idea of what the words meant, but by the way Gracie paraded around while singing, it took all her concentration just to mimic the words, to hell with the meaning. By morning, it was Yelena's anthem.

Nights with Gracie blended into days of growing familiarity with the neighborhood. She located all the essentials, the local Orthodox Church, the market, and the ice cream store where she fed her nieces whatever their hearts desired. These two young girls were a healing potion for Yelena, not to mention an ongoing language lesson. Nadya and Anna liked to talk. Daily Yelena's vocabulary developed and her language skills improved in tandem with her spirits. One day this personal progress brought her an offer Henry didn't want her to refuse.

Nadya and Anna were engaged in their new favorite pastime, helping Aunt Yelena cook, bake, chop, roll or stuff whatever the dish of the day happened to be. On that particular late autumn eve, the kitchen table was covered with a thin layer of dough being pulled by Yelena into a sheer, paper thin sheet that would be cut into squares, filled with spinach and cheese and baked to a golden buttery brown. Henry burst through the door with his tool box, lunch box, and a bundle of good news. Stopping short at the sight of the sea of white dough covering his kitchen table and Yelena circling it like a dervish, rolling pin in flour-covered hands, rolling, pulling, sprinkling, rolling, he stood mesmerized. "What's this, girls, more gold?"

"No, Daddy, this isn't gold, this is pita, can't you see it's pita?" chimed Nadya.

"Pita? What's pita?" Henry asked with surprise. He'd never seen Ljuba perform this ritual.

"It's what we put the gold into," his daughters declared with new found domestic dominion. Henry shook his head, put down his day's load and gave in to the temptation to touch the dough, inadvertently poking a hole in it, earning him a tap on the wrist from his youngest. "Daaaaaaaadddddddddyyyyyyyyy, doooooooonnnn'tttt!"

"Oh, sorry, Nadya, I should wash my hands first." Henry moved past Yelena to the sink.

"Hello, Henry," she greeted him. "How's the business?"

"Business? Uh, business is good." He replied, eyes glued to the table. "Hey Yelena, you got quite a production going here." She smiled.

"You'll see, it's going to be..." and before she could finish her own sentence, her nieces sang out.

"Delicious!!!!!" Their perfect synchronicity made them double over with the giggles. Yelena looked up from her dough sculpture and shrugged at Henry, as if to say, *what's a girl to do, the truth will out*. It made him wonder where she got this new sense of irony.

Oy, he had created a monster, or perhaps this was simply another side of that slippery Slavic temperament infused with exposure to late night cable. He thought he'd seen it all, married to Ljuba these seventeen years, but these Slavic sisters always seemed to have another pellet of unpredictability stuck up their sleeves. The pendulum that swung from intense sincerity to cool indifference baffled him, but he pressed on.

"Yelena, I have some news for you," he announced.

Just then Ljuba emerged from the bedroom, freshly showered and alert, "What kind of news?"

"Hi honey," Henry moved to embrace his wife to soften her up for the scoop. "Well, uh, a job...for Yelena." Yelena stopped rolling and looked up, her face covered in white flour, a deer caught in the headlights on a snowy eve, she clearly comprehended the word "job."

"What kind of job, Henry, and where?" queried the ever protective Ljuba.

"A good one, whatdya think?"

Henry coughed and cleared his throat before answering his wife's second question.

"Manhattan, actually."

"Manhattan." Yelena repeated, as if it were a town in East Africa.

Henry waited, hoping to enlist support from any one of the four females in the room. No one stirred. So he dove in.

"Okay, well, you see a buddy of mine's wife is too pregnant to work anymore, so she's taking several months off. The pay's decent because it's the shift, uh, later, in the day....it's...well...it's nights actually. The night shift, you might say. Nights." Ljuba glared at him, but he kept going. "And I figure, 'nights!' wow, that's perfect for the night owl here, and...."

"What's the job, Henry?" Ljuba implored, while Yelena was riveted as if she were watching the French Open when Monica Seles from Novi Sad, Yugoslavia, by the way was about to beat Steffi Graff after a four hour and twenty minute match, except that Yelena couldn't care less about tennis. Anyway, she was on them, like white on rice. Watching, listening, following them back and forth. She understood, "night," but couldn't filter, "shift" or "owl" or much else. Before she could inquire as to her new career, Henry spoke.

"Cleaning lady at a newspaper office." He began to hum, always a bad sign. No one moved, until Yelena broke the trance and resumed rolling out the dough. She had understood, and they all knew that she knew.

Ljuba intuited it was all right to say, "We'll think about it, Henry." She coupled that response with a look he knew well which read, "This conversation is over for now. Dear."

After dinner, the three muses were on the sofa bed, far past the girls' bedtime, and the questions were flying. "Are you going away to work, Aunt Yelena?" Anna wanted to know, she worried it would take their aunt away from them. Yelena hugged them close.

"I don't know, sweetheart," their aunt replied. She was crocheting them hats, and Anna, who was pensively watching each stitch, remained unsatisfied with the answer.

"Well, where's your husband, Aunt Yelena? Can't he work for you?" Nadya queried.

"He's with God, honey." Yelena whispered. Then Nadya whispered back, as if the mention of the G-word demanded hushed tones.

"Well, where is God?" she inquired so softly and gently as if He, the big G might be listening.

"Everywhere," Yelena gently replied. Nadya jumped right up and started looking around the room for God.

"Is cousin Marko with God, too?" she asked innocently. Big sister Anna answered this time.

"Yes, Nadee, cousin Marko too, now go to sleep." They nestled back into Yelena's arms and slept. She watched them a while, felt their breath on her chest, and watched their purity preserved one more day. Certain they were asleep, she set aside her yarn and needles, reached for the remote, wondering if Gracie might have some clues about working in Manhattan, and once again she studied the ways and wiles of Miss Allen until she slept.

CHAPTER TWENTY-TWO

YELENA WOKE UP WITH HER ANSWER. Yes. She would work. Why not? It would mean she could contribute to her sister's household, buy things for her nieces, and send money to Aunt Sofia. Simply to be useful would feel good. Yes. She would go to work and clean. She would begin anew, she would enter in, she would bring this elephantine grief and funnel it into a menial activity, and bit by bit, the elephant would get eaten, or at least diminished to a manageable size. It was a huge decision for her, yet people made them all the time, everywhere on the planet. They got up, they went to work, Henry did it, she did it at home in the village every single day. Barnyard inhabitants don't permit a day of rest. She worked and she worked hard. Why, then did it feel like such a big deal now? Was it the strangeness of the place, the strangeness of herself? She didn't know who she was here, she wasn't yet defined. Like an unidentified flying object in a foreign land, she traveled unrecognized by most. But still, she would go, she would work. After all, it was only an elephant.

The next evening Henry came home from work early in order to accompany Yelena to her first day/night of work. She dared to put on the red turtleneck sweater Ljuba bought on their first outing, then promptly took it off, embarrassed by the brightness of the hue, and donned a wool vest that Aunt Sofia had made for her. Navy blue and grey, with two modestly decorated pockets, very practical and undeniably unglamorous. Yelena was finishing dressing in the bathroom when Henry called out, "We gotta get going, Yelena!"

"I'm coming," she responded. Yelena had taken to lingering in the bathroom, sitting on the edge of the bathtub, lighting a candle which Ljuba kept on the sink counter, and praying. It was the only private place in the apartment, and even that was debatable. She missed the church loft at home, her sanctuary. But here on the edge of the cold porcelain tub, she lighted with folded hands, bowed head, petitioning God's daily provision of strength. That day she lingered, pleading for some angel guidance to make her capable of the new job. Of course she knew how to clean, but could she clean in English? She even felt a minute drop of excitement to be doing something new. Grief and guilt followed swiftly in the wake of that moment. Was she betraying her son's memory by taking work? She feared feeling farther from Marko as she took this new step. That's impossible, of course, but it washed over her nonetheless. How could healing cause distancing in the heart? Can hearts ever distance? Does distance have the power to separate hearts? She thought not. She finished her prayers, faced herself in the mirror, ran a comb through her long black hair and blew out the candle, opening the bathroom door to an impatient Henry, her ready escort into the city.

Rush hour in midtown Manhattan seemed to Yelena like a savage cry for mercy. She'd never seen or heard anything quite like it, not even in her country's capital city, Belgrade. What was the big hurry, she wondered. Not that she couldn't keep up. Her pace was rapid, her rhythm undaunted, but why and wherefore? That word haunted her like a phantom dream. Why this? Why that? Why anything? Marko, Marko, Marko tapped out like the Morse code with each step of her existence. Even with the kindness of her sister, the strongest of blood bonds, the crux of feminine fellowship, an essential of life, even with that rock to stand on, even with Henry's sincere efforts on her behalf, even with the delight of her angel nieces, even so, she dwelled in Gethsemane, alone with the reality that she lived, and her son did not. Why? She was powerless over it.

Henry made conversation all the way to the subway stop. He rambled on about the guy, Casey, who would be her supervisor and how he was a friend of this buddy of his, Jerry, whose wife was pregnant and had to stop working to have the baby. So Yelena would just be filling in really, nothing permanent, just for a little while. And nothing too strenuous, and she'd get used to the hours and so nothing to worry about, absolutely nothing, nothing, nothing. Yelena watched him closely. She'd never heard Henry so talkative. *He must be as scared as me,* she thought. She caught every word he said, and was proud to note her progress in English, especially in comprehension, if not verbalization quite yet.

The subway stopped at Fifty-ninth and Lexington, and they walked across town, passing Central Park, where Yelena was surprised to see horses in the streets. She approached one to pet it, but Henry grabbed her hand, "Those aren't pets, Yelena. Besides they're blind, most of them."

"That one isn't blind." she concluded for some reason Henry didn't understand.

"No? Really? Well, maybe you're right, I thought they were all blind, but maybe not, maybe they're just stupid," Henry decided.

"They're not blind, Henry, and they're not stupid. They just don't know where they're going. Like me. So they're afraid. Like me."

Henry was stunned. That was more than Yelena had revealed to him or anyone about how she felt in her first couple of months as a New Yorker. He was touched, and put his arm around her.

"Come on, Yelena, I'll show you where we're going, and he grabbed her hand, and they ran across Fifth Avenue, against the traffic light, causing a cab to swerve, Henry to curse, and Yelena to cross herself and utter an old Slavonic urgent plea for divine help: *"Bozhe Pomozhi!"*

The near miss did the trick of getting her adrenaline going and getting her focus off her grief. Moment to moment survival has a way of doing that. They laughed when they reached the other side, like convicts that had just shed their chains. A few more blocks of brisk walking and they were in front of the building. Yelena looked up. Countless stories high, a veritable mountain of a building, she perceived.

"Let's go, kid." Henry ushered her swiftly through the revolving doors. All the foot traffic was going the other way. It was the end of the workday for the white collar world, and the beginning of the magic hour for the maintenance teams and other aberrant late nighters. They walked into the chaos created by the brains of the world, and with an uncomplicated understanding, would set the world of grey matter straight, as if Yelena were to become the "Sorcerer's apprentice" for the newsroom.

The elevator doors opened up to a sea of empty desks set in cubicles, cluttered with papers, books, computers, coffee cups, paperclips, all imaginable human collectibles stacked up to form an environment where acute intelligence and some imagination created the media miracle called a newspaper. Amazing, and they do it daily. Part genius, part fable, part hard core truth, it fed the masses like manna from heaven. For Henry, of course, holier than the Kabbalah was the sports section, which he worshipped on his bathroom throne every morning. The comics he saved for his commute to work, when humor was more needed as much as a bus token. For Yelena, this looked like the biggest mess she'd ever seen, and could not fathom how she'd get it clean tonight.

Casey, her boss, a heavy set man with more of a waddle than a walk, came toward her, chewing an unlit cigar, and shoving a racing form under his arm and an accompanying pencil behind his ear. He smiled warmly at his new employee. "You must be Helena."

"Yelena," Henry corrected Casey, still posing as Yelena's voice.

"Oh, excuse me, there, Yelena. Nice to meet you. I'm Casey."

She met him with a good hand shake, and returned, "Nice to meet you, too, Casey." First round, a point.

"Let me take your coat, show you around," he continued. Again Henry jumped in for his sister-in-law.

"Thanks, Casey." He gave Casey Yelena's coat, then put his hand on her shoulder to reassure her. "Well, I'm going to take off now, and I'll meet you here later to take you home. Okay, Yelena?"

"Okay," she managed, realizing she was about to be on her own in this unfamiliar floor of wild disarray.

Casey spoke up. "Listen, Henry, I can take her to the subway, it's on my way." "Thanks, anyway, Case, but it's her first night, so I'll make it back later. I figure, she'll eventually get used to it, you know." Henry shook Casey's hand, kissed Yelena on the cheek, handed her a bag lunch Ljuba had prepared for her, turned and hit the elevator button. "See you later, kid," he called back to his sister-in-law. She looked after him like a lone pup.

"Okay, kid," she waved.

"Say hi to the family, Henry," Casey called out, as the elevator doors closed. Too late, he was gone. It was just Yelena and her supervisor, the kind, sweaty, gentle-spirited fat man.

"Let's get you a wrapper to work in, so you don't spoil that nice vest you got there." He guided her into a little utility room behind his office. There were a couple of lockers, two restrooms, a vending machine for candy, one for coffee, and a couch covered with magazines. Even the cleaner's area needed cleaning. He gave her a locker, a key, a clean blue cotton wrapper, and guided her to her cleaning cart. Instruction was about to begin.

Standing at the foothill of a mountain, Yelena had no fear. Facing the loss of her son, hovering over his grave, drowning in endless grief, falling into a chasm of sadness, even then, she never lost her faith. Boarding the ship to come to a foreign land, she felt a sense of awe, confusion, and an existential perception that it didn't matter what happened to her next, but still she kept her courage. But right then, in the face of a strange, albeit jolly instructor/boss, in the face of this new job which at first glance looked like one could never get to the bottom of the piles of stuff, and in the face of being trained in a new tongue learned mainly from dialogue off a television show featuring a fabulous lady named Gracie, Yelena felt nervous as never before. From head to toe, fear paralyzed her. She couldn't imagine why. This job should be a cakewalk compared to her recent history of personal challenges. But this was unmapped territory. It was a new horse whose gait she hadn't gotten the hang of yet. So she did the smart thing. She stood still, like a pigeon stuck on an ice pond. Out of the stillness comes yearning, and she was yearning to be elsewhere. Home, for example, or in Ljuba's bathroom, praying or even packed like a sardine on the subway, anywhere but here. But the mind doesn't always control the feet.

"I'll wait for you out on the floor, take your time," Casey urged her toward the restroom to change; to change from everything she'd always been, to all she would become in the future. Little did she know.

The restroom was painted a putrid green, but was clean, as the forceful fragrance of Lysol testified. She took off her vest, then another sweater, and left on her white t-shirt over which she put the blue wrapper. The belt went around her small waist more than twice. She made a hasty bow in the back and took a look in the mirror. Goodness, she thought, this is what they wear to clean here in America. It seemed too thin a thing for the job, but oh well. She took her scarf and tied it around her head, covering her shiny black mane, then dutifully folded her clothes and placed them in the locker Casey indicated was hers. Stepping out into the main newsroom where Casey awaited her with her new chariot, a large gray cleaning cart. The Serbian Cinderella thought she would die there. No particular reason, just another short lived, exaggerated, baseless, gypsy intuition.

Casey escorted her and her cart to the edge of the rows of cubicles, surrounding desks, computers, and trash cans. "All right, sweetheart," he opened with, "here's what you gotta do. Nothing's trash till it lands in the basket. I don't care if the coffee cups got mushrooms growing out of them. You don't touch nothing until *they* throw it away. Journalists can be a touchy bunch." He stuffed some snuff in his cheek, and she was immediately transported to Aunt

Sofia's kitchen table where she'd seen her dear old aunt exercise the same strange habit, daily. "Know what I mean," Casey added, sensing he was losing her attention. She nodded, reassuring him and herself that she was with it. He added, "God forbid you toss their Pulitzer Prize, right?" At which point, he picked something off the floor, read a half typed page, and crumpled it up, and tossed it into the bin on her cart.

He winked at her, "Don't you do that, kiddo."

Yelena nodded again, "Right, Mr. Casey."

"Call me Casey, kid," he smiled, revealing the dark juice of tobacco about to slip out if he spoke another syllable before spitting. He pulled out his red bandana handkerchief and with expert timing provided the landing pad for the tobacco juice. That drill repeated itself every few minutes, and it was more than fascinating for Yelena to behold. They continued down a row of cubicles, just about empty now, with only one or two writers still at their desks, ready to wrap it up. Apparently, this was more or less the daytime news floor. Casey continued, his own version of a college professor lecturing to freshmen, "This here is your territory, and all the way around to the filing area. They like those floors mopped every night. These here with the carpet, you can vacuum. Take your time, you got all night, right? Ha ha."

Yelena joined him, in what she couldn't imagine was funny, "Ha,ha."

Casey gave her a double take. "You're a good looking woman, but not much the brains department, eh?"

Yelena couldn't have seen this coming, but as naturally as a bee goes to honey, Yelena calmly and confidently replied with a Gracie-ism, "I've got brains I haven't even used yet."

Casey paused and stared at her, uncertain of what he had heard, cleared his tobacco-ridden throat and replied, "Well, hang on to them, you won't be using them here." He smiled. She smiled, suddenly realizing all she'd learned from Gracie Allen on late night TV was all she needed to know to get through this job, and the mountain became a molehill, right before her very eyes. She would manage it just fine. Casey turned her loose in the vast arena of cubicles, and went back to his office to catch the sports news while Yelena commenced cleaning.

CHAPTER TWENTY THREE

THERE WAS A SIMPLE SATISFACTION THAT came from affecting a change, however minor, from a smudge to a shiny surface, from a dusty corner to a sharp right angle, from an overflowing trash bin, to one ready to receive. It was an activity that actually took Yelena into a realm where for a matter of minutes, Marko's memory wasn't howling. She could see clear cause and effect at the end of her fingers. It was she who was making a change, and briefly in control of something. It was a meditation not unlike her farm chores were, like the task of moving milk from an udder into a pail. A specific, necessary mission to be accomplished in a focussed, concentrated way. Daily. Repeatedly. Without fail. It was hypnotic. She loved it and missed it. Now the chores of this new barnyard, a news office, provided her with a goal: picking up after the creative men and women working there. Yelena noticed the heavy stone in her heart had shifted inside her slender body, allowing her a fleeting sense of lightness of being. The reality of doing was an antidote for her mourning. For the first time in a long time, she stood upright, shoulders back, and embraced the purpose before her. To clean. She went about her business with the zeal of a convert, the conviction of a new devotee, the pulse of a woman who had not yet given up the fight.

By the time the midnight break came around, she felt almost guilty for having spent several hours away from her grief, as if she had abandoned the house where she'd been born. She found a secluded aisle between two rows of file cabinets, where she made herself a private dining area, wedged between archives of American news. She sat down on the floor, stretched out her legs, took off her shoes, and let her bare feet feel the coolness of the cement floor, and drifted back into the archives of her heart.

A genuine desire to sleep overcame her. Fatigue rested heavily on her eyelids. Now, of all times. She shook it off, opened the lunch that Ljuba packed for her: slices of chicken, a tomato, a chunk of fresh bread and some black olives. She wasn't hungry. She leaned her head against the sturdy metal cabinet and felt the hum of machinery beneath her. It was cold. She placed some cleaning cloths under her to muffle the vibration of the heating or cooling system, she wasn't sure which. And then it hit her, like a club to her gut, she was so very far from her own pocket of earth on the planet, where her own patch of land squished willingly between her toes, and where the flowers she'd planted over Marko's grave were surely sprouting up by now. The file cabinets began to blur. She pulled a photo of her son out of the pocket of her skirt, studied him, and felt the rain fall from her eyes, drop by drop onto his black and white glossy smile, onto the hand he trustingly placed in hers, the hand that said, "I know I'm safe with you, mom."

What had happened? How did that eternal grasp fail? Did motherhood blink long enough to rip her heart to shreds? And why? Why…a crooked yet irresistible question that made her want to pound her fist against the floor to make it yield an answer. She wept. At last she was truly alone to weep, no one waiting to use the bathroom at Ljuba's, no one pulling her away from the gravesite, no one telling her lies about how it would get better. Any mother could tell you it wouldn't. Never. So she wept a tidal wave of tears, with no one around to interrupt or console her. She wanted none of that. The enormous office of her new employment, occupying the entire floor looked like maybe it was just big enough to hold her sorrow. She needed this opportunity to unleash her soul's darkness far more than she needed lunch. The time and space had been given to her at last.

That is, until Jake turned the corner, searching for the source of the sad sound and found Yelena bent over her beloved photograph. He couldn't have been more surprised if he'd rounded a bend in Glacial National Park in January and found a blooming cactus. Leaning against the slate grey metal cabinets, which housed the tomes of news stories, yarns of unsolved murders, glories of Olympian victories, accounts of twisters on the Eastern coast, quakes in claustrophobic Asian cities, drug trafficking in China, reports of quintuplets born to rookie cops, all forms of wonderment in the reportage of daily human life in this metropolis and the world…there against the safe deposit box of media, rested the trembling shoulders of a weeping widow, certain she was alone with her heartache with the crumpled vestige of her loss cupped in the palm of her hands: the picture of her boy, her only son, her child, her one and only, who would own her heart forever.

If Jake, the down on his luck journalist who'd taken to working nights in search of that one story that would put him over the top, who in the comfort of all-night sirens, occasional gun shots, screeching taxis and the odd human cry, found the appropriate backdrop for his creative muse, the man who sought erasure of the sham of his ex-marriage in noiseless all night restless writing, if this man, Jake, found the image of the foreign beauty nestled up against the brittle drawers of this burg's biography, a shock, then Yelena's view of this rumpled thoroughbred, framed by the unflattering fluorescent tubes of defiant light, was nothing short of traumatic. She had thought she was alone at last. After the long journey, after the unfamiliar though loving new home base complete with the otherworldly lullaby of cable television, after the somewhat indecipherable instructions of Boss Casey, and after the countless aisles of American dust she had already cleaned, she thought she had earned a moment of solitude. After one tumbling domino of chaos and heartache after another, she thought she'd finally found a pocket of time, to pull her mantle of sorrow from across the continent to cover her naked head like a curtain dropping at the end of an act.

No such luck. Instead, she looked up to see a man, easily as stunned as she was. Two elk caught in fluorescent headlights. Both shocked still, but each with different words to focus the feeling, mapped out with alphabets that shared no more character than a wooden spoon did with a velvet hat. Two worlds, two individuals, two voices, one sentiment. Surprise. The unpredictable and the inevitable have just met. The unexpected guest in each other's lives had arrived. Who was he?

And who, pray tell was she?

It had been a short time since Yelena had landed in America, these several weeks. She could keep count by the number of phrases she'd learned from Gracie, but it was a bit of a blur, her time in America. Words didn't produce themselves to describe her state of being yet. She had sat down in a cool, safe place, in the solace of metal cabinets, with a parapet to rest upon and weep awhile, when this *other* appeared. Much easier to keep a door shut tight than to have it cracked open just enough for a tear to pass through it, which could easily lead to a tsunami. She could feel it in her gut, which never lied. Her breath stopped. His too was staunched for a beat. All sound arrested. Where was that pounding air conditioning? Where her beating heart? What of the crashing of the tears on her face? It had all gone quiet, and then after an interminable gestating pause, the silence broke with a single syllable from this tall handsome buck, "Oh."

With that single sound, a symphony closed in upon itself, the musical rest was swallowed up in a minor key, and that mere glimpse of silence would be the last of its particular kind that these two creatures from different worlds would ever hear again.

A born journalist, reporter, investigator, and curious cat, Jake was skilled at taking in a scene in a flash. He trained himself to memorize everything from the color of a person's eyes to the mole on their cheek, or the size of their shoes in a three second glance. It was his work. It's what he loved; it's all he ever desired to do. Well, that and pitch for the Yankees, but he forgave himself that failed dream when he broke his elbow, slamming it against a boat when he pulled his kid brother out of a river, one summer, long ago and faraway.

The kid couldn't swim, and Jake's intuition and swift response saved the boy's life. At eleven Jake was a hero, a god in his mother's eyes, a savior to his brother. He bought his brother ten more years till he died of leukemia at twenty. Jake had never forgiven himself for not being able to save his kid brother from that. Such are the demands on the life of a gifted young man, who did so much good, only to grow up feeling like he fell short when it really counted. But feelings aren't facts, thankfully, and the facts about Jake Thompson are distinctive.

He was born in his parents' home in an Irish hood in Brooklyn. His mother, Mary, was as surprised as he must have been that he didn't wait for a hospital gurney to greet the planet. The first son of a Scotch/Irish mother, and a Czech father. That combo guaranteed he'd be tall and a drinker, and probably hot tempered, and somewhat brooding. His real name, Tzimpozli, was changed when his father opened his own butcher shop in Brooklyn and Thompson was as close as the sign painters could come to Tzimpozli. They didn't have the stencils for "z," so they renamed the family on the spot. Janos, Jake's father, was furious, but his mother, with that bent Irish sense of humor, thought it was hilarious. That was the yin-yang that kept that couple together, and the family all around it.

Naturally, the frailty of Jake's younger brother, weighed heavily on his mother daily. Nevertheless, she had a healthy pride that the rest of her family, Jake and her three daughters, would prosper, so she kept her grief to herself as best she could, in service to the healthy ones that would remain, not the least of which was a demanding husband. Jake could recognize grief when he saw it and he sized up the situation accurately when he caught sight of the beautiful creature folded against the filing cabinets.

Though he read the picture of loss as clear as day, he'd never before witnessed it in such a one as she. He felt like he knew her. He figured it was her grief he recognized. Neither one would ever know they rode the same "L" train for two stops, two months ago. Whatever it was that made this beauty weep, he wanted to make it go away, to be her hero, to come to her rescue. His heart shifted in his chest, reorganizing itself for what was to come.

"Would you like a glass of water?" He offered. This was a new experience for Yelena, an American man speaking directly to her, without telling her how to channel surf, or how to clean the newsroom floor, or how much money cabbage cost in Queens. It was a sound she hadn't heard in a while, the kindness of a stranger. A tenderness, the likes of which she heard only in her own mountain home, except that over there, it usually came from a man of the cloth. Yet, here stood a tall stranger, offering her water, in a foreign tongue, in an unfamiliar place, at a most embarrassing moment. She accepted, "Thank you."

He disappeared as fast as he'd appeared to fetch the water. It gave her a moment to travel a compressed journey of wonderment. Who is that? How'd he get in here? Did he hear me weeping? Will he harm me? Am I going to lose my job? The questions barraged her as she dried her eyes, put Ljuba's lunch away, restored her headscarf, and was about to gently replace Marko's photo into the safety of her pocket when Jake was already presenting her with a cup of cold water. Their eyes locked. Jake was both fascinated and instantly drawn to this beautiful, sad, exotic woman.

"Here you go, one water straight up." Yelena drank from the cup, without taking her eyes off Jake, partly out of interest, partly out of caution.

"Thank you." His eyes broke from hers as he caught sight of the photo still in her lap. He cranked his head around to see it.

"Is that your boy?" Perhaps this would open the conversation, and lead to an invitation to sit down next to her on that appealing cold cement floor. He could only hope. She looked down for what seemed like an eternity to Jake.

"Yes," she replied slowly, "my son," as if she'd never said those words before, as if she'd never seen the photo of his smiling face before, as if she'd never identified herself as his mother before. Jake was still campaigning for an inroad.

"Nice looking kid. Is he with his father?" The journalist wanted to learn if the lovely lady was in wedlock. He held his breath.

"Yes," she replied, and he exhaled his disappointment, but pressed on, as his profession had trained him to do.

"Where's that?"

"Heaven." Yelena looked him in the eye again. She would learn all she needed to know about him by his response. She held his gaze steadily and watched a shadow soften across his angular features.

"I'm so sorry" he said slowly, as he gently positioned himself to sit down next to her, to halve her grief by osmosis, perhaps by his very presence, to leaven that moment of torture for her, "Is this seat taken?" he asked and then landed on the floor, wondering why one would choose to sit on that cold pallet, but so be it. He joined her there.

Seated right next to her, shoulder to shoulder, his long legs blocked the way toward the newsroom. On the other side of her was her cart, which blocked a quick getaway for her, if needed. How did this happen? Moments before, she was alone with the memory of her son, then suddenly a handsome someone appeared and planted himself against her, and was reaching into his pocket for something, she knew not what, but feared it could have been anything from a knife to a gold coin. What did she know of the bizarre customs of this country? *Dear God, get me home, I don't want to be here, I shall surely die of suffocation.*

Meantime Jake produced a photo from his wallet of a young man of about eighteen or so. He held it out to her. She glared at it, recognized the similar eye brows, and put two and two together. It was her turn to exhale. He was not going to kill her, he was showing her a picture, okay.

"Your son?" she managed. Jake was triumphant. She spoke! Oh speak again sweet angel! "Nice looking kid," she mimicked with complete sincerity, thinking it part of her endless self-education. Jake smiled.

"Yes, he is. My Tony is a good-looking boy. Boy, heck, he's almost twenty! Still lives with his mother, well, most of the time, anyhow. But he's a good boy, and I love him." They stared at the picture of Tony together, then Jake flat out flirted with the young childless widow, "Looks like me, don't you think?"

Yelena nodded in agreement. "Where's your mother?" she asked, attempting to keep the conversation going, something she'd never done before in her life in English, that is. Jake didn't quite get her question.

"My mother?" Then he understood that she was asking about Tony's mother. Possessive pronouns weren't the easiest thing to grasp in English. "My mother is dead," he explained, "but I think you mean Tony's mother, and she's here in New York. We're divorced."

This time, Yelena turned to him in sympathy, "I'm sorry." Jake's impulse was to say, *what the hell, I never really loved the bitch anyway. Besides, if we were married, I might not be sitting here next to you, you doll, you, but we're divorced, praise God, and so now you can be mine.* Of course he said none of this, but nodded instead, accepting her sympathy, which for all he knew, could have been for the death of his mother, rather than the divorce. They weren't quite synched up yet.

He couldn't resist waxing philosophical though, and added, "Well, you know, you make one mistake to correct another mistake and everybody ends up miserable."

"Like war," she replied.

"Yes, actually, divorce is like a gang war," Jake responded, impressed by her use of simile.

"I saw some gangs in Queens," Yelena countered.

Jake was most willingly being reeled in, "Well, there you go, then," he said, flashing her his winning smile that had worked for him for decades. Though he hadn't cause to use his charm much lately, he took it out, dusted it off, and risked it all with, "What's your name?"

"Yelena."

"Yelena," Jake repeated it. "That's a beautiful name. I'm Jake."

She only nodded and looked him in the eye once more. It was a little unnerving, he couldn't quite read her.

Determined to stay in the game, he took a Hershey bar out of his pocket and offered it, "Would you like to share some of my dinner?" They sat silently chewing the little squares of chocolate, as if it were Beluga caviar.

"Where are you from, Yelena?"

"Shar Mountain village," she replied between crunches of the almonds in the chocolate bar.

Jake waited for further description of where that might be, while his journalistic mind was already placing it somewhere in Bulgaria, Romania, Russia, but his need for precision unsettled him.

Maybe she read it on his face, so she threw him a crumb. "A beautiful place where there is no peace."

"That could be a lot of places," Jake coaxed.

Yelena's eyes suddenly started scanning the file cabinets and counting the squares of tile on the floor. If she uttered the name of the place of her birth, her grief might overtake her, and she wasn't ready to enter that cavern of sadness in the company of a stranger, so she searched for an objective way to describe her beloved, bloodstained village.

"It is between Bosnia and Kosovo, near Montenegro. Always a battle going on there."

"Ahhh, yes, that's a rough and tumble spot these days. Is that what happened to your family? The civil war wipe them out?" Jake pressed. Yelena, unable to say more, rose to go back to work, the only anesthesia for her pain. Jake jumped up to apologize.

"I ask too many questions. I'm sorry, please, forgive my chronic journalism." Yelena only caught the word "sorry" since her tears were threatening to blind her again. She kept her head turned, and mumbled, "Thank you for the chocolate," as she headed toward her cart. He followed her, hooked.

"Don't go." But she continued recalibrating for work, retying her wrapper back on, fixing her babushka, placing the lunch bag in her cart, putting on her gloves. Jake, choosing to be oblivious to the behavior which was so clearly dismissing him, carried on with the conversation. "So, how long you been in New York?"

Yelena, continuing her prep, threw back, "Only some few many several weeks."

"And you already got a job. Man, that's an impressive work ethic." Yelena didn't catch that, not only because her vocabulary fell far short of his, but because she was focused on the tasks at hand, counting on them to keep her emotions in check.

The best she could come up with was, "I live with my sister." Jake had fallen for her, without even knowing it.

"And that was my next question, where do you live?"

"In the village of Queens." She took a beat, then, "With the queen." She smiled, thinking she made a pretty good joke.

Jake melted, "Now that's a smile worth a thousand words in ten languages."

Yelena was keeping up as best she could, returning to her work, with Jake in tow like a puppy. "I only speak three languages."

By then Jake was volleying very well, and was shameless about shadowing her, "And that was my next question...what are you, anyway, a Gypsy mind reader?"

Like two lines eschew in space on a trigonometric graph, their conversation continued, "Gypsy, I don't speak."

Both at the net now. "But English you do! And quite well, I might add."

That elicited another smile from Yelena, "Yes, I do."

Pshaw, Jake looked down, suddenly a little shy himself, as he found they were standing so close to each other their clothes were touching, and he whispered, "Well, I for one am glad, because my Slavic is a little rusty." They breathed in unison.

Finally, Yelena said, "Ya djelam tyepyer. Izvinitzye, pozhalyusta."

"So's my Russian," Jake replied, looking into her eyes.

Then Yelena translated, "It means I have to get back to work." And with that, she turned the cart around, walked past Jake down the corridor of file cabinets that had just served as their Verona garden wall. Lost in thought and completely captivated, he leaned against one of the file cabinets, jamming his elbow into the handle of one of them. "Ouch."

CHAPTER TWENTY-FOUR

SHE WAS GONE. Was she real? Did he down too much Irish whiskey tonight in an effort to neutralize the pain and drain of his dear ex Sigrid, and so conjure a spectre to save him through slow and graceful torture? That's it. She was the ghost of cleaning ladies past, the spirit warrior of the dying world of journalism, the phantom female expressing the tragedy and treasure of the time he lived in; loss, strength, depth, beauty, all rolled into one persona? Did she show up to castigate him for doing nothing of consequence in the living or writing department since the breakage of his marriage? Perhaps she was sent as a haunting reminder that it was about time he moved back into his own life? Or did he just have the plain ol' D.T.'s?

Who was she, anyway, a cleaning lady? Really? Come on, that had to be a cover for something. She didn't look like any maiden of maintenance he'd ever seen, and he'd seen plenty of cleaning personnel come and go since he'd been on this self-imposed "work at night" program. He'd been particularly attentive to the janitorial staff in the last couple of years, since they often were the only other living beings in the building with him at 3 a.m. Jake had a nice friendship with the last cleaning lady, Carmen.

She was a tiny thing with the strength of two oxen and hailed from Puerto Rico but had grown up in Harlem. Need one say more? A Latina in Harlem either learned to fight or was sliced before she could vote. Carmen had reached forty, so he figured her a fighter. Plus they'd become drinking buddies. She'd share a shot with him, just before heading out to face the middle of the night subway life. She traveled armed. More information than he needed or wanted, but she'd shared it with him when she got loose-tongued one night when a heavy rain kept her at Jake's cubicle a little longer than usual; she'd stopped to buffer herself with an extra shot of whatever he had open. Then some months ago, she confided in Jake that she was pregnant for the fourth time and needed to lay off the sauce for the baby's sake. He supported that idea and occasionally bought her an orange juice when he slid out for nicotine. So Carmen was gone on baby leave, and with two others at home under four, she wouldn't be coming back to work anytime soon.

Before Carmen, there had been an African-American woman, Regina, whose five by five fleshy frame housed a soulful voice that wafted to heaven nightly with gospel melodies that could have made even a stinker like Jake take Jesus as his own personal savior. A good southern Baptist woman, she didn't drink, and worked hard at converting Jake to abstinence, to no avail. They had some good talks about the Gospel, each with their own view of Jesus' miracles.

Jake insisted that if Jesus' first miracle was turning water into wine in Cana, why wouldn't a nip now and then be acceptable in the eyes of the Lord? Regina would laugh till her whole body jiggled like a gallon of primer getting mixed at the hardware store. She'd remark how happy she was that he knew the Good Book, and then would point out Proverbs 20:1: "Wine is a mocker, strong drink is raging: and whosoever is deceived thereby is not wise." He agreed with her completely, and thanked Jesus he was made wise before he ever had a drop, which got her digging for more Biblical material, maybe something to handle his pride besides backing up her campaign to get him hooked on apple juice. It all slipped right by him.

Nevertheless, she enjoyed Jake and when her sixty-year old knees rebelled against her desire to be in constant motion and service to her Lord Jesus, she retired. Jake knew he'd never see her again, gave her a cool fifty when she left, which she refused until he said it was "for the church." That helped the bill find its way into her pocket. Jake was sorry to see Regina go. Her pipes filled the nights at the office with a sense of hope. He missed that.

So with his history of good relations with cleaning personnel, he was expectant of another simpatico partner on the graveyard shift. What he wasn't expecting was that she'd be radiantly beautiful, young and enchanting. Plus, even with an accent as thick as London fog, she still proved to be a bit wittier than he is. Hmmm. That stimulated his competitive juices, and if he were going to be completely honest, she stimulated rather more than that.

Jake watched her disappear behind the tunnel of files, and spied between the cracks in the cabinets to catch sight of her moving with the smoothness of a lioness, connected to the earth, yet ready to spring from it to protect what it loved. She had touched him, the loss of her son, so recent, so raw. What the hell was going on in that country of hers? Of course, he knew what had been reported, but he also knew enough about the news business to know that was only half the story, if that. He was thinking with his heart now, something he'd trained himself not to do, but it was rambling along the lines of: What the bleep kind of mountain village did she come from, that made her a widow and childless at such an early age? He knew civil wars were the bloodiest, that brothers shot brothers, and kin turned against each other. Hell, our very own American Civil War still held the record for numbers dead, some 600,000 and the brutality of the killing that continued even after a so called truce had been reached was despicable. He also knew that in civil wars, there was that magical thing of value called land. The one thing that nobody was producing more of, good old mother earth. Men were willing to kill to have it, die to own it, become barbaric to rule it. Dirt.

For centuries, it brought out the savage in all of us. He also knew that there were religious conflicts on her precious turf, not unlike the other powder keg on the planet, the Middle East, but he didn't understand the depth of what exactly ailed them, and from whence hailed the divisiveness. How could he know really? History had become like the news, or the news was the new history, constantly being rewritten, perpetually in flux depending on which country was publishing the account. Where and what was truth, he had no idea.

For a moment he flashed on Regina's view that Truth was Jesus himself, and that's why he couldn't answer Pontius Pilate directly when asked the very question Jake was asking now, what is truth? Regina said that when Jesus was in the presence of it, He was it, and He couldn't speak around it. Regina held that the world convulsed the moment that question was asked, and that now all the wars fought since were in search of that answer. That thought flared up in Jake and kindled his desire to know the more about Yelena's homeland. He wondered if multiple relative truths might have collided with the One absolute Truth, wrenching her country into civil war.

Jake bee-lined to his computer to begin the pursuit of understanding what made this new cleaning lady tick. He was in search of what this is that convulses the world, as Regina would say, because frankly, his own world was rocking some. He'd never really understood Regina, but felt she knew something he didn't. Heck, do all these cleaning personnel have to be smarter than he was.

Yelena found her way around the sprawling office, accomplishing her duties with alternating automatism and fierce focus, as the emotional roller coaster of the last twenty minutes flooded her mind. Her "lunch break" had been the first real private time alone, or so she thought, when she could shed her tears for her Marko on American soil. Her grief was large-sized, it needed two continents to absorb the salt of her salt. Jake was the first man she'd spoken to, without the presence of Henry or Ljuba, since she came to this country. Casey's introduction doesn't really count, she reasoned, since that was more an instruction manual, than an actual conversation. It bothered her that she'd opened up to Jake. It was like she broke a precious relic and in so doing, sacrificed its power to heal. She'd shown the image of her son to a stranger. It objectified him in a way that made her uncomfortable. She hadn't completely admitted he was truly gone. She'd stated aloud that he was in heaven and she hadn't even accepted that herself yet.

There was a mountain of denial that grew inside of Yelena. It created a giant delusion, not so much to save her from pain which she was more than willing to suffer, but to keep the reality from being true, to prevent the fact from boldly announcing itself over and over again, demanding to be recognized. Yelena walked from desk to desk, cleaning, dusting, organizing, working to regain her balance, as if she'd been walking on a ship in a storm, searching for her sea legs, missing at every stride.

The disturbance went higher on the Richter scale when she thought about how kind Jake's eyes were, when she remembered that he too had a son he loved, and in his eyes, she'd seen a flicker of his imagining a loss he could not endure. She felt it was a split second of simpatico that humans give to each other without uttering a word. It is the true act of goodness.

Work had been the cure when she lost her husband, Radmilo. That day, before she had even broken the news to her Aunt Sofia, she'd fled to the barn to feed the animals and start an early milking, much to the cows' curious concern. Maybe the sheer movement toward a specific activity would redirect the course to read other than it had. Perhaps she could become a compass that would pull the centrifugal force of the earth in a direction that did not include the horror of the news that her Radmilo had been killed in a truck accident. It didn't work of course, but it provided her a plateau on which to hold her breath, and stop the world till her heart was ready to pulse again. So she applied this ineffectual but familiar prescription to her chafed consciousness, and threw herself into her cleaning.

Terrifically intent on leaving each cubicle that she entered completely transformed and well-ordered when she left it, she worked in "the zone" and had almost forgotten Casey's primary instruction. Don't throw out the Pulitzer unless they've already pitched it in the trash themselves, or some such tutorial. She had just cleared a desk of several torn up missives when she remembered Casey's words, and so carefully fished them out of the trash and placed them exactly as she'd found them on one particular desk. It seemed ridiculous to her that if someone had already partially discarded something, why not do for them what they can't bring themselves to do and broom it? But alas, she smiled slightly to herself, indulged this human vanity and replaced the rejects, only to look up to find Jake staring at her from across several cubicles burning a look into her like a laser beam of wonder.

He couldn't figure out this crazy activity either. She mouthed the word "Pulitzer" as she held up the ball of paper and placed it in perfect position on the desk, exaggerating a bit for Jake's benefit. He laughed out loud, a new sound for her. Lest he detect her blush, she turned to commence cleaning another cubicle filled with potential prize winners scribbled on yellow pads, then crumpled into balls of self-doubt. She heard Jakes's radio snap off and his computer clicked rapidly under his ready touch. Suddenly it was completely quiet on the entire floor, but for the tapping sound of Jake's keyboard. She kept her head down, her nose to the grindstone, continued cleaning and thought of her Marko.

CHAPTER TWENTY-FIVE

JAKE HAD HIS WORK CUT OUT FOR HIM. Determined to understand the incomprehensible, the Balkans, he pounded on the dusty keys of his computer, entering the following words in his search engine: "Kosovo," "Serbia," "Bosnia." One thing lead to another as it is wont to do, and before he knew he was up to his elbows in the horrors of that land, not only in the recent civil wars, but for centuries. He had no idea. Neither did the grand establishment he worked for. They never mentioned the historical hysteria of the region. He nearly admitted to himself that his drive was as fueled by the beautiful Yelena as it was by his peaked curiosity of her homeland, but decided to stay in denial about that for now and pretend he was actually a journalist in search of the truth, if not a good story. The night tapped on, and when he came up for air, he thought to survey the floor for the lovely Yelena. Instead he got hit with his mundane reality.

His eyes drifted to the three messages stuck to the top of his monitor screen. "Your ex-wife called." "Sigrid called." "Call your ex, ASAP." All three left within a half an hour of each other. Certain that this was not an emergency but rather more of her relentless insistence to control him, he'd decided to wait till tomorrow when the phone rang. *Christ,* he thought, *this better be good, it's after midnight and she hunted me down, knowing full well if I'm here, I'm working.*

"Hello, Sigrid," he said, glancing up at a photo of his son standing at the center of the Brooklyn Bridge, and wondered how this dame hooked him, transported him from Vinegar Hill, the Irish town of Brooklyn all the way to Park Avenue and halfway back again. Her one honest act was giving him a son. Beyond that, their cohabitation was a nightmare. He lived in mid-town now, alone in a studio that served as home plate while he got his bearings after the barely year-old divorce from a twenty-year marriage.

Jake met Sigrid on the job. He was covering a fundraiser for the Whitney Museum of Art, and she had been helping Daddy, a.k.a.

Chairman of the Board, host the event. The exhibit featured photographs of extraordinary, dramatic events in International Sports. They were nine by twelve feet high, amazing really, airbrushed photographs, silkscreened, some directly onto the wall, which gave a heroic, larger-than-life feel to the captured iconic moments portrayed. Not much for museums, Jake was surprised that he actually liked the exhibit.

He was smiling at an image of Willie Mays sliding into third in the pennant playoffs in 1962, a game he remembered well, when Sigrid came up behind him to snoop over his shoulder at his notepad. He was scribbling some notes and looked up because the waft of her perfume was so strong that he'd started to cough. "Dust from third base?" she asked. Clever girl, he noted, wanting to jot that down for his review.

"Yeah," he answered, "kinda makes me thirsty."

"I thought it might," she replied, and with the swiftness of a fox at a chicken coop, she produced a glass of champagne from behind her near naked back. Always the perfect hostess, he would come to learn.

"Why thank you, young lady" he managed, before he swallowed the fundraiser-regulation-size drink in one gulp.

"Sigrid Manchester," she offered her hand, "and I'm not so young, nor too lady-like to talk to a reporter."

"Journalist, please…and did you say Manchester?" Something registered with Jake. He knew who was buttering this slice of bread.

"Yes," and before he could say "Jake Thompson," she'd linked her arm in his, and they were off to meet Daddy and his entourage. Then twenty years went by.

Jake whizzed through that memory in less time than it took to pick up the phone. When he heard her voice, it jolted him back into reality. They had a troubled son. Maybe she was calling about him. Tony, the light of his life, his raison d'etre, was the weld between the two I-beams that had formed his marriage to Sigrid. Though the crack in their marriage was unredeemable, he knew he'd be joined at the hip in some way to Sigrid forever because of Tony.

"What's up? It's after midnight." He cut to the chase with Sigrid as a rule.

"It's Tony," she replied, uttering the only two syllables that could make him sit up faster than a bolt of lightning.

"What happened?" he demanded. "Is he all right?"

"Fine," she taunted him. "It's just, well, he left the latest rehab for the second time, and they're threatening not to take him back this time, and then he'll need to stay with me, and I just can't right now, Jake. I have the Green Art Fundraiser at the Tavern in Central Park next week and the visiting artist from Holland is staying with me, and I'm simply swamped," she spilled.

"Sounds like he's already there," returned Jake, referring to the noisy music in the background, "where in the world are you?"

"Me? Oh, home, that's Philipe, my new trainer. We've been doing some weight work."

"At this hour!"

"You should be glad I'm up, or I wouldn't even have heard the phone when Tony called, and besides why not now, you could do with a little ab training yourself."

"Thank you Sigrid, dear. I appreciate the reminder, now what is it you need from me exactly."

"To give Tony a place to stay this weekend, and drive him back up to rehab next week."

"Done. Tell him the doorman can let him in right now if he likes."

"Thanks, darling, you're a dear…and…."

"Good night, Sigrid, have a nice bicep." He clicked off, looked at the pictures of war-torn Bosnia on his monitor and realized the radical change of his bio-chemistry in the last twenty years. Today he would no more fall for a socialite like Sig than he would put his hand into a tar pit. He gazed at the screen and realized that the reportage of human tragedy was what his life was about, though he didn't foresee the one spinning in his own backyard.

What was he thinking, marrying a woman like Sigrid? Then his eyes found the photo of Tony again, and he remembered, clear as day. Tony, his son, she was carrying his son; he married her and was a willing prisoner for a couple of decades for the love of his son.

Suddenly, his head hurt and he wanted to take another stroll around the premises to check up on the Shar Mountain native, when he heard the sound of a vacuum switch on and he knew she was busy. What a difference, he noted. Sigrid has Philipe for white noise, and Yelena has the hum of the Hoover. The world was an absurd place. No one would ever believe anything he set down on paper about his life; it was too tawdry and too typical and way too timely. *Let it go, Jake. Go get a cigarette,* he told himself, then threw on his coat and hit the elevator.

Hovering over the Hoover, Yelena freed this American newsroom of dust, in a steady, unbroken rhythm that provided temporary relief from her grief. Cutting through the dirty carpets, leaving behind a clean path, making a difference, even if it was only on the floor, gave her hope.

By the time the first shift of Yelena's new job was completed, she had cleaned every inch of the place. At the end of it, Jake was asleep at his computer. And out of cigarettes again. She made a pot of coffee in the utility room, and as she was leaving, she placed a hot mug of coffee on Jake's desk for Grendel to find when he awoke. She pressed the elevator button, resisting the temptation to turn into a pillar of salt. As the lift doors split open, Jake awoke and nearly knocked over the java with his giant-sized yawn. He looked around for the coffee fairy. Eyes on the back of her head felt his glance but then the doors slid open and shut behind her, as her stomach felt the flip of the fast fall of the eighteen-story trip back down into the pre-dawn of a new day in Manhattan.

The early winter air bit her cheeks as she looked around, attempting to recollect which way she and Henry had come from, so she could retrace her steps to the subway stop, when Henry called out from across the street. "Yelena, over here!"

Yelena broke into a full smile, first one Henry had seen since she'd set up camp at his house. She was relieved not to have to navigate home alone. "Henry!"

Henry was gallantly jaywalking across Sixth Avenue, "How'd your first day go, Yelena?"

"It was fine, Henry. Thank you for coming to get me. Maybe I'll find my own home train tomorrow. I have to learn, right, Henry?"

"That's the spirit, and you're welcome, honey. You want a coffee?"

"No, I want to sleep." He took her by the arm and they descended into that miraculous underworld of Manhattan and neighboring boroughs, where the writhing labyrinths of transportation abide. The subway car rocked Yelena to sleep. Henry had to wake her when they got up to change trains. "Hey, Yelena, you better pay a little bit of attention if you're going to do this yourself tomorrow."

"Oh, yes, Henry, I better watch and wake up!"

"Okay, kid, you could do it that way, or you could wake up and watch, either way."

Yelena gave Henry one of her deadpan looks, one that made the sweet and sour plumber from Queens smile, especially when she got up exactly as the train pulled into their stop in Queens, and turned to Henry with, "Let's go Henry, we don't want to miss the stops."

Admittedly, Henry had a familial love and baffling wonder thing going with regard to Yelena. He had met her late husband at their wedding and found him to be one helluva nice guy, though only a humble truck driver. Rad, as Henry called him and Yelena were so obviously crazy about each other that it often embarrassed the company they kept. Perhaps not the village women, as Henry recalled, but he found it a little awkward, especially when Ljuba expected similar demonstrative affection from him over there in the village. It had been years since they'd made the journey. Certainly not because Ljuba didn't suggest a pilgrimage every single year, but because, quite frankly, Henry was not confident it was an altogether wise idea, what with the civil tensions there, and news reports of ethnic hatred. Now this horrible event of Marko's death clinched his suspicions. He hadn't yet inquired about the details. He knew they had to be horrific, and it made him shudder with gratitude at how he vehemently denied Ljuba and the girls their pleas to visit their Aunt Sofia last summer. He breathed a prayer of profound relief, like a guy who nearly gets hit by a bus, and is spared by a sliver of divine intervention.

God, what a crazy country and what madness they bring on themselves, he thought. But as he watched Yelena walking, head up, gait swift even after her graveyard shift at the newsroom, he conceded that the women "over there" were rather amazing. His wife certainly was. He often stood in silent admiration of her for the way she handled so very many things all at once, like a sorceress without a wand. Ljuba was a beautiful woman and he wondered why he didn't tell her that every once in a while. Henry loved her, for sure, and was fond enough of her kid sister. Hell, Ljuba was a like a mother to Yelena, and though they had about six or seven years between them, they were like two peas in a pod. Henry had a slight longing for a brother with whom he might have shared that closeness. His older sister was a flight attendant in San Diego. Here he was in New York, his hometown, raising his own family and caring for his own widowed mother, so he rarely saw his sister. He was however, the ever obedient, loyal son; he was the recipient of his mother's praise, and her uber-vigilance, matzo ball soup, and brisket, at least two, three

Sundays a month. Another thing his wifey Ljuba was great about; another thing he never acknowledged.

Yelena caught him frowning, "What's the matter, Henry? Tired?"

He felt like saying, "No, just sick of my self this morning," but instead replied, "I guess I am Yelena, and I didn't work all night like you did." He gave her a pat on the back, "I'm proud of you."

"Me too," she replied. Surprised by the speck of pride from the pious widow, he threw her a look out of the corner of his eye. She caught it and threw it back, "I'm proud of you too, Henry." Trumped, again, he slipped the key in the door, delivering her safely home.

Exhaustion hit Yelena when they walked through the door and she threw herself on the sofa bed. The kids were asleep in their own beds. It was barely dawn. She searched briefly for Gracie on TV, her nightly lullaby and guidepost to American living, but couldn't find it, so she quickly succumbed to sleep. She slept like a log, right through the kids getting up and off to school and Ljuba's sending Henry to work with his lunch. Yelena sawed on right through Ljuba's trip to the market and back.

CHAPTER TWENTY-SIX

SEVERAL HOURS LATER YELENA AWOKE to the smell of garlic and onions frying in oil, and the inspiring aroma of fresh coffee. Through the screen of sleep, Yelena watched her sister preparing a meal she knew was marked for her and thought how lucky she was to have Ljuba. How would she even be able to breathe, let alone put one foot in front of the other, show up at this new job, and manage her moods, without her beloved sister giving her confidence that she would survive this terrible loss?

When Yelena's husband died, Ljuba got on a plane with her toddler daughter and stood by Yelena through the Orthodox forty-day mourning period. It seemed like it would be more like forty-years mourning this time. When Radmilo died, Yelena was comforted that she still had Marko to love. But now she had no one but Ljuba, who did what she could to march Yelena through each day.

At times, Ljuba, the tower of strength, was confounded as to what to say to Yelena to alleviate the pain. She couldn't fathom losing one of her daughters or Henry for that matter. Ljuba thought she would probably die on the spot if Yelena's fate had befallen her, and she admired her sister's grit. Each one thought the other was the source of strength and generator of faith. It kept their sisterhood in perfect balance.

Yelena broke through the sound of her sister's shuffling preparations, "Sestro!" she called. Ljuba walked over to her sister, spoon in hand, and leaned over the sofa, ready to shake her awake if required, but found her sister already stretching, yawning and coaxing herself into the day.

"Aha! You're awake! Finally!"

"Alive and hungry!" her baby sis replied, music to Ljuba's ears. As grief is not known to be an appetite enhancer, Ljuba could only take this as a small sign of progress. After breakfast, where Ljuba delighted in every mouthful her sister took, she inquired as to her sibling's first day of work. "It was fine, a little strange, a lot of mess, and I think it's going to help me right now," Yelena rambled in their native tongue.

Ljuba let go a sigh of relief, quelling her initial fury with Henry for sending Yelena off to work so fast. Turned out he was right, it would help her to heal. Yelena started to clear the table, a habit well engrained in her by Aunt Sofia, when Ljuba shooed her away.

"Well, I'm glad your job is fine but I think that means we have to practice your English, so no more Serbian in this house unless you need to curse. That I'd prefer you do in our mother tongue so my children don't understand it."

"Ljuba, I'm shocked! When have you ever heard me curse?"

"Have yourself a nice, hot shower Yelena, before I take an inventory of your tempered Serbian tongue. I have a student coming shortly, so I'll clean up."

"Fine," Yelena complied. "Just wait till I inventory you!" Ljuba shook her head and smiled, not entirely certain whether Yelena even knew what she was saying.

Yelena emerged a full hour later from the bathroom, looking radiant, and donning the contentious red sweater. Ljuba nearly gasped, but she kept her attention centered mainly on Jose, whom she tutored biweekly. Yelena was beautiful. She was always the beautiful one, and Ljuba the wise one. It had not caused jealousy or competition between them, because Aunt Sofia had taught them, "one sun beam is never in competition with another sun beam." So it was between them, each reflecting different qualities and appreciating the differences in each other.

"Yelena! You look wonderful!" Ljuba exclaimed.

Feeling like she was caught with her hand in the cookie jar, Yelena responded quickly, "Well, the other sweater was quite dirty from the dust at that place, so I...."

Ljuba jumped in, "No explanations necessary. I'm almost done with this lesson, and then we'll go for a walk together." Ljuba turned back to her student Jose, while musing that there was something strange about Yelena this morning. And she had a feeling she knew what it was.

Late that afternoon, the two sisters stood in front of St. Steven's church, a mere five blocks from Ljuba's apartment. Yelena was surprised. "I didn't know there were Orthodox churches in America."

Ljuba laughed, "Are you kidding, honey, there are tons of them, and thousands of Slavs for each one."

"That's good for America!" Yelena replied.

"That's debatable," Ljuba countered.

"What's 'debatable?'"

"Never mind." Ljuba grabbed her sister's hand and they went in. They stood in front of the altar and lit candles, three each. For Yelena, one was for Marko, one for Radmilo, and one for her dear sister Ljuba. For Ljuba, one was lit for Yelena, one for her own family, and one for the mystery she sensed was going on in Yelena's life. They crossed themselves three times, and exited. Yelena felt she had found a sacred haven, and she memorized exactly how to get here. This is where she would come to grieve. Now she could breathe easily, she'd found a space she could call her own. The churches were often empty in the afternoon, and she could make this her regular stop before she went to work. There was so much she wanted to talk over with her Heavenly Father. To sit there, surrounded by the waft of incense, burning candles and beautiful icons fed her Byzantine soul and made her feel closer to Marko.

Ljuba walked her to the subway stop, and wished her a good evening at work. They kissed on both cheeks as always, only this time Ljuba noticed a faint waft of her own perfume that her sister had donned. She was happy to share it, but couldn't quite figure why Yelena wanted to wear it to clean cubicles.

CHAPTER TWENTY-SEVEN

YELENA ARRIVED IN MANHATTAN A BIT EARLY and took a little stroll around the area to see what she could see. All one could do is look up, straight up. This was the single most pronounced difference between her life at home, and her life here.

At home she looked out. Up, too, but mostly out to the horizon and across many layers of mountain ranges. From the top of the hill where her little church was she could turn around a full 360 degrees and see only mountains, and the vast sense of space that accompanied them. They were high and grand, 13,000 feet in some parts, utterly majestic. Her mountains held her dreams, her secrets, her tears.

But here in New York, she looked up and saw the vertical obilisks called skyscrapers, high rises, super structures like she'd never seen. One could not find the horizon. She hadn't yet discovered that Manhattan was only seven miles wide and eleven miles long, and an island at that. All she experienced was this compression of space, darkening her heart and crimping her neck. Though limiting the wonders of Mother Nature, the city certainly peaked her curiosity about mankind. This mountain range of steel kept a hidden eye on her tears, not to absorb them for they never could, but to serve as a silent witness or quiet presence on which to wipe the sleeve of her wrenching past. Who knows, maybe this stone and steel fortress would provide her with something? Money to send home to Aunt Sofia, yes, a place to come each day, yes, and what more could she expect? *Nothing,* she thought. Yet she did expect, and the expectancy quickened her pace, all the way up to nearly bumping into someone at the thick glass door of the news building. It was Jake.

"Good evening, Yelena!" he said with a welcoming smile. Instantly shy, she looked down, suddenly the red sweater seemed so gauche and wrong and shameless that she wanted to disappear.

"Good evening, Jake." She managed.

"That's a beautiful color on you."

That's it, she would never wear it again; it goes right into the trash tonight when she gets home. She knew she should never have let Ljuba buy it for her, obviously a terrible mistake. From now on, it's her native black, at least for the next twelve months. What in the world was she thinking wearing red?

"Thank you Jake," her manners contradicted her inner monologue, and what of it.

The interminable ride on the elevator, in which she could barely look Jake in the eye, began day two of work. Like the second jump from an airplane, the second day of employment could be a lot more difficult, she sensed. She headed to the employee locker room, where she donned her wrap which would thankfully douse any flame of life from the red sweater. She gathered the supplies to load onto her cart. Casey was lighting his evening cigar. There was "No Smoking" on the floor, but both Casey and Jake broke that rule as soon as the day employees left. Night standards were different, and the night owls ruled at this rag.

"Hello, Yelena, so you decided to come back for more, eh?" Casey sputtered between puffs on his Corona.

"Oh, good morning, Casey." Yelena replied, busily tying the belt around the most unflattering wrapper.

Casey just nodded, thinking, morning, evening, what's the difference, at least she showed. He took out his deck of solitaire, and settled in for the first round of his nightly "tournament with self." Casey would gladly have played a few hands of poker with Jake instead, but the dictates of Jake's conscience sent him right to his cubicle to work every night, even though Casey and he both knew that Jake hadn't been able to write a hundred words that hung together in any coherent manner for several months. He was lucky he hadn't been fired, but his past performances and awards, including a Pulitzer for a story he did on Turkish opium dealers some years ago, kept the powers that be patient with him, for now.

He was going through a rough patch, they told themselves. Broken marriage, troubled kid, bachelor digs; it wasn't exactly the Park Avenue life had lived with Sig for two decades. Either way, Jake was in transition, and the suits decided to see him through it. Not the usual corporate way of handling non-productivity. But somehow the humanity of a fellow baby boomer had slipped into the scene, and was counting on Jake regaining his assets and then some. This ally of his, one of the chief editors, was a recovering alcoholic and believed in second chances, and wasn't about to deny Jake one.

Jake's rhythm had found a new gear since yesterday. Casey was
surprised when Jake skipped the stop at his desk for the traditional shot
before his evening work. Instead, he'd gone straight to his desk, jumped
on the computer and his fingers began to fly. Casey also noted at least
three trips to the coffee urn in the first couple of hours, which told him
two things: One, Jake wasn't drinking whiskey because he had too much
good Irish blood in him to chase it with coffee, and two, Jake was
working on something, otherwise, he wouldn't impede the promise of
his usual mid-evening nap with caffeine. "None of my business," Casey
concluded, and kept dealing himself winning hands at solitaire. Each
victory was rewarded with a shot.

Jake didn't know what to make of what he was reading about
Bosnia, Serbia, Kosovo, the Balkans in general. There lay the powder
keg for the First World War, reportedly started by a fervent young
student, a defiant Serb that earned his country infamous headlines
that have hardly ceased since that first shot rang out. Yet Jake, in the
true tradition of journalism, discovered another school of thought
that said it was a German soldier taking the identity of a Serb in order
to break into the desired conflict in Europe that would, they thought,
finally let Germany ante up in the game of imperialism, which the
Fatherland had long coveted.

All right, he thought, let's say that's hooey, and it was a Serb not
a German, after all. Well frankly, who could blame them? The
expansive Austro-Hungarian Empire had shackled the Serbs for
more than a few centuries, making it a minor miracle that one of the
hot blooded Slavs hadn't tried to pop the Arch Duke sooner.

As Jake rifled through the library books he'd picked up on the
way to work, his mind pondered these historical boundary disputes,
and sensed the beginning of an inside track into understanding that
mysterious, mystical, most desirable territory leading to a warm water
port, that sections of the Balkans provided. He felt like he was back
in grad school, or in the Peace Corps in Nepal, or on that risky
assignment in Turkey when he was a daring journalist in his twenties.
He was completely caught up in what he was doing. He loved it. He'd
been hungry for it, for years. What the hell had happened, he
wondered. He'd been turning up at the office after hours for months
searching for inspiration. Zero. Zip. Zilch. Divorce happened, that's
what happened.

Splitsville left him with baseball games as his main occupation,
either on television or better yet, the radio, anchoring him to a past

he knew he could never retrieve. He'd been dead inside since his marriage died. Like a lot of writers; he was a romantic, he'd married for keeps, never thought he'd be riding the caboose of divorce, never, not him, not a good Catholic boy. He'd been clad in a cloak of failure since the day Sigrid called it quits. That's what you get for marrying outside the faith, his mother would have said, with an emphasis on *the,* like there was no other, and never would be.

Jake was intrigued as he poured over the materials about Yelena's homeland. No matter how riddled with problems the ol' US of A was, we'd never experienced the kind of bloodthirsty, vengeful daily combat of neighbors slitting neighbors' throats that the Balkans had been sustaining for centuries. How long can a grudge last? A millennium, if you're from Kosovo. He wondered if the shortened memory Americans boasted of was an extension of the Christian ethic of turn the other cheek, or a poverty of dignity and lack of true identity. Who knew? Who even thought he'd be researching the civil strife in the easternmost part of Europe that even he had presumed was virtually over by now? Just goes to show you, he registered, how incomplete the reportage of world news is. Incomplete and inaccurate, that would be the bumper sticker on any Smith Corona on wheels he drove, if there even were such a thing anymore.

So, as he scavenged through the clippings, history books, and articles on the internet, a light went on in his journalistic brain that caused him to admit he knew absolutely nothing about what really had gone on over there. Neither did any of the Americans that were reading the daily newspaper he worked for. Okay, Jakey, go to work, this could be the woman, I mean, story you been waiting for.

Something caught his eye. A picture of an old woman on the front page of his paper, some months ago. Dressed in black, her boney body was bent over a young man's corpse, apparently her son. Her tormented, heavily-grooved face looked up, obviously under the command of a staff photographer and click, her grief was immortalized. As if she needed a photo taken to know she was living in hell. Jake looked closely at the grainy shot, and saw that a small gold cross hung from the old woman's neck, and from the neck of the neighbor or sister who was offering a supportive hand on her shoulder. Yet the caption read, "Muslim woman grieves her son, slaughtered by Serbs."

Wait a minute, something is wrong here. Last time he checked, Islamists did not sport gold crosses of the Orthodox kind or any other kind. He couldn't be the only one that noticed that this photograph depicted a Serb grieving, while his beloved newspaper held the position that the Serbs were the only perpetrators and the Muslims the only victims. It infuriated Jake how quickly his paper picked sides on a conflict long before they knew what the hell they were talking about. The truth was in the photo finish. If this Serbian woman had lost her son in a war, as the photo implied, odds were that it was by the hands of an Albanian Muslim, not a Serb. Yet the caption of the front page stated the opposite, and the opposite of the truth is, uh, what's that again, oh that's right, the opposite of the truth is a lie.

This fueled him to dig more deeply into the Pandora's box of facts and falsities, now with teeth gritted not only against this sickening misinformation, but for the flagrant mendacity in the field which was his chosen profession. How'd you like to be that dead man, or his mother, he thought. Raped, pillaged, murdered, photographed, and then inaccurately captioned, for all the world to see. Okay, maybe just the Western world; maybe in China they got it right. He kept digging.

A newspaper man for over twenty years, Jake got high on the smell of ink and the sound of a printing press as a young rebel fresh out of college, primed to right the wrongs of the world, and to heal injustice. It was clear to him that it might take some doing, but he never doubted he was up to the task. Must have been his Irish mother's indefatigable spirit unleashed in him. He never allowed a margin for error, failure, or default. Kids nowadays, he heard himself say, more often than he would admit, are afraid to take a risk, afraid to follow their dreams, they're always thinking of the back-up plan. Back in the day, we never had a "back-up" plan he thought. However, that would not be true for his son Tony, who carried the curse and the passion of an addict, and came by it honestly with Irish DNA. Though Tony had thrown caution to the wind more than once, Jake never felt that Tony dared as he had dared at his age.

Now, next to a woman, widowed and childless, so young, and somehow driven from her ravaged mountain village, Jake suddenly saw himself as a tame pony by comparison. What courage it must have taken for this lady to walk away from her home, if only to catch her breath, and to come all the way to Queens of all places. *There were problems and then there were problems,* he thought. Jake's broken marriage paled next to the loss of a child. How does one go forward after that, or drink a glass of water even, or read a sign on a bus? Function plunges to zero. It must. He didn't know how to approach Yelena. She had a moat of sadness around her. But at least he could learn of her world, of the circumstances that drove her to find solace on the cold floor of the file area in a newsroom in Manhattan at midnight. Why the hell hadn't he gone over there to cover that conflict? he asked himself. Where was Mr. Dare when the Bosnian conflict first hit the front pages in '91? Now a few years later, what kept him from boarding a plane to the exotic land of Byzantium, where all hell was still breaking loose and new levels of human hatred were railing?

There was something murky about the whole deal. He didn't know why, but from the jump he had sensed he was only getting part of the story. Everybody was only getting part of the story. Where could he get the scoop, except to go to the actual site? Something kept him from moving on that instinct. That was most uncharacteristic of Jake. He had taken a backseat in this conflict and watched, stewed about it some, but mostly waited like a coyote at a birdbath, knowing the feast was just around the corner and that it would be bloody, as only unwanted truth in the newspaper business could be.

Now it was time to fess up to some facts. Here's what he learned: First, Kosovo was the Jerusalem of Serbia. It had hundreds of monasteries from the eighth century through the sixteenth, and the idea of the devout and willful Slavs giving up their bedrock of Eastern Orthodoxy was as likely as the Pope turning St. Peter's Cathedral over to the IRA. Secondly, he learned that the Ottoman Empire dominated the Serbs for about four hundred years, and that the famed Battle of Kosovo, in which the Serbs were ultimately defeated, was still celebrated and revered, not as a loss but as a day of glory for the Serbs. The truth was that they fought magnificently, and though the Turks triumphed, the Serbs had inflicted sufficient casualties to see to it that Greece and Asia Minor did not become Turkish.

Jake wondered if the Greeks, the self-proclaimed fathers of Western Civilization, remembered to say thank you. He also learned that the Serbs didn't take oppression well. They were scrappers and fighters and valued freedom more than life itself, though they spent little time living it, because the Turkish Empire segued into the Austro-Hungarian Empire. The world was forced to notice that this didn't sit well with them when Arch Duke Ferdinand got it right in the jugular, providing the straw that broke the camel's back and invited the globe into the First World War. He learned too, that after World War I, Kaiser Wilhelm said he hadn't been licked by the 500,000 Russians in 1917, but by 60,000 audacious Serbs who wouldn't quit. And they didn't quit, not in World War I nor in World War II, when Serbian soldiers were the only ones to get behind Nazi barriers to rescue American fighter pilots that were shot down by the Germans.

Jake learned that the Serbian peasants also risked their lives daily by defying Hitler and hiding Jews in their silos. Serbs loved to go against the grain, and countless thousands of them died in camps with their Jewish brothers, a gift from the Croatians for Serbian defiance against the Nazis.

He learned further that Tito, who united the Slavs in 1948 into what came to be known as Yugoslavia, was actually German by birth, though reared in Croatia and so happily sold the Serbs down the river when he gave preferential treatment to the northerners, Slovenians and especially Croatians, a perk they enjoyed for their obedience to the late Fuhrer. Tito's disdain for the southern Slavs was evident when he opened the borders, unequivocally, to the Albanians, who slowly and insidiously took labor from the Serbs, paid no taxes, yet demanded their language be spoken in the schools, filled up the local mosques, built dozens more and finally flagrantly made a decision to make Kosovo theirs.

That wouldn't sit too well with New Yorkers, he thought, if the Cubans in Miami moved up the eastern seaboard and decided to call Manhattan Havana, just because they out-populated the native New Yorkers. Fat chance, inhabitants of the Big Apple would let it become the Big Banana! Crazy, yes. Unimaginable, no. Different from the Yugoslav situation? Not really. They had intelligentsia in Belgrade just like in New York, he surmised. So why didn't somebody do something to stop this madness before it all went haywire. Why indeed? "Y" is a crooked letter that rarely yielded straight answers. The so called intelligentsia were no better than the country folk who could recite classical poetry and whistle a Puccini opera start to finish. He knew them from the pubs in Ireland when he traced his roots years back, and he knew they were probably no different in Montenegro. Those pure spirited folks just didn't fit into this world today.

There was a time for that kind, but it was rapidly disappearing into the mist of a past barely remembered, hardly recognized for its fleeting yet deep substance in the face of a superficial world. Jake longed for that world, though he never really knew it. Can you long for something you've never had, nor never known? He did. He yearned. It startled him, embarrassed him before himself. Guys don't *yearn,* he thought. Not guys from his hood in Brooklyn, not guys he defined as guys. Yet a few hours of pouring over the pictures of Yelena's land, what it looked like centuries ago, what its people revered, and what it was reduced to today by the blackguard called revenge, that wretched human desire to get even, got Jake's gut churning. There before him on his computer screen or in newsprint or in the shiny pages of the history books was this dedication to revenge, pronounced by and to the Serbs. A vicious cycle of hate. He couldn't figure Yelena into this mosaic. *How would this gentle beauty fit in?* he pondered. As he did, the instinct that he had trusted all his life, that told him when to go left and then the avalanche fell on the right, that same gut that spoke with the certainty of an oracle in telling him, "take the next train," landing him a great story of a heist, that same gut level, sixth sense that he once ignored his fated wedding day when it said to him, "Sigrid is not for you," dumping him into a vat of a vacuous, virtueless, vindictive marriage from which he still sported the war wounds, that gut was telling him now, "Stop. Listen. Follow." It was telling him there was a sword of fire inside this most womanly woman Yelena, the fawn of fear that walked away from her village to a foreign land and into her sister's arms to heal. There was something terrific in her, he felt it with all his being, and he feared it.

CHAPTER TWENTY-EIGHT

YELENA, ON THE OTHER HAND, felt anything but terrific. The finality of Marko's death was dragging her to depths she didn't know she had. Like a free-fall of a lead weight into a endless, waterless well, her grief held no promise of ever arriving at its bottom, a place from which one might begin to look up. Instead, it held her hostage, and when hope would bait her into thinking that just maybe this was as bad as it would get, a new ring of the inferno of reality, that Marko was gone forever, would reveal itself and lengthen her sorrow by leagues.

Her daily reprieves were Gracie Allen and Jake. Not necessarily in that order. Both were derived from a world unknown to her, even though they obviously had journalists in her country, and television. Even her remote mountain village boasted the presence of the magic box in individual homes since the early-1980s. Before that, watching the tube was a collective pastime that transpired at the village pub, known locally as the "cafana." It was generally understood that the cafana was for the men in the village to unwind after their days' work by watching soccer and swallowing sinful quantities of Slivovitz. Watching soccer made them thirsty. It was a sport that Slavs excelled in, a game that could unify or divide people faster than any politician, party, or partisan platform. It was a game that demanded enormous endurance, great physical fitness, precision of thought, strategic vision, unfathomable skill, nimble feet, eyes like a hawk, legs like a jaguar, and a heart as big as the Black Sea. Slavic men came out of the womb with these qualities, some with soccer balls balanced on their heads when they popped out, their mothers already applauding them as they bled out their afterbirth. Perhaps that's what made it difficult to keep Slavic men happy in marriage for their mothers had already presented them with such a high level of entitlement at suckling that their wives had to figure out how to match it or beat it.

So with that backdrop of Yelena's life to date, it was easy to understand that the ingenuous spirit of Gracie and the guileless manhood of Jake were appealing to Yelena. Jake possessed humility and kindness, and talked to her with an equanimity that was unfamiliar to her. He held her gaze as if she were a goddess. She wondered if all American men were like this. Henry didn't seem to be, but maybe Ljuba had molded him into an honorary European man. He did seem to yield to Ljuba on most issues; Ljuba ruled, Ljuba rocked, Ljuba reigned in her household, no doubt about it. Like their mother, she was the queen, the Queen of Queens.

Gracie, however, was rather non-referential. Yelena viewed her as a fable or myth or archetype of American womanhood. She rapidly became Yelena's own personal hero. A woman who thought for herself, whom her husband listened to and cheered, and who had the most amazing power of all, the ability to make people laugh. What a woman. And Yelena liked Gracie's short hair and sparkling eyes, and thought she looked like a doll, in her perfectly fitted clothes. It wasn't like Yelena was foolish enough to try to emulate her physically, as they couldn't have been more opposite in body. Yelena, with her dark, gypsy black hair, deep dark eyes, olive skin and cheekbones as high as Mt. Everest, contrasted radically with Gracie, who had honey colored hair, light eyes, fair skin, a round face, a tiny frame, and a distinctively sing-song voice. Gracie was not just from another planet, but rather from another solar system altogether. Who was like that?

Yelena's English improved every day, and every day, more of the incongruities of Gracie's logic were revealed to her, and she was in awe before them. Do they let women talk this way in America? Yelena guessed yes, since Gracie was all over the tube with that mouth of hers. When Ljuba caught Yelena watching the show one night, and explained that those were reruns of an old show, Yelena's response was, "Oh, she's not working on this now, I wonder where she is, I'd like to meet her, have a talk with her. There are few things I'd like to ask."

Ljuba shook her head, chuckled and wondered when to break it to Yelena that Gracie was dead. It was like telling a child that there was no Santa Claus or Tooth Fairy. And it seemed like that would have been more bad news for Yelena. *Loss was not what we wanted more of,* Ljuba thought. She decided to let it go for the time being.

Ljuba was in the kitchen fixing Yelena's dinner when she got a call from Henry that he wanted her to come to pick him up at the shop and drive him to his final appointment of the day. "I was just making Yelena's food for work. Can you wait twenty minutes?" she pleaded.

"I'd rather not, honey. This is kinda an emergency call, overflowing you know what. Just come as quick as you can. Yelena won't starve." He hung up. Ljuba instructed Yelena to pack her own dinner and was out the door to rescue her beloved of fifteen years of marital bliss. Maybe not full time bliss, but often enough to make it last. It didn't hurt that they also had created two beautiful daughters, whom they both adored, and for whom they'd jump in front of a train. It was impossible to conceive of losing one of them, as Yelena lost her only boy. The thought of it flooded Ljuba and Henry with daily compassion for the young, childless widow.

"Go, don't worry about me, I'll be fine. Go help your Henry," urged Yelena.

Ljuba vacated quickly, and Yelena found herself completely alone in the apartment for the first time. There had always been someone else there, either the girls, or Henry or Ljuba or all of them at once. It was a small place, and with one ounce less heart, Henry could have understandably recommended a room at the local YWCA for Yelena. They were stuffed in there like potatoes in a dumpling. They slid on each other's towels, wiped each other's tears, ate each other's leftovers, poured over each other's daily events. It was amazingly harmonious.

But just then, in that late autumn afternoon, an amber ray of light cut through the vintage Venetian blinds, landed on the flowery patterned sofa, and Yelena stilled her task of lacing up her boots, paused her preparation for work, and listened intently to the ticking clock and gurgling radiator, as if they were carrying a message from the celestial, especially for her. It was so quiet. *It's never quiet here,* she thought. The days and nights were normally rampant with honking horns, steaming pipes, shuffling neighbors, screeching subways and searing sirens, not to mention the loud nature of her own family. She double knotted her boots, looked around the room, as if for the first time, and realized that while she'd registered the soundtrack, she'd not taken in the full picture. She watched the clock, noted its mantra. *It's time to go,* she thought, but didn't move. Frozen in the reality of that moment at twenty past four on a fall afternoon, a moment galvanized in her. Marko would never hear the clock, the radiator, the subway, the siren, the honking horns, or giggles of his cousins. Her womb went numb. There were no tears welling up to the familiar ponds in the moats of her eyes, no trembling of the lower lip, no heaving of her chest. She was for that moment devoid of all feeling, of life itself. Still. Like the room. Not alive, not desiring to be alive without her son. She wanted nothing. And in the absence of desire, there was a kind of death. All was dead silent, but for the clamoring reality that he was gone.

Her fingers rubbed the edge of the pillow she slept on each night. Unconsciously, she moved them back and forth as if to uncover a clue hidden beneath the pillowcase that could reveal a reason to live life without her son, without her husband, without a purpose. She got up from the sofa, put on her jacket, and walked to the subway without packing her lunch. She stood in the subway car like a robot, standing, as she always did, holding onto the strap, as was her custom, reading the advertisements, practicing her English, whispering the words she saw scrawled across the signs that papered the train car; ads for travel, ads for headache medicine, ads for refreshing drinks, maps of the upcoming and foregone subway stations. She stood there speaking English in a stage whisper to the stale air of the subway car, oblivious that she was weeping. Like a dedicated soldier, she performed her practice in her new tongue, accompanied by soundless, centuries-old tears.

CHAPTER TWENTY-NINE

THE QUIET OF LJUBA'S HOME met its complement in the noise that greeted Yelena in the newsroom. Chaotic, willful, angry expletives flew from the mouths of several newsmen, writers, journalists, gathered together in their shirtsleeves, hurling remarks at each other, in full frontal attack. Maybe her English wasn't perfect, but she had a pretty good idea that these folks weren't having a friendly chat. She disappeared into the utility room where she caught sight of Casey listening to the professional brawl. "What's happening, Casey?" Yelena inquired of her employer-mentor.

"Nothing to worry about, doll. It's just a bunch of newsmen arguing about who's gonna cover what features next month. This happens every four weeks, like the moon, these "girls" strut their stuff and try to out macho each other. That was too much metaphor for Yelena to make sense of, but she nodded and figured there was no need for concern since Casey seemed amused by it all. She got into her wrapper, gathered her equipment together and started her work.

"A little early today, aren't you, doll?" offered Casey. Yelena nodded. Noticing her quiet demeanor, Casey queried, "You all right, sweetheart?"

"Okey, dokey," she replied, making him smile. He turned to witness the hotheads breaking up, knowing they'd be continuing this over beers at O'Neill's, and he had a moment of envy that he was stuck there for the night, and would have to forgo swilling a few with them. They loved Casey. Everyone did. The guys often invited him to join them. But duty and the eternal consolation of sports news kept him tucked happily in his nightly nook. Casey relaxed.

Yelena, engaged in her cleaning, glanced out of the corner of her eye for Jake. No sign of him. *That's fine,* she thought, *better not to be happy tonight; it's too sad a day to be happy.* Without knowing it, she employed logic not unlike that of her new idol, Ms. Gracie Allen.

Lunch time came around quickly. Yelena was focused on her tasks and the time flew. Shortly after Casey left, round midnight, she started to get hungry. It felt like years since she'd eaten which was not at all accurate. *No matter,* she thought. Jake's not here, she'll just sit and rest for a while, then finish up her work and maybe head home early tonight. She could use the rest. She sat down in her usual spot against the file cabinets, removed her scarf, untied her wrapper, and leaned her head against the cool metal cabinets. It felt good, comforting, and oddly reassuring to have the firm hard surface holding her head. Despite such an unyielding pillow, she fell into a catnap easily enough. Who knows how long she drifted, maybe minutes, maybe longer, but the smell of fried food found its way to her nostrils and she awoke, hungry and happy to see Jake standing over her with a huge bag of food, splattered with the MacDonald's logo.

"Wake up, Yelena! Soup's on!" He joined her on the floor of their Manhattan picnic table betwixt the file cabinets of the Daily Journal, and laid out a feast of fast food. "This," he proclaimed, "is America!!" He popped a French fry into her mouth reassuring her, "These aren't really French, don't worry!"

Jake made her laugh, and she came to life. Who would have guessed this same dead soul who sat on Ljuba's sofa hours earlier with little reason to ever move off of it, was now flushed with the blush of flirtation from the attention of a handsome man who thought to bring her lunch? *This,* she thought, *is America.* They dined voraciously.

"Now then, for desert, I'm going to show you a national treasure." Jake teased.

"Really," she managed, between fries and dripping catsup. She could have been an ad for the sloppy burgers she'd seen on television. Out of the same bag that previously held their dinner, Jake produced two Yankee hats and a baseball. "This," he began, and she finished, "is America!"

"Yes, indeed," he rejoiced. He pulled out a large box of wooden matches from the same bag, and cleared their food wrappings from the floor and created a baseball diamond made of matchsticks. Cleverly, breaking off the red sulfur tips to set as bases, and producing a second box of matches with blue tips, he magically formed Yankee stadium. He patiently instructed Yelena on each aspect of the game, culminating in a grand slam, hit by his very own matchstick bat, and his blue-headed player raced around the sulfur bases, sliding into home plate. "Safe!!" Jake proclaimed.

Yelena understood only a fraction of this lesson on Americana. Soccer was her native bravado. But Jake's enthusiasm was not lost on her, and she cherished his zealous introduction to the great American pastime, which she felt she could learn to understand, and maybe love. By the third inning, the diamond sport was winding its way into her heart, and she couldn't have been more enchanted.

After having played a full five innings, and acting as umpire, first and third base coach, the entire infield, and the top of the batting order, Jake sat back, discovering for himself the cool relief the metal file cabinets offered, and said, "So, Yelena, how do you say baseball in your language?"

"Soccer," she replied, delighting in his delight in her. The shape of the playing field may have differed in their respective patriot games, but the vast divergence was rapidly being erased by the tenderness in Jake's eyes when he looked at her.

Later that night, when Yelena was finishing up her work, Jake was huddled over his computer, printing out images of the Balkan civil war, and reading accounts from various European newspapers, touching the fringe of the world she had fled that had stripped her of everything she loved, yet still held her love. He wanted to understand, but he kept being struck by the ancient grudge that stiffened their headstrong resolve and their righteous indignation. One wants to ask, is this the people? or their leadership? In a country like the former Yugoslavia, where the leadership does not seem to have been elected, it remained ambiguous. *Even in the United States,* he thought, *where we do supposedly elect our leader, does he really speak for the people, or is it the political party policy that speaks?* He just couldn't get his mind around the fact that the Serbs' reference point for present-day hailed from several centuries ago.

Kosovo, the Jerusalem of Serbia, had mountains filled with plutonium. How appropriate. The place was as beautiful as God's day, and rightfully was the cradle of Eastern Orthodox Christianity, yet it also laid claim to being the hot bed of Eastern Europe where warring factions could converge and detonate any semblance of civilization that their Greek neighbors bequeathed them, millennia ago.

Jake was struck too, by the radically different reportage on the reason for the war, if actual reason could ever be discerned for a civil war. On the one side there was the instigation of the Albanian Muslims wanting to take Kosovo and claim it as their own. On the other, the German inspired secession of Croatia, leading to the violent expelling of two hundred thousand Serbs from the Krajina region where they'd lived for generations. It would appear that from the North and the South, the Serbs were getting bumped. You didn't need to have a Slavic temper to rebel against that. And it got ugly.

Who killed whom first will never be truly known. It was civil war, after all; neighbors kill neighbors, brothers, brothers, and this war had the added fuse of religion, Islam versus Christianity, then further divisiveness between the Catholic Christians and the Eastern Orthodox Christians. When one looked at the whole picture, it was somewhat impressive that they hadn't all killed each other or themselves decades ago. It was inexplicable that these people had all lived together more or less peacefully for as long as they had.

Or maybe that was the problem, too, too many years of denial. Too long a stretch of making nice-nice, turning the other cheek in a tinderbox of resentments. It went against the grain of the primitive manhood that said, "Don't hurt my people, or I'll get back at yours." "Don't take my home, or I'll burn yours." "Don't desecrate my temple, or I'll bomb your place of worship." All those "don't's" add up to the most uncivilized and irreverent human emotion, revenge. It ruled them, it fueled them, and it was about to snuff them out as a people. Sure, someone would be left standing with a smoking gun, but what would he have in his heart to pass on to his sons? What would remain in his soul to bequeath to eternity, to his god, whatever he may call him?

Lost in his thought, confounded by the dilemma that was tearing apart that region and even the globe for that matter, Jake didn't hear Yelena approach, coat on, coming to say good night.

"Wow! Is it morning already?" Jake jolted up in his chair.

"Yes, indeedy!" Yelena lobbed, proving once again her talent as a mimic. Yelena glanced quickly at his computer screen which had photos of a war torn village, looking a lot like her own. She was able to discern the word Srebenica, a town near her own, and the words "horror" and "war," both of which she could translate.

"What are you doing, Jake?" she asked, staring at the screen.

Not wanting to upset her, and knowing her sensibility toward the events in her homeland was as fragile as a butterfly's elbow, he treaded lightly, "Just doing some research, learning more about you."

"You don't need that machine, I can tell you about Srebenica, Jake. I can tell you more than you want to know, more than you'll believe, more than any newspaper can report. I can tell you the truth, about Srebenica...what really happened, and what really started the horrors. And I can tell you of many, many places just like it." Yelena's voice had an intensity Jake hadn't heard before.

"Really." He stared at her in fear, thinking of all that he'd seen of the world, and that it might be a mere pebble on the mountain of terrors she had witnessed. "Well, we'll have to have that talk. I want to know everything. But right now, I'm buying you breakfast." He grabbed his coat and they were out the door, into the Manhattan morn. Dinner at midnight, breakfast at dawn, five days a week, a rather eccentric consistency of a budding something indeed.

CHAPTER THIRTY

LJUBA WAS DOING HER PART to lift her sister's spirits. She'd always believed in the standard American means toward that end, shopping. Ljuba claimed it was the world's foremost mood elevator, even if their initial shopping spree had resulted in Yelena breaking down in the fitting room. Ljuba saw it as a breakthrough, especially when her sister finally wore the red sweater that had caused the sea of tears. Makeover was the other method Ljuba relied on. Haircut and color, her own personal panacea when Henry was grinding her patience. Clearly, Ljuba understood that Yelena's hurdle was far greater than an irate, errant husband, but she could only offer what she knew worked in her own experience, so a trip to Salon de Charles was slated for the two sisters that day.

"Yelena!" Ljuba called, waking her earlier than usual on a chilly, late autumn morning. "Yelena, are you awake?"

"Now, yes." Yelena yawned.

"Good. Get dressed, we're going to Manhattan early today to get our hair done."

"What hair?" Yelena queried.

"Well, yours, actually. Let's go. Coffee's on the table, we'll eat in the city."

"Hair done," Yelena murmured the new expression as she trundled to the bathroom to prepare for this adventure which she would have been happy to forego. "But I just got back from Manhattan, Ljuba!" she called out with a mouth full of toothpaste, that promised to whiten, brighten and heighten one's very existence when used as suggested. Yelena was daily struck by the promises that American packaging included on their everyday items. At least it provided Yelena with material on which to practice her reading skills.

"I know you just got back from your shift, sister of mine, and I was about to ask why so late?"

Yelena pretended not to hear that question and gargled for a full minute to ensure Ljuba would drop it. She wasn't ready to say what was up with her and Jake, because she didn't have a clue herself.

On their way out the door, Ljuba grabbed the mail from their mailbox at the bottom of the stairwell. "Oh, look, a letter from Aunt Sofia!"

Yelena grabbed at it, but Ljuba had already stuffed it into her faux leopard shoulder bag. "We'll read it at the salon; we're going to be late." She picked up the pace, as they headed toward the subway around the corner.

"Read it where?" asked Yelena, lagging more than a few paces behind her fireball sister. One needed more than a quick gulp of caffeine to keep up with Ljuba.

"Never mind," Ljuba commanded, "I hear the express train coming, let's run." And since at no time known to man had anyone ever said "no" to Ljuba, they ran. They caught the express, and were planted in "Charles' Salon of Style" on Fifty-first and Lexington in no time at all.

Ljuba had been going to Charles for five years, ever since her natural honey brown hair had become flecked with grey. It quelled her raging hormones to be all golden blonde in the most superficial and temporary way. *So sue me,* she thought, *I need change.*

Charles, a kind and talented African-Cuban from Miami knew well the yoke of minority existence, so he warmed to Ljuba immediately. The first time she happened into his garden apartment hair salon on Lexington Avenue, she was primed to file divorce papers, but after Charles' worked his magic, she danced out, feeling gorgeous and irresistible. She had suspected Henry was stepping out on her. Hovering around forty, her kids in school all day, Ljuba felt alone with her whitening crown when she found her salvation with Charles' *"Makeover Special $25: Cut and Color on Tuesdays Only."*

By the grace of the Mother of God, it had been a Tuesday and she couldn't have been happier than if she'd won the lotto when she got "the works" from Charles that first Tuesday. Not only because she looked ten years younger with her new "do," but because she and Charles became fast friends. She shared the tribulations of her homeland with him. He could relate, as his family hailed from Uganda, then Cuba. He ended up arranging for Ljuba to tutor his sister's son in English. The boy was flunking everything at school except baseball, and Ljuba took on the job, which started her home tutoring career. So she and Charles had a mutual aid and admiration society, and he was over the moon with joy to meet the sister whom he'd heard so much about through the years.

"Pleased to meet you Yelena, and please accept my condolences for your loss." Classy man. Yelena nodded a thank you.

Charles's talent as the transformer of darkness into light kicked in. "Now you sit right down on this throne, pretty lady, and let's talk transformation." They did, and within minutes, Yelena's long black tresses were being chopped into a fashionable "do" that she was neither sure about, nor resistant to, for she was caught up with the letter that Ljuba had agreed to read, once she was in the chair. So Charles chopped, Ljuba read, and Yelena listened with the poise of a pony waiting for the rider's click to jump the fence.

Ljuba read, translating as she went, "'Zorka went up to Belgrade to visit her sister, and had her hair frizzed. Vlado hated it, so she threw him out, and then went after that young policeman.'"

Charles threw in, "You go, Zorka girl!"

Yelena remained attentive.

Ljuba continued on, overlapping Charles's stream of remarks, "'…and he turned out to be more interested in her daughter, so she banned him from the place, and then Vlado came back.'" She glanced up at Yelena to see if she'd had enough, "What a mess, huh Yelena?"

"I miss that mess, Ljuba."

"You don't need to be there right now, baby," Charles chimed in.

Ljuba read on. She scanned the letter for something cheery. "Dushka has taken to cleaning the church, and chasing after Father Voyn, begging him to teach her to be a nun…and Miriana is pregnant again."

Charles continued a running commentary, "Hmm, hmm, hmm."

"What else, Ljuba?" Yelena implored.

Paraphrasing, Ljuba offered, "No word about the three boys still missing. The spirit of the village is low, the tension of the war, worse every day…Uncle Anton, still healthy as an ox, at eighty-eight, thanks to Aunt Sofia…amazing woman." Ljuba folded the letter slowly and neatly, as if that action would somehow smooth out the madness of her homeland.

"Aunt Sofia is just like mother was."

Ljuba nodded in agreement. "Our mother, I miss, and our Aunt Sofia, of course, but the chaos over there, no thank you."

Yelena, shocked at the sacrilege Ljuba had uttered, jerked her head toward her sister and proclaimed, "Well, I miss everything!"

"You got to hold still girl or what you gonna be missing is an ear," Charles cautioned. Ljuba chuckled at Charles's light touch amidst the jarring tragedies of life. Yelena softened.

"You'll read me the rest later, Ljuba, yes?" Yelena pleaded.

"There is nothing else, Yelena. They haven't a clue about the killer. Aunt Sofia is not even sure they're still looking."

With that, Yelena faced the mirror obediently, and let fall quiet tears, while the river of dark hair fell to the floor.

CHAPTER THIRTY-ONE

A MERE TWO HOURS LATER, THE TWO SISTERS were striding through Midtown Manhattan, with the confidence of newly inaugurated politicians, or freshly foaled mares, or simply the radiantly beautiful Slavic girls that they were. Dignified when they had nothing to be proud of, and forward thinking when the past had them tethered at the ankles. That was Ljuba and Yelena.

Ljuba broke the silence. They hadn't spoken since the letter, except to applaud Yelena's new look. Ljuba had always admired her sister's natural beauty, and with her new hairdo, she was almost glamorous, in an earthy, womanly way. "I love the way they decorate for Christmas here, don't you, honey? We don't have that at home."

"Yes, it's nice, a little early, though isn't it?" Yelena managed a reply. "I mean Christmas isn't until January."

"Well, here they celebrate it in December, and they start the ball rolling before Thanksgiving." Ljuba was losing Yelena on all this "American" lore. She could tell her sister's mind was across the great pond. Undaunted, Ljuba tried another tack, as they marched across Fifty-seventh Street. "So how's that man you have lunch or dinner or should I say, midnight snacks with? What did you say his name was...Jake?"

"He's fine, I guess." Yelena answered politely.

"What do you mean, you guess, don't you know?"

"Yes, yes, he's fine, he's nice, he's very interested in the Balkans, so we talk a lot about what's going on over there," Yelena confessed.

"Well, maybe he's interested in the Balkans, because he's interested in a certain Balkan beauty." Ljuba tentatively tested the waters, to no avail. Yelena gave her a side glance, shorthand for, "Knock it off, sis."

Finally, they reached their destination, a deli on the corner of Fifty-seventh Street and Sixth Avenue. Shedding their coats, they plopped into a booth and ordered soup. *One nice thing about New York*

City, Ljuba thought, *most restaurants were over-heated.* So no matter how chilled-to-the bone one became, after walking in the cold November wind, the payoff was to be happily peeling off jackets and sweaters and plopping comfortably in a warm leather booth. Ljuba persisted grilling her sister about Jake, anything to keep her mind off the letter.

"So...tell me."

"Like I said, he's very interested in the history of our country, and I told him all about it. He wanted to know about Srebenica too, and I told him what I knew and what I'd seen for myself. He said that wasn't the way it was reported here."

Ljuba looked away, embarrassed that she had not been more outspoken to her neighbors who, upon learning she was Serbian, looked at her like she was *armed and dangerous.* She cancelled her New York Times after the first splash of misinformation about the recent Balkan Wars hit the stands. She listened to Belgrade news, Italian news, and the BBC on the Internet, as their stories were not so anti-Serb. They reported atrocities on both sides, unlike the American press. Especially in Srebenica, when most Western media left out the killing of Serbian children that preceded the atrocious retaliation the Serbs carried out against the Muslims. Which came first, the chicken or the egg? It was infuriating, and Ljuba felt helpless, and a bit ashamed that she remained a silent victim of spin.

"Really, Yelena, he sounds like a good man."

"Mm-hmm."

They slurped their soup awhile. Yelena dipped one of the over-sized dill pickles sitting in a tray on every table into the soup and crunched into it. Ljuba winced. Yelena had always had strange eating habits. Aunt Sofia always said that was just her way, but Ljuba insisted it was for shock effect, and she confirmed her own theory when she caught Yelena glimpse out of the corner of her eye toward Ljuba to see if she was watching. They both broke into laughter, causing the waitress to walk away until they'd calmed down before she could take their sandwich order. That broke the tension between them, and the siblings surrendered to a delicious, chatty lunch, during which Yelena confided Jake's fascination with baseball and the strife of their homeland.

Bundled up again, they walked toward Yelena's place of work. Ljuba was now captivated by Yelena's telling, in Serbian, this time, so she could get it exactly right, of a news report Jake had found about a Serbian woman in Srebenica whose daughter was raped and killed by a gang of Bosnian Muslims. "Do you think he could get a copy of that report?" Ljuba queried. "I would like to see, just once, that American reporters told the Serbian side of the story, in any newspaper."

"I don't know, I could ask him," Yelena replied, "but you can't do anything with it.

"I can't?" Ljuba replied, scheming a way to restore herself to standard bearer for truth and justice. After all, she was the one who chased down the dog catchers to save Yelena's pup. Yelena looked at her with admiration, and shook her head, while Ljuba glanced across the street at a handsome man. He was waving at the two sisters.

"Don't look now, but I have a feeling, this could be your Jake and he's headed this way. Either that, or St. Peter has answered my own prayers," Ljuba announced.

Jake ran across, dodging a cab and a bicyclist to get to the pretty pair before Yelena entered the building. He was smoking a cigarette, something Yelena hadn't seen before.

"Yelena, wait!" he called. She and Ljuba turned and stopped at the front door of the building. Before he was within earshot, Ljuba managed, "Oooh, cute."

Yelena elbowed her to shush.

"Hi Yelena!...uh...Hello." Jake waited for the introduction which Yelena swiftly provided.

"Oh, Jake, this is my sister, Ljuba," then gesturing to Jake, "and Ljuba, this is my..." caught in a damned possessive pronoun trap, with nowhere to go but forward, she finished, "my...Jake." Jake rescued her by extending his hand to Ljuba, at the same time, he stroked Yelena's shoulder.

"Yes, I'm her Jake." Yelena turned bright red. Ljuba looked him up and down like he was cattle she was about to buy, and a warm smile spread across her face.

"Nice to meet you, Jake, I've heard a lot about you." That's it. Yelena was officially looking for a sewer cover she could crawl under, but Jake and Ljuba were off to the races in conversation and Yelena was left in the dust of her own shyness.

"You have! Well, whadya know about that," and with that Jake squeezed Yelena closer to him, bringing her out of her flustered state, then spoke to her with some urgency and intimacy, "Yelena, honey, look, I gotta do something for my son tonight, so I'll be back a little late. I wanted to let you know, you may be dining alone."

"Dining?" Ljuba remarked.

Yelena gave her sister a look, to silence her. Ljuba looked up at the sky, giving Yelena the illusion of privacy. "It's okay, Jake." Yelena reassured her man. "You just take care of Tony." Jake kissed her on the temple.

"Nice meeting you, Ljuba." He hurried away, but turned to say, "You look beautiful, Yelena, something's different. Beautiful!"

Ljuba couldn't help herself. "Something's different!" she muttered to Yelena. "Very observant...and he calls himself a reporter?"

"Ljuba! He has his son on his mind now, not my hair salon," Yelena defended.

"Never mind, I like him." Ljuba conceded. "And it's your hair style, not hair salon." She kissed her sister on both cheeks, gave her a warm hug and released her to her evening's work, while she headed home to Henry.

"Not hair salon, hair style," Yelena reiterated to herself as she walked into the building, both doors being held open by two handsome young gents. That was a first.

"Thanks, doll faces," she pronounced, flipping them a Gracie-ism, as she punched the elevator button. "Going up, fellas, or are you waiting for the local?"

They weren't sure if they were being mocked or seduced, but they were enchanted either way and held the elevator door open for the new queen from Queens.

CHAPTER THIRTY-TWO

BREAKTIME CAME QUICKLY THAT NIGHT. Yelena kept a steady pace as if the harder she worked the greater the possibility of Jake making it back in time to join her. No such luck. She nestled onto the cool floor, propped herself against the file cabinets and sat hands in lap like a school girl. She didn't open her lunch. Hungry, yet unable to bring herself to eat, she wondered if this was a new stage of the grieving process; immobility. She had kept moving since the day she walked from Marko's grave, a few months ago. It felt like an eternity. Her life had become a perpetual pendulum sweeping between merciless sorrow and brief relief. Somewhere between those two extremes was a small breath of air, a tiny slice of light that had no history, no future, no sadness, no dread, just a still small voice that called to her, "now, and now, and now, and now." Her head was spinning. She got up from the floor and took a walk.

She approached Jake's cubicle. It was unlit. It looked lonely. Normally it was the hub of activity in the midnight tomb. Usually Jake's desk was the firefly that lit up the night and drew to it all living things that hopelessly tried to capture it, to hold it close and behold its glow. Yelena emptied his waste basket of wrappers from Hershey's chocolate almond candy bars, balls of crumpled second thoughts, old racing forms revealing Jake's habit of horse betting. A man had to have some diversion while working out his divorce settlement.

Yelena tried on his seat for size. It swiveled. She liked it. It smelled like Jake. A combination of dark tobacco, whiskey, coffee and after shave. The aroma of an unattached man. The ones that gathered at the elevators at six o'clock sharp to rush home to their wives all smelled vaguely of chicken soup, pipe tobacco and polyester. Not so her Jake.

She glanced up at the picture of Jake's son, which was pinned to the bulletin board just left of his computer screen. The beautiful boy was smiling and pointing at a large fish he held in one hand, obviously his own personal triumph. Tony, she whispered his name, wondering if she'd ever meet him. He looked to be about fourteen-years-old then, and there was a long-legged woman in shorts, and a big white hat standing behind him, looking the other way, toward the lake. Yelena figured that to be Tony's mother, Jake's former wife. She was a tall woman, and seemed to be a fancy one, Yelena imagined.

It wasn't exactly a Norman Rockwell portrait of the perfect American family. The photographer, probably Jake, barely included the blonde, disinterested woman in the photo. It was as if she purposely turned the other way, or like she had just dropped in from another family altogether. The disappointment of the photographer permeated the picture somehow. Yelena thought she must be going a little nuts, reading into things so much, best to go back to work.

Feeling a little self-conscious being at Jake's desk without him, she tentatively dusted around the many piles of papers, emptied his ashtray, capped the whiskey bottle in the open bottom right drawer, cleaned his ceramic coffee cup with the Yankee emblem on it, threw away an empty pack of Marlboro's pausing to read the label aloud, then stepped back and noticed that the cubicle looked just as dirty as before she started. She dusted the computer screen, as if that was the single thing needed to put straight his messy work station. It was futile. She collapsed into the chair again and noticed a pile of poorly Xeroxed articles about Bosnia. She flicked on the desk lamp and began to peruse stories and photos about the horrors of her homeland, in Bosnia, Kosovo, other parts of Serbia, and even Dubrovnik, which had always been considered untouchable because it's surrounded by a medieval wall.

While it was hard for her to understand every word of the articles, it was obvious the situation had worsened since she'd left, a few short months ago. The images pulled her right back to her village on that fated day when she couldn't cross the field fast enough to save her son from slaughter. Suddenly she was jolted from her nightmare, when Casey called out from across the floor, "Yelena, whadya doing, cleaning his desk with a Q-tip? For Chrissake, forget about it, he likes his mess, leave it, go home, he won't be in tonight."

"What? How do you know that, Casey?"

Pointing to his temple, "Just using my kidneys," he teased. "Go on, call it a night."

"Okay, Casey. Thank you."

"You need me to walk you to the subway, Yelena?" he offered.

"No, thank you, I'm fine, I'll just use my kidneys," she replied, dead serious.

Casey shook his head, topped it with his wool cap and hit the elevator button, "All right, sweetheart, suit yourself. Security guards will lock up. I'll tell 'em."

"Okey dokey," Yelena called out. She carefully replaced the articles into the pile and prepared to depart for the night.

The subway was sparsely populated. Late on a Friday night the week before Christmas found most folks at home with their families. Family. That was one loss Yelena would never recuperate from. How she arrived at this Christmas season, in a cold subway in New York City, she couldn't fathom. She wished the answers had been in the clippings on Jake's desk, she wished they could explain why she no longer had a son, for that matter why her husband, Radmilo had to die. He could have protected their son. She was flooded with questions and didn't realize that she was staring straight ahead, crying. A young black man approached her, "Miss, Miss," he ventured.

Yelena grabbed her purse tight to her chest, and proclaimed, "Don't come near me, I'm a whole lot wilder than I look," she cried.

The young man backed away slowly, "I just wondered if you'd like a handkerchief," and he passed her his clean, white, freshly ironed handkerchief, and backed himself into a seat a few rows from her, never taking his eyes from her, more frightened by her, than she, him.

She accepted the offering, and gingerly patted her tears, looking at him across the starchy cotton as she blew her nose. The next stop was hers; she went to the door, which brought her very close to the young man. She reached into her pocket, and this time the young man pulled his schoolbooks up to his chest in fear. Yelena produced a white linen handkerchief, freshly laundered and pressed, with a crocheted blue trim around the edges, and gave it to him, "Please," she said, "take this. Give it to your mother." He did, and she stepped onto the platform and headed up the stairs, into the crisp starry night in Queens.

When Yelena arrived home that night, she felt burdened with what she'd seen in the newspaper clippings. It was strange, as if she was guilty because she was too far away to do anything about what was going on in her Balkan home. What was happening over there? It seemed to have mushroomed into an even more wretched conflict, if that were possible. Would that she had stayed, she could have done something, but what? What could she have done? When it counted, she failed to protect what she loved, so how could she be effective now? Was Aunt Sofia safe? Uncle Anton? Was her son's grave undefiled?

She ached to go back, and yet desired to stay in the safety of her sister's home, in the anesthetic regularity of her job, and truth be told, she wanted to keep seeing Jake at work every night. She settled into the solace offered by the handmade quilt that Ljuba had put on her bed to make her feel at home. Yelena anchored herself to it. It was a quilt their mother made when she was a young woman and pregnant with Ljuba. Fabulously colored patches of cotton donned one side, and a mixture of black and grey woolen squares were on the back side. Another original creation of their mother's that turned out just like its creator, extraordinarily beautiful and authentic, yet practical.

How she and Ljuba had longed to know their mother better, longer, more deeply. She could have passed on so many of her talents to them. Now she sat with the product of that talent, and wished that a swatch of color could transform itself into her mother's very presence, as in the fairy tale of *The Little Match Girl*, by the Brothers Grimm. They couldn't have invented a better nom de plume for the stories they wrote, she concluded, after reading them in the original German in school.

Yelena glanced out the window and saw rain turning to snow, as it landed on the iron railings of the fire escape. It was getting colder, the days, the nights, the drudgery of life without her boy. Day after day without him, and now Christmas without him. It was unimaginable.

"Marko" she whispered. "Marko." She'd not uttered his name in so long.

Ljuba had decorated the apartment with lights trimming the windows, a wreath nailed to the door, and a small, but perfectly shaped evergreen tree, powerful in terms of its luminescence. There was a colored light fastened to each branch, and homemade ornaments in between each one, and the finishing touch, a cascade of shiny silver tinsel. Yelena reached for the cord to plug in the tree. The beauty of it made her gulp back tears. Not wanting to wake the household, she flicked on the television with the remote, which she now had complete dominion over, just in time to hear "This concludes the *Burns and Allen* series. Starting next week, James Stewart and Lionel Barrymore in *'It's A Wonderful Life'* a will run nightly through Christmas." *My God,* she thought, *was everything coming to an end tonight?* She clicked it off, shoved the remote on the lamp table, and knocked over a photo of Marko. She gingerly picked it up, held it to her heart, curled up on the bed in a fetal position with her coat and boots still on and eventually fell asleep.

The next morning, or what amounted to a few hours later, she barely moved when Henry shook her shoulder, alarmed to find her still in her clothes. Fatigue had turned into utter exhaustion and Henry mistook it for worse. "Ljuba!" he called out to his wife in alarm.

That woke Yelena and at the same time Ljuba came out of the bedroom, half dressed, "What is it Henry? You'll wake Yelena!" Then Ljuba noticed Yelena was still in her coat and the Christmas tree was on, and the photo of Marko was still clutched in Yelena's gloved fingers.

"Yelena, what's happened? Are you hurt? Did you just get home?" Ljuba entreated. Yelena laid there, looking up at the Christmas angel on the top of the tree, and rolled over.

"There's your answer." Henry concluded. "She's probably drunk."

"Oh please, Henry, you don't know my sister."

"I'm getting to though, aren't I. I'm definitely getting to know the gal, and she's full of surprises."

"Go to work, Henry, you'll be late." Ljuba tossed him an apple, "Your lunch. Bye Henry."

"You're going to the moon, Alice...to the moon," he called out as he closed the door and hustled down the stairs. Ljuba stood over Yelena, watching her sleep, fully clothed, and silently agreed that things looked to be getting worse, not better, for her little sis.

CHAPTER THIRTY-THREE

JAKE HAD BEEN MISSING FROM WORK for three nights. It was two days before Christmas. Holidays bring out the best in the depressed. Yelena was fighting her demons by devoting her dinnertime to delving into the clippings on Jake's desk. Unsure exactly what she was seeking did not dent her search, but it did cause her to most uncharacteristically slack off considerably in her cleaning duties.

Casey was standing at the entrance to the utility room when she came out, wrapper in hand. Not looking where she was going, as she swiped a stray hair off her forehead, she didn't see Casey and nearly ran right into him. His mere size, not to mention his larger than life presence, probably made that occurrence a rarity in Casey's experience. People don't usually miss seeing a man like him.

"Whoa! Yelena! You all right?" he queried.

"Oh, sorry, Casey, I didn't see you."

"Really. How you doing? You okay? I mean, looks like things are a little rough around the edges for you, these past few days."

Yelena looked down again, this time in shame, "Uh, yes, I am a little rough, as you say, I'm sorry, Casey, I know I'm doing a bad job and I'm sorry...I...I," she stammered.

"I'm not so worried about the sticky floor in the coffee room, or the stalls in the men's room that need toilet paper, or the carpet that needs vacuuming in the foyer, I'm worried about you, Miss Yelena, you!" he persevered. "Is it Jake? Is it the holidays? Bad news from home?"

"Yes. It's maybe everything." She welled up with tears, and Casey decided not to push it any further. "I'm so sorry, Casey."

"Quit saying you're sorry, will ya? It's all right. Take it easy, Yelena. Things'll get better in time." He summed up the conversation with, "Jakey'll be in later. He called."

Yelena brightened noticeably. Casey, the kindest of men, felt that he'd done his good deed for the day, and each of them went back to their corners like prize fighters, Casey to his cigar and sports section, Yelena to her cart and cleaning tools, and almost indiscernibly primping, prompted by the news that Jake would be in that night. Casey caught this while looking over his newspaper and almost indiscernibly shook his head.

Come midnight, Yelena was actually hungry for a change, and settled in at the filing cabinets to eat what Ljuba had prepared for her, with the hope that a certain someone would arrive.

She'd caught up with her cleaning duties that evening, things were looking spic and span, even to the by-then somewhat bleary-eyed Casey, who was taking one of his many evening naps after a yuletide nip. Yelena unwrapped her culinary treasure, and was about to bite into a provolone cheese sandwich, when a red rose appeared between her mouth and the rye bread. She looked up and saw Jake attached to it.

"Don't eat the rose! It's for an enchantress named Yelena!" Jake proclaimed.

"Enchantress?" Yelena didn't know that one.

"Like a charmer, a siren...uh...a gypsy," Jake clarified.

Yelena caught it on the third try. She smiled. "Glad to see you, Jake."

"Glad to hear you're glad." Jake nestled down next to her and offered the other part of his gift. A packet of chestnuts.

"Kestin!" Yelena took them with girlish glee.

"Kestin?" Jakes's turn to query.

"Chestnuts is *kestin*, in my language." She bit into one of them, still warm from the coals of the street vender. Yelena bit right through the shell.

"Wait a minute!" Jake cried.

"Now what?" Yelena teased.

"Don't eat the shell!!"

"Really, in the old country we do."

But Jake caught the twinkle in her eye, and got that she was teasing him.

"Yeah, right." Jake delighted in her.

"I'm a whole lot wilder than I look," she declared.

"You are, are you? Well, now where did you learn that, I wonder?"

"From my late night teacher, Gracie Allen." Yelena boasted.

"Oh, she comes over to the house after work, does she?" Jake played along.

"No, silly, she's on television, but I'd love to meet her one day."

"I'll bet she'd love to meet you too, but you'll have to put that off for a while, a long while I hope." Jake reached to touch Yelena's hair. "Did I tell you I love your hair cut?"

Yelena was fixated on the bandage that was wrapped around Jake's hand.

"Jake, what happened to your hand?" She could see there was dried blood under the surface of the outer gauze wrapping.

"Aw, nothing, I'll tell you later." He gazed at her and knew he was getting into deep waters; she did enchant him; and he did not suspect anything but genuine guilelessness from her. "Hey, Yelena, you wanna come over and have dinner with me tonight at my place, it's only a few blocks from here?"

Yelena was surprised by the invitation, but recovered with, "Well, I don't know if I can tonight Jake, 'I'm expecting a headache.'" She tried to keep from giggling at her own joke, well, at Gracie's joke.

"Oh Gracie, you really know how to curl my toes. Let's go, you're coming over, and I'm cooking us dinner. "Wrap up that sandwich and stick it in the fridge in the lounge, Casey'll eat it later, believe me. Come on, I'm hungry, you must be too." He helped her up, and they stood very close, feeling each other's breath on their cheeks. Yelena put the rose between them and smelled it, never taking her eyes off of Jake. They breathed as one. Jake thought he'd better back it up a little before he scared her away.

"Let me grab something from my desk. Get your coat, darlin'." Jake went swiftly to his cubicle, and Yelena went to put away her cart and check with Casey about leaving. She found him sound asleep and figured it best to leave him be. She figured she'd done all she could do tonight, and that leaving now would not cause friction with her boss, especially if she left him that yummy sandwich. He was, after all, just a ravenous lamb in wolf's clothing.

She paused in front of the mirror in the locker room to run her fingers through her short hair, which she still wasn't used to, and to apply some rose-colored lipstick and pinch her cheeks. With all she'd been through, she still radiated a beauty that no sadness could mar. Yelena never quite saw it in herself the way others had and the way Jake did from the moment he discovered her on the floor against the file cabinet, weeping.

Jake was checking a couple of phone messages on his office line, and quickly emailing a couple of responses, while he created the illusion of a good day's work by piling the manila folders in a different configuration and labeling them, "to edit." Yelena walked up behind him quietly; he didn't hear her, as he listened to the recordings on the phone line. The news came onto the television which was always on when Jake was there, and she heard, "Civil War...the former Yugoslavia...ravaged villages." She watched images of bodies lying dead, children standing alone in the middle of a muddy road, men crouched in ditches holding rifles with hand rolled cigarettes hanging from their mouths, not moving while the ash formed a fragile ledge that landed on their clothes at regular intervals. She reached to turn up the volume and put her face close to the screen in the hope she'd understand the newscaster's rapid-fire report. Though she only caught every third or fourth word, Jake turned away from his computer for a moment to listen as well.

"Throughout Croatia, Bosnia and Serbia, the horrifying conflict continues, with massive war crimes being committed on all sides of this brutal civil war. Since the Croatians drove 200,000 Serbs from their homes in the Krajina region, where they had lived peaceably together for decades, vengeful crimes have been dominating the scene. Atrocious retaliatory acts, reminiscent of the Second World War, are creating a divisiveness in this country that may well be irreparable."

Jake gently touched Yelena's shoulder. She was frozen at the screen. "Yelena, honey, let's not watch this now." She looked up at him.

"When, then?" The size of her pain was more than Jake could counter with reason. He pulled her toward him.

"You know what? I was planning on a coupla rare steaks, a bottle of Chianti, baked potatoes. How's that sound?"

"Good, Jake, but...." and she stretched to see the screen behind him. He slipped his hand behind his back and hit the off button. The screen went blank. "But, Jake...please, I want to see."

"Not tonight, honey." He helped her on with her coat, flicked off the lamp over his desk, grabbed the bag of groceries he had already bought on his way up there to invite this woman to dine with him that night, and walked with her to the elevator.

Goliath stirred as they passed him. Casey looked up, opening one eye. Yawning, he managed, "Where you two think you're going?" He glanced at the glow in Yelena's cheeks, a far cry from what she looked like when she came in that evening, so he relented. "All right, go ahead, knock off early, the dirt will be there when you come back tomorrow, I suppose."

"I cleaned all the dirt, Casey." Yelena offered.

"Oh yeah? Well, then, here you go." And he handed her a check.

"Thank you, Casey. Merry Christmas." She kissed his bald head.

"Yeah, yeah, Merry Christmas, to youse two, too."

"Thanks, Case, you're a champ." Jake handed him a gift-wrapped quart of scotch. "Merry Christmas, old pal."

"Hey, now you're talking, and you're gonna leave me here to drink alone?"

Jake gazed at Yelena. "What do you think, Case?"

"I think you both better get going before you get stuck here. We're getting a storm tonight, you know." Noticing the sandwich in front of him, "Well now, well now, this looks tasty, whadya know, Santa came early," and he winked at them.

"See you, Casey." Jake put his arm around Yelena, who was busy studying the figures written on the check. They reached the elevator, and she looked up at Jake.

"I read it twice, and I still don't like it." She couldn't deliver it with a straight face, and they both burst out laughing.

"Oh Gracie, you're a pistol."

Casey looked on, in concentrated assessment. *No telling where that would lead,* he thought. Then, as they were getting into the elevator Casey remembered, "Hey, Jake, you wanna ten point spread on the 49er's this Sunday?"

The elevator doors were closing, and Casey heard, "No thanks, pal." Casey had no choice but to tear the Christmas wrapping off the Glenfidich and have himself a holiday toast just to wash down the provolone, of course.

CHAPTER THIRTY-FOUR

JAKE'S PLACE, A TRUE BACHELOR PAD, cluttered and weighted down with books, stacks of newspapers, photos, piles of laundry, clean and dirty, separate but equal, and golf clubs in various locations around the apartment proved that married or not, a man has his own particular sense of order. Deep inside, the male species seemed to relish bachelorhood, and yet they also seemed to flourish in marriage. No matter. It was fine with Yelena. She didn't blink an eye at the mess, nor did she have that dangerous female impulse to start rearranging anything. It was just fine. She was off duty, happy to be out of the cold, and content to be with Jake.

"Sit down, make yourself comfortable," Jake said as he scurried to clear a chair laden with clothes, "and take off your boots if you like."

"Thank you." Yelena was intrigued in this new environment. First, it was the only other home she'd been in besides Ljuba's in the United States. Then, there was the other "first." It was the first time she'd been alone with a man under eighty years old since her Radmilo died five years earlier. She shed her boots, walked over to the window, and beheld a very different view of New York than the one from Ljuba's fire escape in Queens. Jake's place was on the eleventh floor, so she spotted small moving particles disguised as people. She caught a sliver of Central Park, where the horse and carriage drivers were huddled against the wind. Then her gaze fell upon the window sill which was loaded with framed photographs of Jake and Tony and the former leggy woman.

Jake was at the bookcase next to the window searching for a Coltrane disc, which he popped into his boom box. Everything seemed temporary in this apartment. Everything except the books, the photos and Jake himself. Yelena turned to him with a framed photo in hand. He was closer to her than she imagined, and she bumped against him.

"Oops," Jake offered as he put his arms around her shoulders. She held the picture up between them, preventing him from embracing her more closely.

"Is this your wife?"

"Ex-wife, yes."

"She's beautiful, don't you think?"

"No, I don't think." Jake added, "I mean she wasn't beautiful on the inside, and frankly, not in any way to me, anymore."

"Well...," Yelena began. But Jake nipped further conversation about the dreaded Sigrid in the bud, and took the frame out of Yelena's hand, placing it face-down on the window sill, without taking his eyes off hers, nor letting her out of his arms.

"Dance with me, Yelena." The Coltrane was beginning to make him move. Yelena removed his arms from around her waist gently.

"I can't Jake, it's too soon after my son's death. I can't dance."

"I'm sorry, Yelena, I wasn't thinking."

Yelena gave him a slight smile, enough for him to know she forgave him, and that she probably always would.

"Hey, how about some slivovitz?" The sound of a Slavic word mispronounced in his mouth, made her chuckle and she lit up like a sunbeam.

"You have slivovitz?"

"Sure do, picked it up at the Polish deli, just in case you ever decided to visit me on a cold winter night." He was already on his way to the kitchen to grab two shot glasses and the bottle of the infamous plum brandy, which could provide balm and bravado in one swallow. As he poured out the stream of white lightning, he disclaimed, "Maybe this isn't like the homemade stuff you're used to in your village, but I'm hoping it's good." With that he clinked glasses with Yelena and they looked at each other in a moment of recognition that each was in need of something they could not quite name, but it felt like the other might be the one to fill that need.

"To your son Marko." Jake said softly.

"And to your Tony." Yelena countered. "Zhivali."

They clinked glasses and Jake attempted, "Zhivali!"

Yelena laughed.

"What did I just say?"

"To Life!"

"All righty then, to life!"

They drank. He coughed. She took hers down as smooth as a young colt cantering through a meadow.

"Wow." Jake said hoarsely. "This stuff's got a kick."

He swallowed again, this time with more finesse, finishing off his glass. He refilled both their glasses. The sound of the liquid splashing into the shot glasses, like a promise of rain that would make spring flowers grow, trumped the Coltrane.

"You just have a seat here on the sofa and sip your Slivovitz, and dinner will be ready and rare in minutes. Relax."

"Okay, Jake," Yelena sat on his couch and looked around the room, like a child in a toy shop. Everything was strange and wondrous to her. She liked the feel of his bachelor pad, it was unpretentious, just like him. On the coffee table, she noticed a book of photographs of Brooklyn. She remembered Jake's mother had lived in Brooklyn and so she paged through it with great care.

Suddenly from the kitchen she heard, "Ow!!" followed by some indecipherable expletives.

"Jake! Are you all right?" She went to him and found him standing at the kitchen sink, holding his already bandaged hand under cold running water. He looked at Yelena with a brave smile.

"Broiling pan was a little hot." Yelena noticed the hand bleeding from the previous wound, and the burn probably creating a good bit of pain on top of that.

"Here, let me," she said as she gently but firmly applied pressure to his wrist to stop the bleeding. Jake winced and whistled at the same time, as she slowly undressed his wound. "We should change this."

Before he could protest the treatment, for fear of her seeing a grown man cry and thereby risking diminishing his manly charm in her eyes, he yielded to her direction and followed her to the bathroom. She had him sitting like a boy on the edge of the bathtub, while she cleaned his hand with alcohol and antiseptic and applied a clean bandage. He was mid-story about the event that caused the wound the other night, and it served as a great diversion from his physical discomfort. She listened to him intently, while she treated the wound with professionalism and respect.

"And then what happened?" she asked.

"Well, this son-of-a-bitch who's been selling my kid drugs, pulls a knife and I manage to kick it out of his hand, but he cuts me with this razor blade, which he was wearing around his neck like some kinda goddamned medallion. Ouch! Yelena, that...."

"Hurts? I know, I'm almost done, I'm sorry, but he cut you very deep."

Jake continued, braver now for her compassionate acknowledgement of his suffering, "Anyway, well...I nearly killed him...I just wanted to get back at him for what he'd done to Tony...so we threw a few punches, I had him pinned and then...."

"Go on," Yelena urged.

"I don't know. I stopped."

"What stopped you, Jake?"

"To tell the truth, I don't know." Jake pondered a moment, then continued, "Civilization?" trying that one on for size. "Who knows? I hated him for what he'd done, but all of a sudden I was over him, and could have slit his throat with his own damned razor blade in a flash, but he just...he looked so pathetic, so weak, so small, so...I don't know...sick."

Yelena finished the bandaging and looked at Jake, waiting for him to go on, but he was done; he had no more to say about the event. He was back in the present looking at this bewitching woman, who had now performed just the right amount of mothering for him.

"You know, you're good at this, Yelena."

She nodded, knowingly, "Yes, because I was a nurse's aide in Belgrade for one year before I was married."

"You were a nurse?" Jake continued to be bowled over by her.

"No, nurse's aide," she clarified.

"That's nice. You're a nurse, you speak three or four languages; you are just full of surprises."

Yelena turned from him to wash her hands. It was close quarters in the bathroom, to put it mildly.

Hungry to know more about this woman, Jake asked, "So, how'd your husband keep you back on the farm, after you'd seen Belgrade?"

"I think you're teasing me, but really Belgrade is beautiful! It means White City, you know."

"No, I didn't know that," Jake replied, hypnotized by his proximity to her full body.

"But we thought the farm would be a better place to raise a family, safer, and...." Yelena stopped short with sudden sadness at the realization of that grave miscalculation on their part. Jake picked up on it and immediately rescued the moment.

"Hey, let's eat. I just lost a lot of blood, I'm hungry!"

There was that smile of hers again; each one was a victory to him. "Okay," she agreed, but neither one of them moved. There was something mesmeric about the closet-sized bathroom, forcing them into tempting proximity. Yelena broke the spell, as she reached for a towel to wipe her hands. She failed to locate one, so she wiped her hands on her skirt.

"You need a cleaning lady, Jake," teasing him about the messy bathroom, and she started to walk out.

Jake stopped her by grabbing her hip with his good hand, "I know." Yelena attempted to get through the door, again. Jake held with, "And a nurse." This time she didn't move. "And a cook, maybe," he said.

"Really." Yelena started to squeeze past him one more time, more from nerves, than any real desire to move away from him. But he held her close to him, more aroused than he could ever remember, he moved to kiss her. He barely brushed her lips. He felt her body yield almost imperceptibly, but yield it did, to his touch. Then like a gentle wave rushing to shore where it would surely be absorbed into the sand, leaving no evidence of its fleeting existence; just so, Yelena gingerly freed herself and went to the kitchen, leaving him alone in the bathroom with his racing pulse. Jake stood there for a minute or two, glanced up at the shower head and contemplated taking a cold one.

By the time they finished eating the juicy rare steaks prepared by Chef Jake, they had both settled into a more relaxed posture, mercifully aiding their digesting the feast, at the very least. Jake had eyes only for the candlelight flickering in hers, and Yelena's gaze was pulled toward the window, as if on the other side of it lay the answer to how and why she was there in the first place. She was struck with incredulity, mixed with a minute measure of actual contentment. They'd had a fine dinner and delicious wine to accompany it.

"You're a good meal, Jake." She did it again. Found a funny bone he didn't know he had. He couldn't stifle a laugh.

"You mean cook. Yeah, I'm an okay cook. Thank you." He followed her gaze out the window. It hadn't stopped snowing since their first Slivovitz, hours ago. It was a veritable blizzard out there.

Yelena got up from the table and went to the window. She could feel the cold wet air through the glass. "We have snow like this in our village, now." A weariness crept in as her mind drifted to her village which would be entirely blanketed in snow. She yawned. Jake came up behind her and looked out over her shoulder. The wine allowed him to dare again to hold her and placing his arms around her waist, he pulled her up against him. She didn't resist this time.

"Yelena, you want me to drive you back to Queens now, or you could take a snooze here, and I'll drive you in the morning when the snow hopefully has stopped."

"What's a snooze?" She turned and looked into his kind eyes. If she'd been taller, there wouldn't have been room for both their noses between them.

"A short rest people take if they don't sleep well at night. And since you're busy studying Gracie Allen all the time, I doubt you ever get enough sleep, so you may need a snooze about now."

"It's true, I don't sleep well," she confessed. "I have bad dreams."

"Nightmares, huh?" Jake took her hand.

"No," she said, as if to make some cryptic distinction, "bad dreams." Jake took the correction, nodded and led her by the hand to his bedroom. She followed with the courage that one earns from enduring so much of life's bad luck. It could no longer hurt or frighten her. She had the eloquent grace of one who had already lost it all. That was true power.

"You can rest in my room, and I'll take the couch." Jake turned on a light next to the bed, and pulled back the covers for her. He went to close the window.

"You can leave it open, Jake. I like the cold air when I sleep, I mean, snooze." She was sitting on the edge of the bed, and he thought she looked so small all of a sudden, though she was very much a full bodied woman. He took her face in his hands, and whispered, "You need anything, I'm just in the next room, Gracie. Okay?"

"Okey dokey." Jake ventured a light kiss on her perfect mouth then reluctantly proceeded to the living room, leaving her to rest. He then did something he'd never in his life done before, which was to clean up after dinner on the same day the dinner was eaten. Miracles do happen.

Yes, indeed they do. After Jake had cleaned up, quite efficiently by his standards, he took off his dishwater-drenched shirt, stretched out on the couch and lit a cigarette. Sleep would elude him that night.

No matter. He had plenty to think about, to sort out. Who was he kidding? There was nothing to figure out. His gut told him all he needed to know, it always had. Come to happen, it always would. This woman, this gypsy woman touched him in a place he didn't know he had, an unknown turf. He could never say that out loud, it sounded gooey.

Here he was parked in his own pile of garbage from the past: his divorce from a woman he had long since stopped loving, his ceaseless concern over his son's recovery which for today was on track though he worried hourly about Tony. Yet right there in the next room was a wonder, taking a nap because she was exhausted from her daily job, depleted from the stress of living in a foreign land, and despaired over how to put one foot in front of the other on the earth that had swallowed up her eleven year old son. *My God,* Jake thought, *how did she even get up in the morning, let alone manage to be kind and gentle and even make him laugh? What drove her? How was she put together?*

Jake was inspired by Yelena's strength. When he thought about her, he felt like he wanted to be a better man, a better father, a better friend and who knows what else, just better. He let the circles of smoke around his head nourish thoughts of loving Yelena.

In the next room Morpheus was playing a different scenario. Yelena had fallen into a deep sleep almost immediately. Nothing in her body could resist the collapse into a comfortable bed which did not double as a sofa. It was not entirely a restful sleep. Her unconscious was flooded with images of Marko. It had been that way since the night of his death, maybe even before that. A mother dreams of her child. It's natural. But this time, she dreamed she saw Marko struggling with the Masked Man near the truck in the field. She heard Marko cry out for her, she was running to him, breathless from calling back to him, just like she did on that black day, except that in her dream no sound came out of her mouth. She screamed out to him, with more and more force, "My son, my son, I'm coming," but no sound was emitted from her, no matter how hard she pushed. Her whole body wanted to make a sound.

The force of the effort in the dream awakened her suddenly. She let out a cry, which was heard and felt. The agony of that cry created a sound vibration, not in the dream, but where it counted; there in Jake's bed she echoed her raging fury of not getting to her son in time to save him. *What could she have done if she'd reached him a minute earlier?* she had asked herself a hundred times. The answer was quick and simple: She'd have taken the blow for him or torn the predator to pieces. She was certain she'd have saved Marko somehow. If only, if only, the most haunting two words in any language.

Yelena hadn't realized how loudly she'd cried out. She realized she was sitting up in the bed, sweating from the fevered pitch of the dream with Jake at her side.

"Yelena, what is it?" he stroked her back. "You're soaking wet."

She sobbed.

"Shhh, shhh, it's all right, I'm right here." She spilled out her dream to Jake.

"In my dream, I call to my son, but he cannot hear my voice. He is fighting with a Masked Man, the man they will never find, the man who killed my Marko."

This stopped Jake short; he'd never asked for the details of her son's death; he thought it too tender and raw a topic still.

"Your son was murdered?" he asked. She nodded, burying her head in his chest.

"Oh my God," was all he could manage. He rocked her gently, searching for something to say to ease her pain, but the horrific offense of Marko's demise was too huge a crater for any mere word.

He reached for a towel he had on a chair near the bed. Thank God for a piece of clean laundry nearby when he needed it. He wrapped it around Yelena. He kept stroking her moist back and he felt her spine soften.

"When Marko was a child," she said, "when he would get afraid at night, he only had to hear my voice, and he would be calm and go back to sleep…but now in my dream…he…I…." she couldn't finish. Jake held her tightly, and then lifted her chin up to dry her tears.

"Everything is going to be all right, Yelena. There is nothing to be afraid of." She looked at him as if she were seeing him for the first time. Jake kissed her. She let him. Again and again and again she received his kisses until she melted under them. The towel dropped and he laid her back on the bed, removed her wet blouse, caressed her breasts, holding each one in his mouth, warming her. He moved slowly, knowing she could stop him at any time. *She was part wild mustang and part fragile Czech crystal,* he thought. *Had he gone too far?* He went back up to her face to look for disapproval. Finding none, his fingers explored her shoulders, neck, and more. There was a sweetness to his touch, as if they had shared this all before, and were recreating it together that night. He buried his head in that mysterious crevice between neck and shoulder.

"Yelena, I'm crazy about you." He whispered so softly, it was as if in case she didn't want to hear it, he could act like it had not been said. Too late for that. Her reticence was a turn on; her stillness drove him to kissed her passionately. Finally, she returned the kiss, and they made slow, deep, earth-moving love. Yelena never imagined another man would ever enter her after Radmilo, but when Jake moved himself into her, it was like he belonged there all along, like a traveler who'd finally come home from a great odyssey, like a deserter who, once returned, wondered why he'd ever left. It was at once a strange and familiar union that rocked them both into a sexual cradle of oblivion.

The bough ultimately broke, like the nursery rhyme predicts, and eventually they returned to earth. Afterwards they lay together, inseparable, wet, warm, steam rising from their bare bodies. The cold winter air slipped through the slightly open bedroom window. A dried out potted plant that sat on Jake's fire escape fell against the window cracking it open a bit more. Snowflakes floated into the room, as if to bless their union. Jake watched each white prism land and melt, making a claim to the oak floor. Still locked in a primal embrace, their breath slowed. She slept. The first time in three months, she actually slept a real deep sleep.

CHAPTER THIRTY-FIVE

AT DAWN A SLICE OF SUN CUT THROUGH THE PANE OF CRACKED GLASS creating a larger puddle of melted snow on the bedroom floor. It never would have occurred to Jake to do something as logical as close the window before they went to sleep. He'd hit heaven in Yelena's arms, and reason had been cast aside.

Jake carefully arose. He didn't want to awaken Yelena, nor did he himself want to fully awaken from his own delirium. He shut the window, and stood in a small circle of melted snow. It was all he could do to resist splashing in the puddle. He felt like a kid again. He looked over at Yelena's shiny black hair feathered across the white pillowcase, like night on ice. He wanted that vision to last forever. He lit a cigarette. Maybe the nicotine would elongate time. But Yelena woke up at the sound of the match. Jake turned and took a good look at her in the light of day. Just as he had suspected, she was perfect. He smiled at her and took a deep satisfying post-coital drag on his cigarette. She reached her arm out for the cig. He offered it with, "You smoke?"

"Never," she replied as she inhaled the tobacco, with a surly grin. It was the act of one who had smoked once upon a time, didn't any more, but enjoyed the naughty relapse. *Okay,* Jake thought, *she said she doesn't smoke, but then she just took a drag like a convicted felon.* He thought he'd better watch closely, she was rather unpredictable. Anything could happen, and anything did.

Yelena returned his cigarette, then rose and began to dress. Jake watched, hypnotized.

"Ready for breakfast?" Jake tentatively queried. Her long look at him nearly shattered him, as it was coupled with a determined zip of her skirt. A slight smile in the corner of her Slavic mouth gave him hope.

"Stay, Yelena."

"I can't." Her look meant more than that she simply couldn't stay for scrambled eggs and bacon. She dressed deliberately and swiftly. He offered a second drag. She declined. He noticed her hand trembled with the buttons of her blouse. She hoped he wouldn't notice her hands shaking. She was flat out afraid.

There was enough going on inside her troubled soul, she wasn't about to add romance to it. There was simply no room. Grief had eaten up any longing for love. She wondered how it happened that she ended up with Jake inside her last night. What made her do such a thing? Who was she becoming? Her thoughts sent a shiver throughout her whole body and Jake went to her and held her.

"Yelena, you're going to have to stop running one of these days."

"I know," she conceded but moved away from him.

Her boots had dried from their jaunt last night. They were about to get christened with the fresh slosh of snow on this Christmas Eve morning. She hoped they wouldn't leak, as she purposefully laced them up. She yanked at the laces a little too hard and broke one, making it impossible to complete the task.

Jake watched, attentively. "Here let me," he offered. He got on one knee before her to doctor up the broken lace to insure a dry foot. He was silent, though he knew what he wanted to say, if he could find the courage. It flew from his gut to his conscious mind as fast as a horse out of the gate. I love you, don't go. Stay. I'll take you home later, or never. Your wish is my command. But the award-winning journalist spoke not a word. The wordsmith simply double tied her boots, and then patted them as if he were sending his protégé out on the ice to skate for a gold medal.

She paused at the door. He grabbed his jacket. "No, Jake, don't come with me. Please."

He started to speak, but she interrupted him with, "Thank you." Halfway out the door she turned and managed a smile with her eyes burrowing into his. "Merry Christmas, Jake." When he heard the elevator doors close, he dropped his head and thought, *Yeah, Merry Christmas, Jake, you idiot.*

Chapter Thirty-Six

IT HAD ACTUALLY STOPPED SNOWING, yet the wind sent gusts of snow into the air, giving the impression of a continuous downfall. Yelena pulled her collar up around her neck and wrapped her neck scarf around her head. She thought of Aunt Sofia, as she tied the scarf under her chin. *What would she have said about this outrageous behavior of hers?* She shuddered at the thought, even though she'd never known Aunt Sofia to be judgmental about a single thing. No matter. Yelena stood in plenty of judgment against herself. What in God's good name was she thinking, sleeping with Jake? Where were her scruples, morals, spiritual virtues? Gone, gone, gone, melted away in the presence of the handsome, kind Jake Thompson, the only palpable refuge she'd felt in the raging storm of her recent life. Except for Ljuba. Ljuba was a safe harbor, and that was where she was headed, directly to her big sis, her mentor, her best friend, her Ljuba.

It took Ljuba all of fifteen seconds to perceive what had happened with Yelena that night. It was fully dawn by the time Yelena put the key in the door, and found, of course, Ljuba up with coffee made. Ljuba looked at her sister and hummed. Yelena told her to be quiet, and she went to the bathroom, took a shower, and came out wrapped in a warm robe and a towel around her head.

"Coffee, sis?" Ljuba thought that was an unobtrusive place to start. Yelena nodded, as she sat speechless. Staring at the Christmas tree all lit up, she wished she could close her eyes and wake up in the open field behind her Aunt Sofia's house, with her boy, alive, healthy and bronzed by the sun. She wished to come to and have the last three months be a big mistake that never happened, and never could happen, to anyone, anywhere. So she poured out her evening to Ljuba, expecting chastisement, and instead, got two perfectly fried eggs placed before her, along with a thick slice of warm bread, freshly made.

"Eat." Ljuba commanded. That meant she was getting ready to speak, and she preferred it if Yelena had a mouthful when she pontificated.

"Well, I don't know, Yelena," she began, when in fact she knew very well exactly what her counsel was going to be. She liked to start with an opening that would make it seem as if they would both arrive at Ljuba's conclusion together. "I mean, you see him everyday, you have lunch together, or whatever you call it. You talk, you share your experiences. Hell, Henry and I were already engaged after three weeks, and I think I'd only seen him twice during that time. But of course, we talked every day, two, three times a day, really." Ljuba flew into a memory of their courtship, "I remember once he called me so many times that Uncle Anton threatened to have the phone removed so he could listen to his radio news without interruption, and once…." Ljuba looked up at Yelena, and saw that she was not buying it, so she changed tactics. "Okay, maybe that's not a good example. But, honey, you've got to at least begin to look forward."

"Why, Ljuba? Why? Better yet, how? How am I to begin to look forward, huh?"

Nothing she could say would sit right with Yelena when she was at odds with herself.

"I mean, I understand, honey," Ljuba persevered, "but Jake is a good man, after all."

"How do you know that, Ljuba? Huh? You only met him once."

The phone rang, and in the midst of their whispering debate, it invaded the morning like a 22 rifle gone off in a china shop.

"I know, because he's calling to make sure you're okay." Ljuba topped her, picked up the phone triumphantly, with her sweetest voice, as if this were the most normal hour of the day to be calling someone. "Hello-o…yes…yes, Jake, she's fine. And how are you doing?"

Yelena, not trusting what her sister might say, reached to grab the phone from her hands, though she herself had no desire to have a conversation with Jake just then. On the other hand, if she wasn't going to talk to Jake, nobody was going to, by golly. Ljuba dodged her, and held onto the phone.

"Well, she's in the bathroom," Ljuba lied. "But listen, while I've got you on the phone…" she continued.

Yelena was chasing her around the kitchen table. The ruckus woke Henry, who stepped into the living room, gazed at the two of them in the kitchen, couldn't make sense of it, shook his head and went back to bed. Meantime, Ljuba was in the middle of an invitation to Jake, and Yelena was doing her best sign language to communicate to her sister to "get off the bleeping phone, and don't you dare invite him to anything, whatsoever." Oops. Too late. There she went.

"We'd love to invite you over for our family Name Day Celebration – it's called 'Slava' and it means Glory…yes, that's right, 'Slava'…uh-huh…a very special holiday for us…anyway…yes…yes, she'd love it, it was actually her idea…."

By then Yelena surrendered. She knew Ljuba was easily as stubborn as she was, and there was no stopping her.

Ljuba went on, undaunted, "It's on the twenty-seventh of January…yes, just a few weeks from now…Great!…anytime after six. No, she's still in the shower…but I'll tell her, yes…and Jake, bring your son, we'd love to have him, too. Yelena told me all about him. Of course….We'll expect you both then. Bye-bye, Jake."

Ljuba barely got the phone back to its cradle before she let out an "Ooooooo, sis, he's is sooooooo nice." Yelena sat at the table, head in hands.

"We'll have to plan a special menu for Slava this year," Ljuba announced as she refilled Yelena's cup with coffee, and grabbed a notepad and pencil, so they could commence their plans. Yelena wanted to disappear. Ljuba wanted to create something new, or perhaps simply witness the newness of life's opportunities God provides each day. "We are so blessed," Ljuba said as she began scribbling on the pad. Yelena played with her eggs with a fork, appetite gone. Ljuba noticed, but without looking up, whispered, "Eat, honey, they're getting cold."

Yelena looked at her sister with astonishment, admiration, and rapidly evaporating anger.

"And by the way, Yelena, don't forget that Henry and I are leaving for a couple of days right after Christmas for our anniversary. We're just going to New Jersey, to a hotel he likes, and you'll have the girls. Henry already talked to Casey, told him that'd you'd miss a few days. You should maybe let Jake know." Yelena shook her head. Ljuba was indefatigable, barking orders, writing a grocery list, drinking coffee and counseling her sister to keep moving forward, all at the same time. Those two Serbian sisters, nothing quite like them.

CHAPTER THIRTY-SEVEN

MORE THAN A WEEK WENT BY before Yelena was back at work. Jake phoned everyday. Everyday she avoided his call. Her nieces, however, were having a good time talking with him on the phone. Apparently Jake's fathering instincts were intact; he had a way with kids. Of course, Yelena loved mothering them while Ljuba and Henry were away. It took her mind off of her concerns about the night she spent with Jake. How unexpected, unpredictable, uncharacteristic, and unmanageable it all seemed. She chastised herself endlessly. What was she thinking to suddenly become the lover of a man she barely knew? And yet. There it was, that repeated refrain "and yet."

And yet, she did know him, she felt close to him. Was it because he was basically her only new friend here in America? Or was there the kindred understanding of two individuals who loved their sons, one lost, one in trouble? Perhaps it was simply that they suffered similar challenges, maybe it was that their hearts wrenched in like manner. Or did they? Americans were so cool compared to the Slavic firebrand. And yet, maybe not, maybe all was one. What was going on inside her? It was as if she was afflicted with post- traumatic stress disorder from the loss of her son, and the move to a new country, and the cure she chose was the additional post-traumatic shock of making love to a man she'd met only two months earlier. Was that what was meant by "the hair of the dog that bit you?" If you live in terror, do something to terrorize yourself even more? Not funny.

Yelena had one foot in her new life in New York, and one in Byzantium. Centuries lay betwixt her stride. How could she reconcile such vastly different ways of life? She couldn't and she wouldn't. She would be who she is, and always had been. She would continue to be faithful to her own values and to the memory of her son and the memory of her husband, and the memory of what it was like to be a woman in her village, despite the fact that the taste of Jake a week ago had turned her inside out. The screeching brakes of the train pulling into her subway stop graciously brought her conflicting thoughts to an unarguable halt.

Yelena ran up the stairs into the Midtown Manhattan winter with a spring in her step. Refreshed from a short while away from the grind, and renewed by the precious time spent with her nieces, she carried herself with the sway of womanhood, unselfconscious, confident and ingenuous. Nevertheless, she caught the eye of a gentleman on the street, who turned his head around twice to take in the gait of this filly. Then the man who happened to be Jake suddenly realized he knew her, and yes, in the Biblical sense. *Wow,* he thought, *I forgot how ravishing she is!*

"Yelena!" he called out. She turned and flashed him that smile that made him feel sixteen, all over. "Happy New Year, beautiful," he continued and stepped into tempo with her rhythmic walk.

"Happy New Year to you, Jake!"

"I've missed you, where you been? You don't take my calls, I mean, your two personal assistants, Nadya and Annie take my calls, and I trust you got the messages, but I'm in a quandary here. What's happening? Between us, I mean?" He poured it all out in one breath. That was not his intention. He meant to be cool, coy, test the waters, but instead, like a blushing bridegroom, he showed his hand and there was nothing to do about it now but wait. They walked on a few strides, his heart stopped, and she finally replied.

"What's a quandary? Is that a giant hole in the ground."

"No, Gracie darlin', that's a quarry. Quandary is a…well, kinda like a mystery, or a confusion." He smiled at her. "Let's take a little walk. Casey will forgive you if you're a few minutes late. Hell, he'll be happy just to have you back after a week." He took her elbow and steered her toward Rockefeller Center, where he knew they could sit and talk for a minute. Jake needed some answers. He didn't do well with unresolved things. Made him skittish, like the high-strung thoroughbred that he was. Close as they were the other night in his apartment, and then as far from her as he felt when she didn't take his calls, well, it had him confused. It had been decades since he'd hung on the response of a woman, waited for it, needed to have it. They walked in silence and before long they found themselves at skater-filled ice quarry of Rockefeller Center.

New York was doing what New York did best, creating a picture of unmatchable magic on the ice in the middle of a grey winter eve. Splashes of radiant colors moving as if suspended in space, sculpting out that ethereal sound of frozen water being scraped by a blade, leaving signatures of sharpened steel. Jake himself never had grown jaded to this particular holiday scene. It gave him a sense of well being, as if no matter what was happening in the news, Norman Rockwell was nearby reassuring New Yorkers that America was going to survive, because skaters were gliding on the ice, not falling through it. He and Yelena leaned against the rail, looking down at the rink, listening to the holiday music, watching the flood of brightly clad bodies illuminated by the tower of Christmas tree lights. Yelena was spellbound.

"Beautiful, isn't it?"

"Yes," Yelena breathed, "very beautiful."

Jake put a packet of chestnuts and a rose into her gloved hand. He would make this a ritual between them since last time she charmed him by pretending to eat them with the shells on, feigning an old country custom It did make him wonder what other tricks she had up her sleeve. She slayed him with her guileless humor.

"Thank you."

They stood in silence for moments that felt like hours to Jake, until he placed the Barney's bag he'd been carrying on the ledge in front of Yelena, and commanded her to open it.

"What is this?" she asked.

"The answer to that is on the inside of the box." As often happened, the giver was more caught up in the revelation of the gift than the receiver. He hoped he purchased well, and won Yelena's approval. He awaited the verdict, holding his breath, like he was about to win the World Series for the Yankees if he just threw one more perfect pitch. Things went to slow motion as Jake watched Yelena tear open the gift-wrapped box from Barney's. She smiled as she relished the soft fur lining of the fashionable silver suede boots. She stripped off her glove and her hand disappeared inside the boot. *Its lining felt softer than the tummy of her baby rabbit,* she thought. *Maybe it was mink!* Yelena couldn't imagine how very expensive a gift like this must have been. She blushed, reluctantly retrieved her hand from the padded cell of luxury and gently pushed the box toward Jake.

"Thank you," she murmured, "but I cannot accept them." Turning back to the ice skaters, she hoped that Jake wouldn't notice the tears welling up in the corners of her dark hazel eyes. How could she tell him that deep in her soul she felt she deserved no such joy as he had given her? The loss of her son had excavated a part of her that could never be filled with any human affection or aftermath.

She should have gotten to her son in time. She should have saved him. She should have been killed, not him. Those were her daily stirrings since that fated September day, mere months ago. But she'd never reasoned it out so clearly before. Here it was, an invitation for joy. How could she accept it? It didn't fit. She didn't know how to carry joy. It was like being invited to a ball, for which she had no gown. She couldn't go. She couldn't accept. She couldn't step forward. She couldn't go back. She couldn't redo, or undo what was done. She just couldn't. She could not.

"Sure you can," Jake said in that easy way like water lapping onto a dry rock, making it shine. "Just say, 'you're a prince. Jake, how'd you know my size.'"

"I can't." She took a deep breath, and froze before the exhale. So did Jake. He knew what was coming, and wanted to duck. "You see, Jake, the other night, well…that was wrong. I'm not married…and…"

"I know. I'm not married either. That makes it all right," Jake blurted, hoping that if he said it fast, he would stave off the rejection galloping toward him, ambushing his heart.

"Not for me, it doesn't make it all right. Not at all…" she stammered. "I'm sorry, Jake, I…I shouldn't have…I…maybe I had too much slivovitz."

"Oh, Yelena, don't take it back."

In that dark hallway of not knowing your own mind, nevertheless having to define yourself, in spite of your ignorance of yourself, one searches for a way to explain oneself. All Yelena could manage was, "Maybe I'm too old-fashioned, but I can't do this like this…I…"

"Okay, then, we'll get married." Jake was ready to get down on one knee when she startled him with a substantial increase in volume, which surprised him.

"What! No…I, I can't."

Jake went in for the kill. "You mean you can't tonight. But next week? or next month?…or even…next year?"

"I don't know…" she confessed, "I don't know myself anymore."

"Yelena, you can't mourn forever."

"Maybe you are right, Jake, and I am wrong about everything. I don't know. I can't explain it. I only know that I'm not done yet."

Unrelenting, he persevered, "Not done with what, Yelena?"

She looked him in the eye, which nearly undid him, but he held.

"I love you, Yelena." It was barely audible, but there it was, the profession of truth.

"You don't know me."

"Oh great, now I don't know you. Great. First, you don't know you, now I don't know you. Nobody knows anybody anymore, great. Okay, it's one big mystery."

Yelena was riveted to his every word, and he thought he was making some headway so he ventured on. He wouldn't let the old world ways win out.

"You know what, Gracie, I DO know you. But you're right, I'm rushing, and excuse me for that, but I just don't want to lose you." He lowered his head and wound the string from the Barney's package around his hand, hoping to collect his thoughts into an irresistible argument. He made another attempt.

"And what is it I have to know, anyway? You have a secret identity or something? I know the important things about you, Yelena. I do. What more is there to know? Three months we see each other every night, talk together, eat together, work together, what? Oh, okay, do you like waxed or unwaxed floss? Now that I don't know." He spoke with the velocity of an auctioneer at a county fair. As often was the case between them, she responded with an entirely different rhythm.

"What's a floss?"

Jake paused only to take a breath, and stifle a chuckle; she killed him, and on he rolled, "You know what, Yelena, all right, here goes, here's what I know: you're strong, you're soft, I know you ache, yet you endure, and you're funny as all get out, but you don't even know it. You're the real thing, Gracie, and I like it. I mean, come on, life flies by. It's over after the opening paragraph. Look what happened to your son..." he stopped mid-sentence. He'd gone too far.

Yelena turned to him and suddenly looked like a stranger. All at once the curtain fell, and he had no idea what was behind it. "Thank you for the chestnuts, Jake, and the rose." She walked back toward the news building, and he quickly gathered up the boots and followed her.

"And you got manners, which is nice. And morals, which is radical...and it ain't over till the fat lady sings, and she's not even in costume yet..." This metaphor, totally lost on Yelena, did not stop Jake. Undaunted, he followed her, continuing to talk to her back, then offered his final licks. "And anyway, your sister invited me to your...uh...your...Glory Day, or something!"

Yelena paused, and threw back, "Slava!"

"Yeah, Slava." Jake stood still and watched her go, while he tossed the boots back into the Barney's bag with every intention of seeing them on her feet one day. He didn't know how, but he was determined to make that happen. That was the key to the kingdom with him, regarding his journalism and everything else, his fathering, his loving, his being. Adverbs never interested him. "How" something was done was immaterial. "That" it was done, was all that counted. Within legal bounds, of course...well, mostly.

That he was going to Slava was what mattered in that moment. It's all he had to hold onto. How she'd treat him when he got there, well, that was something he and Miss Scarlet would worry about tomorrow, or some other day.

Wet snow began to fall, unable to make up its mind whether to be rain or snow, but set on being sloppy. Great. Fine. No problem. He walked on, Barney's bag in one hand, smoldering Marlboro in the other, a perfect balance of testosterone and testosterone. Jake was not a quitter.

CHAPTER THIRTY-EIGHT

THE WEEKS THAT FOLLOWED FOUND YELENA MORE ALONE THAN EVER. She barely stopped for lunch at work, and Jake barely stopped soliciting any scintilla of attention from her. Throughout this rift in their romance, he pushed on in his research about Bosnia, Kosovo and the volatile history of the Balkans. He was convinced it was not just because Yelena was a Balkan beauty that he found himself fascinated with this strangely complex, mystical, primitive yet sophisticated culture of this Eastern pocket of the European continent, but also because it seemed never to have been fully understood or accurately portrayed in the rest of Europe, not to mention in America. He took it as his own personal challenge. He was going to be the one to do it, to unveil the mystery, to illuminate the arcane caverns, to unravel the yarn of Serbia's past, and in doing so, maybe he'd come closer to understanding this woman who had captured his heart. Who knows, the Sunday magazine feature he had in mind, and the book that would follow, might also heal him from his phantom failures of recent months. Anyway you turned the page, he was back in the saddle, on a mission, to find the Holy Grail of Bosnia, Kosovo and Montenegro – all of which was Serbia at one time or another.

What had happened? The more he learned about the long history of conflict over there, the more that the West's perception of this sovereign nation appeared to be predicated upon major misinformation communicated by yes, even his own beloved newspaper. Was he ready to take that on? Not one to buy into conspiracy theories of any sort, Jake was struck that all the heinous crimes of the war had been attributed to one side only, the Serbs. No civil war had ever been recorded or reported that way, because that was not the way civil wars went. One side wasn't planting flowers while the other side made bombs, it just didn't work that way. That much he knew.

One night he actually decided to go in to work early, which is to say, four o'clock in the afternoon as opposed to his customary 6:30

or 7:00 in the evening when it was safe to assume his colleagues had more or less fled for the day, sparing himself their random pejorative remarks about the erratic hours he kept. And lo and behold, this particular day, he found the editor of the Sunday magazine feature section sitting on the edge of his desk, presumably waiting for him, or just snooping as bosses are wont to do.

She, Ms. Tamar Schenkin, was talking on his desk phone while flipping shamelessly through the papers on his desk. Tamar Schenkin. Jake was sure that there had once been an "a" on the end of Tamar but that her pursed jaw and sour face had sliced it off years ago. A terrifying woman from Tennessee, with a Ph.D. in Southern U.S. literature, she had written a book entitled *From Faulkner to Williams and Back Again,* which got her on some list for some time that impressed some somebody and landed her a job that she was only marginally qualified to do. "She would grow into it," some said. Well, she was his boss, that's all that counted, and she showed no mercy with her editorial pen when it came to Jake's writing.

She'd had it out for him since he'd stopped "producing" during recent months, when his marriage had officially crashed, and he had refused a number of assignments out of the country. He simply knew he wouldn't have been able to deliver at that time, especially with his son having serious troubles. Tamar was unforgiving. She found it to be a sign of weakness, a missing chit in the DNA of true manhood, and she was going to whip that sensitivity out of any man that was on her feature staff. She was a believer in the Southern "pull yourself up by the bootstraps and get back on that pony and ride" philosophy of life. He believed that as well, but they were on different time frames. Hell, even Napolean gave his troops a night to rest before Waterloo. He thought he'd merited the same respite since he had produced award winningly well before the crack in his armor. Tamar saw things differently. She had replaced Jake's notion of a gentle southern belle with the image of the peculiar monsters in Goya's paintings, hungry at all times, looking to swipe, destroy or devour with the flick of a paw, anything the monster's yellow eyes deemed delectable. Therefore, it was understandable that Jake approached his very own cubicle a bit cautiously that day.

"What's this about?" she demanded, waving a bundle of clippings about Bosnia in his face.

"Tamar, hello! What a lovely surprise." Tamar was the only woman besides his dear ex-wife Sigrid, of whom he was certifiably frightened. Her lipstick was always over her lip line, like a bad Joan Crawford imitator. Her suit was always too tight, her stockings always smoky black and always had a run in them going up the back, making her look as if she might be a distracted and possibly talented misfit. Not so. Her shoulders were sporting dandruff, her coif was a day slept on, and she smelled vaguely of cheap cologne covering body odor. He couldn't imagine what Mr. Tamar looked like, and her left ring finger proclaimed that there was indeed a Mr. Tamar. Jake pictured him in a skirt, with a lollipop made of cyanide, waiting for the moment to swill it into her nightly martini, or suck it down himself.

"Cut it, Jake. They tell me upstairs that you've requested every article about the Balkans written since cave dwellers scratched news on the wet walls of Lascaux. Where're you going with this? The Balkans have calmed down now. NATO got it under control. Everybody knows what happened; we've done the overdrive on those stories. Nobody cares anymore. There are a few other things to be writing about, Jakey."

"Really, Tamar, like what?" He couldn't wait to hear what she thought was a priority for news reportage.

"Like a drug cartel that made a major slip-up in Montclart, Colombia, and the president is peeing all over himself with the opportunity to look good on the war on drugs, so I want a nine-article series on this to start running in two weeks, which means you leave on Saturday, and you pack for a couple of seasons."

"Do I have a say in this?" Jake was practically begging, as he felt his knees go weak at the thought of what he calculated would be a least three to four months south of the equator, far away from New York and his Serbian siren.

"Yes, Jakey, you do. You get to say, 'Yes, Tamar, I'm going right home to pack and to burn the Bosnian notes and win you a Pulitzer Prize for this series of articles that you'll be editing, and that may well lead to a PBS series.' Then I say, 'Good boy, Jakey, so glad you came to your senses, because Kosovo and all that jazz ain't gonna get us any kudos from no damned body.' Got it?"

"Loud and clear, Tamar, loud and clear." He couldn't resist, "But fyi, Tamar, dear, it is actually the Balkans that would be your prize winning feature series. What has truly gone on there has yet to be reported, and yours truly is to going to change all that, and let the world know the truth, and win you a prize in Sweden. I mean another one. P.S., the drug stories in this burg are coming out of the wall everyday, there's no real noteworthy mileage in them anymore. They've been done to death, excuse the pun."

"And what, Mr. Thompson, do you consider the truth, as you call it, to be over there in the big, bad Balkans?" She straightened and crossed her arms, and worked her height to her advantage. He hated that, as much as he did when she called him Mr. Thompson. Nostrils flaring, she was waiting for him to bite and fight fire with fire. For a moment, she almost looked sexy in a predatory kind of way. He thought he best not go there, so he didn't.

"Well, Ms. Schenkin, for starters, the KLA is not made up of so-called ethnic Albanians, but rather a group filtered out of Afghanistan under the auspices of you know who, our very own little cave dweller, Mr. Bin Laden, the Al-Queda ring leader."

"Right, and why would they want to bother with Bosnia or Kosovo or the damned Adriatic for that matter, one might ask."

"One certainly might, mightn't one? And one might answer thusly: A: Plutonium in the Shar Mountains, you know plutonium, dontcha Ms. S., one of the primary ingredients for nuclear weapons? B: A warm water corridor to the East, you know the East dontcha Ms. S, Turkey, Russia, China, you've heard of them. And C: Call me crazy, but dare I say it, the creation of yet another Islamic nation, right in the middle of the Jerusalem of Eastern Orthodoxy, where more than 1000 Orthodox monasteries have existed for hundreds of years, a tad before the Albanian Muslims migrated illegally to Serbia during World War II, while the Serbs were busy rescuing American fighter pilots from behind enemy lines. That enemy at that time, Ms. S., would be Adolf, with an f, you know, the guy your grandparents found so hospitable in Poland.

With that, she picked up the pile of clippings she had tossed into his trash basket and walked off with them.

"We'll just see about all that, won't we now. In the meantime, pack. I hear khaki is good down there, this time of year." She breathed between her gargantuan teeth, and stormed past Jake, leaving a definitive waft of bad breath behind her.

The gauntlet had been thrown down, but by whom? All Jake could think of was that "Slava" was the next night, and that he would be leaving a few days after that. Now that was a juxtaposition of events he would not have chosen, and could not have seen coming. A lousy deal on all fronts; where was the glory in that?

CHAPTER THIRTY-NINE

SLAVA. GLORY DAY. HOLY DAY. Day of the Protecting Saint of the Household. Day of the former Pagan Deity of the Home. Day of Celebration of Christian Conversion. Day of Trading Many gods for One God. A most Sacred day. And yet the occasion called for a not so solemn Dionysian celebration that was unlike anything Jake had ever witnessed in the ol' U. S. of A. The tradition dictated that just about everyone the family knew or was acquainted with, come and grace their home and eat and drink and celebrate, well, Glory, he guessed. The custom was distinctive to the Serbians, and in fact, in Yelena's village, Slava could last up to three days, in order to accommodate all who wished to come and be blessed by the sacrosanct anniversary of the family's acceptance of Christianity, several hundred years before.

This ancient religiosity would come to be the greatest mystery of all to Jake, regarding his newborn love for Yelena and her world. He couldn't figure how the reference point for their everyday life and current customs hailed from so many centuries ago. Nothing short of half a millennium, usually. *Small wonder there was mounting chaos over there,* he thought, *they've had it going for quite some time, they're in the rhythm of mega yesterday.*

This day, however, this Holy Day which celebrated and praised their faith was like a huge birthday party. Hospitality was offered to all friends, acquaintances and even passing strangers. No one was turned away, nor should anyone refuse the invitation, not that it would ever have crossed Jake's mind to refuse. Jake and Tony dressed in their Sunday best and rode the train up to Queens, bottle of slivovitz from the Polish Deli in one hand and a large bouquet of yellow roses in the other. Jake sat there, looking dazed and with a slightly pouting look on his face.

Tony couldn't help but laugh, "Dad, what's up, you look like you're about to throw up. I thought this was a party we're going to, not a funeral, for goodness sake."

"Never mind, wise guy, I just...uh...my shoes are too tight and my feet are killing me," he confessed.

"Yeah, but they sure are shiny." Tony chuckled again. Rarely were the tables turned in a direction that permitted his son the upper hand over his father.

"And look at you, what are you, Batman, with the running shoes! How'd I let you out of the house like that, huh?"

"I don't know. I guess you were too busy thinking about which socks you were going to wear. And I guess you couldn't make up your mind, huh."

"What?" Jake looked down, and saw he had one brown sock on and one black one. "Oh, for Chrissakes!"

"Don't worry about it dad, it looks nice, it's cool, you've got that, absent-minded professor thing working real good."

"Well. Not good. Well. Adverb, not adjective, Tone."

"Well, well, well, said the Prince of Denmark." Tony topped his dad. Jake muffled his delight, looked out the window at the stations flying by on the express train, and thought hard about what he had to tell Yelena that night. Conflicted would be a mild description of his insides at that moment. "In love" might be another way of putting it. His son noticed his dad was in this most rare and vulnerable condition. And he liked it. He respected that his dad had this softer side.

Jake and son, two restless mustangs heading up the block toward Ljuba's brownstone, gave an impression of having been let out of the barn for an evening run, Jake leading the way.

"Hey Dad, slow down, what's the rush?" Tony queried.

Jake ignored the question, and shoved the bottle of Slivovitz, brightly wrapped in that distinctive liquor store blue, red and silver gift bag, into Tony's hands. "Here, you carry this, I'll take the flowers."

"Okay, Dad." Tony watched his dad's every move, like he had never seen him before in his life.

Immediately, Jake grabbed back the liquor and handed Tony the flowers. "No, on second thought, you give 'em these, I'll take that."

"Okay."

"No, here, you take both of 'em," Jake decided and loaded Tony's arms with all the goodies, leaving his hands empty, and uncertain as to where they should land.

"Okay, Dad." They continued clipping along at quite a pace. "A little jumpy, aren't you? What is she, royalty or something?" Tony wanted the scoop on this dame.

"Never mind, smart guy, gimme those." Jake took the bouquet and the bottle back into his own custody and carried them both, balancing them skillfully while he reached into his jacket pocket to check the address written on a matchbook. They had arrived in front of the building where Yelena lived.

"Okay. This is the place. Behave yourself now, son."

"Yeah, you too, Dad. Don't worry about me."

Jake took a deep breath and Tony provided him with a little manly reassurance, "You look good in that jacket, Dad."

"Do I? Thanks." Jake almost smiled until he realized he had no way to ring the bell or open the door, and was completely dependent on his son for assistance.

"I'll get the door, Dad." Tony loved his new role as savior, and stifled a smile behind his father's back, as he let Jake pass through the door first, fumbling with the flowers, as if he were going to his junior prom. *What a guy,* Tony thought, *I love this guy.* They were buzzed in and they ascended the stairs to the third floor, passing a couple of guys enjoying a cigar and a shot. They greeted Jake and his son in a foreign tongue, but with great warmth.

This Slava gig was in full swing. It was impossible to decipher how big the apartment was, or even what it looked like, since every inch of it was filled with people, pressed together, gaily dressed, clinking their wine glasses and talking non-stop at full volume, having a jolly time. Jake took it in like a kid at a carnival. There was a palpable sense of joy and well-being amidst the guests. They'd barely passed the threshold before they were enfolded into the flock of festivities. Though Jake had done his customary research on the holiday, he mainly learned of its religious significance, the holiness of the day. But the level of laughter and celebration in that flat reflected more of a feeling of a V-Day celebration on the streets of Paris. It poured out onto the fire escape and he later learned that even the bathroom had become a place for conversation and connection. There, two women lingered over their lipstick application, soon to be blotted off onto the filter tips of their Kools.

Yelena wove her way from the kitchen toward Jake. She squeezed past guests with varying levels of blood alcohol content, and met his arms ready to receive her with her warm smile that lit up those fiery gypsy eyes.

"Sretna Slava, Yelena!" he blurted in Brooklynese.

"Oh! How did you learn how to say that, Jake?" She laughed and gave him a big hug, melting away their recent hiatus, and returned the greeting with three kisses on the cheek, as tradition demanded.

"Some guys in the hallway coached me," he admitted. "This is my son, Tony."

Tony extended his hand, and she surprised him with a big hug.

"Welcome, Tony, how wonderful to meet you," Yelena beamed, and when she looked directly into his eyes that so reflected his father, she almost began to weep.

Possessing his father's sense of grace and timing he responded quickly, "The pleasure is all mine, Ma'am."

"Call me Yelena, honey," she said, and guided them toward the kitchen where Ljuba, Henry, the children and Father Risto eagerly awaited meeting Jake.

The kitchen was doubling as a dining room...actually, the whole apartment was. Two long tables had been joined together to make one extended one that started in the kitchen and ended in the hallway which led to the bedrooms. The table was flanked with people, though no one was seated yet. They were all swimming around, eating exotic appetizers and enjoying the glorious aromas of the imminent feast.

"Wow, it smells good in here," Tony couldn't help himself. He had the appetite of a healthy young man, and gave his father a thumbs-up on Yelena and the whole scene. Jake was pleased, like the parent in pursuit of the pup's approval.

"I hope you both have hunger." Yelena teased. Jake had never seen her like this, so completely at ease, happy even, in her own element, with her family and friends, honoring a tradition that obviously had great significance to them all.

"Don't worry, Yelena, we got plenty of hunger, don't we Tony?"

"Way hunger, Dad. Way."

"I want you to meet my family." She introduced Jake and Tony to everyone standing around in the kitchen and even to some of the folks who were all the way across the room. They shouted introductions back and forth, and exchanged "Sretna Slavas" and toasts, and it all felt as if they'd known each other a lifetime. It was loving, tribal, inclusive, meaningful and so very Yelena. Jake loved it, and he noticed his son, was smiling and happy for the first time in a long time. Tony was bookended by Annie and Nadya who were smitten with having a handsome boy in their midst. They were giving him a tour of their Queens palace, explaining to everyone that he was their new cousin. Where they got that, no one knew.

Jake had an immediate simpatico with Henry. They were both smarter than they would ever let on, each one a man's man: drinkers, cigar smokers, lovers of women and considered a Sunday football game, feet up and beer in hand, to be heaven on earth. New York men, Brooklyn, Bronx, didn't matter, they knew who they were, and they acted like it. Henry sized Jake up-and-down. He didn't want just anybody hanging out with his "sis in law." He would give it some time, before he'd pass his final judgment. If anyone tried to take advantage of Yelena, he'd be sorry, that was for sure. Henry had his own tribal rules; they weren't necessarily Slavic, but they were your basic rules of the jungle.

"Oh, you brought us some slivovitz, thanks! You wanna a shot, might help you get warmed up, here." Henry was already pouring out three shots, for himself, Jake, and Father Risto.

"Thanks." Jake held up his glass and made another attempt at Sretna Slava, followed by "Zhivali!"

"Ahhhh, Zhivali, Zhivali," chimed in Father Risto, "you speak our language, eh?"

"Not really, Father, only three words, Sretna Slava and Zhivali," Jake said apologetically.

"A good choice of words," Father Risto laughed.

The frenzy of the "cocktail hour" seemed to have come to a pinnacle, so Henry took the helm. "All right everyone, gather around, we're going to have the prayer and blessing by Father Risto, and then, you guessed it, we're going to eat like kings. I happen to know the cooks."

Yelena and Jake stood very close to each other during the prayers. Father Risto chanted something in Old Slavonic and poured wine from a small glass pitcher onto the round Holy Bread, which he broke in half and kissed one end, then offered it to Henry and Ljuba to kiss, then their daughters, a ritual reserved for the family of the household.

The priest held everyone's attention with his simplicity and focus in the performing of each of the rites, and he maintained a subtle good humor about each act. So that when Annie called out, "Father Risto, can Tony kiss the bread?"

Father Risto didn't miss a beat, but offered the bread up to Tony to kiss it.

"Now you must show him how to cross himself, Annie."

Father Risto waited patiently while Annie patiently instructed the well-brought-up Catholic boy in the way of Orthodox genuflecting. Jake found the moment filled with such warmth and kindness, that his eyes filled with tears. Yelena squeezed his hand, and his macho side demanded he cover his emotion with a fake cough. Yelena's tenderness was not lost on him, not at all.

The short service was completed with a recitation of the Lord's Prayer, first in Old Slavonic and then in English, followed by an "Amen" in unison. Even Henry's Jewish mother, Miriam, joined in the blessing. Then the table, laid with beautiful white china with a silver pattern, crystal wine glasses, bread, olives, figs, wine, goat cheese, was suddenly surrounded with hungry, happy, freshly blessed guests. "Priatno!" came the cry from Father Risto and various guests, which Jake figured out meant, "Enjoy" or "Bon appetit." Indeed.

Henry pulled out the chair at the head of the table for Father Risto, and complimented him, "Father, thank you for the blessing. You do that so beautifully, it's enough to make me convert." Father Risto chuckled as if he'd heard that a hundred times before, and then from across the table came Miriam's voice, like a great bell, tolling a warning.

"Over my dead body." That only made Father Risto laugh more loudly, and with his innate grace, he responded.

"Oh Miriam, you look so lovely tonight, you must come to sit at my side."

This softened Miriam immediately. She was widowed. And Father Risto was a very handsome man, though married and faithful, he could certainly charm the ladies with his Christly sweetness. Miriam was cool, but she relented, "Well, thank you, Father, I'd be delighted." She smiled and slid over to his side, only to be intercepted by Ljuba's plea for aid.

"Save that seat for her, Father. I need her help with the lamb first," Ljuba smiled.

Meanwhile, Yelena was heaping large helpings of stuffed cabbage onto Tony's plate, and then Jake's. "I made this," she announced to the two beautiful bucks on either side of her.

Jake whispered to her, "A Yugoslavian dish made by a Yugoslavian dish."

He smiled, she blushed. Tony shook his head, rolled his eyes at this corny side of his dad, and dug into his plate. Oblivious that his son was listening, Jake continued his boyish flirtation, "It smells so good, Yelena."

Henry caught that exchange, and looked at Jake, waiting for the punch line. He couldn't imagine that any measure of love or infatuation could bring that statement out of any sane man, since the smell of the stuffed cabbage dish was the only thing about it that Henry abhorred. Seeing Jake was sincere, Henry just shook his head, and figured he himself must be the only one in the house with functioning olfactory glands.

Jake continued, "Your favorite, huh, son?"

Tony couldn't resist, "Actually, Dad, I like the 'other' Yugoslavian dish better."

Jake, slightly embarrassed at the realization that his son had heard him, "All right, smart alec, just eat."

Father Risto raised a glass of wine to make another toast, continuing to unify this group in joy, "Sretna Slava!" Various guests echoed the toast, most with their mouths already full of roast lamb, bread, cheese, olives, cabbage, pita, figs and the liquid inspiration of their lives, red wine.

The preparation that was involved during the weeks before Slava was nothing short of arranging for a royal wedding. It all meant so much to those who prepared for their guests, whom they thought it a privilege to feed and honor. Every detail was tended to by the loving hands of Ljuba and Yelena. In Ljuba's household, all was under her command, and Yelena was a willing worker. Even Henry fell into line. And though his mother, Miriam, longed for this to be a Bar Mitzvah celebration instead of a date marking Christian conversion, she still participated in the festivities wholly and lovingly. It was a profoundly religious holiday celebrated in a wildly pagan manner, reflecting another one of the many fascinating incongruities of the Serbs.

Slava marked the actual date when their family took the religion of Christianity as their own and forsook their pagan gods, if not their heathen ways. Historians have often remarked that the level of indulgence in food, drink, laughter, music, and storytelling, reflected more the pagan ways that they were leaving behind, than the Christian ways they were meant to begin embracing. Nevertheless, it was a kind of Mardi Gras of the Soul, when a particular family said good-bye to their old ways, forever, and agreed to the spiritual adventure of this strange, new clan of Christians instead. The good part was that they got to celebrate their good-bye to the pagan ways, over and over and over again, every year…a pretty good deal. It would be hard to say a final farewell to this much fun.

The meal went on for hours. Jake had never tasted anything so delicious, and neither had Tony. Roast leg of lamb that literally fell off the bone; it had been so tenderly roasted. Strudels bursting with fillings of cheese and spinach, held together by thin layers of dough, so thin that Tony whispered to his dad, "Do we eat the tissue paper, too?" Roast pork and roast chicken were also part of the fare, as well as spicy sausages called *cevapcici*, which sounded more like a dance than cuisine. Music boomed from the stereo, dancing pipes and accordions, wailing strings of mandolin and base, and a strange instrument called the *gusle*, a primitive string instrument that sounded like a violin bow rubbing against a violin bow. The dissonant sound it created was the backdrop for folk tales, usually cried out by the eldest member of the clan; folk songs of war heroes, loss of lives, undying courage, and God.

Jake thought he had died and been transported to the Middle Ages. He loved the conviction behind it all: the dedication to honor this custom, to commemorate the significance of the holy day, to celebrate so generously with their unconditionally open hearts. *What a people,* he thought. *How did this jibe with all that he was reading in his research?* He had so many questions, and now when he was inside the circle of Yelena's family, he would have to cap it by telling her he was leaving for a few months.

Suddenly, he detested the "career opportunity" that Schenkin had dropped in his lap like it was a treasure map to a mountain of gold. Gold he didn't desire, want or need. But it was a job he had to take, or Tamar would make his life living hell at the paper, he was certain of that. She demanded obedience. Now he resented the assignment and it hadn't yet begun. He got jerked out of this dark reverie by the strong smell of Turkish coffee being placed before him, followed by Yelena's gentle voice, "I'll read your fortune, drink it."

Jake thought he was imagining things, but she was serious. Another medieval practice, reading the grinds left in the coffee cup after the thick elixir had been imbibed, a curious way of reading the future. Jake smiled and took the cup to his lips. Over the lip of the cup, he glanced toward the other end of the long table, and saw his son taking on a challenge for chess from the eldest family member there, Uncle Jovan.

"So you play chess, young man?" Uncle Jovan asked between puffs on his corn cob pipe, which looked like it had been around since the Austro-Hungarian Empire.

"Yes, sir, I do." Tony responded with zeal, and began helping him set up the pieces. His two little helpers, Annie and Nadya, had not left his side since he arrived, and now they were going to be his good luck charms as he took on their ol' Uncle Jovan.

"Well, let's go, then. Prepare to lose," Uncle Jovan challenged.

"All right, sir, thank you. Same to you," Tony replied while Nadya and Annie shouted loud hurrahs, when he moved his first pawn forward.

Jake took this in with a grateful heart, then glanced back down at his nearly empty coffee cup. "You're going to read my future from this? It looks rather dark."

Yelena laughed and took his cup, then stopped laughing abruptly.

"What is it?" Jake demanded, "What do you see?" He was suddenly a believer when he saw her expression change from glee to doom and gloom.

"Nothing," she said. "I'm so out of practice, I can't see anything clear. Except, the cup reveals you just had a great meal."

"Well, that's certainly true," Jake concurred. "Yelena, let's get some air."

They rose from the table, Yelena clearing the last few cups. All that remained now were half-filled wine glasses and innumerable red wine stains on the white lace table cloth, with a huge bowl of dessert fruit and multilayered cakes in the middle. Jake noted that no one had run to pour salt or carbonated soda on the red wine stains. They just took it in stride, like all else that night, as if they were all in constant recognition that more important things were going on than spilled wine, like a conversion to God, for one. Besides, it was good luck, they claimed. Oy gevalt would be Henry's response to that. Jake rose from the table thinking that in all his years married to Sigrid, he'd never once sat at a joyful table like this one.

Yelena followed Jake to the door, grabbing a shawl from the back of a chair, and mentioned to her sister that they were stepping out for air. "About time," was Ljuba's sisterly reply.

As they passed the other end of the table, Yelena gave Uncle Jovan a kiss on the cheek, and advised him, "not to beat the boy too badly," in Serbian, of course. She wouldn't for the world, compromise Tony's pride. At the same time, Jake ruffled his son's hair and winked at him, as he noticed he was setting up to take Uncle Jovan's queen. As they stepped into the hallway, they heard, "Oh my God, he got my Zhena, already!" from the voice of the ebullient octogenarian.

Jake paused, "What's a Zhena?"

"The queen," Yelena replied.

"All right! That's my boy!" Jake rejoiced.

"It also means wife," Yelena added.

"Ah-hah! Now I'm beginning to get the hang of this culture of yours. Very interesting, my dear, the wife is the queen, hmmm!" And he put his arm around her, and as they closed the door behind them, they heard Uncle Jovan bemoan again, "Oh no!!!" followed by the cheers of Nadya and Annie. Tony had found a fan club for the first time in his tender, troubled twenty years. Yelena and Jake shared a chuckle as they strolled down the three flights of stairs.

They paused at the door. When Jake had arrived it was still light out, and now the night was pitch-dark, with a few snow flurries making their presence known. The wind came through the door. It jostled it open a bit and let in a sharp chill.

"It's cold out there, Jake, maybe we should get our coats." She started to head back up the stairs, when Jake grabbed her by the arm and spun her around into his embrace, then he backed her into the corner under the stairwell and held her close.

"Yelena," was all he could say. He held her for what seemed like a long time. She surrendered to his embrace. Finally, he said, "I know a little more about you now, you pagan gypsy queen, you." She smiled, happily nestled into his shoulder. "Thank you for asking me here tonight." She looked up at him and her eyes burned into his heart. He kissed her, and he felt her body fuse into his completely and whatever it was that kept them apart these past weeks evaporated. They were pressed together so tightly that the icy hallway suddenly felt like a sauna. Jake stole one more kiss to brace himself for the news he was about to break to his love.

"Yelena, listen to me," he began, finding it very difficult to say what he had to say while looking into the bottomless river of her hazel, brown eyes. "I'm being sent to Montclart, Colombia for a few months, to do a series of feature stories down there about drugs. Now that I don't want to leave New York my boss decides, I'm the only man for the job. I don't want to go, I don't want to leave you, but I must."

"Is it dangerous?"

"No. I don't think so, anyhow. It's just far, very far from all I love."

"Tony."

"Yes, Tony." He paused and took a breath, "And you, Yelena, you."

There was a pause that felt like an hour to Jake. He waited for her response to his profession of love, such as it was.

"When will you go?"

"You understand, I wouldn't go if I didn't have to, and if I didn't have piles of bills from my kid's rehab, I'd probably can it. But this could get me back on track, and if I'm going to create any kind of life for us…." He stopped, fearing he'd gone too far, too fast.

Yelena reassured him with a look that said this time he need not worry. She wanted him as he did her, even if she didn't know how to express it yet. And she was sorry he was leaving.

"Okay, Jake."

"Don't worry, I'll write and call, and before you know it, I'll be back."

"Okay, Jake." Beat. "When?"

"Saturday." He choked on that one, but recovered with, "And while I'm gone, I want you to think about how you can't live without me."

He kissed her again, before she had a chance to protest. There was something she wanted to say to Jake. "Jake, I…."

But before another syllable fell from her lips, the upstairs door opened, and Nadya and Annie and Tony came running down the stairs, all three calling out, "Aunt Yelena! Dad! Mrs. Mandich! We won! Tony won! Tony beat our Uncle Jovan." By the time they reached the bottom of the stairs, Jake and Yelena were there to catch them and applaud Tony's victory, and their own mixed triumph, in the hallway in Queens.

CHAPTER FORTY

MONTHS FLEW BY, THREE TURNED INTO FIVE, for Jake's journey. New York's summer humidity had already hit. It could suck the energy out of Superman. Barely summer solstice and nearing the last day of school for the kids, the village of Queens was experiencing power failures from too many air conditioners running on high, and a serious shortage of fans at all the local appliance stores. The heat was front page news. That particular June morning, Henry was delayed in leaving for work, as he was busy adding to the strain on the local power grids by installing an air conditioner in the kitchen which would hopefully cool off the entire apartment.

Yelena had trouble sleeping in recent weeks. She just couldn't get comfortable. Maybe it was the heat. Maybe not. No mountain breeze to take the edge off the moisture that virtually flooded her forehead as soon as head touched pillow. She was sitting at the kitchen table, directly in front of a small fan, sipping a Turkish coffee and writing. The girls had just flown out the door for school, jumping for joy that it was the last day and a half day at that, and Ljuba, having fed the troops, had gone into her room to dress.

Henry paused to pour himself some coffee, necessary fortification to finish the a/c installation. "Care for more coffee, Yelena?" he asked, approaching her with the coffee pot without waiting for her to respond, so he could disguise his desire to read over her shoulder with refilling her coffee cup. He imagined it to be a letter to Jake. Though it was in English, it had that funny European script that hands accustomed to the Cyrillic alphabet used, so he couldn't make out a word of it. It took him years to be able to decipher the signature at the bottom of the Valentines his wife had given him, even after they were married. *Odd lot,* he thought, *the whole bunch, but you gotta love 'em, they got heart,* he mused. "Whatcha writing, Yelena?" She made what she hoped was a subtle move to cover it with her hand.

"Nothing," she responded.

"Jake should be back any day now, eh?"

"Yes, that's what his phone message said last week," she confirmed.

"He did a helluva job with those articles, last one was printed last Sunday. I guess they traced the money trail on nine of those cartel leaders, right to some small wire transfers to New York. Man, oh man, 1.5 tons of cocaine, that's a lot of dough. Makes you wonder if some Colombian cops didn't pocket the other half a ton, you know what I mean? Hard to stay honest in a place like that." It was like the coffee had Henry high as a kite; he just kept yapping about Jake's articles; and it was all burning into Yelena's ears. Henry didn't notice she was about to explode. "He could win an award for that work, you know."

Ljuba came out of her bedroom in her bathing suit, and that shifted Henry's focus, fast. A woman of forty-five, she still had a great figure, and it didn't go unnoticed by her husband.

"Where you going dressed like that, babe? Jamaica?" Henry whistled at her, wrench in one hand, coffee cup in the other, he reached over for a kiss, which she accommodated, then pointed him back to his task at hand.

"I'm taking the girls to Jones Beach when I pick them up from school later, you knew that." She rushed around gathering towels, and making a picnic together lunch for them. "Would you like to join us, Yelena?"

"No, thanks, Ljuba, I'm working tonight, and I don't want to miss. It's payday." Yelena got up from the table with great effort and a sigh, placed the paper she was writing in her pocket, and took her cup to the sink, where she paused and looked out the window onto the fire escape. There were several potted plants there now, her doing, and one of them was a large red geranium with sturdy stems that often served as a young sparrow's resting place. The bird was poised on the geranium's branch and singing sweetly, welcoming in the summer equinox. Yelena felt homesick for the farm, and all the natural life there, which was so absent in New York. She leaned over and puked in the sink.

Ljuba ran to her side, "Yelena, honey, are you all right?" Yelena nodded, and apologized.

"It's kind of late for you to be getting sick to your stomach, you're six months now." Yelena nodded again and rubbed her very pregnant belly. "Why don't you lie down in my room, for a little while?" Yelena nodded for the third time and conceded, walking slowly into her sister and Henry's room, murmuring an "I'm sorry" to Henry as she passed him. He pretended not to see the whole incident. But when she was out of earshot, he launched into Ljuba.

"Number one, you're not going to the beach looking like that without me. Put something on. Borrow a suit from your sister, one with leggings."

"Henry, how sweet of you to think I'd turn heads at my age." She continued making sandwiches with no intention of changing out of her two piece bathing suit.

"Number two, remind me what we are telling our daughters about this again? That it just comes with the territory at this particular office? The last cleaning lady got pregnant, so the replacement is obliged to."

"Be quiet, Henry, she'll hear you."

"Fine with me. It's about time we discuss the pink elephant in the room, and I'm not referring to your sister per se, but the situation!"

"Henry!"

"And another thing Ljuba, my little beauty queen, when exactly is what's his name coming back, anyway? They've got a correspondence going like Olga Knipper and Anton Chekhov, but we never really hear anything definitive from either of them!"

"Enough with the literary references for God's sake. Everybody knows you're the most over-educated plumber in five boroughs. Gimme a break, Mr. Mensa." Ljuba tried to deflect his ire by peeling a piece of spicy salami, his favorite, and popping it into his mouth, but he was quite skillful at speaking and chewing simultaneously. Gifted guy, no doubt about it. His tirade continued.

"And, by the way, a brother-in-law would like to know: is he marrying her or what?"

Just then Yelena emerged from the bedroom, announcing that she was going for a short walk to get some fresh air; it would help her feel less nauseous, she reasoned.

"See you later, crocodiles," she threw to them on her way out. The door shut. There was a moment of incredulity between Henry and Ljuba broken by Henry's "Oy!"

Ljuba then squirted the mustard at him to go with his salami, and ran to the bedroom to throw some clothes on.

"Where you going?" Henry pleaded, not wanting to be left alone with the air conditioner.

"I'm going after her to have a sisterly talk. That all right with you, Einstein? I just hope she didn't hear you, is what I hope."

Thankfully, the city blocks to the Orthodox Church in the neighborhood were short ones. Yelena felt that was no accident. Ljuba stayed close to her roots, even if she only attended services on the big days, Easter and Christmas, and the occasional funeral or Christening. Ljuba was straight with God, and Yelena never doubted her sister's goodness and Christly ways. Yelena, on the other hand, had inquired about the local parish almost immediately upon landing in Queens. She was perfectly willing to attend a Catholic church if need be, she just needed to have a sanctuary. Ljuba had accompanied her to the Orthodox church, St. Steven's, the very first Sunday of Yelena's arrival last October, and Ljuba knew her sister well enough to know that if she was troubled, that's where she'd be.

And she was.

Yelena had waddled down the aisle with a candle in her hand held like a baton about to be passed off in a relay race. She was not the only one in church. Middle of the day, in the dead heat of summer, neighborhood parishioners found the cool, quiet haven of church an oasis from the intense humidity outside. Yelena lit her candle, kissed the icon, crossed herself, and prayed. It was really more of a breathing exercise than a prayer. The pregnancy had her panting most of the time, and she was worn out from the walk over. She wondered if she wasn't going to give birth to a full-grown child rather than a newborn, she felt so heavy. As she inhaled and exhaled, all that filled her mind were the words, "Help me, help me, help me." Yelena felt as if she were on the edge of a cliff. Jake's coming home, and what will happen now? She heard the heavy oak door of the church open and a shaft of light shot down the aisle next to her and then she heard the door bang shut and it made her jump. Before she turned completely around, she could smell Ljuba's suntan lotion, and wasn't surprised when her sister slipped into the pew alongside her.

"How did you know I was here?"

"You're kidding, right? Where have you always gone when you were scared, since you were six, huh, sis?"

Yelena got off her knees and sat in the pew next to her sister.

"Jake's due back any day, now, right?" Yelena nodded but stared straight ahead at the icon of the Virgin Mary holding baby Jesus.

"Well, that's a good thing, right?" Ljuba made another attempt to get her sister to talk. Nothing. They sat in silence and watched the candles flicker. Finally, as Yelena turned to look at her sister, tears welled up in her eyes.

Suddenly Ljuba read her clear as day. "What?! You told him, didn't you?" Not a word from Yelena. "Oh my God, sis, you are a piece of work! Will you just once in your life not doubt yourself? And believe that someone really loves you; because this guy does; I saw it in his face the first time I met him; and I saw it on Slava; and I hear it in his voice every time he calls you from Medellin or wherever the hell he is. Come on, for the baby's sake, have a conversation with the man. Jesus!"

This last expletive aroused the attention of the priest, who had been behind the altar in quiet prayer. He peaked around the golden lattice altar doors, raised his eyebrows, Ljuba waved him a "don't worry about it...I got it all under control" wave, and he ducked back behind the two archangels painted on the doors. Ljuba chose to lower her voice, to keep the Father happy.

"What exactly are you worried about? Ljuba implored.

"I'm worried about me loving him!" Yelena finally spit it out, and Ljuba softened.

"Oh, Yelana, come on, love is love; it will take care of itself. It's infinite, honey. There's always more where it came from."

"And where is that?" Yelena queried, as much fascinated by her practical big sister waxing philosophical, as she was in need of a solution to her fear.

"God, you silly goose." Ljuba tweaked here sister's cheek.

"Come on, sis, what's the problem? You got a heart as big as the Adriatic; there's plenty of room for Jake and the baby." Then Ljuba gently added, sensing what was at the root of it all. "And room for your son's memory too."

"I hope so, Ljuba, I just hope so."

"Buck up kid, you got a couple of lives to live."

"I really am a piece of job, aren't I?"

With that, Ljuba, stifling a laugh, put her arms around her sister's shoulder and gave her a squeeze that reassured her that at least for that moment, all would be well.

The Priest emerged from behind the altar and nearly tripped on the carpet. He'd obviously been sampling some of the communion wine. That set Ljuba and Yelena howling, lamely attempting to muffle it until they made it down the aisle and out the heavy doors, and down the front steps, and then they let it rip, and had a laugh that could have healed just about anything. Girls again, arm-in-arm, they strolled down the street, as if they'd never known the pain of loss. Church never left them where it found them, that was certain.

CHAPTER FORTY-ONE

SLIGHTLY LEAVENED BY HER TALK WITH LJUBA, Yelena showed up at work more than an hour early. It was hard for her to gage how long it would take her to negotiate foot traffic, with her additional bundle, and she didn't like being late checking in with Casey. Casey, the ever accepting, silent, steady beacon of light greeted her that day with a manila envelope overflowing with clippings. "Jake Thompson" was written in blue marker across the front of it. Casey, the self-appointed godfather of the child on its way, gently handed Yelena the envelope.

"Hey Yelena, early today, you doll, you. Listen, do me a favor and dump this on Jake's desk, willya?" He beamed at her like he had a secret, but he wasn't the type for intrigue, so he blurted, "You know Jake is due back this week, any day now, don't cha?"

"Of course, I know," Yelena reassured him. "I hear from him all the time, Casey, I'm not a night stand, you know," she said with her best, "did-I-forget-to-tell-you-I-have-dignity" voice.

Casey stifled a laugh. He guessed this new phrase was another "Gracie-ism" or maybe she was just whacked by the syntax of the English tongue. Anyway, he knew that she meant "one night stand," and he never would have taken her for that. No how, no way.

Yet he did have his concerns over this new babe in the womb. What Jake's take on it would be, and what was the future of his best betting pal. He also pondered whether this beautiful, young, newly-childless widow was going to become a single mom or what?

Casey worried about Yelena like she was his daughter. He also asked regularly for a chance to feel the baby kick. It was his favorite thing. He had done it with his four kids, practically daily when his wife carried them. "You must have driven her nuts," Yelena would say to him each night as she gently placed his hand on her belly, and they waited together for the kick of the little boy or girl working the trampoline in there. Casey's response would be, "Well, she didn't have far to go, after all she married me and stuck for thirty-eight years."

This would lead to the ritual of Casey pulling out his wallet and showing Yelena pictures of his four kids from infancies to graduations to weddings and birthdays. He was a proud father, no doubt about it. It made Yelena remember Radmilo's endless pride and affection for Marko; how much they had adored each other.

Casey completed this nightly ritual, and Yelena wrapped herself in her ever shrinking cleaning wrapper. She began her rounds, starting with depositing the manila envelope Casey gave her in Jake's cubicle.

Dropping the packet of clippings on his desk, Yelena noticed there were five others already piled up of similar size and apparent content. One of them was so full that some of the articles were coming out, like stuffing leaking out of a turkey. As she did a perfunctory straightening up of the desk, she and her belly got caught between the swivel chair and the desk and as she turned to free herself, she knocked a hefty envelope onto the floor and the clippings came pouring out. She was dismayed at her clumsiness. Barely six months pregnant and she was already as big as a house. She got on all fours to pick up what had spilled, and got caught up in what she saw.

Photographs of villages burning, men with guns threatening old women and children, and faces of villagers not unlike her own neighbors. She tried to read the captions. Her English had improved since last autumn, but her reading skills were clearly a work in progress. She could make out a word here and there. Disturbing words like, 'Kosovo, Serbia, village, killings, Muslims, children, Balkans, war."

She sat back on her heels and studied the clippings, lost in a reverie of horror. The faces of these people all looked like someone she knew. It was so familiar, so immediate. She rifled through them as if she were searching for something particular, though she knew not what. Her breath became short, she felt sick. Then suddenly a hand was on her shoulder and she gasped, startled and afraid.

"Hello, beautiful," came the familiar and smooth voice of Jake. She looked up at him in shock, she managed to stand, revealing to Jake for the first time, the fullness of the life she carried.

"Whoa!" he said, "and hello again!" Quickly recovering from virtual shock, he took her in his arms, as best he could, and covered her with kisses, and whispered in her ear, "My baby, yes?"

She shook her head, and watched his face panic, momentarily until she quickly responded.

"Our baby!" At which Jake picked her up and put her on his desk, knocking over more files and envelopes, without caring a damn about anything but this woman he loved, and whom he finally held captive for the moment.

"Why in the world didn't you tell me?" he demanded, more than a little annoyed. She produced several unfinished letters from the pocket of her skirt, and shrugged.

"I did tell you, many times in my mind, but I don't know. I didn't have exactly the right words in English to write what was in my heart."

"Oh, Gracie," he melted. He stroked her hair, her hands, her stomach, with touches of unconditional affection. "And now that I have your attention, I have come bearing gifts for the Queen!" She laughed and felt free of all care and worry, as the concerns of this morning evaporated in the atmosphere of Jake's divine energy of goodness. He showered her with scarves and woven fabrics from Colombia, coffee, hand painted ceramic cups, a beautiful white Alpaca sweater with an eagle knit into the design, a bright red poncho, fur-lined slippers, and finally a small black velvet box placed gently on her knee. He kissed her. "Your Highness," he began on bended knee, and she laughed and her leg jiggled and sent the box sailing to the floor.

"Oh Jake, I'm so sorry, I'll get it." She got down from the desk and retrieved the box before he could. Swift she was, for a pregnant mare. She placed the box in his hand and was about to assume her position of royalty on the desk, so he could complete his mission on bended knee, when her eye caught a particular picture on one of the clippings that were spread out on the floor. Yelena looked at it, looked away, then looked again and gulped.

"What is it?" Jake was afraid all that bobbing up and down from the desktop had disturbed the baby. He soon saw it wasn't that when she bent down again and with one smooth move grabbed the clipping and leaned against his desk to brace herself.

"My God," she cried, "my God!" The world slowed to the elongated pace of a nightmare, where every detail is so precise and at the same time, so utterly unidentifiable. Who was this face that she was staring at in newsprint? Out of the context of her village, she couldn't place it in her cognizant intelligence, but from the depth of her soul, she recognized something deep inside herself which she'd sensed all along. She was looking at her son's killer. It seemed impossible, and yet she knew it was true.

"What is it?" Jake lifted her up by the shoulders, wanting to pull her out of that mesmeric moment, whatever it was. "What's the matter? Yelena, tell me, honey, what is it?" he implored.

She was shaking, nearly convulsing with the truth that had just sliced through her, "That man, I know that man, he's....he's wearing a gold cross in his hat....why....why..."

Jake hadn't had a chance to look at the photo: he was focused on bringing Yelena back to a calm state of mind. "Honey, so what, he's got a cross...I don't understand...."

"Read it to me, Jake," she demanded, grabbing the article and shoving it between them. He had no choice but to deal with this flimsy piece of newsprint. That which had been his whole life; newspaper, news stories, news clippings, was now rammed between him and his imminent marriage proposal and he had to deal with it. One quick glance at the caption of the picture, and the words Shar village, and he knew this story was going to be news of the bad kind.

"Honey, not now, let's put this stuff away and take a look at it later. Let's go get a coffee now, and let me tell you how much I missed you...." He barely got the last few words out before Yelena, like a wildcat after raw meat, grabbed the clipping, pulled away from him and began struggling through the English herself.

"In a small mountain village, southeast of Bosnia, a Muslim schoolteacher was ar...ar...arrested...on sus...sus....'" She struggled with the words and she knew in her gut they meant. She handed it back to Jake. "Read this to me, Jake, I beg you...."

"...suspicion of murder of..." he stopped, unable to utter the next phrase, for fear of the avalanche he knew it would bring.

"Please, Jake..." she held his look with such fierceness, he'd never seen that side of her, and he wasn't about to cross it.

"All right," he murmured, more a concession to himself than to Yelena, as if he knew he'd have to put his foot on this jagged edged rock if he wanted to cross the stream, and so he continued to read. "...murder of an 11-year old...Serbian boy and the kidnapping of three older teenagers, who had been missing since last September." The reality of what he was reading hit him like a baseball bat to the knees. He stopped and looked up at the love of his life, helpless to take away the pain of what this meant to her.

"Read, Jake, read." Unrelenting, this mother bear demanded to know all.

"...an unmarked grave was found in a cave near Shar Village, where the bodies of the three." He gagged, "Oh my God, I don't believe this...." He forced himself to go on, knowing there was no turning back now; he had to completely traverse this channel. He barely gave himself a millisecond to catch his breath before Yelena entreated him again to continue. She was hanging on every syllable.

"...teenage boys were found, dismembered, mutilated and beaten.'" He let the clipping drop onto the desk. That was all they needed to know about this story, he took Yelena by the shoulders again and matched her frankness, "You know this guy, Yelena?"

"Zima's Omir!" spilled from her lips.

"What?" Jake still not getting it.

"My best friend's husband." She became quite still and responded almost robotically, as if there were a conversation going on inside her head, and another one that was being uttered aloud.

"What?" Jake looked again at the photo on the desk.

"My neighbor, my Muslim neighbor."

"I...I...don't under...." Jake stuttered. Yelena grabbed the clipping from him and crushed it in her hand.

"My son's murderer!" She began to shake and erupt with hatred that was volcanic. "He killed my Marko....It was him!" Tears streaming down her face, she cursed Omir with clenched teeth, spitting out expletives in Serbian. Jake could only imagine what they meant. He was afraid she would explode.

"Easy, Yelena, take it easy, honey...are you sure?" Jake tried to hold her, but she was hysterical by then.

"Yes, Jake, yes, I'm sure! That's my son's cross he is wearing..."and she collapsed onto his desk in uncontrollable sobs.

"My God," Jake whispered as if to the Man Upstairs, Himself. He held Yelena by the shoulders, and did his best to steady this justifiably inconsolable mother.

CHAPTER FORTY-TWO

TWO DAYS LATER, WITH NO SLEEP, food, nor refuge for her heartache, Yelena was strangely calm and determined as she packed her suitcase. Her face was drawn and pale, and her sister looked at her with grave concern and equal determination to keep her little sister in America, as Yelena had conviction to return to her village. She had already called Aunt Sofia to tell her she was coming, who also did her best to discourage Yelena from making the trip.

Ljuba approached her sister, carefully. Yelena had walked around the apartment for two days as if all her layers of skin had been peeled off. Everything made her jump. Needless to say, Jake called endlessly, even came over, but Yelena sat non-communicative, until he finally had no choice but to kiss her cheek and promise to call the next day. They all worried for the baby. Would this emotional trauma cause a premature birth, or trouble with Yelena's heart which had been a challenge during Marko's birth. Doctors had told her she had a heart murmur which indicated a weakness of heart during shock or trauma, and childbirth itself was both shocking and traumatic, albeit glorious. She had proved the medical profession wrong when her heart roared like a lion's through the birth of her son. Now, she paced the apartment like a jaguar about to spring for its kill. There was a restlessness, an actual sense of danger, that made even Henry, the indefatigable, keep his distance from her. Truth be told, neither Ljuba nor Henry nor Jake knew whether they wouldn't be exactly the same way, had they received the news that Yelena had. Yet her decision to pack and go back to what she claimed would be a trial, had them all worried beyond words.

Henry's perception was that Hannibal Lecter was going back to the village for the trial of Hannibal Lecter. No good could come of it was his view.

When Jake visited the next day and was once again met with little, though not unkind, communication from Yelena, Henry offered to buy him a beer at the corner tavern. Henry wished he could comfort Jake, but his best effort was in a couple of bottles of Guinness.

Henry found Jake to be a stand up guy, despite Henry's earlier harsh judgment, which turned out to be unfounded. He searched for something helpful to say, while they silently slurped their ale at Tina's Tavern.

"Tough timing, Jake, I guess you and Yelena were hoping and planning for a happy time around the baby." Henry was careful not to make his conversation sound like a shotgun demand from a protective brother-in-law.

Jake pulled the velvet box out of his pocket and placed it on the bar. He carried it with him each night, thinking maybe the conversation with Yelena would allow for his proposal. Not to be.

Henry nodded in approval that Jake had intended to do the right thing. It was hard to see exactly how things could possibly work out. They drank down their dark ales and ordered two more.

"She seems determined to go back there for some reason," Henry threw out, just in case Jake wanted to spill his guts about the situation.

"Like I'm gonna permit that to happen." Jake mumbled, then sucked down a good long gulp of Guinness. Henry couldn't resist a small smirk.

"I don't exactly see my sister-in-law as someone who waits for permission, but what do I know." He then mimicked, and topped Jake's drinking pattern. It's a male thing.

"Well, you married her sister. That seems to have worked out."

"Same DNA, different temperament. Ljuba got out of the village at a younger age, mellowed out here in Queens."

"Yeah, right. Queens is such a mellow place."

"I'm saying she's maybe more vocal, but I get the last word. She knows it, our girls know it."

"Huh." Jake broke the tacit male rule that at a bar they look straight ahead and talk, rarely, if ever, at each other, and turned straight to Henry in surprise.

Henry took that as a cue to go on.

"Ljuba confided that when Yelena's husband Radmilo died, she had become hardened and unrelenting. She's a tough one."

"Not always, Henry, not always." And he downed the rest of his drink

Henry turned to look at Jake, to see if more was coming. Nope. So he threw out a couple of bills on the bar for a tip, and they hit the door.

CHAPTER FORTY-THREE

BACK AT THE APARTMENT, Nadya and Anna helped their aunt pack, as if she were going on a vacation. They pulled out special items of their own to send with her, so she would think of them while she was away.

"Pooh will protect you, Aunt Yelena," Nadya offered, "and when he comes back with you, he'll tell us all about your trip, in case you forget something that happens."

"Thank you, Nadi." Yelena could barely look at her little nieces. The tenderness of these two girls had cleft her heart.

Anna had a more sophisticated gift, a small plastic picture frame, with Anna's school picture in it and her phone number written under it. "Just in case you get lonely and want to call me up to talk," she said, as she placed it on the top of her aunt's clothes in the small suitcase.

Yelena grabbed both girls and hugged them close; her tears fell into their shoulders, her first release of emotion since two nights ago in the news office.

"Don't worry," Nadya said, "you can come back and live with us again. We'll be waiting for you, right Anna?"

"Right." Anna replied more soberly. At twelve, a girl already understands so much, too much maybe. Enough to be less convinced than her little sister, whose innocence she envied at that moment.

"Okay girls. Go read your library books, remember the summer reading club meets tomorrow. You don't want to get behind. Off you go." Ljuba sent them into their room, so she could have one more shot at talking her sister out of getting on that midnight flight.

Ljuba looked at her sister stuffing Pooh into the suitcase, which made it hard to close. As evidence of her dual-mindedness, Ljuba helped her close the suitcase at the same time that she was attempting to convince her to stay.

"Yelena, you're pregnant, for God's sake!"

Yelena sat briefly on the suitcase, an old wife's tale that it would bring good luck to the journey. Then she shifted to the hassock, to finish lacing up her boots. She glared at her sister.

"Ljuba, tell me the truth, did you know about this?"

Ljuba was silent and looked away.

"You did, didn't you? How could you keep this from me?"

"Because I knew you would do this, and it's dangerous, damnit!" Ljuba took her sister by the shoulders. "Look, sis, I didn't know for sure, but I'd heard rumblings. Aunt Sofia had mentioned it when I called her a couple of weeks ago, but I was afraid to tell you! I mean, you've got a child in you, for God's sake; you can't be running back there in your condition, it's not safe!"

"So what! I must go, and you know it, Ljuba. And we both know you'd do the same if it was Anna, God forbid!"

At this point, Henry walked in from the bar without Jake. A little tipsy himself, he took off his jacket and stood at the kitchen table, listening to the two sisters argue in the living room.

Yelena continued. "Anyway, it's not that dangerous, it is their strict religious law not to harm pregnant women. I'll be fine."

Two glasses of Guinness can buy a man unfettered permission to speak, and Henry was no exception.

"I doubt that law extends to Serbian women who happen to be pregnant, after all, you're infidels. I guess we all are." He sat down nearly missing the chair.

"Can it, Henry, for once!" Ljuba retorted. "And where's Jake?"

"Went home, I guess." Henry managed, obviously hiding something. Yelena looked up at him for a long moment. She searched Henry's face for a clue. It was odd that Jake didn't come back with Henry from the bar. She returned to her packing. Ljuba picked up the cue.

"Well, what did he have to say about this?" Ljuba implored Henry.

"He thought she shouldn't go, or take him with her."

Ljuba turned to Yelena, "And?"

"And I told him, thank you but I'm going alone. I have to. There'll be a trial, I know it." Yelena explained.

Henry groaned on that statement, thinking how corrupt the court system must be there amid all the civil strife. Yelena looked at him, read his thoughts clearly this time, and responded by putting on her sweater, picking up her suitcase, prepared to leave. She would not be deterred. She went into the bedroom to hug the girls once more. This gave Ljuba an opportunity to ask Henry, "Where is Jake, really?"

"Taking care of some business, don't worry about it." Henry whispered which gave Ljuba a modicum of comfort.

Yelena came back in from the girls' bedroom to say good-bye to Ljuba and Henry. She hugged them both silently and a little longer than usual.

"Be careful, Gracie," Henry said as he gave her a couple of extra twenties. "Take a cab."

"No thank you, Henry. I know the trains now."

"I'm going with you to the airport, Yelena," Ljuba insisted.

"No Ljuba, I'm fine. I found my way here all the way from Shar Village, I can find my way to the airport."

"Just make sure you find your way back!" Henry moved to the couch, a larger landing pad. He had to admit it was going to be nice to have it as his own for a little while.

"I love you sis. I'll call you at Aunt Sofia's."

"I'll be fine Ljuba, don't worry. I'm not afraid." Truer words were never spoken. Yelena waved and waddled out the door, down the stairs and into the subway that would transport her directly to JFK.

CHAPTER FORTY-FOUR

JFK INTERNATIONAL AIRPORT WAS AS BUSY at nine o'clock at night as it was at nine in the morning or midnight for that matter. It hummed with the energy of movement or static. Going or waiting. It was the place of constant flux, a vestibule of transition, like the wings of a theatre where one prepares for the entrance into a scene.

Yelena waited in line at the ticket counter, exhausted from standing on her tired feet but centered and confident that her feet were exactly where her mind was, and that felt right. The gentleman in front of her had a gigantic knap sack, hair down to his hips, and more jewelry than seemed possible to get past security. He took a full thirty minutes to choose just the right seat on the plane, which she could only hope wasn't next to her considering, the stench and all. Finally, he sauntered toward the boarding gate.

"Next," came the call, which she thought might well be the last word she heard here in New York. She handed over her ticket, her passport, her seat assignment, and waited patiently, when she felt someone brush against her back, slap down his ticket on top of hers, with a rose on top of it.

"Two together, please. One aisle and one adjacent, as near to the bathroom as possible."

"Excuse me, sir, but I was taking care of the lady here," spoke the lovely ticket agent with some authority.

"I appreciate that, and now I'll be taking care of her," Jake shot the agent one of his you can't resist me smiles, as he put his arm around Yelena.

"What are you doing?" Yelena whispered to him, as if the agent wouldn't hear them, when in fact she was less than a yard away from them, on the other side of the counter.

"I'm going with you, baby," Jake stated, adding the baby more for the agent's benefit, to establish familiarity, and to avoid what he intuited could turn into a scene. Yelena was wound as taut as a corporal's army cot in boot camp.

"No, Jake, you're not." Yelena held her ground. The ticket agent settled into watching the two of them like the semi-finals at Wimbledon.

"Yes, Yelena, I am," he shot back.

"No, you're not," she returned.

"Ye-es, I a-am!" he claimed.

"No-o," Yelena matched him.

Jake knew he'd have to go to the net. "Why, Yelena?" he entreated firmly.

"Because...because...I.... I love you."

Now the ticket agent was completely engaged, and wouldn't dream of interrupting this soap opera, though the passengers in line were getting restless. Even so, Jake and Yelena took much less time than the Woodstock throwback who had preceded her in line.

"I been waiting months to hear you say that, but not as an excuse for us to be separated!"

"It's not an excuse, Jake, I mean it. It's dangerous for you there!"

"And what about for you? You're pregnant for God's sake!"

That jolted the ticket agent out of her reverie of watching this argument, and popped her into her professional posture. "Excuse me, ma'am, sorry to interrupt, but you are not more than six months pregnant are you? Because we have certain restrictions on the overseas flights."

In perfect unison, Yelena replied "No!" while Jake declared "Yes!" This caused Yelena to get serious. She pulled Jake aside. The ticket agent did not take the next customer but stayed fixed on their drama and waved the next passenger in line to her colleague on her right. Yelena was emphatic and intense. She was not about to lose this fight.

"Don't do this, Jake, because if I have to, I'll go by boat, and if I go by boat, it will take longer, the longer it takes for me to get there, the longer it takes for me to come back here. I want our child to be born in America. If I don't get on that plane right now, our child will be born in the Shar Mountains."

"I don't understand why you're going in the first place, Yelena!"

"For my son." Yelena stared him down.

"Oh yeah, well, what about OUR child, huh?"

"For our child too! It should grow up to know about honor—what it is. And integrity."

It was like a firecracker with a very short wick had been lit. And it went off in Jake.

"Integrity! There must be a language barrier here, because integrity does not mean revenge."

"In my country it does."

"Yeah, well, we're still here on American soil, Gracie, and let me tell you something about integrity. Here it means keeping something whole, unified. Like you and me, together, for example. And revenge...revenge blasts lives to pieces, which is what your country's been doing for centuries. That's not integrity, it's insanity. And you know what? I understand it. I do! I know that feeling. I wanted to tear that drug dealer to pieces for what he did to my Tony. But it doesn't do any good."

"You don't understand my people, Jake!"

"Yes, I do. I've been researching it since we met, Yelena. Six centuries of hate. The Turks...blah, blah, blah, and The Battle of Kosovo 1389, and oh so many lives sacrificed for freedom. Freedom they never got. They lost the battle, but they still celebrate the day, now that's Byzantine! And what, you're gonna get even and your pain of losing Marko is supposed to disappear? Never happen. Let it go, baby, there's no mileage in it. It's a death trip."

"Well, it's MY death trip."

Jake grabbed Yelena by the shoulders. By then, they had drawn a crowd, and the agent had to call for security. She'd never quite heard a marital quarrel like this one, and she didn't know where it would lead. Though she didn't understand half of what they were saying, she frankly wanted to hear more of this debate. It was fascinating as hell.

Jake began to sound threatening, "And what if I don't let you go. I could stop you, you know."

"Then I will hate you forever," Yelena replied coolly, looking him straight in the eye. This stopped him. He'd never seen her like this. He was talking to a stranger.

"This is not you talking, Yelena. You're not like them."

"Yes, Jake, I am. This is who I am. I am not like you."

"What's that supposed to mean?"

Yelena paused for a moment, as if she might not say what she was about to say. It weighed heavy on her tongue. Then it shot out like a bullet released because a slippery finger accidentally pulled the trigger. And there was no taking it back.

"I would have killed my son's drug dealer."

Jake froze. Time froze. He held his gaze on Yelena, then looked away, as if to wipe away the last remark.

"You're crazy," he whispered, uncertain if he meant her or himself.

Yelena figured it was for her, and sealed it with, "I'm loyal to my son."

Jake stood looking at this stranger he loved, a woman he thought he knew, did know, did love, still loved, and a gulf of fury opened up between them. A muscular Security Officer stepped between them.

"Is there a problem here, ma'am?"

"Yes, sir, this man is salting me."

"Salting?" More brawn than brain, Mr. Security couldn't make the leap.

"She means assaulting, officer," Jake clarified, "and I wasn't assaulting her, but no problem, we're done here. I'm going." He grabbed his ticket off the counter, and left the rose.

Yelena watched him go. The Security Guard broke up the crowd of gawkers. Yelena slowly bent over, loosened her sandals and slipped them off. She took her boarding pass, inadvertently knocking the rose off the counter, her vision blurred behind her tears. Then she pulled herself together, lifted her chin, rolled back her shoulders, and boarded the plane home, barefoot.

PART THREE

The Return

CHAPTER FORTY-FIVE

FATIGUED, HEAVY-HEARTED AND LADEN WITH NEW LIFE, Yelena trudged up the dirt path leading to her Aunt Sofia's house. No longer did it feel like home, nor had Ljuba's apartment in Queens. She was in that dreaded pilgrim limbo, belonging neither here nor there. The visit with Ljuba was meant to be a short term thing to help her heal her inconsolable grief. That didn't happen, but something else did. She fell in love, though she had difficulty admitting it. And she was very pregnant. It made her tremble with joy and trepidation.

So much had happened since the last time her bare feet sunk into the mulch on the path. In the previous twenty-four hours alone, she'd been on a subway, a jet, a train, in a taxi, and now on foot to finally arrive, but where? Not her own home, but her Aunt Sofia's home with Uncle Anton. Marko was dead, and Yelena was still only half alive. The shift in her inner geography was as dramatic as the moving of the earth's plates which caused the devastating earthquake in Skopje in 1963.

She was just a baby then but later she'd heard endless stories about it. Now, inside the belly of her soul, her own terrestrial plates were having a major paradigm shift. She was walking through the rubble of her being, searching for survivors of her old life.

She glanced up from the path and saw a familiar site, something that could anchor her floating thought. It was Uncle Anton asleep on his chair beneath the arbor. A clean white bed sheet drying in the breeze had shaded his face. He didn't notice when the sun climbed higher and made its way over the laundry line and directly flooded the eighty-six-year-old visage of peace. Yelena paused and beheld his fully whitened mustache moving up and down with each breath, bringing her back to a past so remote, she felt like an intruder. A few boarded up windows, the overgrown garden, overturned baskets, scattered tools, and a pervading sense of disarray frightened her. This was not the way she'd left it.

The disappointment of her diamond village, now dilapidated and unkempt, paralyzed her momentarily, and then she recognized that what was beyond corruption remained, her beloved Uncle Anton. She set her bag on the ground and moved to the clothesline to move the white sheet a few inches to keep her snoring uncle in the shade, but he adjusted himself back into the sun, then looked up, squinting, sensing someone's presence.

"Sofia! Is it time for coffee!" he murmured.

"In a little while." Yelena didn't move, giving him a moment to realize it was not his Sofia, but his devoted niece.

"Thank you, dear."

"You're welcome, uncle."

"Ah, hah! Yelena! It's you." He reached for his cane and heaved himself off the chair and met her embrace.

"Look at you! The lost lambkin finally came home! And you're fat!!!" he cried with childlike delight. She made his day, the day of an old man, who counted each day a gift.

"Uncle Anton," she embraced him tenderly, "look at you, asleep in the hot, mid-day sun! She patted his knee. "Where's Aunt Sofia?"

"What? Oh. She's fine, dear heart." He replied, turning up his hearing aid. He was religious about inserting it each morning, like a soldier pinning on his medals, but he usually neglected to turn on the volume.

"I'm glad, uncle, but where, where is she right now?" Yelena added the emphasis necessary to make herself understood.

"The orchard, honey, the orchard, where else?" And with that, Uncle Anton sat back down to finish his siesta. He hit the mark on his chair just right, returning to the shade the drying laundry was providing him.

Where else, indeed, Yelena thought, as she headed toward the orchard. Actually, there were a thousand places Aunt Sofia could be in the middle of the day. Her hands were never idle and she was always on the move. Pruning, milking, weeding, weaning, cooking, kneading, serving, cleaning, loving. She was the ultimate woman in Yelena's eyes.

Yelena walked toward the orchard, and they spotted each other immediately. Aunt Sofia had the x-ray vision of a mother lion. She always had one eye on her cubs, no matter how far away they were. Yelena smiled and waved as she moved toward Aunt Sofia, who was up on a ladder shaking down some plums, no doubt for the summer brandy-making. As happy as it made Yelena to take in the scene of her Aunt in her very own orchard, vital and well, it pained her to look two degrees to the left of the orchard, toward the field, the place of no return, and no mercy, the infinite expanse she was unable to cross in time to save her son. It looked larger now and smaller at the same time. *Why couldn't I have gotten there in time?*

It was a ceaseless, chastising mantra that brought her no peace. She shifted her focus back toward the plum trees, bearing the brandy-to-be. The plums were a good size, which meant a good batch of Slivovitz this summer. Aunt Sofia would make it strong, as she always did. No matter which direction Yelena looked, there was the hand of Aunt Sofia in it. Grace. That's what the woman had, and there was no end to it. Yelena reached her just as she was leaving the last rung on the ladder, touching earth with her calloused feet that had earned the dominion they had over the ground.

They embraced for a long moment. She heard the skip of breath in her Aunt's chest. Aunt Sofia buried her head to hide the cry that betrayed just how very lonely she'd been without Yelena all these months. Yelena stroked her head, like she would that of an infant.

Aunt Sofia, never one to indulge herself in the luxury of pain or sadness, felt sufficiently comforted, so her spunk returned, "Well now, you're back!" She took a step or two away from Yelena and took a good look.

"And now there are two of you, that means double trouble!" Giggling and sparing like school girls, the months of separation evaporated and they were off to their usual banter.

"Who taught me 'trouble' in the first place?" shot Yelena.

"Don't know, wasn't me." Aunt Sofia took two plums from her apron pocket and offered one to Yelena.

They both chewed in uncharacteristic silence. Then Sofia began to hum an old folk tune, and gave a sideway glance to Yelena. Each was determined not to be the first to mention the obvious.

Yelena broke the silence. "How are things around here now, Aunt Sofia?"

"Crazy," she said between bites. With few, if any teeth, it was hard for Sofia to accomplish mastication of the less than ripened plum. "Yes, indeed, crazy. Like you! What did you come back for, Yelena?"

"What do you mean; this is still my home, isn't it?"

A silence passed between them, as they both acknowledged and denied the lack of truth in that statement.

"It's very bad here now, Yelena. You must know that." Aunt Sofia's voice sobered to a frightening chill.

Yelena was silently sorting out what that meant.

"So why did you come?"

This was the first of a litany of questions Aunt Sofia had for her niece, not the least of which was regarding her belly.

"I came back for justice, Auntie."

"Really." Aunt Sofia gave a penetrating look. "Not for revenge?"

"What's the difference?" Yelena threw back glibly.

"God." She chewed quietly. "God is the difference, child."

Aunt Sofia went back to gathering the plums and putting them in a bushel basket, which she then lifted onto a flat wagon that would hold maybe three or four baskets, making it rather heavy to roll up the hill to the house.

Yelena marveled at how imperceptibly Aunt Sofia had changed in her older years. Her energy remained the same, her tasks, the same, her demands on herself, the same. Only her face showed the ravages of grief and longing for that which she would never have again in her time, peace in her village. Each line on her face mapped out the journey of her love for others, her vigilance and duty to her family and home. Every wrinkle proclaimed her love for this small piece of land that she had nourished and maintained in order to have it feed and sustain her family to follow. A simple, complex, deep soul of a woman, Aunt Sofia seemed unshakeable. Nothing could rock her. Yelena had always, ever since she was a child, had looked to her aunt for strength. Now more than ever, she hoped that she had inherited a pint of the full stream of divine goodness Aunt Sofia possessed. She needed it to carry her through this time.

Yelena picked up the shears that her aunt had been using to clip the plum branches, and began clipping.

"Leave it, dear heart, don't bother now. Relax from your trip, and we'll put you to work tomorrow." Aunt Sofia teased.

Yelena was about to protest and insist on helping, when they both heard the husky voice of Zorka in the distance, singing out, "Sofia I'm coming to help you, in a few minutes…."

Yelena and Aunt Sofia exchanged a glance that said it all. Yelena was not in the mood for Zorka and her thousand questions, not quite yet. Aunt Sofia understood, of course, especially when she caught Yelena glancing up toward the church.

"Why don't you go ahead, and Zorka and I will get the clipping done. Then I'll make her push this wagon up the hill."

"I'll come back down to help with the milking," Yelena offered.

"You will not." Case closed. Aunt Sofia had spoken. She wanted Yelena's baby born healthy and full term. The women in the villages around there were infamous for premature births because they kept doing heavy work up till the end, while their husbands held down the chairs in the cafe with their buttocks.

Yelena took off the babushka that Aunt Sofia had given her months earlier, and put it around her aunt's head. Aunt Sofia's jaw dropped. Her look of shock was not from her niece's act of kindness, but from the new coiffure that her niece was sporting.

"What happened to your hair?" Aunt Sofia was sure she must have been in an accident or something.

"I cut it. American style."

"Uh-huh. Hmmm," was the only response Sofia could muster. She clearly did not approve. She heaved the last bushel up onto the cart, and sat on the edge of the wagon to catch her breath. Yelena stretched and rubbed her belly, and breathed the sweet air, readying to make her jaunt up to the church. Aunt Sofia watched her like a hawk.

"So. Ljuba says the father of your baby is very nice."

"Yes, he was, very nice." Yelena replied with a dejected sigh.

"Was? Is he dead?" The thoughts tumbled into Aunt Sofia's brain that the man had died and that was really why Yelena came back, and maybe she would actually stay, and raise her child here, and not pursue this crazy Omir situation, and, and, and....

"Of course he's not dead." Yelena decided to delay her walk up the hill for a moment and join her aunt on the edge of the wagon for the inevitable, intimate query.

"Aunt Sofia, tell me, where is Omir now?"

"In jail." With that Sofia shoved some chew into her left cheek.

"Waiting for trial, right?"

"He must be," she said with her mouth full and her eyes focused on retying her snuff bag that had a lovely flower embroidered on it, compliments of Dushka.

Yelena sought to gain more attention from her aunt than the tobacco was getting, "Will there be justice?" she implored, finally winning her Aunt's attention.

"Always, my little one, always." Aunt Sofia stroked Yelena's new hair, and then she shook her head in disbelief at her niece's choice to chop off those tresses, and rose to respond to the nearly simultaneous call of the cows. "Zorka likes to milk early so she can start her cocktail hour early, now she has my cows trained to get milked at this time of afternoon. Honestly, I don't know if she is helping or hurting sometimes."

"Yes, you do, Auntie."

"You're right, I do." And Yelena and her aunt shared a chuckle that spoke volumes about what they both knew about Zorka's drinking habits and work ethic. Face it, she was never as much help as she was a hindrance, but who could resist her voluptuous energy and zeal for life? Not anyone in this crowd.

The two women waddled off in different directions, moving with great effort, one from old age; the other from new life soon to be born.

CHAPTER FORTY-SIX

THERE WAS SOMETHING INTRINSICALLY WRONG, utterly unnatural for a woman, any woman, or man for that matter, to be walking up a hill in the brightness of a summer day to visit the grave of her son. The error for him to go before his mother was so gross and overwhelming, it was impossible for Yelena to accept it on a rational level. It couldn't be true. It must not be true. Short of breath, more from the realization of where she was headed than from the physical exertion, she paused and took a moment to rest on a boulder.

She looked out and took in the outrageous beauty of her village mountain range. Surrounded on all sides by mounds of granite, one big circle of protection, her birth land enveloped her with a panoply of love. She had felt safe here all her life, growing up as a girl, then as a young maiden in love with her husband, then a devoted mother, until all was demolished in one moment, less than one year ago. She looked out and listened to the wind blowing gently against her skirt. She heard a hawk cry out above, and a faint clanging of a shepherd's bell yoking his flock of sheep to keep them safe. *Each had a way of thinking they were keeping their flock safe,* she thought.

Yelena believed right upbringing, good education and loving parenting would protect her boy from all evil. *What did she miss? Had she neglected a lesson? Had she been too free, too strict?* It seemed all she did was turn her head for a quick minute, and he was gone. The grief had not moved inside her. It was like a stone that would never roll away. It was only an illusion that with Ljuba and Henry and their darling girls, she was recovering from her sadness; that with Jake teaching her a new way of life and loving her as he did, she would be able to face forward; that with this new little lamb in her womb, she would somehow begin again. Never, never, never.

She rose from the rock and pressed on up the hill. All that was racing through her mind was like treachery. There were no new beginnings. Her jaw tightened. She faced the stone wall of the death of her child, and she had not found or couldn't believe in a way around it.

Before she reached Marko's grave, she perceived that it had been fairly well-tended. Red geraniums were at the base of the white stone cross that bore his name and dates, along with a quote from the Gospel of Matthew 3:17: "This is my beloved Son, in whom I am well pleased." Her knees buckled again, but she forced herself to continue. When she reached the mound of dirt that housed her son, she surrendered and hit the earth with fatigue, despair and a strange relief to be close to her son again.

She breathed in the dirt, the moist soil that lay between her and her offspring. She would have eaten the whole of it, if she could have held her son once more. She doubled over with deepened grief, and had it not been for the pain that shot through her stomach, that almost felt like a contraction, she would have lay there for eternity. She sat up and stroked her belly, the pain stopped. Her hands rested there until she felt the familiar kick of the life inside her, as if it were reminding her, "Don't forget about me." It almost made her smile, till she glanced again at the photo of her son implanted at the intersection of the cross. She looked deeply into his young face, and got lost in a reverie.

Yelena and Marko were sitting on his bed, it was winter, and snow was falling outside the window. He was tucked in under a splendidly embroidered comforter, propped up with pillows that made him look more like a young prince than a son of a country peasant and a truck driver. Marko was a bright boy and he loved to read. Often he had books under the covers, over the covers and all over the floor. It was as if they replaced siblings or pets or other friendly outlets. He loved his books. And so their nightly ritual was the reading of one of them, until he fell asleep. He'd been reading since he was four. His mother taught him, as she had grown up with the same reverence for the glorious imaginings one found in the world of literature.

In her mind she heard him say, "Read me the story, mamma," as he handed her a large volume with Byzantine scenes of battle on the cover. It was entitled, *A History of the Battles for Freedom*. He was about eight or nine-year-old, the age where boys seem to love to play hero, warrior, good guy-bad guy. He was no exception, but his battle books were more than mere war stories, they were historic and symbolic, as the text revealed. She wanted to hear him read, "You know how to read, son, and you read so beautifully!"

"No," the young boy had insisted, "You read, mamma, I like your voice."

"You do? Welllllll then...all right, I'll read to you, and then to sleep. School tomorrow." She conceded as she always did. Her son had her wrapped around his little finger, and he knew it, she knew it, the entire village knew it. They shared a special closeness and were so much alike, Aunt Sofia had often joked about that.

"If you put on his soccer shoes, you could go play for him," Aunt Sofia chided one day when Marko had the flu and had to miss a game. Yelena ignored it and enjoyed it at the same time.

That one particular winter night that she'd read to him, the story had gone something like this: "There flies a grey bird, a falcon, from Jerusalem the Holy, and in his beak he bears a swallow. That is no falcon, no grey bird, it is Saint Elijah. But wait, he carries no swallow, but a book from the Mother of God. He comes to the Tsar of the land; he lays the book on the Tsar's knees. And the book itself preached to the Tsar."

Marko's face was aglow with intrigue at a story he'd heard many times over. He was engaged in the narrative, the images, and more than anything, enchanted by the voice of his mother.

A butterfly suddenly landed on Yelena's arm, waking her out of her daydream at the graveside. She stayed still to watch it flutter its wings as if in rhythm with the story she was telling in her mind. It flew away and settled on the clay flower pot holding the bright, fire-red geraniums at the head of Marko's grave. Yelena straightened up and began to clear a few stray weeds off her son's place of rest. The butterfly stayed on the edge of the clay pot, witnessing her every move. In her mind, she began to hear Marko take over the reading of the story, "Tsar Lazar, of honorable stock, which Kingdom will you choose? Will you choose the heavenly kingdom? Or do you choose an earthly kingdom? If you choose an earthly kingdom, Saddle your horses...Gird on your swords...." And then she remembered his giggle; he always laughed at the word "gird".... She continued weeding the gravesite, and dusting off the cross, and wiping the surface of the laminated photo of him embedded in the grave marker, and as she did so, she went on to recite the poem from memory, aloud, as if she were telling it to him, right there on the spot.

"But if you choose the heavenly kingdom, build a church on the open Field of Freedom. Build it not with a floor of marble, but lay down silk and scarlet on the ground. For all your soldiers shall be destroyed, and you Prince, shall die with them." She sat again. She became short of breath, and as she sat, she took the long blades of grass she'd pulled up from around the grave and wove them into a wreath of grass, which she then laid on the grave marker. She stood and looked down at her work, both above and below ground, rubbed her womb, and finished the story aloud along with the vibrant sound of Marko's voice in her mind, in unison, like a prayer they recited, "After the Tsar heard these words, 'Dear God, Which kingdom shall I choose? The earthly or the heavenly? An earthly kingdom lasts only a little time, but a heavenly kingdom will last for eternity....'" Yelena looked up as she heard the approach of Father Voyn. He was lit from behind by the afternoon sun. The swallows gathered around the church steeple at that time of day and they were circling over his head, making him a heavenly vision as he walked slowly and steadily toward her, joining in the ending of the well-known story. Together with Yelena, the Father added his voice to the yarn, "The Tsar chose a heavenly kingdom...All was honorable and the goodness of God was fulfilled." He embraced Yelena, she kissed his hand and kept her gaze down.

"Father," was all she could manage, overwhelmed to see him and a bit shocked to have him enter into her private communion with her son. And she was somewhat embarrassed at her physical condition, though she was certain he would not judge her now, any more than he ever had in her whole, entire life. Father Voyn put his arm around her shoulder, helped her up, and led her into the church. As they walked he began to tell her another story, more timeless even than that of the Tsar. "Yelena, my child," he began, "did you know that I had a son?"

"No, Father, I never knew." Yelena had always imagined Father Voyn as the father of all of them in the village. She waited to hear what he would say next. They walked slowly and in step with each other. The heavy breath of the elderly priest gave accompaniment to their pace. In the distance, Yelena heard the cows being corralled into the barn for their rather early milking. She imagined Zorka's haste, prodding the bovine givers of white water into their stalls, and hastening the pull on their teats, in order that she may get to her afternoon drinks sooner, as Aunt Sofia decried. Later Aunt Sofia would share with Yelena that Zorka had claimed she'd filled her bucket higher, because her cow had a bigger, better bull. It was always a game of *"Gotcha"* with Zorka, which usually provided Aunt Sofia and Yelena with a good laugh. Yelena's thoughts wove back to where her feet were, pressing the grass under each pregnant step, along side Father Voyn.

CHAPTER FORTY-SEVEN

FATHER VOYN OPENED THE CHURCH DOOR FOR YELENA. She stepped inside the cool cavern of the fourteenth-century sanctuary, and finally felt like she had landed home. The smell of the incense, burnt candle wax and the mustiness of centuries-old mold that sadly was chipping away at the frescoes on the walls; those familiar sensorial realities grounded Yelena. She even thought she felt a kick from the baby, expressing delight with where they stood. Yelena rubbed her tummy, thinking, *not yet, baby, not just yet.* But she agreed with her belly that this place was a happy and comforting one. She hadn't been able to exhale a sigh of release since the day when she first saw Omir's face in newsprint in Jake's office. She'd been wound tight like a high wire since that moment.

"Would you like a glass of water," Father Voyn offered. She nodded and he poured out a clear stream of mountain water into a glass with little red roses painted around the base. It renewed her like a baptism. He offered his handkerchief to take up the beads of sweat formed on her face from the heat.

They stood in silence for a moment. She went up to the icon of the Holy Virgin with Child and crossed herself and kissed the icon, and then lit a candle and bowed her head to keep from breaking down. It was impossible not to think of that day last September when she had entered this church and performed the exact same tasks, with a heart-filled with joy and contentment for her life that day. And before the sun rested on the horizon that same day, everything had changed. The stillness of the moment was vast and deafening, evaporating that former life of happiness. *How could something so real, suddenly be an unreality?* Again Father Voyn jolted her out of her ruminating by inviting her to sit with him behind the altar while he prepared a few things for the service the next day.

"Behind the altar? I didn't think women were allowed." Yelena tested him, knowing he was not a "by the book" man of the cloth, but rather one of huge humanity and compassion and that meant he picked his battles and his orders.

"Nonsense, child, you think God cares if it is a man or a woman that stands on holy ground. You know your mother, God rest her soul, used to come back here to clean. Did you know that?"

"Yes, Father, I did." Yelena smiled as she stepped behind the sacred screen of icons into the inner sanctum of holiness, and sat on the window seat that looked out into Father's Voyn's herb garden. Basil and sage and rosemary and mint and even a couple of tomato plants grew heartily. His little cottage was thirty yards away at the edge of the evergreen forest at the foothill of the highest ridge of the Shar Mountain range. He began to clear away the wax from burned down candles and replace them with new ones for the Sunday service.

"Tell me about your son, Father." Yelena watched him intently. He was an infinitely fascinating and unpredictable man. *To think he had a son,* Yelena mused, *and I've known him all this time and never knew.* She got comfortable on the bench, poised to hear a good story. What he shared, she never could have imagined in a hundred years.

"Well, Yelena, he's been dead for fifty-one years, but it doesn't matter because I think of him everyday, and he lives in me. His name was Voyn, naturally. Because I am not a monk, I was able to have a family right after my seminary studies. I was twenty-four-years-old and I met a beautiful girl named Mara." He went to the window to further open the curtains and let the light stream in through the stained glass. Looking out onto his garden, his family of herbs, he continued, "Our son was born in 1931. What a year. The world was a mess, but we were happy. Hard to imagine, but true. It was enough for us to love and watch our boy grow. God was good to us."

Father Voyn poured a glass of water in the chalice and drank it down. "We have good water in these mountains, don't we, daughter? We are blessed that purity flows to us so effortlessly." Yelena nodded, fidgeting with impatience to hear his story, not to mention her restlessness at her own physical discomfort. She didn't quite fit anywhere, anymore. Even more absurb than Yelena's pregnant hips perched on the window seat behind the Holy Altar, was Father Voyn's tall, lean frame pulling a small stool in front of Yelena, and perching himself at her feet. The elegant uprightness of his being, wrapped in his priestly robe, formed a puddle of black cloth around the legs of the stool. As he looked up at Yelena, he appeared to be young and vulnerable, at his eighty-six-years of life. She looked tenderly at him, as he continued.

"Then the Second World War came, and fear was unleashed on the world. My son was only eleven years old then, and I told him, 'there is nothing to be afraid of, my boy, God is in charge of all of us.' And he believed me." Father Voyn looked away and reached into a pocket and pulled out a pouch of tobacco and some rolling papers.

"Father!" Yelena proclaimed in mock chastisement of the sacrilege of his smoking behind the altar.

Without glancing up from the ritual of rolling the black tobacco into the square of onion skin thin paper, he answered, "God forgives these little things." He smiled, licked the paper, sealed his cigarette, reached for a match from a table of drawers near the altarpiece, and struck it on the bottom of his shoe. Yelena watched with absolute attention. She'd never seen this side of him. Here he was before her, like a normal man, needing a smoke, in order to continue his tale. It made her ache for the ordinariness of her life before she lost Marko, before she lost Radmilo, before Ljuba ran off to the States to marry an American, before there was anything but innocence. She watched the smoke curl around his head, forming a fleeting silver halo around his shock of white hair. His exhale released the weight of the world, and thus fortified, he continued.

"June, 1942, the Fascists were all over the Kozara Mountains. I thought we were dead when the Ustashi captured hundreds of thousands of Serbs, Jews, gypsies, killing most of them, including children." Another prolific puff on his cigarette, "Then, Yelena, I confess, I became afraid."

"I had no idea, Father."

"Hardly anyone does, even now, my dear. History books are like politics, you don't get the whole story. Years later, maybe the truth comes out, slowly, and in pieces. Maybe. Then either men don't believe it, or they say they always knew it, and were just about to say so themselves."

Yelena observed a sadness in him she'd never identified with Father Voyn.

"Open that little window behind you, will you please, Yelena?" She pushed the window open and felt the warm breeze comfort them momentarily, then braced herself for what she sensed might be a tough turn in this recounting.

"So I packed up my family," Father Voyn continued. We traveled by night, and in the day we rested in caves. But, no good, because the Fascist bastards…." He paused, embarrassed at the release of such language in front of Yelena and God. "God forgive me," he said, genuflecting, and then continuing in a whisper, as if the horror of it all could not be spoken out loud. "The bastards put us into Jasenovac, an extermination camp that was worse than anything you could conceive."

"Yes, I've read of Jasenovac, Father," Yelena added.

He got up from his stool and went to the window where he could billow the black tobacco smoke directly out the window, looking out as if he were seeing the story he told unfold before him. "Even the Nazis were shocked by the horrors that went on there." He paused, and looked out, still as a black bear at gunpoint. His cigarette ash was about to drop, Yelena watched it intently. It stayed, and so did her acute focus on what Father Voyn told her next. "Eventually half a million of us were eliminated in that camp." Yelena gasped. That figure, for sure, never turned up in her schoolbooks, and before she could ponder the reason, Father Voyn pushed on, as if in a trance. "They separated the men and women. I feared I would never see my beautiful Mara again. I thought she would claw the guard to death, when he pried her away from little Voyn." Father Voyn took a deep breath to buck himself up to go on, while Yelena held hers.

"My boy and I were allowed to stay together…until they caught us praying. They hated that. They considered it a weakness. Or maybe they saw that it gave us strength, who knows. Either way, it scared them, so they put a stop to it. It was forbidden, but of course it went on anyway, in private, or when the guards were not looking. It made me sick to have to hide my faith, and I would have died for it on the spot, but I needed to stay alive to be with my son, so I could protect him, or so I thought."

He put out his cigarette and sat next to Yelena on the window seat, his head hanging down heavy with the memory of a horrible day.

"One day they decided to 'clean out the weak,' as they called it. The women had been across the way in a separate area, and everyday Mara and I tried to find each other, without success until this one day. They took the women first and lined them up along the wall so that we could see them clearly, so that all of us men with our sons could watch our wives become victims of these evil men, and we stood there, impotent to do anything about it. Mara and I caught sight of each other at the last moment. My son and I waived to her. He blew her kisses. Such a lighthearted gesture, I knew he didn't fully grasp what was coming next. Then my son cried out, 'I love you mamma!' She smiled at us raised her hand to wave and call out, when suddenly she dropped to the ground under machine gun fire. My son screamed, buried his head in my shirt, something I planned to do before they shot, but it happened so fast. I didn't want him to witness his mother's death. He wept convulsively, while I tried to stand strong, but my whole body was shaking.

That's all the provocation the guards needed. 'You!' they cried, 'with the kid! Get over here!' We approached slowly, my son's hand tightly clasped in mine. I thought to myself, they'll have to kill me before I'll let go of this boy's hand...and that's exactly what they did, they killed me by putting a bullet through my son's heart. I screamed and went after the guard who did it. He was about to shoot me, and I didn't care, I wanted to die with my family. His superior officer suddenly called out to stop him, because they wanted strong workers kept alive. So he spit at me and walked away. And I stood there frozen, as they took my son's body away and tossed it onto a pile of bodies like a sack of feed. His little body joined those of dead Jewish children and gypsy children and those of Serbian women and children. So little Voyn was thrown together with his mother in a heap of hellish glory for the Nazis, when two soldiers came and dragged me away."

Tears were streaming down Yelena's face as she listened to him, while he moved to the table with the drawer that held his secret stash of brandy. He removed a flask and a shot glass and poured out a shot of Slivovitz, and drank it in one swallow. He offered some to Yelena, she shook her head, touching her belly. He nodded, understanding she couldn't just then. He put the bottle away. Father Voyn was a man of discipline and precision. He did not drink to get inebriated or to anesthetize himself, he drank that shot to feel again. His body had become numb telling the story. He stood by the table looking at the altar, as if wondering how he ever got there.

"Then they sent me back to the work camp, where I began to hate. It was easy to hate. They destroyed what I cherished more than my own life." He turned to Yelena and finally looked her in the eye, as if to say, "this is the important part, get ready." And it was. And she was.

"Suddenly, Yelena, I realized it was *hate* that killed my family. I had seen what that hate could do, the pain it created, the innocence it destroyed, the lives it disintegrated. And Yelena, I made the toughest decision of my life. I decided right then that I would spend what was left of my life, *loving* every person I met, no matter what." He kept his eyes on her to make sure she got what he was saying, to be certain that it landed.

She paused for a long moment, then returned his look. "But, Father, how do you make a decision like that?"

He smiled at the childlike question. "Dear one," he replied, "really, there is usually only one important decision to make per lifetime." He patted her head, as if the blessing he wanted her to receive from this story were complete.

"Now you must excuse me a moment, Yelena. Nature calls. Rest yourself here, pray. Ask God for help. He always answers, you know, even sometimes...."

"...before you call...." Yelena finished the phrase from Isaiah 65:24 before he could, for she'd heard it from him so many times before. He sort of chuckled a bit. It was a strange sound, a kind of mix between a gulp of grief and a gasp for air. Then he walked out of the church to the portable restroom with an imperceptibly lighter gait, now that he had unburdened his heart.

She watched him through the window with renewed respect and deep compassion for what he'd endured. She'd had no idea what he'd lived through, and she supposed that one never does know the path another has walked, which is why one is taught not to judge. *But My God*, she thought, *how could he ever forgive that heinous act of terror, how could he not feel hatred toward the killer, how could he not desire revenge, or some type of justice?* She heard him humming in the distance, and wondered, *how in God's good name, could he ever love again?*

Looking up at the sky through the trees, she realized, that's all Father Voyn had ever expressed; Love. He was love, nothing but love.

No way could she ever get to that level of consciousness. No way. If this was Father Voyn's way of telling her to love her enemies, he could forget it. No way, no way. Forgive Omir? Never. Not a chance. This was the 1990's, not the forties. Besides we weren't at war with the Nazis. This wasn't war. It was...it was...it was...what? What was it that happened that day? And why?

CHAPTER FORTY-EIGHT

MONDAY MORNING, YELENA ROSE EARLY and took the bus into the town center to investigate the whereabouts of Omir Atalov, and the status of his case. It was possible that her talk with Father Voyn the day before, and a good night's rest in her own loft bedroom had nearly tempered her more toward justice than revenge. It was possible, but not certain. Her streak of fierce motherhood ran deep. When she walked down the steps of Ljuba's apartment to go to the airport, she'd honestly had justice on her mind, but when her bare feet touched the earth that covered her son's young body, revenge brewed in the depths of her being, despite all reason and resolve. On the bus into town, she sincerely prayed that this visit to the courthouse would swing the fulcrum toward bloodless justice, and quell the thirst for revenge.

In the village and throughout the area, the news about Omir and her son was well known. It was whispered about, written about, lied about, denied, and all but hailed as fantasy, depending on whom you talked to. Yelena got lots of looks at every turn, looks of compassion, concern of her return, gross critiques of her hair, not to mention her pregnant appearance. Many snubbed her because they believed she brought it on herself for living so long as a widow, or because if she hadn't gone to America she would not be facing this horrible news at this belated moment. Neither made any sense, but such was the essence of village gossip, it had nothing to do with reality.

It was practically required that rumors be ridiculous in order to qualify for dissemination. So Yelena felt a sense of relief when she arrived in the town center, where actual strangers surrounded her, and she could be somewhat more anonymous than she was on the bus from the village. There were, however, disdainful glances, even from strangers, as they assessed the nature of a woman that pregnant, going to town alone, with no ring on her finger.

Yelena approached the courthouse. She was viewed with suspicion. But there was sufficient bustle in the town center on market day to allow her to maneuver undisturbed through the crowd of shoppers and venders to the courthouse steps.

The front of the courthouse was swarming with people waiting in line to pay fines, or gain counsel from their lawyers before appearing in court. It was a mixed bag of chaos, criminality, and dutiful citizens. Muslims, Serbs, Gypsies should be all the same under the law, and in the proximity of a courthouse. But the divisiveness of the groups had become so ugly in recent years, so atrocious in their random acts of violence toward each other, destructive in thought and deed, that it was no surprise when a Muslim man whistled at Yelena, radiant in all her pregnancy, and a Serbian man threw a punch at the Muslim man for looking at one of "his" people, as if he owned her. Stupidity incarnate. The brawl was broken up by a policeman who ran down the steps of the courthouse to stop the incendiary tempers from flying too far off the handle, since the town was now running a few degrees from spontaneous combustion at any given moment.

Yelena immediately recognized him as one of the two policemen who came to her ten months ago to tell her that her son's death would most likely go unsolved. He looked at her, then looked again, and realized who she was, then in what condition she was, and immediately escorted her through the throngs of citizens into the cool foyer of the edifice.

"Mrs. Mandich, isn't it?' he enquired as he held her by the elbow walking up the steps.

"That's right. I remember you. Things changed, didn't they?" She couldn't resist telling one of the cops who told her nothing could be done that she was now here to witness that something obviously had been done; that was her son's killer had been caught, though she had not yet heard about exactly how Omir was found. What gave him away? What evidence? Who was responsible for his arrest? *The Truth,* she thought, *it was the Truth with a capital T that arrested that evil.*

A million questions flooded her mind; she could barely put one foot in front of the other. How grateful she was that this particular policeman, whom she knew albeit in a bitter remembrance, had come to her rescue.

"What are you doing here, Mrs. Mandich? And in your condition," he implored her, as he steered her away from the main desk, toward the water fountain, as if that was what she came for.

"You don't know why I'm here? Omir Atalov is a prisoner here, is he not?" No response from young handsome cop. She persisted with her usual importunity, "I came to learn of his court date."

Suspicious of the proximity of the young officer to the pregnant tomato, a smarmy officer from behind the counter addressed them. The summer heat had branded this large man's shirt with defiant circles of sweat around each armpit, while his collar fought to contain the generous portion of thick black hair that was trying to escape his chest. He held a hand-rolled cigarette between his first finger and his thumb with a feigned elegance that seemed to say, "I may look like a peasant, but I'm really an emperor, so you best obey." The man obviously held some authority, because when he called out to the young cop, a hush fell across the desks peppering the area behind the counter, where Smarmy stood like a world leader.

"What's this about, Omir Atalov? What is it the lady wants to know and why? Step over here, lady," he muttered to himself and made a snide crack to his underlings about calling her "lady" given she was pregnant and without a husband, and without the shame to at least wear a ring to quell nasty remarks. It was mortifying to this particular court official, and he made his thoughts known.

"Come, come, step over here, young lady," again laying on the "lady" for the audience in the cheap seats surrounding him. "Tell me your business here."

Unafraid, and forever untamed, Yelena approached the counter. "You have a prisoner named Omir Atalov, and I'm here to inquire about his court date."

The man chuckled as if he'd never heard of such an absurd idea. *A court date, whatever could she be talking about, what does she think this is, a court?* Toying with her seemed to be the most fun he'd had all day. Of course, she knew he must know the crime Omir committed, though he had no way of knowing that she was one whose life Omir had destroyed, by killing her son. Nevertheless, there was no way she could justify his attitude. She kept her chin up, and waited for him to stop chuckling, then nailed him.

"Yes, a court date, you know what that is, don't you?" The place froze in shock, that she had the cheek to talk to an authority in that way. She pressed on, "You must know that he's being tried for murder." She spoke in the most condescending tone she could come up with – a dicey choice given the fact that they, or rather he, held all the cards.

This flustered and embarrassed the blustering court official. Determined to put her in her place, he leaned over the counter, towering over her with his stink and ugly attitude.

"Who said so?" The whole place broke into laughter. Even some of the other civilians sitting in the waiting area began to chuckle, hoping that any alliance with the Big Shot official might move their own individual cases along more smoothly and mercifully. Yelena didn't flinch.

"What is so funny, gentlemen?" Her anger rising, her hormones taking charge of her tongue, and the summer heat having fried any modicum of mellow she may have had an hour ago, she went for it. "Surely you know his crime, sir, and surely a man of your stature and dignity...." This was beginning to get a round of smirking and chortling. She paused to let the murmurings reach the ears of her target, she watched them redden, then continued, "...A man of your, shall we say 'integrity' would not look the other way with regard to the appropriate handling of this matter and of this so-called man, who killed innocent children." She stuck her chin out the slightest bit to punctuate her brave statement of irony, tears burning her cheeks. Silence hit the air with a bang. One could easily hear the wings of a small fly through an open window, and then she heard a remark from a Muslim man behind her.

He murmured, "There are no innocent Serbs, not even the children."

Fortunately, the guy's wife yanked him out the door, out of range of Yelena who was winding up when she heard his crack. The court official pulled her attention back to his self-appointed self-importance, by blurting out, "The court date hasn't been set yet, and so, little miss...." Yelena interrupted him, before his peanut gallery could chime in with their obligatory chuckling.

"When will it be set?" she demanded.

Now it was his turn to mock her. "Welllll, let's see, I suggest you come back in a few months...and uh...bring the baby!" He looked around as if to telegraph to the office workers that his punch line had been delivered, and they were meant to laugh on cue. Snickering broke out, and Yelena leaned over the counter as if she were going to either climb over it, or lean in and slap the court official. The desire was aborted by the swift intervention of the young cop who had been witnessing this charade from the water fountain.

He grabbed Yelena by the elbow and steered her out with a loud reprimand for the benefit of his superior, "All right, lady, out you go, you got what you came for, didn't you." She caught on to his ploy, and feigned resistance until they were in the foyer, then she confronted him.

"Where is he? You know, don't you?"

"He's not here, they transferred him," he said staring at the tile on the floor, "...or something."

"What do you mean or something?" she raised her voice, and drew a few glances.

He pulled her aside, and whispered conspiratorially.

"Look, Mrs. Mandich, he's been transferred, I think."

"You're lying. You know where he is!"

"I don't know, and that's the truth. I don't know where he went, but I know he's no longer jailed here."

"What about the other men who were involved?"

The young cop swallowed. This he did know for certain and it made even him sick at heart, as those other men were so obviously guilty. "Well, uh, I'm not sure."

Yelena stared at him in shock. He looked away, ashamed for delivering such rotten news, and forlorn for the state of judicial affairs in their country.

"I'm sorry to tell you ma'am, but that's the way it is now. It's open season for the Muslim Albanians against the Serbs. Everyone wants blood for blood. Neither side is behaving very well." He looked away from her gaze. That's all he could muster up to tell her. More would have been salting the wound.

"My God." She whispered to herself, pushed through the revolving door barely in time to puke on the bushes at the entryway. The young cop patted her shoulder gently, as he turned his head away, his heart strong, his stomach weak. He felt sick too, and walked back inside.

Hot, dizzy, nearly delirious and feeling like she was carrying triplets, Yelena leaned against the cool cement of the courthouse until she got her bearings. Now what? Everything was a blur. The humid air was more intense than she'd ever remembered at this time of year. Was it her own body temperature, or the emotional fever from the inflamed conflict that had spread through her village and the neighboring towns? It lit up the area like a match in a haystack.

It set her mind spinning about Ljuba's warnings about going back to trouble, the look in Aunt Sofia's eyes when she questioned why Yelena had returned, and even Jake's insistence that she not return. All the counsel of her loved ones flooded her mind like a tidal wave of clarity. As if blind from birth, she suddenly received sight only to behold the horror of what was in front of her nose all along.

Managing to straighten up to walk to the bus stop, she was confronted by an old villager who used to live down the road from them with her three sons. Her sons had long since moved up to Belgrade and left their mother penniless, homeless, and as it turned out, toothless. Once this woman, Anitsa, caught sight of Yelena, she was hell bent on having a conversation with her, no doubt with the hope of some dinars being thrown her way.

"Yelena! Ayeeee! Yelena! Is that you?" Anitsa cried or rather whistled through her tooth-deprived mouth.

Trapped in what she knew could become a substantial visit if she wasn't clever, Yelena moved quickly to the lemonade kiosk meters away and ordered up a drink for Anitsa and herself. She'd hoped that the drink would absolve her from what she knew was would be interpreted as a rude brush-off.

"Ah, Anitsa, yes, it's me…of course, it's me." Yelena stammered while reaching for some dinars to pay for the two lemonades.

"I heard you were in America, married to a rich horse breeder, but no, you're here!" Anitsa charged ahead.

"No, I mean, yes I was. In America that is, but not now. Now I'm here." Yelena heard herself making third grade level conversation in the hope of staunching it quickly.

"Well," she replied, as she scrutinized Yelena head to foot, pausing to x-ray her belly, with her eyes. "Maybe your horse breeder needed a break from the saddle!" she cackled shamelessly.

"Maybe," was all Yelena could manage in response, while quickly downing her lemonade. Meanwhile, while Anitsa was sipping her drink slowly and deliberately as if she were Lady Astor at High Tea, settling in for a couple of hours of good gossip, Yelena scurried across the road and called back to Anitsa.

"That's my bus, Anitsa! Bye, good to see you!"

Anitsa nearly choked on the lemonade and cried out, "May you be blessed with a boy, to keep you in your old age!" then turned back to the counter at the kiosk, grabbed the change which Yelena left for a tip, as she demanded the vender refill both hers and Yelena's empty glasses. It would seem in her case that having a son, or rather three of them, didn't turn out to be much of a blessing in her dear old age.

Yelena, safely on the bus in a window seat, looked back at Anitsa pleading with the lemonade guy, and she quietly blessed her and hoped she'd win her battle.

The bus trip back up the mountain was slower than the one coming down to town. The old bus sputtered with over exertion every time it stopped to pick up a villager heading back home for the day. Yelena gazed out the window, not really taking in what she was seeing, as her mind played out images of her son's death.

She saw the image of Omir lifting the pipe over her young son's head and wanted to fly out of the bus and return to the courthouse to raise holy hell. She played out that scene in her mind and realized she'd be laughed at as rapidly as she would be escorted to the door. The futility of the situation twisted her into knots inside. What could she do now?

Find Omir. If he was transferred, he was transferred somewhere relatively nearby, she thought, and she must learn the trial date and pursue justice. But where would they move him, and why, she wondered. It made no sense, the crime was committed here, he should be tried here. The vicious circle of irrational circumstances confounded her.

She let her eyes wander out the window to the granite mountains. The bus was skimming them so closely that one could almost touch the lichen that had formed on the great rocks hidden from the sunlight. She then glanced across the aisle to the other side of the bus where the window opened to the view of the ruins of Czar Dusan's palace. Old stone walls, now standing at a fraction of their original stature.

Why had it not been restored, she wondered? Their neighboring European countries to the west, would have taken a sight like that and turned it into a profitable tourist attraction, with history-minded travel guides, complete with all the tourist paraphernalia, t-shirts, hats, cards and candy bars. Why not the Serbs?

What was it that let them forget their rich and profound history? Well, perhaps, they didn't forget it, but they didn't celebrate it. They seemed to remember only the defeats, the "Battle of Kosovo," the invasions of so many interlopers that had tried to call this rich land theirs. With freedom being so precious to them, they had always fought tooth and nail to keep their country theirs. They had won most of the time, albeit at great price.

Now the unbridled immigration of their southern Albanian neighbors, followed by Albanian aggression to claim Serbia's Kosovo as their own, and the so-called peacekeeping forces of other European nations imbedded on their turf, had diluted the dignity they thought they had about their identity. Their fierce resistance to foreign interference had changed their world image as violators of peace rather than the freedom fighters that they truly were and had always been.

As the bus and its passengers rolled around the curves of the mountain roads taking her home to a place that wasn't home anymore, Yelena began to wonder where, in God's name, did home exist for her now? It certainly wasn't the sofa in Ljuba's Queens' apartment. Her mind searched for answers to endless questions about how to live and where, and more profoundly, how and when would the pain of Marko's death end or even diminish? And would she ever stop hating?

CHAPTER FORTY-NINE

THAT NIGHT YELENA ATE VERY LITTLE, despite Aunt Sofia's exhortations about her needing to feed for two, how pale she looked and how she needed to buck up to look forward toward her new life. Aunt Sofia's affectionate chiding and somewhat enervating mothering of Yelena did not land on receptive ears that particular evening. Troubled and confused by what transpired that day at the courthouse, she excused herself from the table and went upstairs to her bedroom, opened the windows and sat looking out at the night, as if awaiting answers to her heart's queries. A warm June breeze blew across her cheeks. She looked out towards Zima's house, and saw nothing but a small light in the kitchen window. It was quiet and still. She'd not been able to go to the door of her friend's home since her return. What could she say to her? *Hey, why didn't you tell me your husband was planning to kill my boy?*

She looked up and caught the tail end of the voyage of a falling star. She wished on it. What came to her was to wish for justice, without defining what that was, how it would look, or even feel. She pleaded with the skies, "Just give me justice; give it to me, please."

Yelena's reverie with the firmament was suddenly rattled by the sound of the downstairs door opening, slamming shut, and the cry of a woman that could have been mistaken for the wail of a wild animal. Yelena stood at the top of the stairs and listened.

"Let the devil take them all," the woman cried.

Yelena froze. She felt a prescient shiver go up her spine, as if she knew that what she was about to hear she would not be an answer to her wish for justice. Shaken by the continued cries from the bereaved female, she slowly proceeded down the stairs. By the time her foot touched the bottom step, she recognized the voice as Velinka's, a woman from the village who lived on the other side of the stream.

Nearly Aunt Sofia's age, Velinka came for coffee maybe once a week. They were old friends and good neighbors. Yelena knew

Velinka well, and had commiserated with her daughter Maya, whose
son was one of the older boys kidnapped that day. It was months
before they found those boys dead in a cave. Clearly, whatever it was
that brought Velinka to Aunt Sofia's door at this time of night had to
be horrific at best.

Yelena took one look at the wild fire in Velinka's eyes and
cringed as she heard "A curse on God, His Mother, Son and all His
Children, and damn all the patron saints and the houses they bless!
Let the devil take them all!" Velinka's nonstop rift of cursing and
swearing against God and all living things matched the old woman's
crazed features. She looked up at Yelena and collapsed into a chair,
dropping her head between her hands as she wept.

Yelena approached her cautiously, slowly placing her hand on
her shoulder. Aunt Sofia poured a shot of slivovitz, and Uncle Anton
remained mercifully unaware of what was about to be announced.
Aunt Sofia placed the slivi in front of Velinka as Yelena stroked her
back, attempting to calm her. "Easy, Vela," she whispered. "Sip some
slivi."

Velinka lifted her head from her hands and slammed her hand
on the table, clearing the slivi, the coffees that had been there from
dinner, and a bowl of sweet cherries, sending them all flying across
the room. This was accompanied by more emphatic cursing. Yelena
and Aunt Sofia stared at each other, unsure of what to offer next in
the way of aid to their friend. Then it all spewed forth out of the
broken old woman, who possessed the ferocity of ten men, "They
found my grandson and the other two in a cave, cut up and beaten
like animals, this you knew....but...but...that they were barely
recognizable, you probably didn't know that...and now...now they
have set the bastards free."

"Who, Vela?" Yelena asked, fearing and knowing the answer.

Then with the steadiness of a sniper, Vela looked her in the eye,
"Omir. Omir Atalov, your neighbor, your best friend's husband, the
snake, the Muslim pig...yesterday they released him and the two other
men who did this."

The others were from the next village over. They didn't even
have a courthouse there. She stared down at the mess she'd made on
the floor, having no recollection of how it all got there. Time stood
still. The unimaginable had come to their door that night, on the tail
end of Yelena's wish upon a star. So much for the hope for justice.
She was confounded. God had disappeared. She picked up the

broken cups, the dish of cherries, the now empty shot glass, and the knife that had been on the bread board. She took it all to the sink, and placed it on the drain board. She turned on the hot water, and let it run on the blade of the knife, till steam surrounded her face. Aunt Sofia came up behind her, turned off the water and took the knife out of her hand.

The whole village must have been awakened by Velinka's howls. It was doubtful anyone hadn't heard her. Velinka eventually collapsed on the sofa, partly from exhaustion, partly the Slivovitz. Aunt Sofia covered her with a light quilt, and sent Yelena up to her bedroom where she resumed her watch at the window. Looking across to Zima's house, she wondered if Omir was there, and if he heard Velinka.

It began to drizzle, light as the veil of a bride, but enough to blur her view. She thought she saw the lamp in Zima's window flicker, or was it another falling star, or a tear of the saints that had been railed against with Velinka's curses. There was no satisfaction in being right when justice would not be served. Righteous indignation was nothing. She felt futile. She would try to sleep knowing it would be a stranger tonight. She reached to turn off the lamp on her night table and knocked over a glass of water, it broke.

Nothing was holding together that night, all the splinters of existence turned into shards of the cold reality of crimes unpunished, unpardoned, unforgiven. Father Voyn's story drifted into her thought as she carefully stooped to pick up the broken glass. She cut her hand on a sliver of glass and pushed Father Voyn's voice from her mind. Unprepared to enter into any similarly merciful act of kindness as the Father Voyn had, she pushed it away from her consciousness. Aunt Sofia heard the glass break and came to the bottom of the stairs.

"Child, are you all right?"

"Fine, Auntie," she replied, "I just knocked over a glass of water."

"Ah," she murmured, relieved. "Get some sleep, you need to rest."

"Yes, yes," Yelena replied, but Aunt Sofia did not hear her mutter. "Sleep, right, how, Auntie, how?"

Yelena stepped carefully around the glass till she landed in her slippers, then quickly gathered the glass chips into a towel and wiped the wet floor, before returning to her post at the window. Staring into a night that reflected back an unyielding silence, she wanted to scold skies for betraying her. The gross injustice Velinka reported came too quickly on the heels of her hope that she might follow a more forgiving path, too close in the wake of the frustrating day at the courthouse for Yelena not to have runaway dark imaginings.

Cracking open the window, she stretched her neck out into the night air to catch a better glimpse of Zima's house through the fog. The clear night was now shrouded in mist as if Velinka's news cloaked it in a curtain of secrecy. Yelena strained to see through the dark mantle, into Zima's home, now a harbor for a criminal. Yelena bitterly imagined Zima sleeping soundly with her killer husband snoring beside her. It curdled her stomach.

However, the reality was that at that same moment, Zima was experiencing the same insomnia as her childhood friend, and for the same reason, though perhaps from an opposite view. Zima too was struck catatonic with confusion. Relieved her husband was out of jail, yes, appalled that he had committed this heinous crime, yes, and even more horrified that it was against her best friend's son. Zima was utterly disgusted that Omir sat drinking like a pig in the next room, betraying the Muslim law and all rules of decency. She could not bear it. She could not bear him. She wasn't at all sure how she would continue to live in that village or anywhere with him, for that matter. Her boys were asleep, thankfully, and believed their father to be innocent, and maybe even justified. This alarmed her more than anything; this despicable, hateful sense of misplaced entitlement that her young boys were learning from their father and from his ignorant, radicalized family who misconstrued the teachings of her cherished Islam. This misunderstanding of her beloved Allah created a stupid self-righteousness in her loved ones. This made Zima sick.

The sad irony was lost on both of these women, who were once friends, now forced to be enemies by the circumstances of radical injustice and unpardonable crime. If only they had kept him in jail and tried him, there might have been a sense of peace for each of them, no matter what the judgment. But the stamina of political and social corruption in their town, torn up by civil hatred, was substantial and defiant.

Zima sat at the window in her bedroom, listening to her husband slobber over his brandy. In a flash she stood up, strode into the kitchen, and addressed the head of household like she never had before.

"You sleep out in the shed if you're going to drink that stuff." She could hardly contain her fury and disgust. "This is still a Muslim household and we keep Islamic law. Either get your booze out of here, or out you go with it!"

Zima stood there shaking, never having spoken like that to her husband, half expecting him to turn around and hit her in the head with the bottle. It would not have been out of character. His violent streak was always at the tip of his fingers, even in his sober moments. But instead, she saw him crumble upon himself. A broken man, not even remotely resembling the man she married.

Meanwhile, unable to discern anything from her bedroom window, Yelena crawled back into her bed, then sprung up suddenly to vomit again, barely missing the sheets and bedcovers this time. She was indeed too far along in her pregnancy for this, but the upheaval of the day made her insides topsy-turvy. Everything hurt.

And so for both women rest remained a faint memory.

CHAPTER FIFTY

THE NEXT DAY AUNT SOFIA WAS UP EARLY and finished the milking, feeding and chores on her own. Knowing full well that Yelena would offer to help, she slipped out, hoping to insure the young mother would get some rest. Aunt Sofia was sure Yelena had not gained enough weight for the coming baby, and Yelena was sure that she was too fat too soon. This baby was advanced, way far ahead of itself, in Yelena's perception.

There was a pall of silence over the household that morning. The only words spoken were to the cows and the cats. Yelena gathered the soiled linens, bathed, dressed and went down to do the wash at the Laundromat at the bottom of the hill.

It was a bright June morning, already the sun beating hot. If one didn't know the sordid events of recent months, one would think the village, the bubbling stream, the mountain range, all of it, to be the most idyllic environment on earth. It had that capacity, but sadly not that reality, not now.

Yelena, still shaken from the news of the previous night and unsure how to respond to it, did what she did best; cleaned. She carried the laundry in a basket on top of her head, a custom both medieval and effective. Zorka and Miriana were doing their wash at the same time, so they kept her company. They had already heard the horrible news, which traveled at the velocity of a hummingbird in that enclave.

The village center seemed foreign to Yelena. The café was already filled with men drinking and it wasn't yet noon. She wondered why they weren't working. She then noted the separation between the Serbs and the Muslims, seated at separate tables, a division distinct like never before.

Boban, the café owner, had always been neutral and served everyone that came to his establishment. He and his wife prided themselves in having Serbs and Muslims as their clientele. They loved their little business and wanted it to thrive. Peace was the path to prosperity, they often proclaimed. And so it was.

As Yelena passsed the café, there were mutterings from both the Serb table and the Muslims. She kept her eyes straight ahead, and thereby did not notice Omir drinking brandy at a table filled with his Muslim colleagues, who were drinking coffee.

After the women got their dirty laundry churning in the machines, they stepped out for some fresh air, which Zorka quickly contaminated with her dark tobacco.

Miriana, typically positive and upbeat, was at a loss of what to say to Yelena. "Oh Yelo, I know that God is good, and His will shall be done." Then she burst into tears, more at the imagining that if the same scenario had happened to her and her child, she'd have gone mad by now or be in jail for homicide.

Zorka was less spiritually-minded about the issue. Her coarseness knew no limits. "That fucking bastard, son of a whore, how dare they let him out of jail. He should be burning in Muslim hell right now as we speak. Him and the other two sons of bitches!" Her voice was as voluptuous as she was, so Yelena shushed her, since the café was a very short distance from them. The morning stillness would carry Zorka's expletives on its back like pollen on a bumble bee. Yelena had no energy for a scene this morning.

"Say something, Yelena," Miriana coaxed, thinking it would ease her pain to talk about it, but Yelena stayed silent and patted the hand of her faithful friend, then walked back into the Laundromat, where the three women sat staring at the whirling white linens, hypnotized by the circular and somewhat soothing repetition of things.

Finally, all the linens clean and folded, Yelena placed her bundle in a basket on top of her head and proceeded back up the hill, having bid adieu to her friends who were waiting for one more batch to dry. As Yelena approached the portion of the path that went right by the café, Boban was pouring beer into a patron's glass from a large pitcher. It was Omir, who was throwing back a shot of whiskey and chasing it with the newly poured beer. Clearly, his Muslim traditional abstinence had been set on a shelf for now.

One of his buddies, high on his own perfume no doubt, called out, "Whoa, look at that juicy piece of chicken, will you? Shall we carry her clean sheets for her, or lay them down on the ground and dirty them for her."

Another chimed in, "Ya, Ya, juicy!"

9

Omir looked over his shoulder to see what his friends were salivating over, and looked Yelena straight in the eye, then quickly turned away and drank another shot.

"Hey, Omir, what's with you, man?" chortled his friend. "What happened, lost your appetite in jail, eh?"

The others couldn't resist the suction of the depraved quicksand of conversation and added, "Well, we know you went after her son, but that didn't work, so how about Mamma?"

Hearing that, Yelena spun around, splaying her clean white sheets into the mud, as she stooped to pick up a few rocks and hurled them at Omir. She missed him with the first few, but hit a bottle which shattered. Then with the force and power of a woman plus one life inside, she grabbed four more and hurled them repeatedly at him, desperately attempting to annihilate the horror of his crime. Gritting her teeth and short of breath, she persisted, hitting everything but her maligned target, till the fifth rock landed just above Omir's eye. This brought laughter from his cohorts, and rage from the café proprietor who wanted order, harmony, and unbroken glasses.

"Hey, stop that!" Boban cried, "What do you think you're doing?" At that moment, he caught a pebble in the forehead. Yelena's rage of the past months was unleashed in a way that could have brought down the mountain. It took Zorka, Miriana, Boban and two other Serbian men in the café to calm her and get her to stop. They feared she'd drop the baby right there. She was the epitome of the lioness in her lair keeping out the snakes and hyenas. She was incorrigible. Indefatigable, driven and unwavering. When one passes into that existential state where nothing matters, then blind courage is unleashed; and from that point of zero fear, one will find the mark, sooner or later.

Yet, Zorka was able to convince Yelena to walk up the hill with her and left Miriana to pick up the dirty laundry and take care of washing it again at the Laundromat. They walked slowly but steadily, with Zorka's arm firmly around Yelena's shoulder. Yelena, in the mesmeric state of a post violent adrenaline rush, barely heard Boban's loud cries about his losses, nor did she catch Omir hiding behind a towel mopping blood from the broken skin on his forehead.

It was obvious to any thinking man that calm would never return to Shar Village. The place had been fatally wounded by the death of a child. Then months later when the three older boys were found dead and a corrupted court turned a blind eye to it all, there was no doubt that long term chaos had come to nest here indefinitely.

CHAPTER FIFTY-ONE

ARRIVING AT AUNT SOFIA'S THEY SAT ON THE BENCH under the arbor, while Aunt Sofia brought water and a towel and, of course, the mandatory coffee to cool Yelena. When Yelena finally stopped sobbing and blew her nose heartily into Zorka's handkerchief, Aunt Sofia thought it safe to head down to the barn to finish her work. The women sat in silence on the familiar bench under the arbor, where they'd shared many a joy and sorrow through the years.

"I love this bench," Yelena said through her tears.

"I know, honey, I know." Zorka comforted her.

"My home, my mountain, my bench." Yelena let flow her tears of frustration and rage.

"Go back to America, Yelena. They must have a mountain and a bench there somewhere." It was Zorka's feeble attempt to change the subject.

"Part of my soul is always missing, back there, Zorka."

"That will always be so, my darling, no matter where you are."

"I miss my son...."

"I know, Yelena, I know...but now you have a new life to think about, and you can't move forward here. We're all stuck in the mud, especially you. Go back to Ljuba, and your American guy. Hell, I would."

"Not yet, Zorka, not yet...." Yelena looked down toward the path they'd just traversed and got lost in her thoughts, when Aunt Sofia came back up from the barn, calling to them.

"Tsst, Tsst, come quick, you two. Mina is spitting them out. Quick! Zorka get Dushka, I promised her she could see this." Yelena followed Aunt Sofia down to the barn to watch Mina, their great and wonderful sow give birth to eleven piglets, one at a time. They were joined by Zorka and her daughter Dushka, and the wonder of birth silenced them all. It brought a holy calm to the women huddled around the pigpen.

A mother never gets to actually see the birth of her own baby. Not the way these mothers were able to witness the nascence of those baby pigs. The sow's travail, unabetted by epidural or even loud cries, was endured with heavy grunts and breathless perseverance that made her heroic in the eyes of the trio that watched her, rooted for her, and all but got inside the pen to help her.

Mina was one magnificent female, working overtime, unrelenting, braced, and encircled by the compassion of the other females who had born the fruit of their own womb. A lack of boundaries, a blending of each other's pain, formed a sense of community in their village that included Mina their blessed sow.

Yelena took the babes as Mina spit them out. Eleven times. Each time, Yelena wiped them free of their blood and placenta and natal sac, with the confident expertise of a former nurse's aide. Then she shepherded each one toward a full and expectant teat. Each time, Dushka would take Yelena's babushka, doubling as a towel, and rinse it out for her, readying it for the next arrival. Aunt Sofia spoke to the sow, gently encouraging her and scratching her behind the ears. Zorka hung back in appreciation and tender love for the way that her own offspring, young Dushka, contributed to the miracle in silent obedience to Yelena's instruction. It was a nativity that sanctified Shar Village on a day when that small cluster of houses needed benediction more than ever. The fact that more than one ethnic group called it home had never caused problems until recent months. It was as if the arms that protected the mountain like a giant Psalm of David had been broken and scattered, leaving no reassurance that all would be well.

Yet in this antechamber of awe, between the trauma of Yelena's encounter with Omir, and what troubles may lie ahead, there was a little pocket of space like a musical rest, that allowed for a moment of serenity to rise above the conflict. It was Life beginning Life over and over again as it had for eons and would for evermore. By the time Mina completed her maternal mission of farrowing in the cloven tribe, the women were nearly as exhausted as the sow. Eleven baby pigs!

As the wonderful alchemy of the afternoon came to a close, and the shadow of dusk was upon them, the women simultaneously came to and realized it was time for them to find their way to their respective supper tables. They labored up from the barn toward the house, commenting in fragmented phrases at Mina's magnificence, and the triumph that all eleven had lived, a rarity in itself.

The sweet fragrance of the fruit trees laced their path as a gentle evening breeze applauded their vigilance. Zorka spoke of the need for a celebratory toast, as if she had ever required an excuse to imbibe. Dushka, walked in radiant wonder alongside Yelena, her own personal hero, grabbing onto her sleeve, now and again. Aunt Sofia, despite her advanced years, led the plodding females. Then Yelena sent Dushka on ahead while she turned back to latch the barnyard gate, which they'd all forgotten about, so high were they on the elixir of life's eternal creation.

"You go on ahead Dushka dear, I'll be right up." Yelena reassured her, and patted Dushka on the back in appreciation for her internship, which produced a smile of rare pride in Dushka.

"Don't dawdle, Yelena." Zorka called. "There'll be no more slivi left you wait too long."

"You drink my share, Zorka. I'm not drinking till the baby comes, you know that."

"Oh, that's right! Good for you, good for us," Zorka cackled and marched toward her liquid reward.

Yelena paused at the window of the barn and gazed one more time at the feeding piglets, truly an extraordinary sight. She was startled out of her momentary reverie by the sound of a man's coughing and spitting and cursing. She turned sharply to see that it was Omir stumbling along the path from his home, toward the shed, to which Zima had sentenced him. Zima followed him like a jailer and picked up her drunken husband more than once, in the short distance between their kitchen door and the door of the tool shed, which was not ten meters from the edge of Aunt Sofia's barnyard. Yelena saw them and froze. They saw her and kept walking.

Omir, with such gall, stupidity or flat out drunken effrontery stared right at Yelena, while Zima had the grace to look away in shame, leaving Yelena enraged and desolate. When they reached the shed, she heard the jangle of keys, Zima unlocking the pathetic domicile for Omir, and shoving him inside. Yelena wondered if Zima was protecting the village from Omir, or Omir from the village.

Yelena waited and watched like a jaguar about to spring onto its prey. She waited for Zima to turn around and look at her, approach her, speak to her, beg forgiveness, something. Yelena heard the shed door scrape shut, and Zima's quick pace rushing up the path to her house, without even a nod back at Yelena. She then turned to latch the barn door, glancing again at Mina's crib, but the sanctity of that event had somehow paled. It was like ice water had been flung into Yelena's eyes, waking her to the reality, that her son's murderer was safely nestled in a bunk in his tool shed, and her son lie two meters underground in the darkness of the earth, on the crest of the hill by the church. An unacceptable incongruity. An unjust juxtaposition. She wanted to vomit again, but instead, proceeded slowly and quietly toward Omir's shed, for what reason, she knew not.

Omir was muttering to himself, and she couldn't make it out, so she drew closer. Branches snapped under her feet and she nearly gave herself away, but found a small boulder to rest on, that was close enough to the window for her to look in at him.

The shed was surprisingly orderly, for a shed, Yelena thought. It was set up like a carpentry workshop. One side had a large workbench and stool, with all kinds of tools hanging in front of it and from it. In the corner near the doors was a pot belly stove, obviously unlit on this summer night, but clearly functioning judging from the aroma of formerly burned wood. Omir was on a narrow bunk built along the far wall. It had a thin foam mattress and an old quilt on it, and a funky old hook rug at the foot of it. There were a couple of wood crates stacked in one corner stored there for the late summer fruit harvest, and various shovels, spades, and gardening tools leaning against the wall under the window alongside of the one where Yelena stood. All in all, a fairly well kept, though dusty shed. Yelena judged that to be because Zima's late father was a cabinet maker, and probably used it when he visited them, years back. He probably hoped his grandsons would take up the craft, but judging by the rusted condition of the blades and saws, Yelena surmised that might not come to be.

Omir sat at the edge of the bunk, drinking. He reached for a blanket at the end of the bed and put it behind him as a pillow so he could sit, resting against the wall. "Ahh, now this is comfort," he muttered. He must have found the bottle a willing listener, because he proceeded to converse with himself, as if he had a companion right there with him. "Better than that filthy jailhouse, eh?" Drink. "Ahh!" Belch. "I'm a Professor of Literature, dammit!" He groaned as it became necessary for him to rearrange his backrest. "Oh my, now that's better." Then he proclaimed, "'Extraordinary men have a right to commit any crime!'" He finished punching the blanket into a shape that assured him would be more comfortable. "Dostoevsky was a wise man. Slav, but anyway, smart. Not Muslim, but, anyway..."

He drank again, and the bottle seemed to give him yet another great realization, for he again proclaimed, as if on a soapbox, or perhaps a courtroom, "I have a right to protect Muslim women from Slavic swine...I have a duty!"

Yelena watched this without taking a breath. A crack in the siding of the shed gave her full view of this spectacle. She didn't want to miss a word of it. She waited in limbo for a clue, a hint, a sign of how or why a man could do what he did. Nothing he said made much sense. She understood the words, but it was all crap. She could well imagine why Zima would have shunned him to the shed. Not only for the drinking, but for the vermin that came out of his mouth as the alcohol went into it. Moments passed without his saying a word, and Yelena thought he'd passed out sitting straight up on the bunk. She was about to creep away from her lookout, when he stood up suddenly and put down the bottle on the wooden bench and pulled back the covers on the bed. Nothing but proper slumber for this criminal.

His private tirade ended with his spewing..."It's our country now," he seemed to say to the pillow. "Our country...well...not yet, but it will be ours one day. All part of our holy Islamic nation...all...all this land will be ours." He climbed into bed, bottle in hand, waxing philosophical, "These local boys...infidels..." He drifted again, then returned. "...we have to cut them, and damnit...get rid of them...all of them...."

The bottle dropped out of his hand and rolled across the wooden planks, empty. He was out cold. Yelena had just stepped down off the round boulder, when Aunt Sofia started calling out for her, or worse yet, Zorka, with her inimitable pipes. Hot tears steamed in her eyes; she felt all the ground shifting under each step. If the earth opened up and swallowed her whole, she would be no worse off than she was then, having just heard the lousy justification of the man who killed her boy. On top of that, it occurred to her that something similar if not verbatim of what she just heard, was the likely defense that got him released from his cell only a day or two ago. It was more than she could bear, she began to rush up the path, when Dushka stepped out of the near darkness and scared her.

"Yelena, where were you? Are you all right?" Dushka whispered.

"Yes, Dushka, I'm fine, thank you. See, here I am, I'm coming." Yelena took her hand for support, which Dushka happily provided.

They proceeded up to the house, with Yelena muttering that she was "fine," as they strode together. The repetition of her assertion revealed, even to Dushka's simple mind, its untruth.

Aunt Sofia waited in the doorway. She had a sixth sense that never failed. Dushka bid them good evening, and went home. Yelena entered the house, removed her shoes, and kissed Uncle Anton's forehead. Everything just like any other evening, except when she sat at her place at the table, and Aunt Sofia placed her chicken stew before her, Yelena pushed the plate away before her tears hit the stew. She fled to the sanctity of her loft bedroom. Aunt Sofia stayed at the table and watched her go. She knew better than to follow Yelena. Better to be still and pray for her.

CHAPTER FIFTY-TWO

YELENA WASN'T THE ONLY ONE RESTLESS. Halfway across the globe, Jake lay awake in his bed, with the noise from the Manhattan traffic below competing with the noise in his head. The anguish of losing Yelena, not to mention his child she carried, would easily justify his drinking himself into a stupor. Not this time. He was clear as a bell. He hadn't had a nip in over a week. He was taking this one straight, sober. Tragedy is clean. How on earth did it come to this? He played the same tape over and over again, in between phone calls to Ljuba. Had she heard from Yelena today? Was the trial progressing? How was she doing? Did she ask for him? Why won't she speak to him? And when was she coming home? Here, home, not their home. To Jake, home was most definitely here for them, their child, their future. The idea of home had Yelena straddled between two continents even before she and Jake were together. A real sense of home was now a battle ground for each of them.

Generally a man of action, Jake was surprised to find himself stuck in his head, circling and replaying the entire scenario endlessly, starting with the insanity of the Balkans, then the heart of this woman who'd stolen his, continuing into his own self examination of whether he was a loyal father if he didn't avenge the one who harmed his son. Barbaric, yes. Uncivilized, definitely. Vigilante, absolutely. Yet, in the darkness of his room, where months before, he and Yelena more out of compassion and kindness than lust, had tenderly conceived a life together, he lay there feeling he'd failed at everything. All the sign posts he'd counted on had toppled.

At dawn the next day, Yelena sprang from her bed, replacing insomnia with the adrenal energy of one about to save the world, when in fact, she simply couldn't wait to see Mina's little baby pigs. That precious parenthesis upon awakening, before the hard facts of one's existence form themselves into sentences, allowed for the youthful essence of this young mother to get up and head for the barn with the excitement of a kid on Christmas morn. She threw a sweater over her nightgown, slipped on her boots, unlaced, and grabbed the two empty milk pails standing in the hallway.

The quiet of the pre dawn majesty permitted only the sound of dew on a leaf. She breathed deeply as she approached the barn, trying not to look over toward Omir's domicile, lest the dark reality of the day before bleed over into her expectancy of the good awaiting in Mina's pen. But the sound of a cup flying into metal, probably the cast iron stove, followed by the demand of an angry creature, "Get back in here, Zima! I am still hungry!" She snapped her head in the direction of the cry, and Yelena caught Zima walking out with an empty skillet and spoon in hand. *All beasts get fed early,* Yelena thought.

Zima turned to shush the cry of that monster through the shed door, as her eye caught sight of Yelena. They locked looks and stopped for a brief moment, staring like wild creatures caught in their own powerlessness of non-understanding. There was a moment where it was possible the two women might have run into each other's arms, crying and comforting each other, but that was not to happen. Instead, the sharp pain of the chasm that had opened between these two old friends forced them each in the direction of their respective destinations. The stone-quiet morning amplified the sound of their breathing, heavy lungs expanding and contracting. One could hear the bees yawn. Omir continued ranting and as he flung open the door of his cell.

Yelena watched Zima's second attempt to quiet her husband. "Shut up, man, Yelena's doing the milking next door!"

Omir didn't even let her finish, he heard the word "Yelena" and he shouted back with the screech of the guilty, "I don't care what that bitch is doing. May she rot in hell, her and her stupid son. It's all his fault, anyway, he deserved what he got, the little bastard. Son of a whore, with no father; he got what he deserved I tell you; I'd do it again tomorrow!"

Yelena shuddered and dropped the empty buckets; they hit a rock and made what seemed like a deafening sound. She thought she heard Zima emphatically shush her husband again, but she couldn't be sure, her heart's pumping was deafening. She couldn't breathe.

Yelena stumbled, recovered and grabbed the milk buckets lying on their side like silver cornucopia vacuumed dry. She entered the barn as the cows greeted her in anticipation of their feeding. She ignored them, they persisted, until she tossed them a handful of grain and directed herself to the task at hand.

The corner where all the cutting tools were stacked beckoned her. She chose the largest, sharpest scythe, placed it across a couple of wooden horses and found a saw and began to work on removing its five-foot handle. She wanted the blade, and only the blade, and she wanted it sharp. Her movements were swift, as if rehearsed. There was no hesitation or doubt, only perfect resolve. It was as if she had been planning this all her life, and maybe she had, maybe that's what motherhood had done for her, it made her decisive, clear, and unequivocal as to what she needed to do. Like a bullet shot from a .22 caliber rifle by a perfect marksman, Omir's words bolted her into action. She was poised for action, no turning back.

Between each push and pull of the saw, she watched the sweat from her brow fall on the handle of the scythe, while she shut out the demands of the bovine duet, until the call of her Aunt Sofia reached the barn. Puzzled by the cows' restless cries as Yelena had the most experienced hand with them, Aunt Sofia pushed open the barn door, penetrating Yelena's mesmeric mission, just as the scythe handle she was sawing fell to the floor of the barn into a bed of straw.

"Yelena!" Aunt Sofia was breathless from rushing.

It must be important, Yelena thought, placing her body between Aunt Sofia at the door and her newly shaped weapon. She quickly wrapped the blade in her babushka, as her aunt announced, "Ljuba is calling from America!" Yelena mumbled some acquiescence to her aunt, about coming to the house to take the call.

There was little or nothing that could pull Yelena off her course now. But Ljuba had always fortified her, so she was not sorry she'd called. She shoved the wrapped blade into a canvas feedbag and hid it in a barrel, cutting her thumb as she did so. She pressed against the gash to stop the blood, and hurried up to the house. She passed Aunt Sofia in the doorway of the barn, who stood looking into the empty buckets, wondering how she got stuck with the milking again.

"Ljuba!" Yelena exhaled a sigh of relief to be talking to her sis. She measured her voice to keep from revealing her newly found conviction which she could not reveal to anyone.

"Yelena!" Ljuba replied, the simple naming of each other's names built an instant bridge, no matter how many miles stretched between them. Distance was no separator of hearts. They proved that daily. "How are you, sweetheart?" Ljuba continued.

"Fine. I'm fine," Yelena replied as she noticed the blood from her cut thumb dripping down the phone receiver. She reached for one of Aunt Sofia's dish towels, white, unfortunately, and pressed it against her thumb to stop the pumping of her life juice, as if that were possible, then grabbed a sponge from the sink to wipe up the blood that had fallen on the floor.

"What are you doing, honey? You sound out of breath," Ljuba returned.

"Well, this baby doubled in size in the last several days. I think I counted wrong, it feels like it could pop any time, now." Yelena justified, and she felt Ljuba smile at the thought of that image.

"Well, then, I guess you'd better hurry back here, so you can give birth to a little American citizen, don'tcha think?"

"I'll be home, soon, Ljuba." Silence on the other end of the phone. Yelena pictured her sister sitting at the kitchen table, the pink phone cord stretched out from the wall, Henry sitting in the living room, with the newspaper in his hands. It was after all, late Saturday afternoon in New York, and he'd be home from work, and the girls, probably outside playing on the front stoop with their neighbor friends.

Ljuba became a little more conspiratorial, "How are you really, Yelena? Have you heard from Jake?"

Yelena welled up when she heard his name, and stuffed the feelings that she couldn't handle at that point. Denial, that great river in Egypt. "What? I couldn't hear you, Ljuba! How are the girls, by the way? And Henry?"

Ljuba knew when her sister was faking, but let it pass. "They're all fine, we all miss you, and Henry especially misses your stuffed cabbage." Henry looked over his newspaper at her and shook his head indiscernibly and let slide, "Oh yeah, right."

Ljuba gave him one of her shut up looks, and pressed on for some answers, "Yelena, honey, Jake calls everyday, sometimes more than once, what do I tell him?"

"Nothing." Yelena had hardened now on the second mentioning of his name. She could not afford to soften now. "Tell him nothing, Ljuba," she emphasized.

Now it was Ljuba's turn to feign a bad connection. "What, honey? I didn't hear you this time. Anyway, as I was saying, I gave Jake your phone number and the address of the village."

"You what?" Yelena's voice awoke Uncle Anton who was having his first of several daily naps. "Ljuba! You shouldn't have done that. It's over between us! I told you that! You knew that! We are two different people, from two different worlds!" Yelena hung up on her sister for the first time that she could remember, wiped the receiver clean of her blood, and walked to the utensil drawer in Aunt Sofia's kitchen and pulled out a knife sharpener, slipped it up the sleeve of her sweater and went upstairs to her room to dress.

Ljuba stood stunned, looking at the phone. Even Henry was surprised. "What's up with little sis?" he asked his wife.

"Henry, she hung up on me! I didn't even have a chance to ask her about the trial or anything!" Ljuba walked back to the phone carriage and replaced the receiver and leaned against the wall, stunned.

"Trial? What trial? Honey, that country has the judicial system of the Druids! And you know it!"

Ljuba was lost in anxious concern, and managed only, "Henry."

"Henry, what? Okay, okay, maybe mixed with a sprinkling of Crusader charity. Maybe. Get a grip, baby, they're living in the Dark Ages over there! It's Medieval, for Chrissakes. They're still working out their calendar thing! Christmas in January! Their Easter is weeks after that nice Jewish boy already resurrected himself for the rest of the Christian world! I mean, don't get me started, they need a calculator just to tell what time it is!"

Henry went back to his paper, turning the pages loudly to punctuate his brilliant speech, and to steal a look to see how his wife was taking this tirade. Fortunately, she knew about that river in Egypt too.

"I don't like the way she sounded, Henry. I'm calling Jake." She picked up the phone and dialed, as if she'd never heard her husband. And this, essentially, was the secret of their enduring marriage.

CHAPTER FIFTY-THREE

LATER THAT NIGHT, OR WAS IT THE NEXT NIGHT, Yelena couldn't keep track of time, something snapped inside of her. She didn't recognize herself. Yet, in an odd way, she'd never felt more like herself. What did that even mean? You either are yourself or you're not. You cannot be more or less yourself, unless you cut something away. What? The fat? Yes, cut away the fat and you're less yourself, or are you then more yourself? These ridiculous meanderings of the mind occupied Yelena as she stroked the blade with the knife sharpener by the moonlight in the loft of the church. She felt sacrilegious prepping for violence in a church. It's not generally where one comes to ready herself to break the Mosaic Decalogue, but the loft had always been her "place," bequeathed her by her mother, who practically lived in the church. It had been her play loft as a child, her dream loft as a young woman, her prayer loft as a widow, mother, and now childless avenger and mother to be.

Nothing made sense, except the gleam of the blade as she spit on it and sharpened it, spit and sharpened, an abnormal rhythm created out of an ordinary mother's extraordinary love of her son. Nothing was bearable to her since she'd been back, but the reality of doing this action made her perfectly present and focused for the task. Spit and sharpen. Simple. An owl cut the night with its wise old sound, and a coyote returned the call, threatening, "I'm gonna get you, you foolish, old bird," with a mighty howl. She joined the consciousness of the coyote.

It was finished. The blade was sharp enough to split a hair. She tested it. Yep. She secured the bandage on her cut hand, and then leaned out the window of the loft and breathed in the sanctity of the night. *Night in the mountains was always holy,* she thought. It's the size, the sheer size of the peaks that one gazes upon, that promise of infinity. From the vantage point of her precious village, you never doubted the glorious beauty of the Shar Mountain range. It was fact.

However, that night as she contemplated the mountaintops, anger rose up inside her when she calculated how the Shar Mountains had let her down. They were meant to keep her and her family safe; that was the promise of the granite gods, and they had betrayed her. She had lost all that she loved. The baby moved inside her, reminding her again that it was farther along than she had counted. No matter, she stroked her belly reassuringly, silently apologizing for the night that lay ahead, and vowing that things would be better, calmer when it arrived. How she would keep that vow, she had no idea, but she made it nevertheless. A pregnant woman can be prophetic.

Yelena continued to commune with her baby, while she rolled herself a cigarette, a taboo for one in her condition, and again she vowed, *only one puff, baby, please don't be mad.* She inhaled deeply and sent the thick white smoke from the black tobacco out into the velvet night, then kept her word, snuffed it out on the window sill and waited.

Who owned these hours of waiting? Who ruled them? Who made them start or stop? She looked out across her beautiful village and beheld the random lights in living rooms and bedrooms and of course, in the cafe. The café blazed with summer lanterns like Chinese New Year in lower Manhattan, and a waft of laughter would inch up the hill from time to time, telling her the men were still celebrating their weekend manhood. Why were they not at home with their wives? What was this need to huddle together and become anesthetized by liquid poison? They all had possessed it. Even her dear, departed Radmilo. They were like large hunting hounds panting and slurping and scratching themselves, filling up on their fantasies and going home to spill them out. She remembered her second date with Radmilo, when he told her he loved her and would promise his heart and soul and body to her forever. Really? Then he went on to explain that men were sometimes "dogs" but it didn't mean they didn't love their wives. She told him she didn't want to marry a dog and said good night.

The next day Radmilo had a beautifully wrapped box of dog bones at his doorstep, with a note from Yelena, saying, "And yet, I've always loved dogs." He nearly died laughing and came to her that night with a ring. They were happy together and he was one ol' dog that never strayed.

The coyotes cried again. They'd caught something, a bird, a cat, a rabbit, who knows? They were tearing into another's flesh, sucking the life out of it as it lived, devouring its very soul, and suddenly she was no longer the coyote but its prey.

Their cries transmuted into the cries of her son. She looked out from the church window and could see a piece of the meadow streaked with moonlight, and she saw herself striving, pumping, racing to reach her boy that dark day, so many moonlit nights ago. She heard him cry out to her like the prey of the coyote, and she felt her heart race to the rhythm of her rapid feet, too slow to save her boy. The whole scene unfolded before her mind's eye, in slow motion, and this time she saw her Marko wrestling with the Man in the Mask, Omir, and she saw their faces close up; she saw her Marko smile up at Omir and call his name, and she saw that her Marko believed that moment of recognition to be his salvation, as if he were going to say, "Omir, it's me, remember, Marko, your sons' best friend, remember? Surely you don't mean to hurt me." She imagined he must have said that to his killer as the pipe was raised over his head, and as she slipped in the rain, and as the entire earth cracked and shattered to pieces in one single blow of a silver metal pipe.

Yelena crushed her already dead cigarette under her booted foot, twisting it into the wooden floor, and then noted the cafe lanterns were dark. The sounds of male power had subsided. Most were inside their wives by now. She took the feed bag that held her weapon, placed it on her shoulder, picked up the shredded cigarette and put it in her sweater pocket, latched the church loft window and descended the stairs, to the church, paused at the bottom, tempted to pray for strength, but afraid that the Holy Spirit would strengthen her compassion instead of her resolve, and she couldn't go back to mercy now. It was too late for that. She pulled the church door shut, and marched down the hillside with the traction of a mountain goat, pausing behind a tall white pine to listen for the sound of her prey. She heard it, right on cue, the muttering of the murderer. She waited, while he proceeded along the path to his cell. She followed, like a mercenary, undaunted, undistracted, undeceived. His drunkenness didn't fool her for a moment. He had no remorse, and neither would she.

CHAPTER FIFTY-FOUR

HER EARS HAD TAKEN ON THE KEENNESS OF A RESIDENT OF THE WILD. She heard the shed door creak open. She imagined he would fall into his nocturnal stupor instantly, so she proceeded down the hill. Thoughts no longer entered her. She was pulsating from pure rage, and passionate purpose. There was nothing more to think or reason.

Approaching Zima's back door, she walked more slowly to avoid cracking a twig under her feet. Her direction determined, she wanted only to reach the shed, strike and be done with the heartache that governed her. The God she hadn't even prayed to that night seemed to have another plan.

Zima's kitchen window opened, "Psst. Psst. Yelena!"

Yelena stopped in her tracks, but didn't turn around. Not wanting Omir to come out of the shed as she knew he would be easier to overcome lying down, she froze.

"Yelena," Zima implored.

Against her will, she turned and stepped closer to the window where Zima stood, only to keep her from raising her voice. Zima took that as a sign to continue.

"Come in for coffee, Yelena," she whispered hoarsely, but emphatically.

Yelena did not move, though the thought that Zima must be insane to say such a thing, hit her like a bolt of lightning. Zima heard her friend's thought. Murder had severed their friendship, but not the fellowship of their subconscious knowing of each other. Yelena adjusted the feedbag that held the sharpened weapon. It moved indiscernibly inside its canvas carrier. Zima, shuddering at the sense that Yelena could be carrying a gun in that bag, pressed her further.

"I know, Yelena, what you're going to do, and I don't blame you. I would do the same if it had been my son."

Yelena, surprised by the tack Zima was taking, turned her head slightly to hear her better, but all the time keeping her eyes on the shed door at the end of the path, her primal destination, the killer in his lair.

"Yelena, look at me." Zima prodded. Yelena remained still.

"Yelena!" Zima's importunity finally turned Yelena around.

"I don't know you anymore, Zima...the two of us...always together...we're strangers now," Yelena murmured.

Zima was encouraged, even by those few words and continued her negotiation. "I don't understand it either. My mother was Muslim, my father half Serb, half Muslim, my husband a Muslim, so what am I?"

Yelena didn't want to hear this baloney out of her friend's lying tongue. She'd heard all she could of justifications, rationalizations, and explanations of how this madness had struck their land, their village, her own precious son. And it was enough. *Cut the crap,* she was thinking when she said, looking straight into her friend's eyes. "You were my friend, Zima. My truest friend! Do you think I care what name you give God. I don't. And I never did. You know that." She blurted that out so quickly and fiercely, she had to pause to catch her breath, then she let spill the deeper reality, "I care only that my son is dead, and his killer lives." With that she turned and strode toward the shed, as if to say, *'but not for much longer...'*

Zima tried to grab Yelena's arm through her window, but she missed and Yelena was swiftly approaching the shed. Zima rushed out of the house, caught up with Yelena and grabbed her arm, spinning her around. In despair, she pleaded with her.

"When you go in there, you'll see, Yelena, that he is already a dead man." Yelena freed her arm from Zima's grasp, but Zima blocked her way and continued, "But you, Yelena, you...you will walk with a hole in your heart for the rest of your days. Him, he's already finished as a man, so I beg you, have mercy on him for the sake of my sons."

It was a full verbal battle now, two mothers fighting for their young. Two women set before Solomon, the Wise, begging justice, but each one unable to let go of their iron wills. Yelena wanted to tear at Zima's eyes, eyes that still had sons to gaze upon.

"And what of my son, Zima? Where was the mercy for my son? My God, did you know this was happening?" Yelena's outrage was boiling up to the surface rapidly.

"No, Yelena, I swear to you, I didn't know what they were planning. But I do know that Omir never meant to kill Marko." Zima had Yelena by the shoulders now and wouldn't let go. Yelena couldn't break free of her grasp, so she turned away, refusing to give eye contact or credence to what Zima was spouting. Zima shook Yelena by the shoulders, and betrayed her own frustration at the entire horrific event.

"Listen to me, Yelena! I beg you," she was entreating forgiveness, as she presented the defense of her husband's crime. "It was Omir's brother Mahmed who came to Omir for help. Mahmed was out his mind because his daughter, Jasmina, had been raped."

For Yelena, this was going from bad to worse, "Marko never knew Jasmina!" she cried out.

"I'm trying to tell you! They wanted to teach those older boys a lesson for messing with the Muslim girls and then…it went too far!"

"How do you know those older boys raped Jasmina?" Yelena continued blowing holes into her friend's reasoning.

"Someone had to pay." Zima mumbled, knowing this hideous logic had caused their lives such misery for such a long time.

"You're mad, Zima! My Marko was innocent and you know it!"

"Yes, yes, yes, I know that. Omir knew it too. He never meant to hurt Marko, he loved Marko!"

"You don't destroy what you love, Zima!"

"When you're eaten up with shame, you do." Zima wept. "Yelena, he's my husband, I saw the best in him once, and I can't forget it."

"I don't care!" Yelena wrenched away from her at last, but the force of that move caused her to stumble, and Zima pinned her to keep her from proceeding to the shed. The two women, warring for their own sense of righteousness were interrupted by a shriek from Zima's son, "Mamma! Mamma!" The words sliced the night air, throwing Yelena into the memory of those words directed to her, so many months ago. Adrenalin rushed through her and she forced Zima off of her and hissed.

"Your son is calling you, Zima. Go to him."

Little Nassir screamed again, sending Zima running to the house to tend to her boy. All the mothers in the village feared for their children's safety, since the upheaval of recent events. There was a sense of "who will be next." Zima flew like the wind to her crying son, while Yelena moved swiftly toward his father.

Yelena didn't bother to peer through the window of the shed to see if her target was asleep. She imagined she'd find him passed out on his cot. She was right. She freed the scythe from the bag on her shoulder as she pressed down on the metal latch of the door, as silently as possible. However, the unleveled wooden slat door scraped the cement floor of the shed as she pushed it open with undeterred purpose and the beast stirred. The moonlight provided a profile of Yelena for Omir, and he leered at her and wrestled his drunken body up from the cot.

"Well, well," his thick tongue spewed, "the mountain has come to Mohammed, what do you know? Come here bitch, I've got something for you."

"No you don't," she replied as she swiftly raised the scythe above her head to strike. He was mercifully a few inches shorter than her and the alcohol in his veins had him off balance and postured in a slump. It gave her a good shot. She didn't expect his own survival instincts to be sober enough to lunge at her, forcefully shoving her back against the pot belly stove, still warm from the logs that had provided his warm dinner. It singed her hair when her head hit it. The blade dropped from her hand and fell on her leg, cutting through her stockings and the flesh of her calf. No question, she'd done an expert job sharpening it. She seemed to be knocked out by the cast iron stove, and her whole body went limp. How could this be? The great avenger, in a mille-moment reduced to being flat on her back, on the floor of Omir's stinking quarters, leg bleeding, head burning and weaponless.

Holding all the cards, the short sodden school teacher now towered over her, blade in hand. He leaned in to affirm that she was indeed unconscious, then threw the blade aside in favor of another kind of satisfaction he thought he'd derive from this woman who'd come to kill him. Yelena, feigning unconsciousness, caught a glimpse of him through her thick eye lashes that provided a dark net through which she could calculate her next move. She discerned the fire poker was inches from her right hand. Omir backed up a stride or two to remove his trousers, which caused him to reel back and lose his balance. *Barely standing, he'd be beating the odds if he were able to erect any other part of his being,* she thought. So she acted swiftly. He landed on his bottom, just as she reached for the fire poker with her right hand and struck him between his legs, immobilizing his manhood indefinitely, she surmised. He doubled over in pain, and she grabbed the scythe, the blade gleaming in the sliver of moonlight that slipped in through the panes of the one window of the killer's domicile.

Omir was curled up in an embryonic pose, crying with pain and pleading for mercy. Yelena would hear none of it.

"Shut up, you pig!" She lifted the blade of the scythe over her shoulder and took careful aim to slice through the piece of flesh, naked on the back of his neck, which held his head to his man-less body. Her eyes were on fire; her hand trembled as she realized the moment of justice she'd been dreaming of, had finally arrived, at long last.

Hallelujah.

CHAPTER FIFTY-FIVE

ZIMA COULD NOT GET HER SON TO STOP CRYING. He'd had a nightmare. Any other night, she'd read to him, make him a hot cocoa and rub his back till he fell back to sleep. He wanted all that and more, but his mother had no time for it that night. She reassured her young son quickly, and urged him back to bed, telling him it was just a dream, not real, that there was nothing to be afraid of. None of it worked, perhaps because while she spoke to him, she was rifling through her husband's sock drawer to find the pistol he kept there. It was not loaded. She rushed into the kitchen and climbed up on a stool in the pantry to get to the box of bullets, all the time, calling out to her son.

"It's okay, dear, don't worry, mamma will be right back, you'll be fine." The little one cried and cried, following her into the kitchen, watching intently as his mother's trembling hands loaded a gun. That set him wailing even more loudly. His older brother Namik awoke and came into the kitchen.

"Where are you going mother?"

"Never mind," she snapped. I have something to do. I'll be right back. Namik, take your brother into bed with you and tell him a story till I get back. Try to go to sleep."

"Where's pappa? I'm scared!" the older son said, knowing a weapon in his mother's hand could not be good. He was eleven-years-old and a boy knows these things at eleven.

"Never mind, I said, go to bed, both of you." She screamed at her boys before she knew what she was doing. Then she approached them to pat them on the head, and they both retreated, as the metal object in her hand instantly stripped her of her motherly attributes. They ran into their bedroom, comfortless.

Zima justified this breach with the thought that she would make it up to them later, and flew out the door toward the shed, fearing she was already too late. By that time, Yelena was on her way down to the creek bed to get rid of the weapon and treat her wounded leg, which was badly cut and bleeding. When she reached the creek bank, she tossed the scythe into the water. It sank rapidly inside the reflection of the moon on the water. *Perfect.* She soaked her babushka in cold creek water and tied it around her leg. The makeshift bandage staunched the bleeding. She leaned against the wet bark of an oak tree and wept. Then she picked herself up and headed around the backside of the hill to the church, the only place it made sense to be at that moment.

Zima reached the shed, pistol in hand. She saw blood on the cement floor, scattered with straw and wood chips. No sign of either Yelena or Omir. Only blood. Blood she was sure was drawn from her husband by Yelena. She called out for Omir, again and again. No answer.

The blood drippings were so fresh and plentiful, she followed them. They made a trail down the path to the creek. Mystified, she tracked them by the generous moonlight, but could not figure where they would lead her. *My God, my God,* she kept saying to herself. *Please let my husband live.* In this time of crisis, Zima did not call out to Allah, she called to her father's God that she'd never really known, but had seen her father secretly cry out to, the night her mother lay dying.

That night, so many years ago, when Zima was only sixteen, the God of her father's understanding granted her mother another summer of life that leavened his heart and faith. When her mother did finally pass on in September that year, Yelena had been there for comfort. Now she would destroy this friend, her oldest friend, her lifelong shelter from the storm. The confusion and demonic chaos of all that had happened in those last months of civil strife and sudden war between neighbors and friends caused the village folk to think and do the unthinkable and undoable, that which they'd never dreamed of doing. Especially not to each other.

Dear God, Zima panted, as she trudged up the hill, almost unconsciously heading to the church. Something inside Zima knew that Yelena would seek her refuge there, she would find her, she would find out where she'd left her husband. *Was he still alive and where?* She knew Yelena to be capable of many things, and she knew the depth of her pain since Marko's death, but if she had indeed killed Omir, Yelena would be dead before dawn. It was a runaway train of terror now, and even the women had joined this battle between their neighbors, against anyone unlike themselves, against integrity, respect, wholeness or principle of any kind. A war, one could say against love, though no man would call it that. For a man it had to be about revenge, about leveling the score, giving one what they deserved. Hadn't that motivation now become that of the life givers too? That is to say, the women of this small mountain village, maybe women of the whole world. Zima paused against a tree to catch her breath, and found herself convulsing in tears that it should come to this.

Yelena lit a candle near the altar and looked around to adjust her eyes to the near darkness of the ghoulish glow of the church. She thought she heard something. "Father Voyn?" she whispered. Silence. Yet she noticed that a candle next to the one she lit was still dripping with warm wax, telling her Father Voyn had most likely just been there. She called again, and crept slowly up to the altar, as if she might find him there asleep. Nothing.

She took the liberty of going behind the altar and lit one of the larger candles, expecting it to allay her anxiety. She sat down on a stool and stared into the flame. Her breath slowed. She rubbed her belly, as if in apology for all that little life had already witnessed from the womb. Gazing around the confined space behind the altar, she noticed a window open, and a fresh cigarette butt in a dish near it. Father Voyn couldn't be far away, she surmised. She went to the window and called out again, and again, no response. Left alone, she was led to do what she was brought up to do, pray.

From the steady flame of the large candle, she ignited several others in a candle stand by the door of the altar, and kneeled before an icon of the Holy Virgin. She'd never noticed before how utterly forlorn Mary's expression was. Though she had the cheek of her golden son pressed up against hers so that there was virtually no separation between them, her eyes mourned with the quiet premonition of an enormous sadness that would one day overtake her. The small fingers of Baby Jesus wound around His mother's neck and gently touched her cheek as if to dry a future tear. Yelena kneeled in awe. She bowed down as low as the pronounced presence of her own baby would permit, and from the position of lowliness, for she was indeed as low as she had ever been in her brief tragic life, she began to speak her heart.

"Merciful, Holy Mother of God," she whispered barely audibly, "pray for me." She was practically speaking into the cement floor, covered with chips of blue and gold mosaic. "I'm lost, completely lost. And alone." She began to weep, as if she felt that God, Himself heard her and suddenly her heart burst. All thoughts and fears trapped inside her poured out freely. "Father, I know that You made me in Your image, Your image of Love, but where is that love now? Father, I'm afraid...afraid that there is no love in me now. It has been annihilated by fear." She paused to listen, as if this dialogue with her heavenly Maker could become palpable and utterly discernible. She heard nothing.

Slowly, she began again, "My love for Marko has turned to hateful revenge. And my love for Zima has turned to envy that her sons live, and mine is gone...and...I can't help myself. I wanted to destroy her husband, for what he did to my boy, as if that would help...dear Father, I need your help like never before." Again she stopped to listen, and a stillness and serenity came upon her, as if she were hearing an angel's message that was reminding her that Love was, is, and ever shall be present.

She sat up and continued, "Yes, yes, you sent me Jake, and I loved him, and then I ran from him, like a frightened pony. He was a gift, but Father...Father, I am afraid to love him. I cannot take the pain of losing what I love. I can't. Not again. Never again. Help me."

Tears streamed down her face, as if she'd had no clue of what was coming out of her in that moment, a sacred moment between her and her King. She felt a leavening in her heart, and continued, "How little one needs to be happy, really, a single little kernel of truth and endless erroneous deeds dissolve." She looked up to the unlit chandelier, as if God dwelt there in the night, and petitioned, "Give me that truth now, Father, show me the way, dear Shepherd. Help me to feel your presence." She paused a long time, barely breathing, and then as if she'd heard a response to her prayer.

"I know that if I betray what I once believed in and loved, that I can never be free. Purify me, Father, refine me, like silver, and grant me the freedom to love again. Teach me to forgive. Pardon me, Beloved Father, teach me, help me, help me. I am your daughter, I belong to you. Amen." Yelena felt a sense of peace for the first time since Marko died. No sooner had Yelena had time to genuflect and rise from her aching knees than the church door flung open.

"Yelena! Yelena! I know you're here!" Before Yelena could respond, the door to the back of the altar flung open and revealed Zima standing ten feet away from her with a loaded pistol extended and pointed directly at her heart. One has funny thoughts at moments like this, and Yelena was no exception. What flashed through her mind, was that this was a most strange answer to her heartfelt prayers. Yet the steadiness she gained from her prayers stayed her.

"Zima. What are you doing here?"

Zima was on a warpath for sure, and rode right over Yelena's question with, "So this is what your little altar looks like inside. Different. And yet, not so different. A place to pray, eh, Yelena, a place to confess your crimes?!"

"Zima, Zima, put that gun down. You don't want to hurt anyone."

"Don't tell me what I want, don't tell me anything, anymore! Where is my husband?"

"You're out of your mind," Yelena murmured to herself.

Zima was fierce. "Where is he?"

Yelena feared her friend, who was so far from her senses, would fire the gun by accident, so she attempted to bring down the heat of this standoff. "I don't know, Zima," she spoke slowly.

"You don't know? Amazing, Yelena, you know, we always had so much in common, so now I guess we've both become murderers. Always one has to be left living."

"Murderer? What are you talking about, I didn't kill Omir!"

"Liar!"

"Zima...I...."

"Then where is he? What did you do to him then, Yelena?!"

"I don't know. I left him on the floor of the shed. Alive."

"You're lying to me. You know you are!" Zima's voice screeched like fresh chalk on a clean blackboard.

Why did bloodshed always bring more bloodshed? Yet how could she have not known this would happen, when she turned her back on love at the airport in New York, and directed her steps toward hatred and the irreverence of revenge? Where did she get the notion that she was returning to her village for justice? There was no justice there, nor had there ever been, only a throbbing determination to get even, in order to be able to go on living with their so-called dignity intact. Maybe Jake was right. No maybe about it, he was right. Six hundred years this had been going on, hatred was what they were bequeathed by their ancestors and hatred was what they bore.

Yelena wanted it all to stop right then, once and for all. She reached out her hand toward her friend, who was holding a gun to her heart. As Yelena reached for the gun, the door behind Zima flung open, pushing her forward, knocking over the candle stand, and causing the gun to go off toward the ceiling. Zima didn't see that it was her son Namik at the door, and in a fit of animal instinct, she turned to fire at that which had startled her. Trapped animals attack, and Zima felt trapped on enemy turf. Yelena instantly saw that it was Namik that was to become the target of his mother's madness and quickly lunged to grab Zima's arm and direct the gun away from the boy.

The gun went off again, but hit the icon of the Holy Virgin, right in the eye, as if this was too much for her to behold. Zima realized what she had almost done, and collapsed in her son's arms who had come to her for comfort from his fearful dreams. The boy was screaming in terror. Yelena noticed the gun had fallen from Zima's hand, so she kicked it across the floor away from its owner. She then reached over to set the candles upright, which were all miraculously still in their holders, and still burning. Zima was trying to quiet Namik, but looked over his shoulder to Yelena and knew this woman had saved her from a terrible act. She had nearly shot her own son. What in God's good name, had become of their lives?

Naturally, Father Voyn heard the commotion from his cottage down the road a patch, and came running in, dressed in his night shirt. He smelled smoke, as he scrambled up the path, and feared the church was burning. He burst through the door, calling, "What's going on? Who's in here?" Seeing Yelena crawling up from the floor, he feared for the baby. "Yelena, Yelena, are you all right?"

Then he realized it was Zima in his church with her son by her side. That was in itself inexplicable, but they seemed fine, not on fire, and not dead. Yelena was fixing the candle stand, when she turned to him, to reassure him that all was well. "Yes, yes, Father...everything's...."

Just then her water broke, right there in the back of the altar. Father Voyn, looked down, at first not knowing what had happened. He was attempting to put together the pieces. Here was a Muslim woman with her crying son in her arms, in the middle of the night, in the sacred sanctuary of the altar. Here also was a woman he'd known all her life, widowed, sonless, and about to give birth, and at his feet was a pistol, that had apparently shot a hole through the Holy Virgin's right eye, a fourteenth century icon that lay on a carved wooden stand against the wall near the stained glass window left open from his afternoon cigarette.

This picture was not one he ever would have imagined in this holy place, but as the water fell to the floor, there was no time to dwell on the sacrilege of what was transpiring. Rather it was time to behold a holy miracle of life, about to unfold. Father Voyn picked up the pistol and placed it in the Holy Communion chalice, as if no one would find it there, then swiftly turned to Yelena, and ushered her to the window seat, which was as close to a bed he could come up with at that moment.

"You're going to be fine, child. God has you in His mighty hands," he said as he gently laid her on the palette.

"Well, He'd best be ready to catch this little one, because it's decided to arrive early." That was the last coherent thing Yelena uttered for the next two hours. The rest were massive wails of pain. The next discernable thing out of her mouth was, "Zimaaaaaaa!!!!!"

Her friend, her best friend, her neighbor, her enemy, flew to her side as she instructed Namik to run down to get Aunt Sofia, to tell her the baby is coming.

"Father," Zima ordered, "run to your cottage and bring sheets, towels, water and some brandy." Father Voyn stood stunned to be ordered by this Muslim woman, in his own sanctuary.

"Go!" She demanded. And he obeyed. There was no messing with these two women: they were about their true Father's business in the real sense of the word. Giving life.

As Father Voyn passed the open window on his way to carry out his orders, he called to Zima, between birthing wails from Yelena, "Zima, there's brandy in the small cabinet," pointing to a small cupboard with two shelves of Bibles and prayer books, and apparently a bit of the liquid spirits as well.

That old dog, Zima thought, but instead, called back, "Thank you, Father. Now Hurry!"

So here it was, just the two of them, soon to be three. Sisters since childhood, they'd marched through all the stages of life together, shoulder to shoulder, multiplying each other's joys, halving their sorrows, that was their journey, one to the other. And only moments ago, revenge and hatred sandwiched between them.

Now what? Salvation, serenity, forgiveness? Probably not all at once. But certainly this bundle of life, fighting to get free of the fetters of its indoor safety nest, was taking precedence over all that had gone before. Yelena's labored breathing, and Zima's sisterly coaxing teetered back and forth between them, an act of non-denominational goodness made manifest on this mountaintop. No one could have planned this, no one could even have conceived it, except the divine Mind.

Zima helped Yelena move to the floor, on top of the sheets and blankets Father Voyn provided. The window seat couldn't hold so much thrashing about and gnashing of teeth. The glorious blessed event of one life spurting out another, complete and intact, is unimaginable by any man, which may be why they stand dumbfounded in the presence of parturition. Yelena breathed with expertise and determination, but the little one was taking its time. It started to show its head then retreated as if to say, "This environment is not what I pictured for my arrival. You guys want to get it together out there, first?"

From where she lay, Yelena looked up at the fresco in the dome of the church. It was of Christ being baptized with the dove of peace hovering over him, like a halo. His eyes were cast down in ineffable humility, and John the Baptist stood just behind Him, no doubt baffled that he, the one alone crying in the wilderness, was baptizing the one they'd been waiting for, the Christ. Yelena wondered how one recovers from so radical a flip of perception.

No time to figure that one out, there came another wave of contractions that sent her screaming and cursing and telling dear Father Voyn to get the hell out of her church. He was mortified until Zima turned to him to remind him that women in travail will often say things they don't mean and don't even remember afterward.

"Glad to hear that." Father Voyn replied, reaching for the slivovitz, which had not served to buffer Yelena's labor pains one bit, but might help him with his.

Zima was an angel. She kept her friend's forehead cool and gave her a cloth to bite on when the pain was unbearable. She reassured her, stroking her head, telling her that the baby would be arriving soon, and all would be well. Yelena looked up at her friend and nodded.

That must have been the baby's cue, because just then, a wallop of a contraction moved the mother ship, and out popped the little head of a babe, still not gender defined.

"Push, Yelena. Push, one more good one and we're home," Zima urged. And there it was, one great heave ho, and out came Yelena's little girl, perfect, complete, wailing like her mom, beautiful, awesome, wondrous.

Zima deftly wiped the baby, wrapped her in a clean sheet and placed her on Yelena's chest, while she dealt with the umbilical cord, and then the after-birth. Yelena wept for joy. Father Voyn got on his knees in prayer, and Aunt Sofia burst through the door with Namik right behind her along with the first rays of dawn, exclaiming, "What do we got, here, girl or boy?"

"Girl." Zima answered, beaming, and reaching out to her son, to bring him close to behold the mother and child.

"Beautiful," whispered Aunt Sofia.

"What a night, Sofia! A holy night!" Father Voyn was giddy with joy, if not a little drunk.

"Name?" Aunt Sofia inquired.

All turned to Yelena who was now aglow with the radiance that only motherhood could produce. There was a moment of silence, as two mourning doves landed on the window ledge and cooed their congratulations. That image took Yelena's eyes back up to the fresco above her head. She thought of the moment of peace pictured there. Looking at the peace in the eyes of this new and early arrival, she answered them, "Grace. Her name is Grace, Gracie for short."

She and Zima enjoyed a conspiratorial wink, while Aunt Sofia chimed in with, "Grace? What the hell kind of Serbian name is that?" Nevertheless, Aunt Sofia went to her niece and caressed her and her baby, and whispered in the newborn's ear.

"You can always change it to Sofia later, honey."

That broke the morning silence into broad laughter that echoed off the stone walls of the little church, which, maybe for the first and only time in history, found Muslims and Serbs celebrating one and the same thing...Life.

Aunt Sofia was the first to return to reality. "The cows will miss you this morning, Yelena, but I guess we can give you a day or two off." She proceeded to the door. "I'll be back with a wagon to get you down the hill, right after milking. The *cows'* milking, not what's-her-name's milk-feeding."

Yelena shook her head in eternal awe at her indefatigable aunt.

Zima walked her to the church door to open it for her. "By the way, Sofia, what took you and Namik so long to get up here?"

"Well, your dear Namik sat down and had three helpings of yogurt and berries with me, and a cup of coffee, I don't mind telling you, before he remembered that there was something he was supposed to tell me about getting up to the church right away!" They shared another laugh and a warm embrace. "Thank you, Zima, for what you did for my Yelena, thank you." Aunt Sofia walked out before Zima could catch sight of the tears in her eyes. Some kind of Slavic pride that would never fade.

Zima returned to the side of her friend, while Father Voyn put Namik to work wiping up the water and disposing of the towels and after-birth into a plastic bag. "You do good work, there, young man. Let me know if you want an after school job."

Zima looked at the Father and smiled, both knowing that would never fly past Omir. Omir. No one had mentioned or thought of him during these last few hours. It was time for Zima to go. "I'll be back in a little while, to help Aunt Sofia get you down to the house. I've got to go now, Yelena."

Yelena kissed her friend's hand. "Thank you, my friend." Zima patted her hand, and kissed the new mother's forehead, then stroked the baby's head. "Thank you for me and thank you for Gracie."

Zima nodded and started out. Yelena called after her, "You'll find him, this morning, Zima. He's alive. I couldn't...." Zima looked at her friend in total trust now and went out, her son trailing safely behind her.

Father Voyn brought a cup of water to Yelena, who lay on the floor of the altar, propped up against the window seat, resting and feeding her baby. He sat on the stool near her and watched in wonder. "Well, this is the most important thing that's ever happened in this little church. We are very blessed, and so is your little Grace."

"Thank you, Father Voyn," Yelena whispered, as Gracie was drifting into sleep. "She's so small, I hope she's going to be all right. She came quite early, you know."

"She came at exactly the time God appointed her to come, and she will be fine, because she is made in His image and He is perfect, so that's all she can be."

"I love you, Father."

"I will pass that on to the Father upstairs, and for the record, I like the name." He poured himself his morning Slivovitz and lifted a glass to Gracie and her mother. "Zhivali!"

CHAPTER FIFTY-SIX

OMIR WRESTLED ALL NIGHT LIKE JACOB WITH THE DISEMBODIED ANGEL in the Book of Genesis. He struggled to get free of the heaviness from the sense of shame that fell upon him like an anvil. Until Yelena had stood over him with the sharpened blade, breathing heavily, eyes inflamed, leg gushing blood, until the actual moment when that woman with child towered over him like an otherworldly creature, equipped with the weapon of righteousness and bedeviled with the thirst for revenge, he had not taken a good look inside his treacherous soul. He saw in her what he feared most, a person who had no thought for the consequences of their act. The most dangerous being that walks the earth is the one inside whom all was already broken.

At that moment he realized his consummate vulnerability both to her and to himself. She no longer cared what happened to her. She had broken her "give-a-shitter" to put it in base terms. He'd seen it in her eyes, and was shaken with terror when he'd faced the mother he had stripped of motherhood with a single swing of a metal pipe. He had not planned the act never intended, and profoundly regretted it. The blow to the head of her son hadn't any legitimate motive attached to it, whereas the blade that Yelena had held to his neck that night was filled with intention. Why hadn't she done it?

As dawn filtered in between the slits of splintered wood that housed his boundless guilt, Omir's thoughts sobered into the grim reality that he, who deserved not a drop of mercy, had been spared by a woman who would have been justified in any court of law in this land, to blithely slaughter him. He could not fathom what stopped her. The shoe on the other foot, the blade in the other hand, he would not have hesitated to obliterate the one who killed his son. He would not have given it a millisecond of consideration. *What did she see,* he wondered, *when she looked down on him, groveling in his own body fluids, sprawled out on the straw scattered on the stone floor? What was her perception that made her choose to let him live?* He was obsessed with this thought. He turned it around and round in his head.

Finally, a sunbeam sliced across his face, and shook him out of his philosophical conundrum. He lifted his head off the stone slab and tried to focus. He ached with the aftermath of the booze he had consumed nonstop since the day of his crime. Yes, finally he said it to himself, *his crime, his sin, his own personal atrocity was unpardonable.* He had killed a child, a child he knew, and whose parents he'd had at his wedding table. The shame nearly drowned him, all at once. He saw his horror, but hadn't a clue what to do about it.

The demands of bodily functions got him up off the floor and out to the back of the shed to relieve himself again. That was where he had crawled to, after Yelena spared him the night before, and he'd passed out back there on a pile of compost, where he lay till a pre-dawn chill made him slither back into his lair. Again, in answer to Mother Nature's call, he found himself on the pile of manure. Dizzy with the horror of his realization and the unmerited mercy he'd been given, he slipped and fell back on his butt, blending appropriately with that particular pile of earth. He looked up at the treetops that were spinning in a rapid circle around him until he lost consciousness again.

Zima descended the hillside after her spell as midwife, the adrenaline rush from the bastion of life keeping her energized. Swiftly, she checked to insure that her boys were back home and safe, then she ran to the shed where Omir was meant to be. She'd believed Yelena. She took her at her word that she had not killed him, though she couldn't figure why she wasn't able to find him last night. As she approached the shed, the morning sun revealed him flat out on top of the heap of manure. Relief and remorse hit Zima in one chaotic moment of wondering why she had panicked in the first place. There he was, the love of her life, who had fallen so low, lower than either could ever have imagined.

And for what? In the big picture, why? Because the Muslim girls were taunted by the Serbian boys? Did they really harm the girls? Did they rape them? They hadn't been killed. But still there was no excuse for the sexual abuse, if indeed those boys were guilty of that. And yet, murder? And what about young Marko? He was innocent. He wanted to be like the "big boys." Is that what comes from growing up with out a father?

And what about those girls? Were the girls looking for trouble? She had seen plenty of that recently. Rebellion from even the girls of devout Muslim families. But the boys should have known better.

Worse, was Mahmed's daughter Jasmina exaggerating or even, Allah forbid, lying? Would they ever know the whole truth? Can one?

Zima's mind whirred with the speed of a hamster wheel, and equally ineffectively. She got nowhere in attempting to sort it out. Who did what to whom, and who would pay, and who must we hate and why and for how long? What had this madness done to her family, what were her boys going to grow up thinking of their father?

It was more bearable to reach into the muck to pull her husband up, than to entertain that line of thought for another second. He stirred when he heard her approach, but couldn't get up. It was like he was in quicksand. Indeed his soul was. His eyes were blinded by the light of the sun which shone directly onto her husband's face, blinding him like Saul on the way to Damascus. Like a spotlight, it held him on a note expectancy, "say something, do something, to make it all go away," she silently pleaded, as she beheld the ravages of the man who was her husband.

Omir was finally able to discern the figure of his wife, bending over to lift him. He was sober enough now to feel the darkness of his sin, and to witness the remarkable wife that would reach down for her man, whose bottom hit so low.

"What the hell...," he mumbled, feigning surprise in finding himself there, as if it would buy him some time to justify his predicament. Maybe because she was exhausted from a night without sleep; maybe because her love for this man extended in spite of herself; or maybe because she'd been in a church half the night witnessing the wondrous demonstration of life; Zima was fresh out of tolerance for lies or denial. She simply didn't want to hear it.

"Shut up, man. For once, just shut up, and get up."

Omir avoided her eyes. He didn't want to see the disappointment in them. That was one thing a formerly righteous Muslim man could not endure, the utter disenchantment in the eyes of his beloved. Yet, he saw it without looking. He felt it, as he got up out of the pile of dirt, while his soul, his manhood, his sense of dignity stayed down in the steaming heap, never to return to him again. *How would he go on,* he wondered? All he could manage just then was one foot in front of the other, to step out of that mound of matter.

With their heads bowed, the man and wife stood before the lump of future fertilizer when Zorka and Dushka, clanging their milk pails passed them on the path to the barn. Neither acknowledged the other. A heinous rift came between lifelong neighbors. What could ever heal this chasm of remarkable dimension of disdain? Certainly not the remarks that fell out of Zorka's unbridled jaw.

"Stinks, doesn't it, Dushka?"

"I don't know, I guess." Even Dushka, with her supposed compromised intelligence, knew better than to kick the fallen horse, but after they passed them she whispered to her mother, "What was he doing there, Ma?"

"Sleeping, probably, or passed out, more like it," snorted Zorka.

"Why?"

"Why, daughter dear, why? Because Yelena had a change of heart, I suppose. Figures, she's too forgiving. Ridiculous, you ask me!"

"She's kind," Dushka stated.

"She's kinda nuts! Stupid, really." was her mother's reply.

Dushka wanted to know more. "But why was he sleeping in the manure pile?"

"Him? Heck, he probably went to take a crap, and it felt so much like home, he spent the night there!" Zorka cackled at her own wit, while her daughter looked back over her shoulder at the two figures hunched over in self-reproach, disarmed by dishonor, slowly marching toward their home, at a funereal pace.

CHAPTER FIFTY-SEVEN

A FEW DAYS LATER, THE SUMMER HEAT FOUND THE WOMEN of Aunt Sofia's household taking longer afternoon breaks. Fixated on swatting flies while waiting for a breeze to bring them some relief, they found neither activity fulfilling. The only worthy act for the gaggle of gals was the witnessing of little Gracie nearly doubling in size each day, proving that though premature, she had that mountain willfulness to be a healthy babe.

Aunt Sofia spent a good deal of time endeavoring to talk Yelena out of naming the child Gracie before they christened her, and Father Voyn concentrated on getting Yelena to call the father of the child.

The truth is she already had phoned him, several times, but to no avail. She admitted to herself in the quiet of the night that she yearned for Jake, but couldn't figure how it would work to have him here. He would be pleased she hadn't exacted revenge on Omir, though she still didn't understand herself why she hadn't let the blade fall on his neck. It was as if a hand held the blade up and wouldn't let her release it. *The hand of God? The hand of Father Voyn's story resonating in her? The hand of Jake's argument at the airport?* No matter, for the sweet contentment of new motherhood, and the warmth of each precious day prohibited her from feeding old resentments. She was taking it one day at a time. The rest she had released, even the need for revenge. She felt free.

That didn't stop the elders in her life from pursuing their will for her. Yelena sat on her favorite bench, leaning against the cool stone wall of the arbor, her eyes closed, with Gracie asleep on her belly; the child's breathing completely coordinating with the breath of her mother.

"So," Father Voyn commenced, making Yelena smile in prophetic anticipation, "when are you going back to Queens?" That got her to open one eye and gaze at him through the persistent sun, in search of the sign of irony that the question belied.

"Who says I'm going back?" she replied, studying him like a hawk. *Did he know something she didn't know?* she wondered, though she doubted it.

"What about your daughter's father?" he pressed. Yelena winced at that remark, because truth be told, she simply didn't know where he was.

"We...we are not cut from the same cloth," she replied with a conviction that she hoped would close the conversation.

But no, Father Voyn didn't cave so easily. He chuckled and threw the metaphor right back in her court with, "Ahh, but that makes for a better, more interesting tapestry!"

"Impossible, Father," Yelena fired back.

"Now that is a word I do not know." With that, he reached for his coffee and drained the cup, humming with the all innocence of an international spy. Why did she always feel like those around her had intricate plans for her future, especially when there was a child involved? The trouble was that most of the time, the elders were right, and the young rebel in her, not always.

Gracie stirred, and Yelena needed to take her indoors to change her diaper. As she walked up the steps of the house, she turned and stared over at Zima's house. She had the feeling she was being watched. She tried to look through the windows, but the summer foliage had all but covered the side of Zima's house that faced Aunt Sofia's arbor. It was odd that Yelena had not seen any sign of her, nor heard a sound from their household since the night Gracie was born. She had in mind to go over there to see her, but Gracie had demanded all her time and attention. She vowed to go to see her friend later that day.

It so happened that Zima was indeed standing at her window, looking through the slightly parted white curtains at her best friend holding her newborn, the miracle child that had landed in her very own hands, just days ago. The thrill of that moment still vibrated within her. When she thought of the amazing affection bonding their friendship, she had a warm sense of well-being inside. Some things were unbreakable. That felt like an unequivocal truth except when she turned to see her husband, bent over a bottle of brandy, his hand shaking as it traveled from the glass to his lips. She quivered with disgust and compassion.

"Look, man, you've got to stop. Your mother and brother are coming tomorrow. They can't see you like this!"

"I don't give a damn," was all that Omir could offer as a justification to keep drinking.

"Shame on you, Omir." Zima went to grab the bottle, but he was too quick for her.

"Yeah, yeah, shame on me, so what?" Omir's introspection of a few nights ago seems to have drowned in the booze. Now all he could do was concentrate on anesthetizing himself.

"Well, I'll tell you so what…you stay drunk while your mother's here and she'll strangle you with her own hands, that's what!" Zima tried that scare tactic, since she'd run out of any other ideas to get her husband to stop poisoning himself.

"Let her! I don't give a damn, woman. Do you hear me? I don't care. I am nothing now!" She watched him pour more liquor down his throat, while she went into the boys' bedroom to get them ready for the afternoon prayer.

Omir walked out, bottle in hand.

CHAPTER FIFTY-EIGHT

THAT NIGHT, YELENA COULDN'T SLEEP. For all her exhaustion after childbirth, she was as restless as a squirrel in spring. When Marko was born she slept for days on end, rising only to feed him, letting her husband take care of his son's other functions. It took her a good two weeks to get up and around again. With Gracie, it was a different story, maybe because she came early, maybe because Gracie possessed some magical grace that let her sleep through the night. Truly a miracle baby, she was.

But that night, it was Jake that was causing her insomnia. She did want to see Gracie's father. She got out of bed in darkness, crept downstairs to the kitchen phone and dialed Jake's number again and again and again. It rang and rang, no one picked up. Not at the office, not at his apartment. *Where was he? She should at least let him know they had a daughter,* she thought, not admitting even to the private sanctuary of her mind that she longed for him with all her being.

The argument at the airport was a blur to her. So much had happened since then. It was as if she needed to recount it all to Jake, to verify its reality. The courthouse, the near murder, the unexpected birth, the awe of being home again, with their most exquisitely beautiful little girl. It was only the cry of her little one that got her away from the phone that night, with no satisfaction of reaching Jake. She ascended the stairs to her loft bedroom which she now happily shared with her daughter.

CHAPTER FIFTY-NINE

WHAT GOES THROUGH A MAN'S MIND after he's fallen for a most unlikely woman? An exotic creature from a land which, before meeting Yelena, was quite unfamiliar to even a well-traveled journalist, like himself. Right out of the ring, after a full eleven rounds with Sigrid the unbearable, coupled with the vigilance required to monitor his son's recent recovery from drug addiction, and of course, the mandatory slow, steady slippage of his career, he meets a woman like Yelena. Even that was an inaccurate statement. There was no one "like" Yelena. At least he'd never met one before. She was like nothing else, and he knew it. *What was he to think of a woman who put her principles before his dashing and rarely resistible charm?* He'd been all bollixed up for months.

He loved her, that much he knew. But he didn't know what to do about it. Usually a man of action, Jake thought this inertia was most odd, almost as if it was happening to someone else. She'd pretty much given him his walking papers at the airport; nearly got him arrested by the burly, brainless security officer, and hadn't bothered to contact him since she got there. *Two and two don't equal five,* he thought. Something was wrong somewhere. But the other night, when Ljuba called, he moved quickly to finish assignments, take care of his son's needs, and get a ticket to an unknown mountain village, to find the woman who told him it was over between them, but who was carrying his child and his heart.

Where could this lead, he pondered as he packed. He'd just gotten his credibility back at work with the Colombian features. This came just as he was about to be written off as a bum that had written his last good story a decade ago. He was getting juicier assignments now, and off he was leaving again, but not on a news assignment this time. There was really no choice, and he knew he'd have to go get her, sooner or later. He felt heroic and terrified at the same time. Ljuba was in his corner. So was Henry for that matter. And the little angels, Nadya and Annie, and even his son, Tony. But the woman he pursued was not.

Then, just before he climbed into the yellow cab headed for JFK, he got the second call from Ljuba. Gracie arrived early. Now nothing mattered but getting there. Equivocation had never evaporated so quickly. He couldn't wait to land in the unknown. Meantime, champagne all around the Lufthansa flight to Belgrade, on him, the new papa.

Plane led to train, and when the conductor blasted him out of his hangover slumber with a bullhorn announcing an accident on the tracks of the depot, Jake realized he had arrived. The passengers were required to detrain about thirty yards from the station and walk the rest of the way. A Swiss woman sitting across the aisle from him who had mastered several languages in her two and half decades on earth, including English, Serbo-Croatian, Russian and of course, Swiss German and French, translated for him, as the train came to a screeching halt.

While he'd slept, a myriad of passengers had come aboard lugging everything from wine kegs to caged chickens, rabbits and even a pet snake. Baskets of food were transported atop women's heads, all covered with babushkas or long scarves in the Muslim tradition. He may have fallen asleep in the West but, he definitely awoke in the exotic East, from whence his Lovely hailed.

He scrambled to get his bags together, and hop off the train ahead of the crowd so he could get the scoop on the "strange accident" as the Swiss lady called it. No matter what, Jake's journalistic blood still coursed heartily through his veins.

CHAPTER SIXTY

THE AFTERNOON BEFORE, Omir had stumbled from his home, made it to the cafe in the village, finished his bottle and accepted the owner's offer for a coffee or two. That centered him sufficiently to remember who he was and what he'd done and so he took his pain to the next bar at the edge of the nearby village, where he bought a round of drinks for a couple of truck drivers, one of whom agreed to his request for a ride into the center of the town several miles away.

Omir had the driver drop him in front of the courthouse. He was beyond drunk. He was at that strange and inexplicable place where the more he drank, the less effect it had on him. Perhaps he was pickled and far beyond the comfort he'd hoped the alcohol would provide. He sat on the steps of the courthouse, contemplating his confession, and rehearsing his willingness to take responsibility and punishment. He straightened up, shook out his leg that had fallen asleep, and looked around.

He was all but ready to turn and walk through the double doors and demonstrate some dignity, when four Muslim women walked right by him. Like a gaggle of geese lead by the mother, heavily hooded in black, even on this sweltering hot summer day, they listened to the eldest babble on about the man she had married, and what a bum he was, and except for his semen, he was worthless. She went on to say how she'd be better off a widow because then folks could rewrite the memories of him, and on and on.

He froze and stared. They nodded a greeting to him as if they knew him, with proper pleasantries, one Muslim to another. He turned away, ascended three steps and stopped. What a disappointment he was to his family, what a calamity, what an inheritance of shame he would leave his boys.

His boys. That was what stopped him. If he died today, they could rewrite the memories of him, proclaim him innocent, perhaps. No court of law had convicted him. Only a few knew what really happened. Most people around there didn't read the newspapers, and even if they did, they gave them little credence, as the editors were Serbs. Only his wife, his brother, his two cohorts in crime, his own mother, his neighbors and the woman he robbed of a son, knew the whole truth. Not so many, really, he rationalized. He was sure his sons didn't know. His sons must not know. He was sure that his family could easily come up with some story about him that would let his sons think well of him, so they might have a proper Muslim life. He would make his beloved a widow, that's what he would do, and his sons would be fathered by an acceptable memory rather than a despicable reality.

Omir turned on his heels from the courthouse, as if he had been touched by a magic wand and was suddenly straight and sober. He walked with purpose and direction to the train station. His mind filled with resolution, like the river of blood rising in the Book of Revelation. He was driven. He would do this thing and be done with the torment of his deeds. He would suffer briefly in exchange for gasping endlessly for a modicum of decency to get him through a day.

His eyes filled with tears as he thought of his beloved Zima. She would weep for him. He knew that to be true. Yet, what buckled inside him was the certainty that a part of her would be relieved, and that broke his heart. *Yelena should have killed him,* he thought. That would have spared him this endless, dusty walk to the train depot, where he finally arrived within fourteen minutes. It was 8:35 in the morning, and he knew the train from Skopje came through right around then, heading up to Belgrade. He would let the pistons carry some of his Muslim blood to the Serbian capital. He heard the whistle blow repeatedly between announcements that were indiscernible to him, as the voice inside his head grew louder and louder. *I am going to die by my own hand, my own doing, my own decision. I must have this final act of will. To spare my family shame, to spare my sons humiliation, to prevent dishonor to my beloved.* The voice inside his consciousness spoke loudly and distinctly, as if it were the invited last words of a man before a firing squad. *"I loved you, Zima, the best I knew how, but not nearly how you loved me, so utterly unconditionally...for this reason, I leave you now and forever....I never meant to."*

He landed on tracks where the switchback turned the course of the train, the train which severed him in two. His blood cried out for forgiveness, as his soul left this earth, leaving a coat of thick crimson syrup on the rails, the legacy Omir bequeathed to his adopted home and ancestry.

By noon, when Jake's train pulled into the station from the opposite direction, Omir's blood had hardened in the sun, and had begun to crack like the pentimento of an ancient fresco.

CHAPTER SIXTY-ONE

THE PASSENGERS ON THE AFTERNOON TRAIN walked toward the station feeling disgruntled and complaining about the heat and distance to the depot. Jake didn't really mind. It was a chance to stretch his long legs and break out of that hot compartment that had cocooned him all those hours from Belgrade. The journalist in him pushed ahead to the front of the crowd to get the story on the "accident" which was the only word he was able to discern from the conductor's announcement given when the train arrived.

Jake nosed his way between the villagers, many of whom were not travelers, but had come from business establishments nearby, in their aprons or work clothes, tools in hand, as if they'd run down to behold a wonder. Indeed they had.

It was a sight that Jake might not have found terribly out of the ordinary in Brooklyn, the Bronx, Harlem or even certain parts of Manhattan. But here in the idyllic surrounding of the Shar Mountains, where the seclusion of the range of granite pulled one back a century or two, one did not expect this event. Extraordinary. Phenomenal and yes, a tragedy. A man severed at his waist, chopped like a hand made rag doll torn apart by squabbling siblings, with all the stuffing strewn around, never to be reassembled. A streak of wretched remorse was spread across two tracks, in two directions. One could only stand in awe of the precision and certainty of success of this "accident." Jake was surprised by his own emotional reaction.

Tears filled his eyes, as he imagined the despair that would lead a man to such an act. He swallowed back grief for an unknown man in a strange land where he'd come to find his beloved. This was something one might see at a photography exhibition at a gallery in Soho in New York, something contrived, framed, labeled, priced and attributed to a new conceptual artist, something with a small red dot next to it, indicating the art dealer had already sold this piece, so eat your heart out, you art lovers, you missed the big opportunity to own great art.

Jake's thoughts swam around in his own life experience, searching for a current context for this image. He found none. He was ripped from that reverie, when he heard the words, "Omir! Omir Atalov! Aeee!!! Atalov, Atalov!!!" His mind snapped. That was the name of the man in the dreaded newspaper article he read to Yelena in his office that day! He peered at a group huddled around the corpse, probably family and cops, and saw a hat lying upside down as if waiting for the dole, and identified it as the hat in the photo. It sent an electric shot through his body. *If this was the murderer of Yelena's son, where was she? Was she safe? Was this really a suicide after all?* His mind raced, as he turned to wedge his way free of the crowd and find his way to Yelena's village. A car pulled up and parted the crowd, and the family, who Jake presumed were the Atalovs, were loaded into it. The vehicle quickly took off up a single lane road up the mountain. He guessed that was the direction he was also meant to go, but how?

The universal words, taxi and American dollars, got him transport, though it took almost an hour to hire a cab that was capable of getting up the mountain road. He threw his bags in the trunk of a little Fiat taxicab that looked like it had a better than fifty-fifty chance of making it up to the village. His heart was pounding with horror and fear. *What would he find in Shar village? The other half of this so-called tragedy or worse?*

Jake marveled at the terrain, hard, rugged, granite giants that dwarfed one and all. The taxi drove past stone ruins of what he imagined must have been an ancient fortress. The driver pointed and said, "Tsar Dushan! Tsar Dushan! Very big," throwing in that bit of history in English, no doubt to enhance his tip. Like all small communities, everybody knew everybody, so when the taxi dropped him in the center of the village, he stepped into the cool, darkness of the town bar. He asked for a glass of water and the directions to the Mandich home. He was answered with a nod and a gesture by the bartender. He felt a grim silence when he exited the bar, and imagined the awful news must have already reached them. Or maybe they were just disappointed he only ordered water. Either way, he wasn't making fast friends. You could hear bees scratching their thighs, the town felt like "High Noon."

Jake's sturdy gait easily managed the hill, and he paused near the top, when he saw a cluster of houses that almost appeared out of nowhere, behind a cluster of olive and cypress trees. He stopped, less to catch his breath than to notice the car he'd seen sweep away the bereaved at the train station a short while ago. He continued toward it, doing his best to stay on the dirt path, away from snapping twigs so he could get close enough to the house where it was parked. He planned to eavesdrop, under the guise of being a "dumb foreigner."

The sound of a woman sobbing confirmed he was at the right house, or the wrong house, depending on how he viewed his objective at that particular moment. He probably would have settled for a snoop through the window, but the curtains had been pulled, although the window was open wide to allay the heat. He could hear voices quite clearly and decided to knock. He hoped that Zima, Yelena's best friend, whom he'd heard so much about from Yelena, would perhaps put together who he was, and not shoot him on sight.

He guessed half right; he wasn't shot. But a dark burly man sporting a sinister goatee opened the door, with instant cognizance that there was an American at his doorstep. Maybe the Yankee cap gave him away. The bearded man was none too thrilled to see this stranger.

"Yes?" he grumbled. "You want something?"

Zima peered out from the kitchen stove where she was apparently tending to a pot of Turkish coffee. Jake thought he saw her smile at him, maybe not. Meantime, the older sobbing woman pounded her fist on the table when she saw Jake, he wasn't sure why. Red Sox devotee?

"Uh, good morning. I, uh, is this the Mandich house?" Jake asked knowing full well it wasn't, and hoping they didn't recognize him from the train platform. He figured they didn't have eyes for anything but the deceased at that particular point in time.

The name "Mandich" sent a bristle through the house you could feel all the way up to the snow-capped peaks.

"This is my brother's house," was the defiant response of the burly one, who continued with, "the Mandich house is up there," giving Jake his second directional nod of the day. Passing the kitchen window as he continued up the hill, he was able to hear the older woman, who had been sobbing earlier, now mutter something derisive that included the word "Mandich" hissed out between her teeth, like venom dripping from her saliva. He heard, "Americans, Americans!" Then, in the mixture of Arabic, Albanian, Slav and English, he grasped, "Damned.....Americans!"

The burly man shushed her, to which the old lady took immediate offense, manifested in a female fist coming down on the table. Again Jake stood back far enough to glance inside when the breeze blew the curtain away from the window. The old woman was screaming at the burly man, possibly her other son. Jake figured right about that, but couldn't translate any more of her tirade.

"Don't tell me to shut up, Mahmed! Show some respect for your mother! That whore carried some stranger's child! She was dirt, as far as I can see, and it was she that brought my boy down...damn her and all like her!!"

"Enough!" Mahmed insisted, as if he knew that Jake could decipher their exchange, which he couldn't, not quite.

The old lady was keening over the table, weeping, "Ahhh, ahhh, I've outlived my only son, and she's to blame!"

"What did you say?" Mahmed got into his mother's face, now. "What do you mean your only son, Mother?"

She cowered, caught. "I never said that."

"Yes, you did!"

Zima interrupted them, attempting to quell the animosity between Mahmed and Azhara, her wretched mother-in-law. Azhara had never thought any one was good enough for her first born Omir, not even her humble and obedient daughter-in-law, even though she was a better Muslim than Omir, and she had given her two grandsons. Still Azhara would not look Zima in the eye, knowing there was no love lost between the two of them. But Zima decided to take the bull by the horns. Grief had galvanized her rage, she took her mother-in-law by the shoulders, and made her face her.

"Stop it! Both of you! Yelena Mandich did not destroy your son! She could have, but she didn't!"

Azhara tried to get loose from Zima's hold. Not possible. "That's right, she spared him, and I daresay that's more than I would have done, if the shoe were on the other foot!"

"Ayee! You dare to talk to me like this!" Azhara cried.

"Yes, mother-in-law, I do, because, if you want to know the whole truth, she saved your grandson the night that I...." Zima stopped, unsure how to explain that night in the church.

"What? What? You defend her!"

"Yes, I do!" Zima walked out and slammed the door.

Jake scrambled to get up to the Mandich house before Zima noticed him, but she caught his eye. He nodded to her, and proceeded up the path.

CHAPTER SIXTY-TWO

GRACIE WAS HAPPILY ENSCONCED IN THE LAP OF Aunt Sofia, who was talking to her newly arrived great-niece, and calling her by lots of different Serbian names, as if trying them on for size since she was convinced that "Gracie" wouldn't stick. Jake froze when he saw them. He saw the baby. There she was, his baby, their baby. Aunt Sofia adjusted a little pink cap on her head. A daughter, Jake thought, my God, I have a daughter. He wanted to fling himself at their feet. Instead, he gingerly approached the scene, glancing around for Yelena, but seeing no sign of her.

Aunt Sofia looked up and saw Jake standing right there in front of the grape arbor, holding a suitcase and shoulder bag, wearing a baseball cap. Not the way she had pictured him, but she knew immediately who he was. Jake dropped his bags, and took off his cap. The gentleman dwelled within him.

"Uh, hello, I'm looking for Yelena Mandich...," he stammered, wanting to grab that little babe and hug her to his heart. "Is this where she lives?"

Gracie let out a wail so Aunt Sofia lifted her up and rested the baby on her shoulder to allow for a good burp. The great aunt nodded at Jake.

"Yes, yes, Mandich, yes! Okay! Oh boy!" which was all the English she could conjure. She smiled her irresistible toothless smile and he took his cue and went to them. Aunt Sofia gently placed Gracie in his arms, and the baby ceased crying instantly. They both chuckled. Gracie looked up at Jake with big brown eyes like her mother's and smiled. He couldn't focus for the tears filling his own.

"Hello, beautiful!" he whispered. Aunt Sofia told him her name, perfunctorily, and with a bit of a frown, "'Gracie.'"

"Ahh, Gracie." Jake sighed. "Good name!" Aunt Sofia just shrugged, as if to say, "It'll do, for now." She put some chew in her mouth, offering Jake some. He declined, causing her to question.

316 One Woman's War

"You, cowboy?"

He just smiled, one of the rare times when Jake was at a loss for words. It was amazing to feel such deep contentment as he did in that moment, looking into his own daughter's eyes.

Then Gracie began to fuss a little, which brought a response from Mom. Yelena's voice wafted down from the second story of the large white stone house.

"It's okay, sweetheart, mamma's going to feed you now. Aunt Sofia, could you bring the baby upstairs to me, please?"

Jake looked to Aunt Sofia for direction, and he got it. The third nod of the day, in the direction of the house, telling him, he could proceed in her stead. He carried his precious cargo upstairs to Gracie's mom.

He crept up the stairs to the loft bedroom, trying desperately not to make a sound. Thankfully, Gracie was making enough googling baby sounds to camouflage his steps. Yelena had just bathed and was combing out her wet hair and slipping into a cotton dress, when she turned around to see Jake and their child standing in the doorway.

"Hello, beautiful," he greeted her.

Yelena couldn't have been more stunned than if the mountain had melted into the stream. Incredulous and thrilled, she put her arms around both her life's treasures, and kissed Jake randomly, endlessly. Gracie did not enjoy her first experience of not being the center of all available attention, and she let that be known. Hard to say from which parent that impulse hailed.

"She's hungry."

Yelena took her into her arms and sat on the bed to feed her.

"I imagine she would be. She arrived early, didn't she?"

"Did she ever!"

"Is she all right?" Jake asked with a taint of fear in his voice.

"She's perfect, Jake. Growing fatter everyday."

"Probably the stuffed cabbage, eh?"

Yelena smiled at him, and Jake exhaled, releasing his concerns that the baby would be fine, and that Yelena wouldn't throw him out the minute she saw him. He sat down next to them on the bed, and watched the fascinating ritual of breastfeeding. *Is there a man on the planet that doesn't envy the baby, in that moment,* he wondered?

Yelena looked up at Jake, while he gazed at their creation, "Welcome to my homeland, Jake."

"Thank you, Gracie, both of you, thank you." Then softly, "Yes indeed, thank you."

CHAPTER SIXTY-THREE

AUNT SOFIA STOOD UNDER THE GRAPE ARBOR, still as a statue, hoping to hear something from the bedroom window that would clue her in to how the reunion was going. Nothing. Perhaps that was the best sound of all. Her first impression of Jake was good, very good. *Maybe not a cowboy, but a very handsome man, and nice, with a sincere smile,* she thought. He held the baby tenderly, and she imagined that he held Yelena the same way. *Must be, or else why would he be here,* she determined. Finding a piece of shade under the arbor, she removed her babushka and fanned herself, looking over at Anton walking up from the chicken coop, where he recouped two eggs. He walked to her triumphantly, one egg in each fist.

"Good job, husband! Now put them in the kitchen before you drop them!" He obeyed, humming as he went, a very blessed man to have been cared for by Sofia all these years, and she felt blessed for having him with her well into their old age. She felt more calm, now that Jake was here, and she was beginning to conclude, the way old folks do, that her desire to leave this good earth with both her girls married and cared for, might just come true. That was her wish, although she was in no hurry to walk through the pearly gates.

The times when Aunt Sofia waxed philosophical were few and far between, and one occasion was rapidly approaching. Zorka. Trailed by Dushka. Aunt Sofia couldn't help but wonder how Zorka managed to move her fat butt at such a pace as to break a sweat. More importantly, what was the impetus for it? Certainly not anything as mundane as a chore, or daily duty. It could only be one thing, gossip, or worse yet, bad news. Sadly, it was both. Zorka huffed and puffed like a bellowing mule making the marathon finish line. When she finally landed on the bench next to Sofia, she joined her in the activity of fanning herself with her own babushka.

"Well, Sofia, God is just!" Always the comment, before the fact, she knew how to hold an audience. Dushka started to talk, Zorka shushed her. No one was going to steal this news from her. Bad tidings, her specialty, but first, she needed to catch her breath. Sofia stared at her with patient incredulity.

"All right, Zorka, what is it this time?" Aunt Sofia yawned, secretly thinking she was the one with the really big news, that Jake had arrived. She wasn't expecting what she heard next from her brazen friend.

"Omir finally did something right." Zorka replied, with a wink to Dushka. Aunt Sofia couldn't imagine what that meant, but had a bad feeling about it. So she took some chew and waited, her jaw keeping time.

"He ended his mess of a life on the train tracks this morning," Zorka blurted out the news. To her credit gasped as she said it aloud, as if reporting it to someone made her finally realize the calamity of it all.

"On purpose?" Aunt Sofia asked, not taking in the possibility of such self-inflicted catastrophe.

"Of course, on purpose! What the hell did he have to live for after what he did?" Zorka regained her horrific vulgarity.

Aunt Sofia crossed herself and kissed the cross that hung around her neck, saying a silent prayer as she bowed her head, letting the sun hit the top of her head where her thinning hair offered little solar protection.

"My God, his poor sons," was all Aunt Sofia could manage.

"His lucky wife!" Zorka crowed.

"Shut up, Zorka!" It fell out of Aunt Sofia's mouth without restraint. It was as uncharacteristic as rain in the Sinai desert. She had never reprimanded any of Zorka's crassness through the years. And yes, this man killed her grandson, but somehow, if Yelena was able to staunch the impulse to avenge the death, the least she could do was have some modicum of mercy. God knows where that compassion comes from, but Aunt Sofia had it in spades that afternoon, and she wouldn't listen to Zorka's hot air one more minute.

"Just leave it, Zorka! No one is lucky at times like these, you hear me? No one."

Aunt Sofia went inside to prepare food to take to Zima's house. It was the custom to bring freshly made food to the house of the mourning, and this bereft Muslim family would not be any exception. How quickly bad news followed upon the heels of good, she thought as she closed the door to her home, and began to work in her kitchen while praying ceaselessly.

Up above Aunt Sofia's activity of bread-making, a much desired reunion was taking place in Yelena's loft bedroom. She listened for the sound of her niece's voice, or her grand niece's cry, or even the boot of the cowboy hitting the floor, but all was quiet and at peace. She dared not disturb Yelena with the horrible news about Omir just yet. Instead, she petitioned as she baked, that God in His infinite mercy would bring rest to Omir's soul. Then she prayed that Jake had gotten down on one knee to propose. That child needed a good father, and Yelena, a good man by her side. Aunt Sofia had pronounced Jake both at first glance.

CHAPTER SIXTY-FOUR

BY THEN, GRACIE HAD BEEN FED AND WAS ASLEEP in a crib next to Yelena's bed. Jake and Yelena sat on her bed, wrapped together in an embrace, gazing at their miracle baby, wondrous in her premature sturdiness.

"She sleeps so sweetly," Yelena said, stating the obvious. Gracie had captured their attention for eternity. It was as simple as that. They could have sat there looking down at her forever. The presence of a newborn was a mysterious elixir. It melted away anything unlike its purity and innocence, including, in this case, the rift that had existed between Yelena and Jake when she left America. It was like it never happened. Jake pulled Yelena down on the pillows so they could lie side by side on the bedspread. He propped himself up on one elbow and looked at her sublime Slavic beauty, and stroked her hair.

"I missed you so." He kissed her mouth, softly, gently, then passionately.

"I missed you too, Jake." She responded with tears in her eyes. "I'm so sorry I left the way I did. Please forgive me."

"There's nothing to forgive." He paused to overcome a second of doubt, then declared, "I love you, Yelena."

She smiled through her tears, "And I, you." Then she began to cry, this time with joy. Mostly, anyway, like any true Slav, Yelena felt even her greatest joy mixed with her deepest sadness.

"What's wrong?" he asked.

"Nothing. I'm fine." She stroked his cheek, rough with a couple days beard. "I just wish you had known my Marko, Jake."

"I do too, honey, believe me, I wish he was right here with us right now." He comforted her with kisses.

"Marry me, Yelena." It was more like a command than a request, and the way he said it made her laugh. This man had her, heart and soul, and she'd never known the likes of him before, that was certain. His sincerity rendered her uncharacteristically acquiescent.

"What's so funny?" Jake said, defensively, which only made her giggle more.

"Are you telling me or asking me?"

"I'm telling you, so when I ask you, you'll be prepared to say yes." He got into that spirit of levity she had created in him.

"You want to live here?" She threw down the gauntlet.

"Noooo, I want to live in America. With you." he continued to caress her face, "And with our children." He smothered a protest with a kiss, then continued, "And so do you!" Yelena sat up and propped herself against the headboard with the pillows.

"Oh really?" she challenged. Jake let her ponder his proposal for a moment, before continuing to build his case.

"Give it another chance, Yelena. You know, we've got a few nice customs there, too. None that are 600 years old, like you got here, but you'll see, they'll grow on you."

"Like what?" she chided him.

"Baseball." This sent her laughing so loudly, it brought Aunt Sofia to the foot of the stairs, hoping to grab hold of something comical to lift her heart. It looked like Gracie would sleep through it all, and permit them this precious consort. Jake got suddenly serious.

"I'm not going back without the two of you. Just so you know that," he stated flatly and unequivocally.

Then Gracie woke up crying, as if to punctuate Jake's game plan. Yelena went to her, and Jake feared he'd lost his window of opportunity to get her to say "yes" to him at long last. But in her typically unpredictable, unorthodox fashion, Yelena lifted Gracie from her crib, put her up on her shoulder, and turned to look at Jake and said, "I want to get married here, in the church on the hill."

"Yes, yes, anything you want!" Jake leapt off the bed and put his arms around his new family, holding his breath in fear that her next words would be that she wanted to live there in the village. God was merciful.

"Before we go back to Queens," Yelena stated with the propriety of a wife.

"Uh, honey, who says we're living in Queens?" Jake ventured timidly.

"Okay, then. Belgrade if you like."

"No, no, no, Queens is great." Jake conceded faster than the speed of light. They sealed their promise with another kiss, accompanied by Gracie's coos, making them both smile till their faces hurt, during which time, Jake got out that small black velvet box.

Yelena sat back down on the bed with Gracie in her arms, and assumed her matriarchal position, while Jake got down on one knee, to smoothly place a diamond on her finger. They were both quiet for a while, taking in the wonder of it all.

"Jake, I have so much to tell you, about what happened to me here." She talked with the excitement that came when one is secure that one's partner won't get up and walk out on you. Something about Jake had always made her feel safe, and the beautiful ring he slipped on her finger made her feel totally his. Yelena wanted to recount every detail of her journey, the courthouse, Omir's decline, and of course, the baby's birth. But Jake trumped her story with what he felt obliged to tell her. It was only right, she should know.

"Yelena, honey, first there's something I have to tell you, too…at the train station when I arrived…." She sat in rapt wonder at what he was going to say next, and gasped in horror when he spilled the news. She rose, gently placed Gracie in his arms, grabbed a shawl, and headed down to see Zima, pausing at the kitchen stove long enough to take a pan of freshly baked biscuits, wrapped in white towel, from Aunt Sofia's hands.

CHAPTER SIXTY-FIVE

YELENA KNOCKED ON ZIMA'S DOOR. The curtains were pulled tight, and if Yelena didn't know the tragedy the family was suffering, she'd have taken that as normal protection from the afternoon sun. But there was not a window cracked or a door unlocked. It was as if they boarded it up and vacated, which in a certain way, they had. Their lives were emptied of what they were before Omir stepped onto the rails. They were shut in, away from the world for good reason. They were all in shock.

Importunity won out. Yelena's persistent knocking was finally answered by an older, thinner, more withdrawn picture of her best friend. Zima's shoulders slumped, her gait slowed, her very being had sunken to a base acceptance of this sudden but somehow inevitable loss. The two women had been through so much together, their girlhood, their budding womanhood, their boyfriends, their families, their religious differences. They had always solved everything between the two of them, whether in the hayloft, a schoolyard, or on a mountaintop. These two always found a solution to the heartache each other was enduring.

It all changed the day Marko died. Yelena had become inconsolable, and Zima afraid. When the revelation of Omir's guilt was made known to them, neither could look the other in the eye or utter a word. The canyon that opened between them was too vast a moat of pain and grief to be bridged by the largest or smallest gesture of this hardcore friendship. Now the scales were unhappily balanced by a terrible fate. Omir took his own life. No wife on the planet would not look to herself to blame. It was not unlike Yelena feeling at fault that she could not save her son.

That was the way it was in their village. The bond that held people together was meant to make them impenetrable against the hatred of the world. Alas, Omir faced something greater that morning, a shrieking, unrelenting hatred of his own self. Beyond all healing, he ended it for himself. What it would do to his family, was uncertain. They'll tell the boys it was an accident no doubt, and someday they may understand the unbearable truth.

Zima cracked the door open, just enough to tell Yelena to go away. Her family did not want to see her.

"What about you, my friend? Will you see me? Please," Yelena entreated. The door closed again, and Yelena listened to the removal of the chain, and pushed the door wide open before her friend changed her mind, and took her into a long embrace. Zima sobbed into Yelena's shoulder, where moments ago her newborn daughter had laid that fuzzy head that Zima had caught when it came into the world.

"I know, I know," was all Yelena could say to her, as she rubbed her back. Finally, Zima broke the embrace, blew her nose, and ushered Yelena into the kitchen to sit at the table. Yelena put the biscuits on the table, and stood silently, holding her gaze till her friend met it, so that the true communion that would lead to comfort could begin.

"Sit down, I'll make coffee." Zima muttered.

"No coffee, thank you, just sit with me, Zima."

"My family is due back any time. They went to town to make arrangements. I couldn't bear my mother-in-law another minute, so I stayed." She began to cry again. Yelena held her.

"Oh Zima, dear friend, I'm so sorry, so very sorry." Finally, they both sat at the table and watched a fly buzz around the bowl of fruit in the center of the oak table that Yelena's husband Radmilo had made them for their wedding day.

"Remember this table...?" Yelena began. Zima finished her sentence as friends often did.

"...and everything that went on around it!" This brought a fleeting melting to both of them. "I want to run away, Yelena."

"I know, believe me, I understand. But my friend the pain will run with you. This I know for sure." Yelena patted her friend's hand, and then went to the window to respond to Jake's voice calling for her. The baby was crying for her. She called to him to say that she'd be there shortly.

"So, your American came to visit the Barbarians?"

Yelena was awed that Zima could even come up with a sense of irony at a time like this. She knew Zima would survive, she had that grit that they say southern American women invented. *Well,* thought Yelena, *they haven't met the southern Slavs.*

"Yes, Zima, he came. He came to marry me."

Zima went to her friend and kissed her three times on the cheeks, the custom for congratulations.

"It's next Sunday," Yelena continued. "And I want you to be Gracie's godmother, and stand with us at the wedding."

This produced an actual chuckle from Zima. "You're crazy." She sat back down at the table as if this news had knocked her over.

"You're right! I'm crazy. Maybe we both are."

Zima stared at her, as if she were waiting for the punch line. "We'll talk more about it next week, Zima. In the meantime, I will be at the service for Omir tomorrow, and I'll bake pitas for you. But I understand your family doesn't want me there, so I'll stay unseen, but you can count on me being there in silent support."

"Thank you, my friend." They embraced once more.

"I'd better go to relieve Jake of Gracie's crying. Besides, your family will throw me out if I'm still here when they arrive. Give the boys my love. Tell them....tell them what you told me...'you saw the best in him once, and you just can't forget it.' I think that will help them."

Zima kissed Yelena's hands and opened the door to the afternoon sun. She followed her out, and sat on the front steps and looked up at the light on the silver leaves of their olive tree that Omir had planted when they married, fifteen years ago. It was still a young tree. Olive trees grew to be very, very old, very very slowly.

CHAPTER SIXTY-SIX

THE MORNING OF YELENA AND JAKE'S WEDDING was overcast and rainy. Hot, humid, muggy, the kind of weather where clothes stick to you, no matter the fabric. The village elders were delighted because rain on a wedding day meant fertility, and when they got a look at Jake, they thought that buck, though not terrifically young, looked to them to have some fine seed. It appeared as if the sun was fighting to show its face, and odds were good that it would be burning brightly right about the time the dancing at the reception commenced.

Naturally, the entire village was invited, because how does one leave anyone out when the event was at the church on the hilltop, visible to all? Women were setting up tables and chairs on the lawn outside the church, covering them with white linen tablecloths and decorating each one with a centerpiece of gardenias and white roses, arranged by their very own Dushka. Tomo, the village baker, had prepared a three layer cake with buttercream frosting and plum filling between the layers. How it would survive the heat, he hadn't yet determined, but it was placed under a make shift tent to keep it dry from the mist and shaded from the imminent sunlight.

The musicians were there early, setting up their amplifiers, and looking for a little hooch to wake them up, having played at two weddings in the city the night before. Food had been prepared by women in the village and carried up to the church, and set on hot dishes or on ice, according to their respective needs. Children had already found the basket of rice and began throwing it at each other, while being scolded by Zorka who, as one could predict, was already a little loaded.

Her husband Vlado rarely went anywhere with her. He couldn't stand her drinking, nor could he stop it, or the verbal abuse it precipitated. But he came that day because he was fond of Yelena, was a good friend to her late husband, and thought it only right to be present for Radmilo's sake. He rested under a tree in the shade, having carried the tables and chairs up the hill single handedly and under Zorka's supervision.

Jake was inside the church being prepped by Father Voyn as to what to expect in the Orthodox wedding service. The tying together of the right hand of the bride and the right hand of the bridegroom seemed like a good idea to him; then there were the crowns they both donned before walking three times around the altar, then the candles, the rings, so much to remember. Jake felt he was getting married for the first time, and in a sense he was. His wedding to Sigrid found them both awash with martinis before the ceremony had even began. It was held at her father's country club on Long Island and he'd had nothing to do with the planning of it. The day was a vague memory, but he remembered waking up in Capri two days later, wondering why the hell they had to honeymoon so far from home. The Yankees were in the playoffs that year, and why in God's good name had he agreed to marry in September?

This wedding day was different. First, it was only the beginning of July and most of the baseball season awaited him in New York. Second, the party was outside, much more informal, and with a most breathtaking view of the Shar Mountains. He didn't mind the actual church either. That it was old was an understatement. As Father Voyn explained to him, "These precious frescoes here are from 1489, exactly one hundred years after…."

Jake decided to show off a little. "The Battle of Kosovo."

"Why yes, my son, very good! You know about this famous Battle?" Father Voyn liked him more every minute.

"Yes, Father," Jake continued, "but isn't it a bit odd, that the reference point for life around here is an event that occurred over 600 years ago?"

Father Voyn took a pause to ponder Jake's question, to determine if it was sincere or a wisecrack. He decided the former, so answered in suit.

"Perhaps, a little strange, yes. Hmm, you could have something there."

"Perhaps." Jake decided to let it go, he was growing fond of the Father too. Especially when he produced a flask with some of their "special" plum brandy. Jake thought a little morning nip might calm his nerves. He'd been trying to get Tony on the phone this morning to tell him the news, but couldn't get through to him.

"Care for a little nip?" Father Voyn offered with a glint of mischief in his eye. "I was nervous as a hen on my wedding day!" Jake graciously accepted.

"You're married, Father Voyn?" he inquired.

"Oh yes, my son, our Orthodox faith provides for priests to marry and have families."

"Where's your family then, Father?" Jake's journalistic impulses were unleashed by the spirits he had just imbibed. He noticed Father Voyn looked away, swallowed hard, then recovered quickly, but nothing got past the kid.

"That's a story for another time, Jake." Then offering him another nip, he added, "Zhivali! That means...." Jake did it again, impressed the Father by finishing his sentence.

"To life!" he said triumphantly.

"Yes, yes, very good, my son, to Life, indeed!" The two men were having a fine time and becoming fast friends, until Zorka burst in concerned over the groom's wellbeing, or so she said. Her innately rambunctious entrance caused the roses hanging delicately over the threshold of the church to tremble. Jake and his new mentor were comfortably settled in back of the altar, where Father Voyn was in the middle of a lesson on medieval church history to a captivated Jake.

"Hey, you two!" she called out. "Yoo, hoo, where are you?" she questioned as she spied their feet behind the altar doors. Jake peeked around the door painted with and iconic image of St. Gabriel.

"We're here, Zorka!" Jake called.

"We're coming outside, right now," Father Voyn added, intending to get her to give them another minute or two together so he could complete his lecture. No such luck.

Zorka immediately shooed them out into the sunlight, where the band was already playing some lively folk music. The guests were walking up the hill, dressed in their Sunday best, finding places to sit outside while they waited the ceremony began. They all wanted a view of Yelena coming up the hill, with Gracie in her arms, accompanied by Aunt Sofia and Uncle Anton.

"So where is that bride of yours, we're almost ready?" Zorka made no bones about flirting flat-out with Jake in front of everyone. Her husband wished he was invisible at times like those. "Maybe she changed her mind, Jake. If so, you know who to call." Jake felt embarrassed for her husband who was within earshot. But Vlado managed to get in the last word, vindicating them all.

"Here, Jake, you want the number!" Vlado offered.

Jake quickly excused himself so they wouldn't see him laughing. He walked down toward the edge of the lawn, looking for a glimpse of his bride. He didn't believe in bad luck: he couldn't wait to see her.

Meanwhile, down at the house Aunt Sofia was sewing Yelena into her wedding dress. Yelena was standing on a chair. Uncle Anton was in his rocker with Gracie in his arms, enchanting her with a silly song. The dress was lace from top to bottom. At one time it had been white, now a faded cream color. It fit Yelena perfectly, almost. The dress belonged to Aunt Sofia and Yelena was overjoyed to wear it. Aunt Sofia was once more petite than this post-birth body of Yelena's and so the dress was being altered on the spot.

"I can't breathe," Yelena complained to her aunt.

"Get used to it." Aunt Sofia knew this was a tight squeeze. Yelena, trying not to breathe, looked down at Gracie who was all in white as well.

"You look like a little princess, Gracie, ye-ess you do-oo!" How brilliant to be able to have your own child witness your wedding. She thought that was a good sequence of events, and was about to relax and exhale, when Aunt Sofia yanked the dress even tighter. If Yelena was not mistaken, she did it with a bit of a vengeance while muttering.

"Gracie. Hmm. Why not Zhivka, Yorda, Alexandra, Ljubica, Milica, Jovanka, Snezhana... Sofia, even maybe.....but no-ooo Gracie – silly American name!"

Yelena tried to laugh, but the seams would not permit it. Instead, she let Aunt Sofia finish her handiwork, and then scooped up her little angel Gracie, grabbed the small bouquet of wild flowers that Dushka had made for her, and marched over to Zima's house to fetch her.

This time Zima opened the door after Yelena kicked the door with her satin clad foot, the only appendage that wasn't carrying or balancing something. Zima was all in black and stood in dour contrast to the mother-bride.

"I can't do this, Yelena," she stated flatly, looking down at her feet. Yelena had no intention of taking no for an answer, but was clever and quick enough to win her cause with behavior rather than words. She handed Zima the baby.

"I have to pee," Yelena confessed, and swept into the bathroom.

"Did you hear me?" Zima called after her, already fearing she was going to get sucked into this one way or another, by her importunate friend.

"Of course I heard you," Yelena answered, "and of course, you can do this, we can do this. Together." With that, she shut the bathroom door and began humming, in order to discourage any further discussion from Zima. The tremor of the door closing caused some framed photos that Zima had placed on a small dresser to fall over. Yelena swiftly replaced them right side up, and as she carefully accomplished her business without undoing Aunt Sofia's fine threads, she glanced at the photos.

It was a gorgeous gallery and testament of Zima's life, and as Yelena studied them, it was also a picture of their life together as longtime friends. There was a photo of Zima as Yelena's maid of honor at her marriage to Radmilo, with Omir standing at her side, her intended at the time. Then a year later, Yelena, pregnant with Marko, witnessed Zima's traditional Islamic wedding to Omir. Pictures of them with their babies together picnicking on the riverbank. A photo of Omir and Radmilo having dug out the truck from a ditch it skidded into during a snow storm, their first winter of married life. Pictures of Marko with Namik and Nassir at the seaside one summer, when they were barely toddlers.

The one that stood out above all was in a colorful, bejeweled frame. It was Yelena and Zima as teenagers, on the top of a mountain, waving their babushkas in victory for having reached the rocky summit in record time, and barefoot. It was a gallery of love and endless evidence of their warmth and support for each other through the years. Yelena flushed, washed and came out to the kitchen where Zima was amusing Gracie with a little ball of yarn. She presented that photo of the two of them on the mountaintop to her friend, determined to get her to create another memory for that altar in Zima's bathroom that very day.

"What can we not do together?" Yelena said sotto voce as she took Gracie back in her arms.

"It's crazy, Yelena, you know that. My family is already so upset with me...," she trailed off, as if once she was no longer convinced it made a darn bit of difference. Yelena said it for her.

"Exactly, so what's the difference?"

"But...." Zima tried to come up with something, but Yelena overrode her.

"Look, Zima, they'll just have to get used to a different way of living together."

"That day, we won't live to see."

"That day," Yelena responded, while grabbing Zima's shawl and handing it to her, "is today, my sister."

Zima looked at her friend in amazement at her hopefulness, and she surrendered, donned the shawl and said, "We'd better go then."

"Thank you, Zima, thank you." Yelena was getting teary-eyed.

"You had better fix your mascara, or you'll look like my mother-in-law." They laughed their way out the door and up the hill to the new set of rules they were making up as they went along, one foot in front of the other, Gracie accompanying them with her gurgling.

CHAPTER SIXTY-SEVEN

FATHER VOYN SPOTTED THEM FIRST, and ushered Jake back into the church to wait inside. He sent Aunt Sofia and Uncle Anton to walk on either side of Yelena, and cued the musicians to begin the processional music to introduce the bride. He then stepped inside the church. Yelena's heartbeat nearly tore open the precious lace on her dress. She never in a million years would have imagined this day, a day with true joy in her heart, after all that had been. The two women walked with their heads high, as a few villagers murmured at the presence of Zima. Before Yelena stepped into the church, she handed Gracie to Zima and stated loudly enough for all to hear. "Here, Gracie, go to your godmother." Yelena and Zima locked eyes, smiling and thinking that was the first step in their little revolution here, since to have a Muslim godmother in an Orthodox family was ground breaking to say the least.

When Yelena stepped into the church, the precious edifice that had housed her joys and woes for her entire life, it was as if her life passed before her eyes. She looked at Jake, beaming, and her heart leavened, what a gift from God. That man of integrity and grace came all this way to marry her, to give her a daughter, to give her a home, a life, and hope for a new way of living, perhaps one with precious moments of peace.

The choir began to sing the traditional wedding hymn and she saw Jake look up into the loft. Tears filled his eyes, tears of joy, unmixed with sadness. She wanted to be inside his heart to hear the words it spoke to him at this moment. She glanced around at the frescoes, all lit up, more brightly than she had ever seen before. There were candles and oil lamps everywhere, showing the patches of amber, and coral and green and gold that someone one six hundred years ago had plastered onto that church wall to honor their heavenly King. That little church, named the Holy Mother of God, looked celestial indeed that day. The choir swelled, Aunt Sofia released Yelena's hand and stepped back to stand with Zima and the baby.

Uncle Anton, bless his heart, with all his deafness and dementia, looking like a count, dignified and upright, with his bright blue eyes, shining brightly, gently placed Yelena's hand in Jake's and loudly spoke into Jake's ear, "You take care of our little girl, son."

Jake took her hand and replied, "I will."

Father Voyn guided Uncle Anton to his place, and began the sacred service, by tying their right hands together with a white cloth, symbolic of the purity of their eternal bond.

"Dragi Brace I Sestre," Father Voyn began in Serbian, knowing most of his audience knew very little English.

"Dearly beloved." Yelena translated to Jake in a whisper, hinting to Father Voyn to realize his main witnesses deserved the tongue they both understood, and so he continued in his beautifully broken English.

"My dear friends. Today we come together to perform the most sacred sacrament of marriage, to join together two very special individuals whose love has triumphed over much already, and whose union will bless the world." He cleared his throat, as if he was surprised at what was coming out of his mouth. "Jake...Yelena...."

The ceremony proceeded with all the glorious pageantry of the Eastern Orthodox Christian tradition; and Yelena and Jake never took their eyes off of each other. Their love was felt by everyone standing in that little chapel. The baby stayed quiet and awake. What blessed one, blessed all. As the choir completed their "Our Father," Father Voyn untied the white cloth that bound them together during the ceremony, as he pronounced them husband and wife. Then he said to Jake with that impish smile on his face, "You may now kiss the bride, before we all do." The place burst into applause and oohs and aahs, at the lengthy kiss this cowboy gave this peasant girl.

The choir broke into full song of "Mnoga Ljeta...Mnoga Ljeta...Many years, Many years, Many years of life together...," as the congregation joined in. And as they stepped out into the day, the sun was shining brightly with not a cloud in the sky. The mist had lifted, the curtain drawn, the light shone forth. All, all was well.

CHAPTER SIXTY-EIGHT

THE CELEBRATION WAS IN FULL SWING. Jake and Yelena were like teenagers. Their joy was guileless, their desire to share it, fervent. They danced together, they danced with others. Yelena taught Jake a "kolo," the traditional circle dance. He did it with great agility and alacrity. It made him an instant hero in that crowd.

Zorka was in one's cups. She flirted shamelessly with anything in pants, while her husband sat against a tree, napping and providing a launching pad for the local flies.

Dushka danced with the other children in the village. She taught them how to make little wreathes out of the wild flowers that grew all around the church.

Miriana was helping with the food, serving, clearing, pouring, rejoicing.

Zima sat with Aunt Sofia and Uncle Anton and took care of Gracie.

Yelena was the belle of the ball. No one could have imagined that she would arrive at a place of gaiety after all she'd been through. It appeared miraculous, but in a certain spiritual sense, it was divinely natural. She was young, she had carried life, she exuded it, it was right for her to share it. Jake had captured her heart, the first day he sat with her between the filing cabinets in his office in Manhattan. His kindness, manliness and sincerity charmed her from the start. Clearly, she never wanted to live without him.

What was she thinking that day at the airport? She must have been mad. In fact, she was, mad with the ferocity of revenge and human willfulness. *Where had it gone?* It seemed to have disappeared, as if it had never been.

The guests frequently clinked their glasses, bringing about kisses from the American cowboy and the Serbian princess. Bride and groom didn't mind that in the least. Yelena glanced over at Zima who was holding Gracie up in the air, making the baby giggle. Yelena smiled at the sight. Then her friend brought the baby back down into her lap, and her face blanched with terror. Yelena spun around to see what caused Zima's sudden change of expression.

Mahmed, Zima's brother-in-law, was coming up the path with a rifle in his hand. His mother, Azhara, was close behind him. Mahmed stopped at the edge of the party area in front of the church, and fired a shot into the air. Everyone stopped cold. Music froze mid-phrase, dancers stood motionless in place.

Zima slowly stood up at her table, and gently handed Gracie over to Aunt Sofia, who steadily and purposefully carried the baby into the church. She kept her focus straight ahead, as if not looking would make it all go away. She felt like she was walking through molasses, but Yelena perceived Aunt Sofia's move to safety as swift and efficient. She was thankful for that, though she couldn't have guessed what was about to happen.

Everybody stood at attention toward Mahmed, as if waiting for their orders. The power of a bullet shot into the air and the leadership it claimed, stunned the wedding party into obedience. These people were not puppets, nor cowards, nor inured to the evil in the world. Yet the element of surprise, the shock of the violent intrusion instantly immobilized them.

"Zima! Get home! Now!" Mahmed commanded.

Zima was shaking and barely audibly uttered "Mahmed," as she edged her way out from behind the table and began to walk toward him. No one else moved. Even the breeze stood still.

Finally, Jake spoke. "What's the problem here?" God bless the American manner of understatement. He did not add to the inflamed situation, he merely questioned the armed offender in a simple way as if to say, "Hey buddy, do you happen to have the time."

As Mahmed was the man with the heavy metal, he answered with a swaggering attitude of dismissal, "I'm talking to my brother's wife, cowboy! My brother, who we buried two weeks ago."

Jake would not be deterred. "Yes, your brother who killed my wife's son."

That upped the stakes and the tension. The guests groaned. Beads of sweat formed on Mahmed's brow. He was not a hardened sinner; he was a mixed up man with a gun. He was lost and dangerous. He cocked the rifle. Jake took a long beat, then spoke again.

"Look, you and your mother are welcome to stay and have some food and drink with us, but the gun doesn't belong here."

Mahmed sneered at the invitation, and returned to his mission.

"Zima, come home with us, right now!"

Zima proceeded slowly, afraid to cause any stir that might cause a sudden action from Mahmed. Father Voyn, strengthened by Jake's courage and directness, stepped forward.

"Please, Mahmed, stay in peace, or go in peace, but don't create problems here. This is a happy day...this is...a wed...."

Mahmed shot at the ground near Father Voyn's feet, sending a loud gasp through the crowd, and knocking Father Voyn back into a table. It caved under the lurch of his body. Women screamed and grabbed their children, running for cover. Miriana and Dushka went to the side of Father Voyn to help him up. Jake's ire was up.

"What are you, nuts? Don't you people ever quit? What's it gonna take? Killing all the children! Put the damned gun down!"

Meanwhile a couple of men had edged their way behind Mahmed but were still some twenty feet away. They needed to get closer to jump him, and that was risky at best. The weapon could go off in any direction.

Mahmed cocked the rifle again and pointed it at Zima this time, who was nearly abreast with Jake and Yelena now. Yelena slowly stepped in front of the rifle leaving Zima behind her. Gently, softly, she spoke to Mahmed. She figured he might be crazy enough to shoot his brother's wife for attending a Serbian wedding, but she didn't think he was mad enough to harm the bride. Not very solid logic, but nevertheless, she took the chance. Now that Yelena had stepped in front of the barrel of the rifle, the men behind Mahmed didn't dare attack. They froze.

"Mahmed, it's enough," she declared. "My Marko and your brother Omir are dead. Your daughter was harmed, and your mother's heart is broken. Look what all this hate has brought us." She spoke as calmly as she ever had in her life. It was working; she was getting to him. At the mention of his daughter, he gulped back his emotions, but the gun was still pointed at her heart. "Today, we try a different way, eh, Mahmed, for your daughter, Jasmina's sake." she continued.

Jake watched closely, timing the moment to move in on him. Yelena continued in a hypnotic voice. "Eh, Mahmed, we must, yes?"

Just as Jake was about to jump, Mahmed began to lower the gun. Stillness was the best offense now. All waited for the gun to be completely lowered, and clear of Yelena, then the men behind

Mahmed would make their move. Mahmed was shaking, but steadily lowered the rifle.

His mother, Azhara, suddenly reached for it, and though reluctant to let it go, Mahmed finally did. The men behind him sprang into action. At the same moment, Gracie let out a cry from the church loft window. Yelena jerked around to look up toward the church where her baby was.

A shot rang out. Mahmed's mother, Azhara, sent a bullet ripping through Yelena's back. Her white wedding dress now oozing red, she fell.

Jake dropped to her side. Zima screamed and tore at Azhara. She scratched at her eyes till she dropped the rifle. Father Voyn grabbed it and flung it into the brush. Mahmed collapsed to his knees, head in hand, realizing what he'd caused. Two men were beating on him, till Father Voyn, Zorka and her husband, Vlado, broke it up. What was the point, they had him pinned. He could do no more harm.

More than ever, prayer was needed now. A circle formed around Jake and Yelena. "Yelena, Yelena!" Jake cried.

Aunt Sofia, called out, "Yelena!" as she ran toward them from the church with Gracie in her arms.

Miriana yelled to her husband, "Go down and call for an ambulance!"

Aunt Sofia reached them, as Yelena opened her eyes and stretched her hand up to touch Gracie's foot. But she missed and her arm dropped as Jake screamed, clutching Yelena to his heart. The world went black.

CHAPTER SIXTY-NINE

DAYS PASSED INTO WEEKS. One late afternoon, Jake stood at the edge of the meadow where Marko had been killed, looking out over the tall hay, nearly ready to be sheared. He pictured Yelena amid the grassy field on the day Marko died. He imagined the way that she must have run to him. She had described to him the night he made love to her in his New York apartment, the night they made Gracie. He could envision his wife, her heart pumping hard to reach her Marko, the horror of getting to him too late. The nightmare of Yelena being shot on their wedding day had paralyzed him. He hadn't yet caught up with his own heartbeat. He had nearly lost his mind.

For the first three days after the shooting, Jake sat continuously outside the Emergency Intensive Care Unit in a hospital where not a word of English was spoken. All he could discern were the words "okay, okay," uttered by the surgeon who'd removed the bullet from Yelena's shoulder.

The blood loss was so great; she was already in a coma when they got to the hospital, which was an endless distance from the village. Each sharp turn on the rough mountain road seemed to seal Yelena's fate. Jake donated blood, so did Zorka, pickled though it may have been, and so did Zima.

Zima sat with Jake everyday for the first week. At night she would return home to the questioning of her brother-in-law's eyes. Was he responsible for her death his tortured eyes demanded? She spoke not a word to him, nor to Azhara. Nightly she tended to her boys who'd been traumatized by the whole event.

It seemed impossible that Yelena would survive being shot at such close range, God only knows where Azhara was actually aiming. The wave of fury and fear that riddled the wedding reception was incomprehensible.

Where was God's grace to restore the lost, to redeem the unforgiven, to renew the unworthy? Where was the balm to comfort the gashed heart of Jake, Aunt Sofia, little Gracie, everyone? Jake's mind ran over and over these questions during the time Yelena was in the hospital.

One day Jake stood outside Aunt Sofia's house gazing at that beautiful meadow, thinking how it had gone from innate innocence to an acre of blood, encased though not protected by the grandeur of the mountain range. If that meadow of hay could only explain the inexplicable, if it could only offer some comfort to the comfortless, or healing to the wounded. The field remained soundless.

Yelena came up behind Jake and gently touched his shoulder. "It's time to go, Jake." Jake's scowl from his vain imaginings brightened when he turned and beheld his wife, dressed and ready to commence a new chapter of their life together, at long last. *Was he dreaming? Did she really live?*

He turned and smiled radiantly at his beloved. He took her right hand, carefully avoiding the bandaged left shoulder. They walked together toward Aunt Sofia's arbor, where they joined her and Uncle Anton for their last cup of coffee before they drove to the train station. They had barely started up the path, when they heard the sound of a police jeep barreling up the path toward the house. Its absurdly muted siren sounded like a wasp caught between a screen door and an oak door.

They were the same two policemen whom Yelena had dealt with that day after Marko died. She remembered how they'd brought her Marko's gold chain that she'd given him when he was christened. They were the same two policemen had helped her to understand that nothing could be done at the courthouse, and that she should just go home and have the baby; the same ones who had shown up at the hospital after she'd regained consciousness to get her to press charges against Omir's brother and mother; the very same one of the two was still admiring her beauty and was secretly saddened she was leaving with the American.

"What's up, gentlemen?" Jake asked, hoping they were not planning on tainting their last few moments at Yelena's home with bad news. The one smitten with Yelena spoke first.

"Well, uh, Mrs. Mandich, glad to see you're, uh, out of the hospital and doing well."

"Actually, it's Mrs. Thompson, now," Jake interjected, surprised to find himself actually jealous of this young lad's attention toward his beautiful wife.

"Oh yes, of course, Mrs. Thompson, then. Well, uh, Mrs. Thompson," he glanced at Jake, in what Jake perceived to be a mocking smirk and continued speaking to Yelena in Serbian. "We've held Mahmed Atalov and his mother Mrs. Azhara Atalov under house arrest for almost two weeks, and it you don't press charges, they're going to be free to go back to their village. Free, Mrs. Thompson, I mean, uh, without punishment." He looked her straight in the eye, as if he was telegraphing the line he wanted her to say next. He waited.

After a considerable pause, Yelena replied, "Let them go." She answered him in English because she knew she'd have to face up not only to the young cop's disapproval, but her own husband's newly acquired thirst for revenge. She met the young cop's stare, anticipating his response.

His words tumbled into hers, commencing with a few choice curse words in Serbian and then, "Miss, I mean ma'am, with all due respect, they nearly killed you, tried to kill you, for all intents and purposes, and so...uh, uh, are you kidding? Let them go free!" The young officer took her compassion as a personal affront to his sense of justice.

"Yes, Officer, I understand that. Frankly, I don't know why I'm still alive, but I am, and I thank God that I am." She paused and then added gingerly, "And so...I forgive them."

"Well, I don't!" blurted out the uniformed Casanova, making Yelena smile. She knew he lusted for her, and she forgave him that, too.

"We've got to start somewhere, gentlemen. Why don't you sit and have coffee with us." She sat, next to Jake, who was holding Gracie.

The two cops looked at each other and spoke in Serbian, "What the hell is this village coming to, I'd like to know." They shook their heads in resignation and sat down to coffee.

"Thank you, ma'am," the quiet, homely cop mumbled.

The one with the broken heart added, "Well, we'll see you're escorted safely to the train station, anyway."

"Thank you!" beamed Yelena.

As usual, there was rarely much instigation needed to uncork the plum brandy, and that's just what Aunt Sofia did, while the uniformed fellows shed their regulation hats and rules to share a shot of slivi for the road.

CHAPTER SEVENTY

JAKE AND HIS FAMILY WERE READY to board the train. They'd already loaded their baggage and the basket of food Aunt Sofia packed for them. It was packed with chicken, fruit, bread, a bottle of wine, a bottle of Slivovitz, a canteen of fresh water right from their own mountain stream, and an entire cake she baked for them that morning. The whole village came to bid them adieu. It was like a national holiday. Even people that didn't know Yelena came to say good-bye. Naturally, everyone had heard about what had happened to her, her son, her offender, and now this latest news of her departure with a real American cowboy. That was the rumor that had spread throughout the area. It was the most colorful one, so that's what the folks circulated.

The important thing to Yelena was that Aunt Sofia and Uncle Anton were there. So was their friend, Velinka, as were Zorka and her daughter Dushka. Even Zorka's husband Vlado showed up, but stood off to the side, by himself, smoking a cigarette as was his wont. Miriana arrived with her whole family, and she too had baked goods to contribute to their journey.

Father Voyn was there in his quasi civies, i.e., no robe, just black with the white collar. He brought a little prayer book with Gracie's name engraved on it for her christening, which Yelena promised would take place immediately upon arrival in New York. Aunt Sofia thought it was good that they would have time to come to their senses on the journey home and change Gracie's name to a fine Serbian one before it was too late.

The train whistle blew the warning for the last boarding call. There is no more nostalgic sound than that of a train whistle announcing the travel to or from one's heart's desire.

"Honey, we'd better board now," Jake urged her.

"I know." Yelena replied, unconvincingly, as she'd not yet given up hope that her best friend would come to say good-bye. She prolonged her farewells with each person, doling out the traditional three kisses on the cheeks with slow deliberation. Jake boarded the train with Gracie in his arms and opened a window, so that he and Gracie could look out.

Yelena went down the line of friends, neighbors, relatives, even strangers, embracing them, and blessing them, each and all. Saving the best for last, she stayed with Aunt Sofia in a long embrace and wept. Then Aunt Sofia chirped through her tears "Yelena, honey, try to think of a nice Serbian name for your daughter. You'll feel better." Yelena smiled and hugged her once more, before moving toward the train. Aunt Sofia waved at her, calling out, "And Jake, don't forget to bring them back to visit next summer…and bring Ljuba and her family too!"

Jake promised with a confirming nod and a final wave from the compartment window. Again he called down to Yelena who still stood on the platform, "You'd better hop up here, honey."

Yelena nodded and with one foot on the first step of the train, she took one more look back, and heard what she'd been waiting for, "Yelena, Yelena, wait!" It was Zima, jumping out of a car that had barely slowed to a stop. She was running toward her friend, when Yelena jumped from the train to meet her. They collapsed into each other's arms.

Yelena cried, "I knew you'd come."

"Oh my friend, my dearest friend," Zima returned. She handed Yelena a bag of pears, and finally Yelena was ready to go, once the necessary and inevitable had occurred.

Now with both feet on the steps of the train, Yelena turned to wave at her family one more time when she saw Mahmed gasping to catch up to her with a thin, young girl behind him. He touched the hem of Yelena's skirt. He was weeping, convulsively, head bowed, "I'm sorry, I'm so sorry…."

"I know, you are….It's all right."

"Please Yelena," he continued, "this is my daughter, Jasmina. I wanted her to know you." Jasmina bowed her head to Yelena and handed her a small basket of fresh figs. Yelena stepped down from the train to meet her. She offered her hand.

"Hello Jasmina! What a beautiful girl you are." Yelena patted the girl's scarved head and smiled at her. "Thank you for coming, I'm glad we met, Jasmina. I hope we meet again."

Mahmed took Yelena's hand and kissed it. Yelena saw his mother, Azhara, standing a little ways off, looking at the ground.

Yelena imagined how hard it must have been for Azhara to revisit the train station, the place of her son's death. She went to her, and wiped the old woman's tears. Flooded with compassion, Yelena spoke gently to her, as she touched the face of the mother of her son's killer. What came from her, she could never in a million years have imagined herself say. "It's all right," she said to Mrs. Atalov. "It's okay," she choked. "I understand...you...you...lost a son, too."

Mrs. Atalov kept her glance down, but nodded. Then Yelena heard the softest, most sincere, "I'm sorry" from this woman whose heart had been cracked in two just like hers had. Mrs. Atalov ceremoniously walked over to stand next to Aunt Sofia. She put her arm around Sofia to comfort her sadness that Yelena was leaving. Miracle upon miracle.

Zima's boys ran up to Yelena to hug her good-bye, and Yelena almost lost it. They reminded her so much of her Marko. Nassir handed her a picture he'd drawn for her. It was of a boy kicking a soccer ball.

"That's your Marko," he said proudly, as his heavily lashed brown eyes, looked up at her with a smile.

"I will treasure this, Nassir. Thank you, sweetheart, thank you."

Mahmed had moved to the open window of the train where Jake was watching all this, clutching Gracie so tightly, as if this radically unpredictable, yet somehow divine activity going on all around him might take her out of his arms. Mahmed stretched up his hand toward the open window.

"Jake, Jake."

Jake ignored him.

But Mahmed's plea persisted, "Jake, Jake...please...." His arm was nearly touching Jake's. "Jake...please forgive me, Jake."

Jake yielded, pulled the window all the way down, and offered his hand to Mahmed, who grabbed it, and put it to his forehead.

Now both Yelena and Jake were leaning out the windows of the train, waving. Yelena snapped a picture of this unlikely group waving their hands, wiping their tears, calling out blessings to the travelers from the platform.

Serbs and Muslims standing together in a moment of harmony. Then the train began to pull out and white handkerchiefs were waving wildly.

Zima ran alongside of the train for a bit, then stood and watched with her boys on either side of her. Jake and Gracie ducked back into the train compartment, while Yelena hung out the window till she could no longer discern anything but the fields of hay bending in the summer wind.

CHAPTER SEVENTY-ONE

YELENA AND JAKE AND GRACIE were seated in the subway car headed up to Queens. Jake's son Tony was standing in front of them, hanging onto a subway strap. He wore a t-shirt that said "Belgrade" that Jake bought for him at the airport. He was thrilled with his new baby sister, and he didn't tire of making faces at her to make her smile.

The surrounding passengers on the subway train were not that unlike the ones they'd journeyed with only days ago on the train to Belgrade. All sizes, shapes, colors, and costumes were chugging up to Queens with them. The chatter of different tongues and the roar of the boom boxes made Yelena reflect on the 'peace' she'd left behind in Shar Village, yet she was perfectly happy to be where she was at that moment. She wouldn't trade it for anything; well almost anything. The memory of Marko sat on her left shoulder like a constant evangel evidencing eternal life in spirit. She accepted that graciously, and listened expectantly for him to whisper in her ear. He hadn't.

Ljuba and the girls threw open the doors with hearty hugs and tears. Henry was putting drinks and food on the kitchen table, and then joined in the clamor of embraces and kisses. Nadya and Annie were over the moon with joy over their new little cousin, Grace.

Dinner was long, languid, delicious, ribboned with champagne and wedding presents, baby presents, welcome home presents, and news of an apartment available in a neighboring brownstone. Life was overflowing with goodness. After dinner, Yelena produced the photos of the wedding and Gracie's first days. The last one was the snapshot of the group at the train station when they departed.

"It was amazing…all of them together," Yelena proclaimed.

"That'll be the day," said Henry, throwing his usual cynical cold water on Yelena's triumphant statement.

"It happened, Henry, I couldn't believe it myself." Jake defended his wife's report.

"Look Daddy, it's right there on the picture." Nadya declared with the clarity of a sixth grader, ready to take on her father in a forensic debate.

"Yeah, yeah, yeah," Henry said. "You guys probably doctored the photo," he chortled, poised to concede.

"Believe it, Henry." Ljuba commanded firmly, then softened it with a squeeze to his thigh.

"It's okay, Henry," Yelena resolved, "you will see for yourself! Next summer we are all going back for a visit...together!"

"Oy!"

Laughter bubbled over, while they clinked glasses brimming with that naughty plum brandy.

Jake chimed in, "Zhivali!"

Yelena cradled Gracie on her good shoulder, and carefully stroked her little head with her bandaged arm. She whispered into her daughter's ear, "To Life!"

Then, like a sunflower suddenly able to lift its heavy head after the weight of centuries had tried to break it, Yelena looked up, and felt the warmth of her son's memory from on high, as palpable as if his hand were caressing her cheek. For the first time she was able to see him in her mind's eye, whole and untouched by death. She felt a soft, sweet movement of air, and then she heard what she'd been waiting for - Marko's whisper as clear as the day, landing like a feather in her left ear - an angel message of hope, "Yes, Ma, yes!"

THE END

Abundant Gratitude

To my sister Daniella Gomez for her ceaseless loving push for me to "get it done."

To my faithful brother Christ Nogulich, a voracious reader, who enhances my love for the written word.

To Marko Perko, a terrific writer with infinite vocabulary and a damned good editor.

To David Mamet, a man of many gifts, whose genius leavens the earth.

To Yael Prizant for profound insights, confidence in me, and soul-sisterhood.

To Susan England for her patient conviction and steady encouragement.

To my dear friends, Deanna Chouinard, Kelly Curtis, Luca Kouimelis, Alice West, who took care of me when the going was rough.

To a brilliant writer and my forever friend, James Trivers.

To my life long love Richard Armstrong.

To dear friend David Bloom whose message to me has always been, "Write!"

To Kim O'Kelley-Leigh for her grace, and to her husband Randall Leigh for painting my vision for the cover of this book.

To Channing Walker and Beverly DeWindt for timely spiritual uplift that always met the need.

To Harry Newman for our conversation a certain number of years ago in New York City.

Most especially, to my parents Helen and Walter Nogulich, who trained their sometimes rebellious second daughter, to never give up. I am endlessly grateful.

And more than all, to the Divine Creator that inspires every thought, word, and deed. My most humble thanks.